In the Manor Of the Ghost

In the Manor of the Ghost

By

Tina E. Pinson

Other Books by Tina Pinson

Touched by Mercy

Shadows Book One: When Shadows Fall
Shadows Book Two: Shadowed Dreams
Shadows Book Three: To Catch a Shadow

To Carry Her Cross
Then There was Grace
Christmas in Shades of Gray

Desert Breeze Publishing, Inc.
27305 W. Live Oak Rd #424
Castaic, CA 91384

http://www.DesertBreezePublishing.com

ISBN 10: 1-61252-942-9
ISBN 13: 978-1-61252-942-4

Published in the United States of America
eBook Publish Date: June 1, 2010
Print Publish Date: February 2013

Editor-In-Chief: Gail R. Delaney
Editor: Gail R. Delaney
Marketing Director: Jenifer Ranieri
Cover Artist: Jenifer Ranieri

Dedication

This is dedicated to those I hold near and dear.

My father, who isn't here to see the compilation of this dream, but I'm sure he watches from heaven.

My family and friends, who graciously listened to chapter by chapter breakdowns. I thank you all for your patience, your candor and encouragement.

To my husband, Danny and sons, Milton, Nathan and Joshua, thank you for bearing up under the assault of cold meals and a wife and mother on extended day trips with her characters.

To you especially, Danny. Thank you for your support. Thank you for backing my endeavors and believing in me even when I doubted myself. Thank you for your love. I'm blessed to have you in my life and on my side

Prologue

Boston, Mass.
November 9, 1872

Hooves resounded from the horses pulling the carriage trailing her. Kaitlin should climb in and get home, where her husband and daughter waited. They left her mother's earlier, but she stayed longer and now she wanted fresh air and solitude.

She studied the toasted orange horizon as she walked; awed and inspired by the way God had painted the dusky sky.

Kaitlin tapped a pebble with the toe of her boot and considered her mother's tea party. So many people converged on her mother's brownstone, eager to meet Kaitlin's husband, the Marquis Jean Marc Dupree, and daughter, Simone Victoria. In retrospect, she wished she'd declined the invitation.

"I didn't think so many would accept my invitation," Kaitlin's mother, Angela, apologized.

The way her mother boasted about Kaitlin's exploits, why wouldn't they?

Kaitlin married a title. A renowned singer, she'd been given an audience to sing for the Tsar and Queen of England allowing Angela and Harold -- Kaitlin's father -- an introduction to noble society.

Kaitlin recalled the crowd when her brother, Graham Franklin, returned from Medical School. Hoping to catch his eye, a bevy of debutantes nearly set up residence on the walk. When Constance, her sister, returned from abroad on the arm of Sir Eliot Dunlevy, the tumult became uproarious.

Kaitlin believed the desire for privacy and anonymity led to Eliot and Constance's move west. She personally would have chosen some place other than the godforsaken, frigid plains of Minnesota.

After a stint around the capital, concluding with a concert for President Grant and a host of dignitaries, Kaitlin needed a break. She had forgotten the maniacal fascination Bostonians had for Europeans -- especially with those of the ton and titled. Why they thought since she had married a Marquis, she knew the hottest gossip and would make them privy to it, Kaitlin didn't know. It was comical that these Bostonians, whose ancestors routed England from their shores, were so intrigued by what happened across the Atlantic. One might say if Queen Victoria sneezed half the nation was obliged to catch her cold.

A fire wagon passed with warning bells clanging, followed by a stream of men. Kaitlin looked skyward and saw the burnt tangerine glow.

Something was burning.

The wagon raced down the road. It stopped right on her front step and was soon surrounded by a clamor of people. A chill snaking her skin, Kaitlin hiked her gown and broke into a run.

*****

Kaitlin slipped past the barricades and pushed through the crowd. Heavy smoke made it hard to catch her breath. Nothing could stop her cry when she saw her apartment building engulfed in flames.

She scanned the lines of blackened faces. Her family wasn't there. Her gaze was drawn to the building, to the raging mingling of fire and life. Kaitlin prayed her family would come out. No one exited -- the agony of her thoughts cut her like a well-sharpened saber. Looking up, her thoughts became flesh.

Jean Marc stood in the upstairs window holding a bundle. Kaitlin knew, with another slice to her soul, the bundle was Simone. Jean Marc, so quiet, protective, so uneasily riled, yelled. Tormented wails for help rose along with tears of anguish and fear as angry flames licked out behind him.

The knife in Kaitlin's gut pushed through and slit her spine, filleting with cold precision.

Pandemonium reigned around her where men held out their arms, coats, and blankets, and yelled for those Kaitlin loved to jump.

Across the space of the yard, over the din of bells, the cries of man and beast, over the conflagration -- eternity settling between them -- she caught her beloved's eyes. She couldn't read them. Perhaps she could, but couldn't bear to hear the message. *Jump,* she bade him. He remained at the third floor window, their daughter pressed to his chest. A sparkle of flame in his tear filled eyes spoke of things to come and time froze. She closed her eyes for a brief moment to dam the tears and looked up to find him gone.

No one had jumped.

Spurred by inner wells of terror, Kaitlin raced for the doors. She groped for the handle, ignoring the pain. The timbers that secured the awning crashed, splinters of flame flickered like fireflies around her head, and fell to her skirts like droplets of orange rain. She stopped momentarily to brush her skirts and continued passed the obstacle. Moving on, ignoring the rush of heat, she screamed for her husband, her child. Her legs ignited with heat, her lungs burned with the smell of seared flesh. She pushed on through the maze of lashing flames, ignoring the screams behind her.

Kaitlin was pulled to an abrupt stop before she could cross the threshold. She fought for release so she could join her family -- in death. She was dragged from the building, thrown to the ground and rolled into the dirt.

Afraid to look at the window and have her fears justified, she closed her eyes against the burning tears. Unaware, as she succumbed to the blackness, whether it was her voice she heard screaming so loudly, so pathetically, or the haunting cries of her husband and child, calling for salvation.

Chapter One

Macleod County, Minnesota
October 1875

Kaitlin Michelle Dupree -- or Franklin, as she called herself now -- trudged through the autumn drizzle. The cool smattering of rain didn't dampen her anger. Her wet cape hung heavily on her slight frame. The hem of her dress, a magnet for the moisture from the blades of grass and weeds jutting along the path, clung to her legs. She walked with head bent to keep the rain from running down her cheeks into her dress, the hood of her cape pulled close.

Clayborne's carriage -- big, black, and ornate, with lanterns and glass windows, and pulled by two coal colored horses -- sat outside the orphanage, waiting to whisk her away in warmth and dryness when she first set out. She turned down the ride.

The drizzle would end and she had no desire to ride in Satan's death coach. She walked the length to Clayborne Manor. Shy of her destination, the rain steadied its pace, fogging the air, giving the mansion looming in the distance a greater air of mystery and doom.

She studied the expanse of nondescript gray brick through squinted eyes. The best of days it resembled a castle. Today, shrouded in a veil of gray, autumn, desolation, it looked like a mausoleum.

"Ma'am, please," The coachman, dressed in a dark cape, a style that matched the rig and the manor, slowed and urged her to climb in the coach.

She put up a deflective hand.

Rebuffed, he shook his head then flicked the reins and passed on, heading home.

"Next time tell him not to send a mortician's rig," she yelled.

Her words were meant for the owner of the carriage. She wouldn't begrudge the poor driver. She pitched a rock at the retreating coach as if its owner would be discomfited by her actions.

She lost her balance and slipped on the muddy path, covering her gloves and the front of her skirt from knees down, with mud. That did nothing to assuage her anger. It bloomed full when she reached the manor door.

*****

Devlin heard her before he saw her. She pounded the door, drumming with a precision that resounded through the manor. Then she began to yell and her voice -- because of her lung capacity, no doubt --

echoed the halls.

From the landing, he watched as Perkins allowed her in and led her to the study. He'd hoped to gauge the woman from a safe distance, but a heavy cape covered her head and body.

He spied Perkins and the housemaid, Marla, with their heads bowed in discussion. From the pointed looks in his direction, they discussed the woman and the plans he and Eliot concocted for her. Did they wonder why he was about to do something so idiotic? Did they hope the woman would agree to the plans and give him his just desserts? He never should have discussed his plans with them. They were unhappy. They would never voice it, but it was loud and clear in their frowns.

Unhappy people were a commonality in his world. Scathing diatribes about him and his holdings were commonplace in the county. Why not in his household? He would ignore it. Either that or fire them. And good helpers were hard to find -- no one, unless they were female and of a marrying age, cared to seek employment at Clayborne Manor. Or even visit these days.

He rather liked it that way.

Clearing his throat to make his presence known, he watched somberly as his butler and housemaid disappeared like mist. He berated himself for thinking the worst of them. They said nothing to warrant his mistrust. They'd been with him through worse times without recriminations. Why did he expect them now? *Why did it matter?* He was the master of his domain. They were hired help. He sighed heavily. Maybe the fact that they'd been with him, faithfully, for years was reason enough. Caring as he did, he desired to know their minds, which compelled him to share his plans in the first place. He would do it again.

Leaning against the handrail at the bottom of the grand staircase, he listened as the woman railed at his lawyer and friend, Eliot Dunlevy -- her brother-in-law -- with clarity and diction. The staff was relegated to the back of his mind.

"What are you doing here?" she growled. "Where is he, Eliot? Where is that monster?" Devlin doubted the raggedness of her breath was merely from the brisk walk to the manor.

"Kaitlin, what happened? The driver informed me you chose to walk in the rain. Why didn't you take the carriage? You could catch your death."

"Death of cold. Ha. Yet, you expected me to ride in that coach from Hades? I could have caught worse!" She flung the wet cape off her arms. "I bet he borrowed it from his father."

"Kate, let's not go into that." Eliot sighed, pulled his kerchief and wiped his face. "You must be freezing. Let me help you out of that cape. You can stand by the fire. I'll call for the maid to bring you a cloth and water so you can freshen up."

Devlin awaited her next move. The young lady didn't disappoint him. She pumped her fist at Eliot.

"I don't care to stand by the fire or clean up. I have enough water on my person. I don't plan to stay long, Eliot. Just tell me where he is so I can give the man -- and I use that term loosely -- a piece of my mind."

Devlin moved closer and watched from the crook behind the open door as she flipped the cape over her left shoulder and threw a sodden, muddied paper to the desk.

"How dare he think he can make such a request and not be made to answer for it. Who does he think he is? God?"

"Now, Kate. Take a seat and calm down." Eliot threw up his hands then motioned her to a chair.

Devlin found Eliot's exasperation a rare treat. Rare indeed when he'd tried to shake the unflappable manner of his friend occasionally and failed. The slip of a woman had put him to shame. His lips twisted into a grin. *She would do nicely.*

"Kate, take a seat. Please," Eliot said more firmly. He drew a deep breath when she took her chair. "Mr. Clayborne will not be joining us."

Kaitlin came out of her chair. "Are you telling me that... are you saying he's demanded this drivel but he won't be here to account for it? Has he no backbone? Is that why the sniveling coward sent you?"

Devlin's brows furrowed. His lips pursed. A sniveling coward. A devil. A monster. His fists balled at his sides. Were it a man making these claims, but it wasn't. It was a woman, a mouthy, stubborn woman.

"As his lawyer, I'm here on his behalf."

"So, you're going to stand back and watch while your employer -- blackguard that he is -- rapes the community?" She slammed the desk, and the dull thud reverberated through the room. "How could you? His demands are immoral. Don't you care about those poor children and young women the home is supposed to shelter from ingrates like him? Have you no regard for their well being?"

Eliot's sighs grew wearier. "He's not a blackguard nor is he raping the community. He's not going to harm the home or those housed in it. It's a simple business deal."

"Is that what you call it?" Kaitlin snapped. Eliot shook his head. "A *simple business deal*?" Kaitlin sniffed. "Ha. It's rape, pure and simple. Those poor women at the home told me all about his past deals. They say he threatens to withhold funds if he doesn't get his way. Now he's withholding funds because he wants some poor girl to be his... his... What's the matter can't the old geezer get what he wants at a brothel? I could strangle the old buzzard."

Blackguard. Old geezer. Old buzzard. Indeed! Devlin's frown intensified. This was too much. He'd celebrated his twenty-eighth birthday, hadn't lost his teeth and he'd *never* set foot in a house of ill repute. He wanted to march in and set the young lady straight. As a lawyer, he could deal with the legalities himself, but Eliot bade him not to show. He would have to confront her once they married. If they married. It didn't seem like such a good idea now. With his sigh he sounded rather like Eliot.

"Katie, I don't know what you're talking about. Where have you gotten such gross, and might I add, asinine, misconceptions concerning the reputation of my client?"

"I've heard them from near everyone in town."

More so from Greta, Devlin figured, but doubted she'd divulge that.

"If a whole town has misconceptions they can't all be wrong? Your client has a sorry reputation," Kate went on to say.

"His reputation is of the highest standard. I doubt the whole town maligned it. Sounds like Greta to me." She sniffed. Devlin wanted to tell her a thing or two about Greta, but he stayed quiet and let Eliot deal with his sister-in-law. "But, let's not go into that. Did you even read the letter?" Eliot asked. He twisted the gold chain on his fob as though he already knew the answer. Devlin had his own suspicions.

*****

"Of course." Kaitlin replied. Eliot pierced her with his gaze. *Well, half of it,* she admitted to herself. "Only an idiot could misinterpret such--"

"Drivel," Eliot finished. She bit her bottom lip, searching for the proper retort.

Picking up the sodden paper, she peeled it open. She scanned the page until she found what she was after. "The man has unmitigated gall. And I quote, 'Mr. Devlin T. Clayborne of Clayborne Manor in Macleod County extends the following proposal...' Proposal indeed. I pity the poor woman whom he chooses."

Eliot lowered his lids as if to keep his eyes from rolling. "Kate, read the letter."

"Fine." She sneered. "To continue, '...if the aforementioned woman agrees to said terms and chooses to reside at Clayborne Manor in compliance with said agreement, then a sum of fifteen thousand dollars will be deposited into a trust fund for the Clayborne Home for Women and Orphans." She flipped the paper. Half of it broke off, fell to the desk, and stuck there like a lump of oatmeal.

She eyed it with a mixture of awe and contempt then turned her attentions to Eliot.

"What is this, *reside at the manor?* Can't you see the immorality of such a demand? If that's not trying to rape some poor girl's dignity and Lord knows what else, then I don't know what it is. Does he actually think he can buy himself a mistress? Most of the young women at the home are children, Eliot, mere children, seeking protection from a cruel and heartless world. Must they now defend themselves from the wolf at their door?"

*****

Devlin shifted his weight from one leg to the other. A wolf laying in wait to prey on some poor unsuspecting female? Goodness, if he didn't know himself, he'd be tempted to find his actions contemptible. Where did she come by such lies? My, but the woman could rail. Wait until he had the little lamb in his office alone.

He shook his head. Why did he still entertain ideas of marriage?

"Just because he donates for their care, doesn't mean he should demean them by offering something so--"

"You didn't finish the letter," Eliot replied.

"I can't very well finish it now," she declared as she crumbled the paper in her hand.

"I meant earlier."

"What else was there? More illicit demands?" She sniffed as if her constitution had been harmed. "I'd rather not be privy to them."

"It was not illicit, nor a demand. He offered to make her mistress of the manor."

"Mistress of the Manor, indeed," the words rolled slowly off her lips laced with disgust. "You mean the *mausoleum*. What a gift," she added sarcastically.

"It is a gift women from counties over have hoped for. He's offering shelter and every necessary provision. Your meals, your clothes."

Kaitlin's giggle held disdain. "Shelter from him, I hope? And what should be worn when entertaining ghosts? Meals and clothes are great concessions for a woman to sell her soul. I'm tempted to accept them myself. I can't believe you're trying to justify this deal. Have you thought how this will affect the poor young thing he chooses? Have you considered her constitution? The man is a devil and if you're willing to have some poor girl blackmailed into spending a life of loneliness, entombed in his mausoleum, you're the devil's advocate." Her head tilted back even as her hands thrust out with fingers splayed. "I have a mind to strangle you both."

Devlin wasn't sure whether to laugh or run in and save his friend.

"Katie..." Eliot's voice hit a lower decibel. His eyes narrowed.

Kaitlin lowered her hands and drummed the desk again. "Don't use that endearment with me. I can't believe you'd hurt a child that way. Why the older girls are in complete turmoil. They're afraid they'll be chosen as companion to the beast."

Devil... beast... such lengthy vocabulary regarding his character. Devlin knew rumors circulated about him, but this was more than he cared to hear. Much could be said for ignorance.

Eliot's eyes rolled. Looking up, he seemed to beg for mercy. "First of all, no young girl or woman will be compromised. Mr. Clayborne is neither the beast nor the philanderer you claim. He is not asking for a companion, he's asked for a wife."

Kaitlin gasped. "A wife? Dear Lord. That's worse. How can you--"

"Kate, hush, let me finish," Eliot scolded.

Devlin waited for her to protest. She stood there, her back still and straight. He wished she would turn. Eliot assured him Mrs. Franklin was comely, but he had yet to see her without her cape. The back of her head, covered with the curliest and unruliest sable hair, streaked with glints of deep reddish gold, wasn't nearly enough for a man to ascertain the rest of the woman. If her looks equaled her demeanor, she must be beautiful. She had a powerfully sassy mouth.

Eliot took a seat. Devlin hoped she'd follow. Kaitlin remained standing. One foot tapped the floor in a disquieting rhythm.

Eliot expelled another frustrated breath. "As for anyone at the home worrying, they do so needlessly. You shouldn't have read them the letter. It was addressed to you, Kaitlin. Mr. Clayborne has already selected the woman he'd like to marry."

Kaitlin seemed to gnaw on that tidbit of information. "Tell me who she is so I can warn her. I'll get her to the train even if I have to pack her bags." Apparently it didn't digest. Given the flare of her cape, Kaitlin's hands were on her hips. Devlin wondered at the face she graced Eliot with. "Eliot, show some good judgment and tell me who the poor woman is," she added.

Eliot rose slowly, trying to smile, battling to get the corners of his mouth up. They lay still, twitching. He gulped hard. "The woman is you, Kate!" Eliot coughed. Though a huge oak desk stood as a barrier between he and Kaitlin, Eliot backed behind the chair.

"Me?" Kaitlin cried in disbelief. "How cou--" Her words died in her throat.

Eliot tensed as though he expected her to fly across the desk.

Devlin nerves were taut. He flexed his fingers. He relaxed when he saw her stumble backwards, but her actions made him feel like crawling into a hole.

"Why?" she asked, her voice wavered as she finally took a seat. "Mr. Clayborne doesn't even know me. I have no desire to marry again."

"I know that, Kate. I know you've scared off other suitors. That's one of the reasons you're the perfect choice."

"One of the reasons," she gasped. "Dare I ask the others? Should I somehow be gratified that he chose me for this... this... Are you asking that of me, Eliot? Are you asking me to be grateful?" Anger mounting, she stood. "Where is he so that I can strangle him? If I have to tear this manor down, I will."

She turned abruptly, gifting Devlin with his first look of her face. He took a long breath, and tried to shut his gaping mouth. She was surprisingly lovely. Her face equaled -- no... surmounted -- her sass. Even with her nose turned up in smugness, with nostrils flaring, and her full red lips set in a pout, she disarmed him. To think most of the eligible men in town called her the *Ice Queen*!

She sounded icy, but Devlin wondered if her coolness didn't belie the truth. Her passion in this matter proved she harbored warmth. Was that what was written in her eyes? They were the loveliest eyes he'd ever seen -- emeralds afire, offset with long, dark lashes. Yes, she would do nicely. A man could do worse than to have her on his arm.

He shook his head. What did it matter? She wasn't for him. He would never let his heart be turned again by a pretty face. His smile melted into a thin line of disgust, unseen walls, thick as manor stones, rose to protect his heart.

*****

"Kaitlin, you can't go after Mr. Clayborne." Eliot caught the back of her cape, reeled her in and turned her around. He held her shoulders.

"Why can't I see the old geezer? Are you afraid I'll knock his teeth out?" Kaitlin seethed. "How dare... oooohh... how dare he think he can buy me? Does he actually expect me to accept this? Even if I did, I'm worth far more than..." Mortified by her argument, she paused to regroup. "What good could possibly come out of such an arrangement?" Sitting, she put her head in her hands. "Isn't there someone else?"

Ironically, and most nobly, she'd marched out to stand up for the women at the home, never thinking she'd end up being the chosen one. She wanted to protest and protect the others. Now she had to save herself.

She wanted to drop to her knees and beg Eliot to talk the man into finding another -- with little regard that it might be someone from the home. She clutched the armrests to keep herself from it.

"Ah, Kate." Eliot knelt to one knee before her and laid his hands on hers. A purely tactical move, she decided. "I know what you're thinking, but you're wrong. Devlin isn't interested in you. Not in the way you think," Eliot amended swiftly. She looked up in confusion. He straightened and reared back slightly when her hands escaped his and dropped to her lap. "Devlin wants to marry you. He's offering you more than any woman could hope to have."

While Kaitlin scowled, Eliot repeated the benefits. "You'd be the Mistress of Clayborne. Half of everything he owns would be yours. He'll give you whatever you want. And he doesn't want anything in return. Don't say a word," he said firmly when her mouth opened. "He's not asking anything for himself, he wants a wife because--"

"I'm not for sale." Stubbornly, primly, she folded her arms across her chest. "I'm not an adventuress. I can live quite nicely without his money, thank you."

"I never thought otherwise. I know you don't need his money. In the event that you accept this offer, Mr. Clayborne has stipulated that you will retain your accounts." Kaitlin stared in bewildered disbelief. Eliot's voice softened. "I told him about you merely because I want to see you happy."

She started to rise then sat back down. She clutched the armrests. "You told him about me to make me happy? I'm happy now. Are you that eager for me to move? I'd have found another house had you told me."

"Kate, I don't want you to leave."

"Does Constance know about this?" Her voice trembled.

"It was partly her idea." This new shock sent a shiver through her being. Her eyes grew glassy, the tears spilled over. "Now, Kate, don't go thinking we're trying to get rid of you. We're not." Eliot reached for her hands and grabbed air as she pulled her hands away, clutching them to her breast in anger and pain. "Kate, we want what's best for you."

"Marriage to the devil is best?" Broken to think that her own sister had a hand in this, she cried in earnest.

Eliot offered her his kerchief. She caught it from him and dabbed her eyes. "Devlin is not a devil," Eliot said. "You've got this all wrong. This has little to do with Devlin. And everything to do with you."

"Me?" her voice squeaked pitifully. "How can you say that? Mr. Clayborne takes a wife and it has nothing to do with him? Will he hire a man to take his place in his bed?"

"Kate!"

"Eliot, don't call me that," she ground out, her tone menacing, and she lifted her fist. "I'm this close to popping your nose. You better explain yourself."

"Oh, dear Lord."

"You better pray," Kaitlin muttered, releasing a flood of hot angry tears.

Rising, Eliot backed and leaned against the desk. "Kaitlin, we don't want to hurt you. You are welcome to stay on with Constance and myself. We'd love that more than anything. But we worry. It's been almost three years since Jean Marc and Simone died. When you wrote to say you'd be coming, we were ecstatic. We wanted to see you get on with your life, hoped you could do so here. While you seem happy in your work, you're quiet, distant. Every time you go into the nursery, you come out with tears in your eyes. You're happy, but there's an underlying sadness. The only other time you're truly happy is in the company of the children at the home. One in particular."

Kaitlin knew the child Eliot spoke of, but she loved the child, not his father. "You think marrying Mr. Clayborne will make it better?"

"Yes, we do," he said earnestly, and found the courage to move closer.

"I doubt pitting me with a stranger will make my life better."

"Devlin *is* a stranger. But he's offering you his name, his house, his lands, his--"

"His bed," she spat the words in disgust.

"No, he's not prepared to give that, nor is he asking."

"Whaaat?" she croaked.

"Kaitlin, if you accept the offer, you will be his wife in--"

"Name only?"

"You could say that. But you will have a home of your own again.

And a..." Eliot words died as a boy, head of rich black silk, thick lashed eyes lighted with happiness, arrived at the door. Kaitlin's face lit with his smile. Dressed in black britches and a creamy white shirt, overlaid with a vest of deep golden brown, he looked rather like a little man. Crestfallen, he looked to his left, then with a blink turned back to her. With what could be a squeal of delight bursting against his chest, he ran across the short distance, giving Eliot little time to move before he jumped into Kaitlin's lap. The boy clung to her then looked up with a smile nearly breaking his face.

It broke her heart.

She fought to compose herself. "Mister Clayborne. How lovely to see you. I thought I was going to have to wait until tomorrow." His beaming smile separated at the lips to show a toothless grin. "And here you are." She kissed his forehead. He blinked slowly then looked down at her dress, and studied his newly sodden pants.

When his eyes met hers again, she saw the question. "You're wondering why my dress is muddy?"

He nodded and blinked again.

"Would you believe I was making mud pies?"

His smile turned coy as he shyly shook his head.

"Would you believe I'm a klutz?"

His eyes laughed, his grin broadened, and his head bobbed as if controlled by strings. He remained heart-shattering silent.

"You're right." She pulled back to her cape. "I have a clean spot though." Hugging him up into her lap, she tickled his stomach, wishing silently that she could hear his laughter. His wiggling when her fingers contacted with his belly, was her only answer. She stilled and bending forward, touched her nose to his. "You're so handsome, Mister Clayborne?"

He stopped to study her. His mouth moved, but said nothing. Kaitlin saw the approval written in his dark gaze. She laughed. "You smooth talker." She tickled him again, hoped for a giggle. She shifted him in her lap. "So, Mister Clayborne, what have you been doing since I saw you last?"

The boy's deeply tanned face blushed behind another dazzling smile as he lifted a folded paper from his vest pocket. Unfolding it like delicate glass, he handed it to her. Kaitlin had a feeling her response would make Eliot more determined to see that she accepted the offer.

Kaitlin was touched. "For me?" His head bobbed, his eyes filled with expectation as she studied his gift; a child's drawing of trees, grass and sun, where a woman and boy walked hand in hand. From the fiery red hints in the woman's hair, she concluded she was the woman holding his hand in the drawing. She wondered why his mother or father didn't walk in the land of the boy's imagination. Eyes stinging, she clutched the picture to her chest and met his gaze. "It's beautiful. You did a lovely job."

Laying his head against her, he hugged her again. He felt so warm.

With an ache, Kaitlin envisioned Simone in her arms. A feeling so dear, she wanted to hold the small boy forever. Were it not for the maid's abrupt arrival, she would have.

"Here you are, Mister Derrick." A housemaid came to a halt in the doorway. Nervously she blew a sigh then pushed a graying strand of hair behind her ear, jerking the cap that sat on the ball of her head. Her attire, hideously hued in splashes of deep green and white, crackled as she brushed her paper-like apron. She, too, looked left and back again, and was seemingly flustered for a time before it dissipated.

Kaitlin wondered if the flush on her cheeks wasn't from the garish outfit. The puffs and ruffles were hardly suited for a child, let alone a woman nearly fifty.

"Sorry. I turned my back and he was gone. A nanny I'm not. Anita keeps a better handle on him, but her Bradley is ailing. This tyke gets away from me more than I care to admit. Don't you, young man?" Her tone was firm, her eyes narrowed in jest, but the smile she wore belayed her love. She held out her arms. "Come along, Derrick, it's your nap time."

The boy hesitated, frowned and slid from Kaitlin's lap. He looked like he might cry as he backed away.

"I'll see you tomorrow?" Kaitlin asked with a frown to tell him she'd be heartbroken if she didn't. She didn't have to fake it. A crooked smile returned to Derrick's face as he nodded. Kaitlin grinned. "Good, I miss you when you're not there." She didn't hear it, but it looked rather like the boy sighed.

From the shadows, Devlin noted the way her dour tone softened with Derrick's arrival, making her all the more lovely. Her fiery eyes melted into gentle jade. He noted the way his son sought Mrs. Franklin's approval and love, the way he reveled in it, and noted, with great satisfaction, the way she readily gave it. Did this woman truly love his son?

Her reaction made him believe she did. He felt the stone around his own heart break ever so slightly -- he wouldn't admit it. Yes, she would do. She had to say yes. If only for Derrick's sake.

God forbid he let himself think it was for his own.

Kaitlin turned to Eliot, who'd yet to say a word. Her eyes were soft. "You just played your ace. You were going to say a place of my own and a son, were you not?"

"The boy has a great need. His mother is gone and his father travels extensively. He needs someone to care for him. I would like to see you both happy. Devlin is seeking companionship for Derrick. He's asking you to be a mother to his child."

Chapter Two

Legs afire, lungs bursting, he pushed into the darkness, running with an uneven gait into the sparse cover of the black walnut grove. He hoped the trees would shield him, give him solace from the Harvest moon and the mob bearing down on him. But dry leaves cried the way, and fingering limbs, like boned hands, reached for him. Slapping. Cutting. Mocking. Entangling. Ripping his cloak free, he ran, praying his heart beat wouldn't echo through the frigid night, alerting those behind to the path he'd chosen through the maze. It tolled in his ears, pealing a dirge in the night.

He covered his heart, felt it pulse against his hand. Thud in his head. He should have never come out. Shouldn't have foolishly believed anyone would accept him. His biggest mistake had been to trust her, believing iced veins could course with warm blood or compassion. It had been lacking in her cold blue eyes as well. He'd been too stupid to notice, too stupid to heed what was so vivid in her stare.

That stupidity sought reckoning now. Only the price had risen considerably. It was much too great to pay. So he ran.

Ran for his life

The din grew. They were gaining on him. He was tempted to turn, and see how close. Tempted to turn, and face them, but she led the pack. She manipulated them with lies about the beast. They would never listen to his explanation, would never allow him a defense.

He was not a molester of children. Not a demon. Nor a Beast. He ran from the beast. A beast led by Satan himself.

In the fervor, the mob would not make the distinction.

The dull smell of smoke filled his nostrils. The taste of it, acrid on a tongue dry and laden with fear, pushed him though he felt near to breaking.

Ducking behind shadows, he skirted the mob. How he eluded them, while his heart chorused the way and his lungs heaved like bagpipes in the night, he didn't know. Sweaty and exhausted, he reached the edge of the clearing to find the manor looming like a beacon in the darkness.

Salvation waited a few yards away.

An eternity away.

After a quick gasp to satiate his lungs, he broke into the clearing. His eyes focused on home. On safety. He sprinted like a gazelle, in swift and fluid motion. Paying no attention to the ground beneath his feet, he tripped on a dog hill and fell clumsily to the frozen earth.

He sat up quickly, cursing himself, searching the night. Torches distorted by trees moved in the distance, glowing like eyes in the darkness, moving in his direction.

He needed to get home.

Spurred into action, he tried to rise -- to walk -- but his leg clung heavily to the earth. A finger of pain ran the length of his body from ankle to head. Crawling, his teeth clamped on his lips, he dragged the screaming limb. He had barely covered a yard when the torches broke the trees.

Lying back with a disgruntled sigh, he prayed the mob wouldn't find him in the winter barren field. If only it were summer, if only the grasses were high. He hoped the mob would be blinded and the clouds would continue to hover like a shield between him and the moon.

Hope dwindled as the clouds pulled back. "I think I see him," someone yelled. And hope died.

He shrank back and tried not to move, praying he'd melt into the field, praying wisps from the breath he desperately tried to hold wouldn't betray him.

With a long slender finger, his betrayer pointed toward him from her place at the head of the pack.

Like a child, he closed his eyes, hoping to disappear, but knew the futility of his dream when he heard footsteps break the frozen ground to his left.

He opened his eyes in time to see the gun. Opened his mouth to scream, it was never heard over the report.

The scream echoing, he sat up shivering, drenched in perspiration. He wiped the sweat from his brow and ascertained his surroundings. He'd come to Devlin's room to wait for him and fell asleep. Sometimes he hated to shut his eyes.

"You, all right?"

A new sensation of fear pierced his heart as he whipped his eyes to the door. "I didn't hear you come in." He peered at the clock on the mantle.

"I apologize for the wait. Eliot has just left."

"No harm. I managed a nap."

Devlin's gaze filled with questions and concern. "You don't look rested."

He wiped the back of his neck, took a long breath and fought to compose his nerves and countenance as he slipped his legs over the edge of the bed. "I'm quite rested. And in a mood to trounce you," he teased as he took his place over the chess board across from Devlin. He caught his reflection in the far mirror. Darkness shadowed his eyes.

Devlin studied him, and his calculating grin said he bought the routine. Did he see the sheen of sweat glistening on his skin? "You seemed rather shaken when I arrived. Would you care to talk about it?"

Blinking as if he didn't understand, he shook his head. "You only startled me. I'd rather talk about your visitor." He slid a white marble bishop along a board made from black walnut and oak. "She seems nice enough." He smiled coyly as he laced his hands together and waited for

Devlin. "Are you actually going through with this?"

Devlin's brows rose. He opened his mouth and cocked his head. "If she accepts, I suppose I will. For Derrick's sake," he added as he swiftly moved a knight and absconded with a bishop. "Derrick needs a mother's love."

He made a play and Devlin another. Then he stared at the board. After a long moment of silence, he lifted his head from play and gave Devlin a cautious grin. "What do you need?"

"Solitude from scallywags like yourself," Devlin said. He smiled. He tapped the chess board. "Take your turn or I'll be forced to call it an evening."

"I won't keep you. You've shortened this round anyway." His lips twisted as he moved his queen in to conquer Devlin's king. "Checkmate."

Devlin scowled. He met it with a grin. He'd never beaten Devlin before, doubted he would have if not for the woman, and the chance of an upcoming marriage. He wondered who would win this new match, and quietly rooted for Kaitlin.

"What's that smile for?" Devlin inquired with a lazy grin.

"Nothing." He lifted his chin. "Ready for another round? I'm feeling lucky today."

"You're sure you're not tired?"

"Not at all," he replied with a measure of arrogance as he cracked his knuckles and reset his battle lines.

Luck didn't keep Devlin from beating him soundly the next two rounds.

Chapter Three

"Here you are." Constance threw open the door. A rush of black passed her and fell into step with Kaitlin. Kaitlin gently patted her dog's head. She wondered if she could be as gentle with her sister.

Constance sighed. "I'm relieved you're here. I saw you coming. We were worried. Eliot went to find you."

Kaitlin scowled. "Goodness, Constance, I'm not a baby. Did you think I'd throw myself off a cliff? You shouldn't have worried. There aren't any on the flats."

Kaitlin started for the stairs then stopped. Constance stood by the open door, tears in her eyes. Kaitlin retraced her steps and hugged her sister. "Sorry, Con. I didn't mean to be rude."

"Yes, you did," Constance laughed softly. She shut the door with her foot. "I'd be mad, too. I'd be furious." She bowed her head then lifted it. "Kate, I never meant to hurt you. I never meant for you to think we didn't want you here. We do! I, ah, oh, I don't know."

"Would you marry him?"

Constance smiled wistfully. "Once, I hoped I might."

"Really?"

"Really, then I met Eliot." Slipping her arm through her sister's, Constance led them to the couch. "You look shocked."

"You wanted to marry that old geezer?"

Constance's laughter spilled with her tears, causing her to choke. She gave Kaitlin's hand a patronizing pat. "Devlin is far from old. He's younger than Eliot. I'm sure I told you about him during my first season."

Kaitlin tried to recall the name. Her sister, three years her elder, shared numerous names that year. "You had so many beaus, I couldn't begin to remember."

"If you consider it you will. I'm certain I told you what a handsome, and I might add... virile man he was."

"You may have. At this point, I find it hard to believe." Kaitlin folded her hands. "If he's so young and virile, why couldn't he find a wife of his own? Why doesn't anyone ever see him? He never brings his son to the home. I heard he was on his last legs."

"You hear a lot of things, don't you? Greta, no doubt." Constance grinned. Pushing her palms against the small of her back, she stretched her belly outward with a grunt. "Kate, he's not the devil's own, he's not dying, and he's not trying to rape the community."

Kaitlin's lips quirked upwards. "You've been talking to the enemy?" Her sister's wan smile confirmed her suspicions.

"He made no demands on the town."

"He made this one," Kaitlin declared.

"It was to you. It was not a demand and Eliot wrote it."

"I'm well aware of that. Still, if the man wants a governess, he should place an ad. He doesn't have to marry one."

"He planned to get a governess," Constance replied. She positioned herself over the edge of the couch. "Eliot talked him out of it."

"Why? Is he so bad no one will work for him?"

With a grunt and a snort that could pass for a laugh, Constance dropped to sit on the couch, her belly protruding before her. "Kaitlin, there are some things you should know. Sit here." She slapped the cushion beside her. Kaitlin obeyed. Her dog stretched out by her feet. "Devlin Clayborne has a line of governesses willing to come at his beck and call. The letters of reference come in by the hundreds."

Kaitlin had to admit astonishment, and listened with greater interest.

"Every governess he's hired to date stays only as long as it takes to learn that the master of the manor is not going to fall madly in love with her. Long enough to get the child on her side and break his heart."

"They would use Derrick?"

Constance nodded. "Eliot and I have seen the way you care for the boy even when you had no idea about his father."

"Did you send me the advertisement for this purpose alone?"

Constance gave a wan smile. "There was no job, save for the one Eliot and I fabricated. Oh, Kate, Eliot and I thought if a woman could love the child beyond the knowledge of the father and his wealth, the boy would have a chance of knowing what it is to have a woman truly love him. To make sure the woman in question couldn't leave the child, Eliot felt it would be better for Derrick and Devlin if the woman were to become Mrs. Clayborne. Then Devlin wouldn't be put upon by every young lady, or old, seeking a husband. And Derrick would have a mama who loves him and not the dream of being the Lady of the Manor."

"Why would Mr. Clayborne agree to that? He has no desire to marry. He doesn't even know me."

"His son knows you," Eliot answered, coming into the room. "And loves you. We were worried about you." Moving behind his pregnant wife, he massaged Constance's shoulders.

"Constance told me," she replied cattily then cleared her throat. "I went to smooth things over at the home. I figured since I read them the letter I should be the one to undo the mess. I told them about the offer and that I was considering it." Her statement caused Eliot and Constance to smile. "Greta assures me that Mr. Clayborne is the spawn of Satan and I shouldn't marry him. She says the manor is haunted. And only a fool would move there."

Eliot chuckled. "Greta has a lot of things to say. And why not? She had some schemes of her own with Devlin."

"Her daughter was one of Derrick's most adamant governesses," Constance added. "She never got over the fact that her daughter didn't become Mistress of the Manor."

Kaitlin blinked. "She never said a word about that."

"Of course not. It's not common knowledge," Eliot explained readily. "Greta came from the east. Her daughters were grown by that time and serving as maids in other households. Greta hired on as cook's assistance at the manor. When she learned Devlin needed a governess for the boy, she wired for her eldest daughter, Uma, to come west and apply. She coached her on Devlin's likes, dislikes, and his history and she got the position. Uma wasn't the most attractive of women, but she played it for all it was worth. When Devlin wouldn't be taken in, she tried more desperate measures."

"Desperate?" Kaitlin was dumbfounded.

"Extremely." Constance laughed. "She hoped to trap him. She put on a peignoir -- with little cover and a lot of lace. Then she slipped into Devlin's room, into his bed, to await him."

"He never arrived, thank God," Eliot replied. "She swore otherwise. She said he meant to compromise her good name and called him a bald-faced liar. When the truth of his whereabouts came out, she was sent packing. Greta was fired from her position. She's probably been waiting for the right time to get her youngest daughter, Ingrid, out here and try again."

"Where was Mr. Clayborne?"

"In jail. Your mouth's gaping, Kate." Constance laughed, and closed it with her finger. "He's not a common criminal... so get that out of your head. He had good reason to be there. He was protecting Eliot."

Kaitlin shot her brother-in-law a look of quiet condemnation and bewilderment. "What from?"

Eliot grinned at Constance. "My wife."

Kaitlin's hand flew to her aching head. "I'm afraid to ask any more questions."

"It's not that bad." Eliot slipped onto the couch beside his wife and hugged her back against his chest. "Is it, darling?" Turning to look at him, she shook her head. The look of longing that passed between them helped dispel the notion that something awful had taken place, and made Kaitlin feel like an interloper.

"I was carrying Michael at the time," Constance resumed the story.

"R*eally* carrying Michael" Eliot threw out his arms to mark a large invisible space before Constance's round stomach. They were retracted when his wife's elbow connected with his ribs.

"Anyway," Constance continued, "you know how pregnant women are?"

"Moody, irritable... beautiful," Eliot finished before the elbow, poised at his abdomen, reconnected.

"Eliot had been working on a case and returned home late the night before. I felt so fat. I believed he didn't desire me anymore. I feared he'd found a lover. I heard him talking in whispers to Devlin about this female client and decided she wanted to tear my family apart. I thought his late hour was because he'd been with her. I stewed the whole day then when he didn't show up at the expected time I marched out, with rolling pin in hand, to confront him. As I walked, my anger flared."

"It was blazing by the time she found me."

Constance's lips wrinkled into a playful sneer. "When I found him, I informed him that I knew about the other woman, and furthermore, he wasn't welcome at home anymore. Having my say, I marched out."

Eliot chuckled. "More like stomped. And she left an irritated judge behind. He wasn't happy with the interruption. He commented that pregnant women should be shut up behind closed doors, especially while their emotions are so a kilter. In defense of my wife -- who'd just tried to bean me -- I flew off. Before I could get to the judge, Devlin -- who was prosecuting the case -- stepped in. I popped him instead. We were held in contempt and spent the night in jail."

"When I heard what happened, I went straight to the jailhouse and apologized. Imagine how stupid I felt when I learned that the client I'd been so worried about was nigh onto eighty."

"Proof that people shouldn't go off half cocked," Eliot said as much for his wife's benefit as Kaitlin's.

"I was not half cocked. I had an extremely good reason. I really don't care to discuss it," Kaitlin informed him, rising from her seat. "I think I'll run up and see if Michael is awake," she added, swiftly changing the subject. With a rustle of skirt and a tapping from the paws of the dog as he followed, she disappeared.

Chapter Four

Kaitlin woke up frazzled early the next morning. Thanks to her mind-boggling dilemma, she tossed and turned all night. Her coif looked like it'd been shaped by a windstorm.

Running the comb through the tangles, she thought of Devlin's proposition. She wanted to wring the neck of everyone involved. Save the boy. She told herself the tears that swelled and burned her eyes were due to the pain of combing her rat's nest. She wouldn't admit she was afraid or angry because her sister and brother-in-law had been so traitorous.

Clearly, Eliot played his opponent -- namely her -- well. His proposal touched her deepest concerns, at her weakest points. It was designed to force her to look in one direction -- toward the manor and Devlin.

If she didn't say yes, the girl's home would lose the money, Devlin would have to find another governess, or wife, and Derrick would be forced to give his heart all over again. She didn't want to do that to the boy. But if she took the offer to be Mrs. Clayborne, would she be happy? The house, a tomb, could be fixed. But she didn't know the man, wasn't even sure she'd ever seen him.

Kaitlin had a powerful desire to take that wagon and catch that train. If only she could talk herself into it.

"You think you know me, Eliot." She pointed at the mirror. Her reflection all but laughed back. "Well, I am not going to allow myself to be roped into anything. Especially marriage. Besides, God wouldn't want me in such a loveless union. Would you?" Looking up, she waited for an answer. "Of course he wouldn't," she assured the reflection with a curt nod when the answer didn't come. Now if she could block out the small voice of her heart.

Repeating the argument all morning, she nearly convinced herself. Then the black carriage from the Manor arrived while she was in the yard playing tag with the children. She froze in her place. The voice in her heart said 'the boy needs you'. The voice in her head called her a 'fool'. In the end, all it took was the smiling face of the child who climbed down and ran directly to her -- plastering himself to her -- for her to make up her mind.

To cement the decision, today as usual, he peeled back her lace mitten, stared sorrowfully at the bared skin and kissed her scarred hand. Touching her so deeply she thought she'd break. He reduced her to a puddle in ways she couldn't understand. She fought for composure.

"Did your father bring you?" She swung him up into her arms with a grunt and hugged him to her chest. The boy was a sturdy six.

Simone would be four, she mused sadly.

To prevent a new onslaught of tears, she walked toward the iron fence circling the home's perimeter, hoping to get a glimpse of Mr. Clayborne. Perkins stepped out from the carriage instead. Dressed in a black suit with white shirt and shiny black boots, he stopped on the step. Expecting him to enter the yard, Kaitlin moved to the gate to greet him.

"Mr. Clayborne will send for the boy at three," Perkins addressed her. His missive delivered, he disappeared into the carriage, closing the door behind him. The driver tipped his hat, gave a shake of the reins, and urged the huge black beasts into motion.

"That's odd," she told the boy in her arms, her brows raised slightly. Perkins usually stopped and talked awhile then headed to the kitchen for coffee and cookies. Maybe Mr. Clayborne found out and put a stop to it. Kaitlin frowned and chided herself for letting her thoughts sway her so easily. Mr. Clayborne wasn't a monster.

He couldn't be and have such a lovely son.

Kaitlin waited until the carriage pulled away, then pressed Derrick's head to her chest, so he couldn't see, and stuck out her tongue. Satisfied with her small act of rebellion, she turned to follow the other's back inside.

She didn't see the tall dark man who stood across the street watching. Nor did she see him smile.

Kaitlin held a music class with the children then, instead of going home, spent the afternoon playing with them. A routine she'd fallen into since journeying from Boston.

*****

After months spent in the country at Graham's home rehabilitating her body, she came to Minnesota hoping to rehabilitate what was left of her spirit. There was no other reason to come to such a cold place, unless she counted her sister, Constance. It helped that she would have employment too.

The advertisement for a teacher had been a Godsend. Her father agreed, her mother questioned the sanity of the idea. "Wasn't that the place where all those poor farmers were slaughtered?" she argued.

Papa rescued Kaitlin by reminding his wife the massacre happened years before, during the war. And Lincoln, bless his poor, departed soul, took care of it. "Minnesota hasn't had the problems since, Mother. It's not as dangerous."

Her mother's fears weren't assuaged. She tried to talk Kaitlin out of leaving.

Eager to test her broken wings, Kaitlin took the job. Knowing Constance and Eliot lived in the area cemented her plan. Constance expected their second child and would need help, and Kaitlin didn't want to be alone. Being with family made spreading her wings easier.

Ever since the night of the fire, when she'd lost her husband and daughter and her hopes and dreams had fallen like ashes, vanishing like the smoke lingering in the aftermath, Kaitlin feared being alone. Much like her old house, Kaitlin's insides -- what remained -- felt charred, vacant, and crumbling. Three years lapsed since the fire and she hoped, in leaving Boston, her mind could find rest from her tormented dreams. She wanted the night to end, hoped to find a way to live again.

She answered the advertisement with mixed feelings. On one hand, she hoped they'd send for her, on the other, she was petrified they would then she'd have to leave her sheltered home in the countryside and travel to Minnesota.

When the letter of acceptance arrived with the monies for travel, she packed her bags -- quickly before she talked herself out of it -- and with her dog, Lady, set out on her journey. Braving the train and the wagon ride, she carried herself so no one saw how much terror lay beneath her thin layer of calm resolve. Reaching Minnesota, she settled into a life with Constance and Eliot. She filled the position at the home, and looked as though she was getting along. Kaitlin told herself she was. But she wasn't.

While she loved Constance dearly, and enjoyed her company, Kaitlin felt empty. Memories of her child and the life Simone would never have, haunted her. Kaitlin spent long hours in the nursery with Michael and longer hours at the home, even after music classes were over. She loved to be near children. Loved holding them, reading to them, playing with them. Without them days were far too bleak, and too many memories of Simone were allowed free reign in her mind. She couldn't begin to think of Jean Marc without falling apart. She still heard him calling her, still heard her daughter's screams. The children made her think of better times.

They also caused distress. After only three months in their company she was also dreaming again -- of family, home, and hearth. Sadly, given what happened to her in the fire, her dreams were futile. Once someone learned how hideous she was, they'd be forced to turn away. Knowing that, she built barriers around her heart, barriers that only the children could penetrate.

She looked forward to her afternoons, further still to the days that Derrick joined the children. Out of them all, besides her nephew, he'd stolen her heart. She cared for the others, but they hadn't taken to her so strongly or poured out such love that her heart was compelled to return it.

Her greatest joy was to see Derrick smile. Her greatest hope was to hear him speak again. She hoped her love would be a catalyst toward that end, and wondered if Mr. Clayborne hoped for that as well.

*****

Greta was inclined to believe the worst. "Mr. Clayborne should have sent the child away for help years ago, but he doesn't want the boy to talk again. Then Derrick would be able to tell the truth about what happened that night to his mama -- no one knows what happened. Why Devlin may have killed her and if Derrick talked again... well, Mr. Clayborne might end up in a noose."

"Oh, Greta, really," Kaitlin had argued, weary of the gossip. "Why didn't you help the boy?"

"His pa wouldn't let me. The child has only started coming to the home. Otherwise, he's been locked up in that house with all the other freaks."

"Greta, that is most unkind."

Greta shrugged. "It's the truth. It's a freak show out there."

"Everyone I've seen has been normal enough."

"You haven't seen everyone. Mr. Clayborne could open a circus. Some even say there's a monster." Kaitlin rolled her eyes and started to turn. Greta clicked her tongue. "Don't believe me. He was probably another manor freak, but Devlin shot the poor creature. Now they say his ghost haunts the manor. Or maybe it's Mrs. Clayborne crying at her accuser from the grave."

Kaitlin walked out without a backward glance, but she heard every word.

She didn't believe in ghosts, but was Mr. Clayborne a murderer? Surely not. Constance thought highly of him. Constance thought highly of everyone, although she had warned her about Greta. Kaitlin hoped Mr. Clayborne wasn't a murderer, not if she was going to marry him. It threw her to think she entertained the idea of marriage. She didn't know what to think about herself or Mr. Devlin Clayborne.

Kaitlin hated that she spent so much time assessing Greta's warning. She prided herself on being a fair judge of character, never judging others strictly on the words of another, and yet, she thought about the monster, ghost and freaks. Greta's sour disposition and icy words became a yardstick by which to measure Mr. Clayborne and those at the manor. What could Greta -- who ran from the carriage, and hid from Derrick -- really know? She spoke from fear.

And Kaitlin had let herself be swept along. God couldn't be pleased that she'd gauged a man by Greta's wicked tongue.

Greta didn't have a kind word for Mr. Clayborne. She counseled Kaitlin on the ills of marriage to him. "It's tomfoolery. I'd skedaddle my backside to Boston, before I got caught up in his foolishness. He's a dangerous man for all anyone knows."

Greta told Kaitlin this enough, throwing the ghost and monster into the conversation every chance she got, that, finally, Kaitlin's anger surged. She had enough when Greta started into another diatribe on the manor side show.

"Can't you say anything nice about the man?" Kaitlin asked. Greta shook her head. "Then I'd prefer not to hear anymore about Mr. Clayborne until you can."

"You'll see how foolish you are if you marry him." Greta marched away, rebuffed and angry.

Greta might have called it foolish, and dangerous, and she might have been mad at Kaitlin, but that didn't stop her from asking about Kaitlin's decision. Other helpers in the home asked as well, but no one cautioned about the monster, or the freaks, and no one sided with Greta. Not one of them considered the offer foolish. Or dangerous.

Probably because the home stood to inherit, Kaitlin concluded. But she knew she was wrong. Greta brought up the money. She factored that in favor of the union -- even as she tried to talk Kate out of marrying.

The girls at the home spent the better half of the day asking the same questions as Greta. They said Mr. Clayborne was evil. They mimicked Greta to such a degree, it sounded like she was whispering in their ears. While it was disheartening that Greta had such a hold on them, Kate didn't fault them, they were only girls, easily swayed by imagination. She'd been swayed, too, and she was a grown woman who knew better.

Who was Devlin Clayborne? Did he have the decent character Eliot said? Did he harbor ghosts under his roof? Kate shuddered at the thought and shook it off soundly. Only an idiot would believe Greta's dribble. The question should be, instead, *could* she marry him?

"Is that what I should do?" she bade heaven for the hundredth time. "Should I do it for the boy?" But what if Mr. Clayborne is as Greta says? What if he killed his wife? What if...? Again she shook her head, amazed at how little thoughts needled.

Still, her heart reminded her, she had said some rather ungodly things about him and she'd never even met the man. It was good that Mr. Clayborne hadn't been privy to her outbursts concerning his character at the manor. She recalled Derrick's scowl and Marla's nervousness -- they both looked left. She put a hand to her face. Had he been there? If so, she'd be beyond embarrassed -- she'd be mortified.

*****

"Dev?"

Devlin turned from the fireplace to Eliot. He wiped his hands on his thighs. "Has Mrs. Franklin made her decision?"

"Yes, but before I tell you her answer, she has a few concessions."

Devlin exhaled and rubbed the bridge of his nose. His offer, by his estimation, was most generous. But then she was a woman. She'd probably heard more about his wealth. "What could she possibly request that I haven't promised?" He took a seat behind his desk and stared down his friend.

"For one, she wants it clear, if she marries you, that she will be the true mistress of the manor."

"Meaning what, Eliot? Has she heard about the gems?

Eliot's lips quirked. "Not to my knowledge. She wants to know for certain that she has the run of the house."

Devlin's thoughts lit in comprehension. He grinned. "In case she wants to redecorate, change the staff, and the likes?"

"If she chooses, she will keep you abreast of any expense incurred or decision made. I won't press the issue of the reasoning behind this request, nor will I recount the words she used to describe your home. As I'm certain you recall them with clarity."

Devlin nodded. She didn't want to reside in a mausoleum. He was comfortable here, and doubted once she met the staff she would need to make changes. He leaned forward on the elbows he planted on his desk. "Tell her if she chooses the offer, she will be in charge of my home. It will be her home. She'll be in charge of the staff, and the daily workings of the manor. I have no problem with that. As for redecorating, I can spare some expense, but she'll need to talk to me. There are a few rooms I would prefer are not changed."

"I'll let her know."

A brow cocked. "She is aware the greatest portion of her time will be spent with my son? That is the reason behind this proposal."

"And that raises her second concession." Eliot cleared his throat. "If, at any time, you decide you don't want to keep this contract, or cannot tolerate her in your home, or around your person, she'll try to be understanding. She would, if it comes to such, like your assurances she will never be stripped from the company of the boy. She is aware that she can't have custody of him, as he is your son, but she wouldn't want to see him hurt further, or herself, by banning visits. Unless the boy chooses that. Then she would honor his wishes and yours in the matter."

"That sounds reasonable. So long as she doesn't hurt my son then I would have no other recourse then to protect Derrick. Assure her that I have no desire to break this contract."

Eliot shifted in his seat. "What will her place be once the boy is grown?"

"I can't answer that far ahead. Who knows what the years will bring? For now..." He sighed. "When the time comes, if we get that far, she will be his mother and will retain the name if she chooses. Are these the only concessions?"

"She has a dog."

Devlin's back stiffened. His lips quirked. He was reminded of Anna's yapping, sock eating, ankle nipping, rag-mop. "It can't remain with you?"

"The dog is attached to Kate, and Constance is fonder of cats."

"And I'm fond of my peace, but if she must..." He frowned. "It will be her home. But I won't have the house destroyed, or the carpets ruined by some piddling little rat."

Eliot laughed. "The rat in question is a huge black dog with the gentlest and calmest of demeanors. Lady is well trained. She does her master's bidding to the letter. I don't foresee problems. There are other concessions, as you can see by your sheet, but the finality of this contract doesn't hinge on them. It does, however, hinge on these last two."

"Well?"

"She wants your assurance that you only want her to be a companion to your son and that you won't, at any time, try to access her bed."

Devlin chuckled incredulous. His dealings with women proved that he should be wary, not her. "She has my assurance."

"She wants your further assurance that should you change your mind, you will disclose that to her honestly and forthwith, so that she can make the proper alterations to her living arrangements."

Devlin smiled at the absurdity of the request. Her worry on the matter was groundless, as he would see little of her, but he nodded. "The final concession?"

Eliot squirmed in his seat and sat back. "She wants to be married in the church by a preacher."

"I will not be made to step foot--" The bellow came, rose, and magically subsided. Devlin would have fought marriage in a church completely if not for his son. She said she wanted to be married in a church, but that didn't mean he had to set foot in one, or had to visit one every week thereafter like Anna had expected him to. He would not be forced to worship the God Anna had committed herself to -- a God who cared little for him and dwelled in the church where Reverend Marlow gave his sermons every Sunday. "I'll work that out."

Chapter Five

"I can't believe his audacity," Kaitlin seethed as she took another turn on the floor. The pale green gown Constance chose for her to wear flapped against her legs, nearly felling her. Kaitlin would happily wear black, it matched her mood. "I should think the man would have the decency to arrive at his own wedding. Am I asking too much for him to come to his own wedding? Am I?"

"Proxies *are* legal," Eliot defended Devlin. He gulped and straightened his collar when Constance fixed her glare on him.

"They may be, but he won't get away with it. Gracious, Eliot, he sent Perkins! Dawdling old Perkins!" Kaitlin pivoted as she headed back across the floor.

"You'll feel better if you sit down," Eliot replied.

Kaitlin marched on, her legs taut. "If he's not here in the next half hour, the marriage is off. And I sincerely hope every daughter of the county is at his door on the morrow. In fact, if he doesn't show, I'll round them up myself." She turned, unfurling her gown as she went. "How dare he? Doesn't he have the decency to show his face to me, just once, before we are man and wife? Am I not allowed to look upon him? Is he so hideous?"

Kaitlin paced two more turns, her anger flaming to new heights as she puckered her lips. She was anxious, had been for the last week during wedding preparations. Couldn't Devlin be considerate of her feelings? Certainly that wasn't too much to ask from one who was supposed to be held in such high regard? Their wedding was already the talk of the town. If he didn't show, she'd be the laughing stock for sure. Her fists clenched at the thought.

"Is he hiding something? Maybe he's changed his mind." She stopped, placed her hands on her hips, and faced her sister and brother-in-law. "Maybe he's going to leave me here. Maybe he is the spawn of Satan like Greta warned me... his name could be misspelled. What's the matter, Constance? I realize it's not the nicest thing to say, but given the circumstances. Is he afraid he'll die if he enters the church? Eliot? Surely you understand how I feel. The man is a stranger to me. At least he could show his face. I'll give him twenty minutes and no more. Constance, whatever is the matter with you?"

"I won't need the extra time," the deep voice sounded behind her.

"It's him, isn't it?" Kaitlin's eyes bulged before Constance could nod.

Kaitlin turned around to find her soon to be husband leaning against the door frame. Dubiously attired in a dark gray, long coat, wearing a sardonic grin, he gifted her with an overwhelming desire to shrivel up and die.

She wouldn't add insult to injury by asking how long he'd been there. "Mr. Clayborne, I presume?" Her voice sounded hoarse and her smile withered.

With a nod, he moved away from the door and stepped toward her, his eyes fastened on her face. When he stood full height, she about croaked. Unlike Jean Marc, she couldn't look him in the eye without craning her neck, which put her at a distinct disadvantage. And Constance was right, he wasn't an old geezer. She could see where Derrick got his dark good looks. He was, as Constance said, a handsome and virile man. With his obsidian eyes trained on her in such a menacing manner, she'd be happy to face down a raging bull.

"I've come as requested. Might I suggest we get this over with?" His face stern, he extended his arm. Where did she get the courage to slip her arm through his when she should be running for the train? If she could master walking out the side door to the front of the church, she'd be extremely proud of herself.

Quietly, prompting herself to place one foot in front of the other, she took her first step, when her boot became hung up on the worn carpet. Trying not to fall, and lose her dignity fully, she grabbed for the back of a chair to stay upright -- she had little desire to manhandle her husband to be.

Her mishap stopped the entourage.

*****

His arm encircling her, steadying her, he caught a glimpse of her crimson face before her head bowed. Eager to get the wedding over with so he could distance himself from the church and the preacher, Devlin fought the desire to lift her and carry her. Instead, he waited.

A deep flush crept up her neck. "Where's Derrick?" she asked.

"Yes, where is Derrick?" Constance echoed, fanning herself. A cool fall day and she was flushed as well.

"I would have brought him, but he's sick. You can understand why I left him home?" he responded curtly.

Kaitlin's head shot up. "Of course I can," she retorted with a scowl, which quickly softened to concern. It surprised him. "Is he bad off?" she asked before her head dipped again.

"A slight fever." Devlin watched in amusement as she wrestled with the carpet and reached down to help.

While making some sense out of the mess, he took the time to think of about what he was doing. He never planned to marry again, not after Anna. But Eliot made such a fine argument and here he stood, in a church prepared to marry a woman he barely knew, all for the sake of a boy.

While his son showed little affection for him these days, he showed it to this stranger bent before him, growing so agitated with the carpet she somehow wrapped in the hooks of her boots. A stranger who, over the course of the next hour, would be his wife.

What had gotten into his head? Did he really want another wife? Perhaps, more than likely not, but the business arrangement would benefit his boy.

The more he looked at her, the more he liked what he saw. She was lovely today. Her sable hair had been pulled up into soft curls. The gown she wore -- thankfully not black -- showed off her trim, womanly figure, leaving little to the imagination like the cape she'd worn the day she came to the manor. He wondered if it might be better if she'd had the cape on now.

Since that day at the manor, he'd come to town and watched her from a distance, telling himself he needed to assess her way with his son, knowing his interest arose from reasons he didn't want to admit. To do so meant he had the capability to feel again. He didn't want to feel. Not for a woman. He would not allow himself to be weak.

Telling himself it was natural for a man to look at a handsome woman, he could study her without counting it as a weakness. It was his good fortune that the woman his son loved was so easy on his eyes. Although, he had no doubt, his son's choice in women had nothing to do with her good looks, but the beauty of her heart.

Could a woman have such a heart? After Anna, he'd be inclined to say no. After the way Kaitlin had been with his son, he wasn't sure. His uncertainty bothered him.

Kaitlin was lovely. Not as beautiful in her features as Anna, but he was glad she wasn't blond like his first wife. He found Kaitlin's dark, mesmerizing beauty refreshing. Her features would complement his. Her clothes weren't as fashionable as Anna's. They were simpler but far from dowdy. Although, glancing at her hands once more, she could do without the white netted mittens she wore. He didn't care for them, probably because Anna had a fetish for them.

"They repel germs," he heard Anna's voice whisper distantly in his memories.

He shook his head. They weren't even married and he compared Kaitlin to Anna already. It wasn't fair. He told himself she wore the mittens strictly for fashion and warmth, but found that hard to believe when they were of open weave -- with no covering for her fingers. And each time he saw her, even while working, her hands had been covered.

Why?

"I'm ready now," Kaitlin replied, arresting Devlin's attention. He met her gaze, caught her sheepish grin as she unwrapped the last bit of carpet from her shoe.

He started to smile then looked at her feet. "Then let's be done with," he said curtly, straightening. He hated himself when he saw the smile fade on her lips and in her eyes. What did it matter? She need not smile at him. He wasn't marrying her for himself. The better he stayed aware of that, the better they would both be.

*****

Kaitlin surveyed her surroundings throughout the ceremony. She knew this room like the back of her hand. She'd seen it every Sunday to date and nothing had changed. It was just easier to stare at the pews and the pulpit then to think about what she was doing.

I must be mad, but if this is what you'd have me do, Lord. Am I needed at the manor? If not, could you get me out of this now? She blinked and waited to disappear. She remained in the dimly lit room, by the stranger who would in the space of a few moments be her husband.

She tried to recall Sunday's sermon, something about hell fire and brimstone, a topic far more soothing on her nerves than staring at the large, dark, and extremely handsome man who held her hand now and stood ready to take marriage vows with a woman he didn't even know.

He was as mad as she.

The boy needs me, Lord, right? I could always go back to teaching music? If not, I could be a Harvey girl? Oh, why did Jean Marc have to die?

The pastor's lips moved. She didn't hear him over the memory of her first walk down the aisle. She thought of Jean Marc and Devlin and compared the two. Her nerves danced.

Marrying Jean Marc was a dream come true. This marriage might well become a nightmare.

Yet here she stood. What an idiot!

Her first wedding was held in a pristine chapel in southern France, with several from the gentry in attendance. No one dared compare this weathered church with the finery of Europe. Those attending now -- though dressed in their Sunday meeting clothes, their finest -- looked liked they prepared to go to work in one of the homes of Paris' wealthy.

None of that really mattered. Kaitlin didn't care if they didn't reach the standard of the people in the life she'd known before. She didn't care if there were no royals in the small gathering. What she really missed and what she wanted now, was to know she made these vows with someone who loved her. She missed Jean Marc so strongly in that instance her tears welled up.

She missed her husband's touch -- he never gripped her hands so callously as the man who stood beside her now.

What was she doing?

She missed Jean Marc's voice -- tenor, smooth and musical. Devlin spoke curtly in deep trembles of baritone.

Could she really find happiness without love?

She missed her husband's eyes -- rich brown, soft, concerned. She looked up hoping for them and caught a chill from the black eyes that stared at the preacher. They bore contempt. Hatred. She shivered and looked at the preacher.

Reverend Marlow smiled at Devlin and bowed his head to her then graciously continued with the service.

Kaitlin could barely recount the ceremony, but she could remember, with clarity, the way Devlin looked at her. Did she see a hint of a smile before his lips met hers to seal the pact they'd spent the last few minutes vowing to keep -- in words she wasn't sure she'd spoken? His eyes were black, foreboding, but shining with hidden words she dare not let herself read or believe he'd even spoken.

By the warmth and the pressure of his lips on hers, she could, for a moment, almost believe that this was her love. Devlin gave more than required under the circumstances. With each passing second, where his mouth molded and searched hers, she found herself wanting things she'd told herself she'd never have again.

Her body defied her mind, almost verbally, as it cried out to be loved again. It'd been so long. Sinking further into the bliss, she fought to maintain her calm. Her heart wouldn't let her. Letting her fingers burrow into the thickness of his ebony hair, along the nape of his neck, she kissed him back with equal fervency.

When he pulled away, she felt breathless, shaky. It wasn't from fear. Had he felt it, too? No, it was nothing. Devlin had put on a show for those in attendance. So why did that bother her, why did she want it to be more than a kiss? More than a business deal? She hated herself for her weakness, hated herself for signing the papers.

Chapter Six

Sitting in the carriage, wrapped in her cape -- her woolen armor -- she thought of the manor. It was as dark and foreboding as her new husband.

Husband. Oh, Lord, what have I done? Does he know you? In her oversight she'd forgot to ask.

All's well. She heard her heart say. So why did she feel so ill?

She wished the reception were longer, because, here in the silence, it felt like the business deal had been secured. There were no smiles from her new husband, no further indication that the kiss meant anything but an exchange for the benefit of the witnesses.

Devlin helped her to the carriage in a perfunctory manner, paying no heed to the townsfolk who'd gathered on the walks to gawk. He sat across from her in silence as the carriage carried them to the manor. After a few moments, he stretched his legs taking up nearly the whole coach and stared out the window. She wondered about his thoughts.

She was tempted to ask him why he glared at the preacher through the ceremony and why, during the reception, when the preacher came to offer congratulations, he didn't take his hand? Afraid of the answer, she kept her question to herself.

She stared at the passing countryside and tried to find something of interest in the bared trees and desolation, but her eyes had a mind of their own. She glanced in his direction. He may be the devil's own, but he was intriguing and easy on the eyes.

"Why do you look at me like that?" he asked without turning.

Her cheeks flushed with the awareness she'd been caught peeking. She averted her eyes.

"Are you frightened of me?"

"No," she said, giving him a quick glance. When she realized he looked at her, she bowed her head and played with the lace on her gloves.

She shivered. She was petrified of him.

"Then why?"

"I was..." She looked up and met his eyes. "I wondered what you were thinking about." *Wondered why I accepted your offer?*

He leaned against his hand and turned to look outside again. Was that a hint of mischief she saw before his head turned? "I wondered what it feels like to be riding in the death coach with the spawn of Satan?"

She about fell out of her seat and blinked so her eyes wouldn't pop their sockets. "Oh, dear Lord," she mumbled and bowed her heated face. Her fears had come to light. "I had no idea. I do apologize for that, Mr. Clayborne. I really do."

"Apology accepted. Do call me Devlin, we are married."

She looked up with a grimace. If only it could be so simple.

"There now, I doubt it will be as bad as that," he said with a hint of jest. "I mean to keep the contract and, hopefully, things will be amicable between us -- for Derrick's sake," he added, probably to remind her of why they were married.

"I'll try, Mr. Cla--"

He cleared his throat.

"Devlin." Her hands warred together. "I, too, want what's best for the boy."

"I know," he said softly. He broke the conversation to look out the window, saying nothing until they reached the manor and were inside the front hall.

"There is a very small staff at Clayborne." With a hand on her elbow, he led her to where the six people in his employ lined up, waiting obediently.

Kaitlin nearly choked. She saw why Greta called the staff a sideshow. The butler, Perkins and the maid, Marla, were normal enough. She sensed them gauging her reaction as she looked down the line.

The woman beside Marla looked at the far wall, offering a profile of the left side of her face. Her face was lovely from the glimpse Kaitlin saw. She seemed to bare no *abnormalities*. The man next to her stood all of two feet, as did the woman at the end of the line, who seemed fascinated by her shoes. The boy between them, the young man who drove the team, stood nearly six and a half feet. Not so peculiar, but his forearms and hands were enlarged in comparison to his body. No wonder he wore the large, black cape to drive the rig. She'd seen a young man with such an ailment at her brother's house once before.

Remembering that young man's feelings about the stares and ridicule, Kaitlin made a conscious effort to turn her head. Looking back up the line, she noticed the scarred face on the woman next to Marla.

She gulped.

She saw no freak show, only people who needed acceptance, and she knew what it meant to desire that all too well.

Yes, some of the staff had peculiarities, but it was their manner of dress, another mixture of garish clothes, that gave their peculiarities a side show quality. They seemed not to mind that they were trussed up like a circus act. She felt appalled for them.

The ensemble, similar to the outfit Marla wore earlier that week, was done in purple and white. The designer had freed the men from ruffles and lace. Still, they overdid themselves. Kaitlin wondered if they were trying to emulate the liveries of the royals by dressing the servants so grotesquely -- even the gaudiest of royals had better taste than this. Was this meant as silent ridicule? Had Devlin chosen their attire? No, she decided when he removed his gray long coat, for the first time that morning, and put it away. His taste was impeccable. His suit was cut and tailored to his tall, lean body. Why did his staff dress so atrociously?

"This is Perkins, my butler. He worked here under my father." Devlin returned to her side.

Kaitlin tore her eyes from the study of their outfits, and stepped to Perkins, hoping he wasn't mad at her for refusal to marry with him as proxy. She wanted to ask, but didn't want to bring it up in front of Devlin. "How do you do, Perkins?" She extended her hand. "There were some wonderful cookies in the kitchen the other day," she added with a wink.

Devlin's eyes narrowed.

"Miss," Perkins said, his composure stoic. His boiled-white shirt, ironed and pleated to perfection, complete with offsetting purple tie, sounded like wadded-paper as he lowered his arm.

Kaitlin blinked to keep from laughing, but she caught a hint of a smile from Perkins and Devlin as she moved down the line.

"Marla, my housemaid, has been here about as long as Perkins."

"Marla." Composed, with eyes on Marla's face and not her outfit, Kaitlin smiled, and leaned forward with a whisper, "I trust the young master hasn't given you the slip again?"

"No, ma'am." Unlike Perkins, Marla smiled fully. Kaitlin followed Devlin aware that the staff and Devlin quietly assessed her reactions.

"Anita has worked alongside Marla for nearly five years," Devlin said by way of introduction.

"How do you do, Anita?" Kaitlin said in greeting. With a hand covering the left side of her face, Anita's head turned slowly, and Kaitlin, looking beyond the scars that maimed her, was gifted to look upon the deepest, most beautiful violet eyes she'd ever seen. "I trust your son is feeling better?"

"Ma'am?" Astonishment tongue-tied her; she looked to Marla and back.

"Marla mentioned that your son, Bradley, I believe, has been sick. I do hope he's well and that you're not having to stand here waiting when you have an ill child at home?"

"No, Ma'am, he's fine," Anita assured her. Her eyes misted even as she grinned. The hand lowered from her face and slipped gingerly into Kaitlin's. "Thank you for asking." Her eyes seemed to silently thank Kaitlin for not mentioning her face. For not staring.

*****

Devlin was further perplexed. She not only took their hands into her own, as Anna never would -- it was beneath her, one never knew what germs were carried among the working class' -- but how did she know Anita's son was ill? He wondered until he remembered the conversation in the office earlier that week and found himself touched by her concern for those below her station and her memory.

With the next three servants, his awe grew. She didn't gawk, she didn't look as one about to laugh or run. She struck out her hand and smiled.

To Henry, the driver and overseer of the stable, she complimented his care of the horses and carriage. To Thomas, the stable boy, Henry's eldest, she stated how proud his father must be that such a strapping young fellow would follow in his footsteps, and apologized for not accepting the offer of the carriage so graciously offered earlier that week. And to Margaret, the cook and Henry's wife, she joked that she would be most happy to have a decent meal again. Margaret looked up from her shoes for the first time since Kaitlin's arrival.

Devlin caught a wisp of a smile before Margaret's head dropped again. He knew Margaret was uncertain about this new addition to the manor, but Henry smiled big enough for them both. And Thomas beamed.

Devlin noted that each servant had listened well, and while they stood erect, they weren't afraid of the woman who greeted them. She filled them with ease. Like him, they probably saw the softness of her heart in her vivid green eyes and in her concern.

He saw it more clearly than he cared to. He cleared his throat. "There you have the staff. All but Ernestine, she'll return in due time. She helps with the duties around the house and serves as my secretary. If you have any concerns with the staff or any changes to be made, Ernestine will be happy to help."

Devlin's staff frowned at the mention of Ernestine. Kaitlin looked at the servants then him.

"Henry is procuring another worker for the stable. You will make Gerrard's acquaintance when he arrives. Anita will take you to your room at the head of the stairs on the east wing, across from the nursery. Thomas will see to your bags. I have business to attend to, but dinner will be served at six. I should be able to join you then. If you'll excuse me?" He bowed and turned to leave.

*****

Kaitlin watched until he disappeared into the office and closed the doors. Her heart sank. What had she done? He all but fled. As if he couldn't wait to get away from her. Perhaps he was busy. Or perhaps he couldn't stand her. She chose busy, but a nagging doubt remained. She would have considered it further but the staff -- her staff, small as it was -- stood quietly, watching, waiting to be dismissed. She wondered if Ernestine had any peculiarities, but her curiosity would have to wait.

"I don't want to keep you from your duties. I look forward to getting to know each of you better. Ah, good day then."

The servants nodded and filtered from the room, until she was alone with Anita -- echoes of their starched outfits wafted the hall long after they were gone.

Turning slowly, Kaitlin studied her surroundings. She felt strange.

Alone. She tried to think on better things. Her room was at the head of the stairs. She sighed when she considered her legs. At the resounding crumple of starched cloth, she turned to see Anita move toward the grand staircase, and fell in behind her.

The staircase was magnificent. Four horses could go up it abreast!

She slowed and peered at the chandelier overhead. It looked like diamonds dripped from the ceiling. In her haste, and anger on her first visit, she paid no attention to the grandeur of the house. With a deep breath, she started up the steps.

Such opulence usually tripped her dreams to fairy tales. Today she imagined how the nightmare would turn out. Given the conditions of the marriage, it shouldn't seem strange going to her own room on her own honeymoon. The conditions were clear. Still, the fact that her white knight had found an excuse to leave her presence was unsettling. Did he find her that awful to be around?

Or is there something else, Lord?

She caught a glimpse of Anita's skirts as she turned on the stairs and, lifting her skirts, hurried to catch up, chiding herself all the way.

"This is it, ma'am." Anita pushed open the door. "I hope it's to your liking?" At the look on her face, Kaitlin wondered how bad the room was.

It was beautiful. So lovely she didn't want to touch anything. At least the person who'd outfitted the staff hadn't been commissioned to decorate the room. No, the person who'd chosen the colors here had some taste.

In the center of the room stood a huge four-posted, mahogany bed with drapes of blue satin. On the far wall a cherry-wood dressing table and chair sat in the shadow of a dressing screen with oriental markings. There was a foot stool made of the same glossy mahogany as the bed, which she knew was of French craftsmanship, possibly Louis something or other -- Jean Marc would have known.

Jean Marc. What have I done?

Covering her heart to hold the ache, her gaze wandered the room. There was a chest, a dresser and a fainting couch to match the foot stool, all done in rich mahogany. Further in the room, she found a private bath with a tub, complete with shiny brass knobs and running water. Unfortunately, she only found a chamber pot, leading her to believe the other sought after amenity remained outside somewhere. She frowned.

"He plans to add the bowl soon," Anita said with a half-smile. "Sometimes we have to heat the water 'cause the pipes freeze." Her hand hovered near her cheek. "I hope you're pleased with the furnishings. Mr. Clayborne had it redone this very week."

Kaitlin couldn't hide her surprise. "He did this for me?"

"Yes, ma'am. Well, he had ideas for whatever room was chosen." Anita nodded with a shrug. She frowned. "Ernestine thought you might like this room. It hasn't been used for a time and needed a touch up."

Kaitlin was encouraged to know Devlin had been considerate of her feelings. She wanted to know more about this man she'd married, wanted to know how a man with such taste in the matters concerning her room could allow his servants to walk around dressed as they were. And why had he disappeared so quickly? She didn't have the courage to pursue that line of thought so she considered Ernestine. Why did everyone frown when her name was mentioned? Was she so awful? She had chosen a lovely room.

"It a lovely gesture on Mr. Clayborne's part, and Ernestine's." And well it was, but Anita frowned again. Kaitlin tucked her questions away.

The room was exquisite, but it lacked a window. That admonition, amid such beauty, jolted her senses. *As long as I have no panic attacks, Lord. Then I'll be all right. I'll try to be grateful and keep my mind on what you would have me do.*

Thankfully she hadn't had many attacks since leaving Boston.

Excusing herself to return to her duties, Anita made her exit. "Marla will be up to help you unpack. I will see you in the morning, ma'am," she said in parting.

Kaitlin noted the way her hand lowered slowly as she turned to leave, and hoped one day, Anita wouldn't feel obliged to hide in her presence. One day she might even gain Anita's trust. One day she might have the trust of them all.

Even Devlin.

She sighed heavily. Given his quick escape, that seemed almost too much to dream for.

Thomas brought her bags up promptly and Kaitlin started unpacking. She stopped when she heard the crumple of starched cloth and turned to see Marla, tray in hand, stop at the door across the hall, open it and enter.

"Derrick," Kaitlin said softly, amazed how the cloud hovering over her senses lifted at the mention of his name. Unpacking would wait. Tossing a gown to the pile of black dresses on the bed, she followed Marla.

Opening the door, she was struck by the small boy. He seemed lost in such a big bed and pathetically replete with pale face and dark circles beneath his eyes.

I am truly needed, Lord. And I am thankful you've trusted this boy to me.

"Is there something you needed, ma'am?" Marla noticed the new addition to the room and scowled. "I'll get to your bags soon as I can."

Regret stabbed Kaitlin. Had the women before her been so selfish? Did Marla think her so petty? "I'm not worried about my bags. I've already started on them. I was concerned about the boy. How is he?"

"He's faring better," Marla said, gracing her with a smile before she turned to her patient, her dress erupting in a symphony of sound. "I sensed you were different," she added softly as she held Derrick's head aloft and leveled a spoon of broth toward his lips.

Dumbstruck, Kaitlin didn't know how to take the comment. Hopefully, the smile meant it was a compliment of sorts. She waited for

Marla to say more and alleviate her confusion, but Marla tended the boy.

Kaitlin made her way around the bed. "Can I do anything?" Marla seemed not to hear her, so she leaned in toward the woman. "Is there anything I can do?"

Marla gasped and turned. Their eyes locked for a moment and Kaitlin came face to face with Marla's abnormality. A fake eye. Had she not been so close Kaitlin would have never of known.

Marla lowered her eyes. "Now, ma'am, you don't have to do anything," she insisted, before turning back to the child.

"Perhaps not, but I'd like to." Not to be deterred, Kaitlin sat on the edge of the bed and leaning forward, took the load of the child into her arms so Marla could handle the bowl better. "He's quite warm." She pressed her lips to his head. "Hello, sweetheart."

"His fever has gone down greatly," Marla assured her. "I stayed the day with him yesterday, it was pretty rough. Today he's resting better. I would have stayed on today but there was a lot to do. So Anita and I took turns," she added as if expecting Kaitlin to scold her for leaving the boy.

Kaitlin knew full well why she apologized and sought to dispel the notion that she might be displeased. "I'm sure you and Anita did everything possible. I would be the last to judge you when I know you have other duties to attend to."

The older woman relaxed. "Yes, ma'am. You are different," Marla proclaimed again with a pat to Kaitlin's leg.

"Why do you say that?"

"It's not meant in disrespect, ma'am."

"Of course not. But why?"

"The first Mrs. Clayborne could barely stand the sight of the boy. Her own son." *Or you and the staff from the looks of it,* Kaitlin wanted to add. "She rarely set foot in his room, let alone held him or touched him the way you are. And the governesses... Tsk," her tongue sounded as if stuck to the roof of her mouth, "they'd be scheming ways to get to the master's room by now with little heed to boy's welfare. I know you're his wife now, ma'am, but you're different. I rather like it."

"Thank you," Kaitlin's voice wavered. *Oh, dear Lord, what have I stepped into*? A mother who barely wanted her boy. A disappearing father. A staff who... Her mind whirled. *How can I make it better?*

Love them, Kate.

How could she not?

"That's very kind, Marla. But you barely know me." Kaitlin swiped at her eyes.

"It's merely the truth I speak," Marla declared. "I sense the tenderness in you, ma'am. As does the rest of the staff. We don't have to know you to see it. We've only to see the way the boy's face lights up every time your name is mentioned. After seeing you today, I have no doubts. You'll be good for this family." She laid the spoon in the bowl and rose. "I'll be getting back to my duties. I'll come back and check on him."

"It's not necessary," Kaitlin called. Marla, with hand on the knob, turned. "If you want to come up, I'd enjoy the company. But if you're busy, you needn't worry. I'll be here. I'll watch the boy. That way you won't have to trudge those stairs so often."

Marla bowed her head slightly. "I'll see." She turned back to the door then to Kaitlin again. "Pull that cord there it if you require anything. I'll bring you some dinner later."

"That would be very kind of you."

"It's my duty, ma'am." Marla replied.

Kaitlin opened her mouth, only to hold her words when she noticed the smile Marla wore.

"I'll return later," Marla said with a wink and slipped from the room, closing the door behind her.

Kaitlin hugged Derrick, she was warmed by the fact that she had made a connection with Marla and hoped she could reach the rest of the staff as well. She exhaled a long breath then put her lips to the boy's cheek. "Now perhaps you can show me how to reach your father."

Chapter Seven

Humming, Kaitlin ran a damp cloth along Derrick's brow and down his cheeks. She stopped abruptly when she realized he watched through partially open eyelids.

"Hello," she whispered and kissed his cheek. Pulling back, she saw his lazy smile. Taking his hand in her own, she gave it a gentle squeeze. He returned the gesture ever so weakly then closed his eyes. "That's right, you rest. Then you'll get better." She pressed her lips to his forehead. "You just rest."

With his hand tucked safely in her own, she whispered a prayer. "Lord, use me as You will, and Lord, heal this sweet child." She continued in silence then, after a time, laid his hand gently beside him and went to explore the room.

Such a large room, twice the size of her own, filled with every toy imaginable. Two large painted, rocking horses, of the finest craftsmanship and vivid colors, set in a continual race at the far end of the room. She ran her hand along their painted manes and down the jewel encrusted saddles and wondered who crafted something so lovely. Did Derrick find them as wonderful as she?

There were shelves of books and a black board with a half-erased picture of a dog. She looked back to the sleeping boy. "Is that what you long for?"

Facing the board again, she traced the outline with her finger, hoping Derrick would be pleased to meet Lady when Eliot dropped her by on Monday.

With a sigh, she imagined afternoons spent in such a lovely room playing with Derrick and watching as he played with Lady. They might sit by the fire and read. Or have pretend races on the lovely wooden steeds. It was idyllic, but in a room so large and christened with so many toys, what else could one think?

Best of all, it had windows, large windows with seats in front of them. Cavernous seats where a person or two -- possibly three -- could sit in the sun and get lost in the beauty of the world outside. Taking a bouncing seat, she tested the plush cushion then the window. When it slid wide to let in the frosty air, she was pleased. She closed it, wishing she had windows in her own room.

"I know I promised I would be grateful for the room given to me." Kaitlin grimaced heavenward.

She sat at the window thinking of all the things she and Derrick could do, when a door on the wall beyond his bed caught her attention. Thinking it to be the bath, she went to see how opulent it might be compared to hers. She found a room, as large as Derrick's and completely empty. It too had a long row of windows!

With the moon beginning to paint golden streaks on the floor, it glowed with an eeriness that made it hauntingly beautiful. She imagined it filled with the furnishings from her room, and found it magnificent. One turn around the room, uncovered a bath, a smaller dressing room and closet off the far end. One look out the window, overlooking the small lake, overwhelmed her with possibilities.

Would Mr. Clayborne mind if she used the room for her own? She didn't want to seem unappreciative, but he hadn't actually picked her room. Ernestine had. Surely, he wouldn't be angered if she changed rooms. Would he? How did she explain her need for windows, without drawing too much attention to her past? Maybe she should move her things and be done with it.

"He did give me run of the house," she told herself, pleased. And it would be right by Derrick. Devlin would see the necessity of such a move. Not that she was far away now. But she could argue, if she were to take the room next to the boy the doors between them could remain open and... Her shoulders slumped. The other room had been prepared for her. She might as well make the best of it for now. After all, she did promise.

Closing the door felt like resealing a tomb, and she had promised herself she was going to brighten up the whole mausoleum. Kaitlin smiled at the reminder. "We'll just start with that room. No one said I couldn't clean it up," she said aloud as she picked up the cloth and dabbed it to Derrick's skin. "It will be a lovely room, Derrick. Bright. Cheery. I'll put sheer drapes on the windows, another layer of pale blue velvet drapes for warmth. It won't be too cold, not with the sun shining through."

She had herself moved in all over again.

Stretching out beside him, she shared her plans. After she talked a blue streak, Kaitlin closed her eyes.

*****

Devlin found her fast asleep with Derrick in her arms when he came to check on his son.

He'd been tempted to knock on her door and see if she were hungry, since she hadn't come down to dinner. It was just a courtesy he told himself, but he'd talked himself out of it. In reality, he couldn't bring himself to face her. If he faced her, he faced emotions that he'd been strangling. And now there she was. The moonlight drifting through the open curtains settled on the bed where she lay with his son. Its shimmering fingers danced on her dark curls and haloed her skin.

She looked more like Derrick's mother than Anna ever had. Devlin couldn't remember a time when Anna laid with their son. She passed him to a nurse soon after his birth. His heart ached with the desire to be a part of this family, his own family, but both the people laying there fast asleep on the large bed were strangers to him.

Try as he might, he couldn't recall a time when his son had lain so quietly in his arms either -- except during his first two years. All Devlin saw now when he looked in the eyes that mirrored his own, was fear. Would there ever come a time when he'd find trust, or love gazing back at him? He ached to think it'd never come again.

Fearing the look in his son's eyes, he visited him in dusky moonlight.

Tempted to touch the tendrils of his son's hair, and possibly hers, Devlin moved to the bed. Slowly, like touching a priceless vase, he leaned across and fingered his son's hair. It was silky like the smooth hair on a newborn pup.

"What would you do if I held you, boy?" With a gentle hand he caressed the boy's head. *What would you do?* He kissed his son's cheek and reveled in the memory of his son's voice. His son's laughter. His son's smile. His trust.

A smile his son reserved for the woman now, a trust that might never be his again.

Taking liberties, Devlin reached out to touch her hair, her skin. He grasped a lock of silken sable between his fingers when Kaitlin stirred. Gently letting go of her hair, Devlin took his leave. He carried the touch of her and his son with him as he slowly closed the door, but he couldn't erase the picture that remained in his mind and in his heart. Though he tried to rid himself of it, it came up to haunt him in vivid detail each time he closed his eyes that night and, he found, while they were wide open.

Devlin's heart hammered with thoughts of Kaitlin, her hair, her smile, her lips. Rising, yet again, he fought the temptation to return to the room for another glimpse. Another touch, another... Afraid to face her, afraid of the yearning in him, he paced his room instead.

*****

He saw the woman arrive in the carriage. She'd been lovely to look upon even from a distance. He wanted a closer look. Throwing off the covers, he donned his cloak, and slipped into the darkened recesses of the manor. Following the path others traversed in times of danger, he fell into the line the ghosts cut before him and made his way to her room. Knowing the darkness better than the light, he needed no candle.

His footfall the ghost of a whisper on rice paper, he slipped silently up the stairs and quietly unlocked the hidden portal so that he might slip through. Once he'd latched the door softly behind him, he allowed himself to drink in the moonlight and tried to recall what it felt like to stand in the sun.

The last time he'd stepped out into the sun, unshielded, his body had been so badly burned it scarred from the blisters and remained distorted in several places. Stepping to the window he touched the glass and stared at the field beyond the pane, recalling how the lush grasses felt beneath his feet. All he had were memories now. Now that he'd been cursed. He turned away with a heavy sigh, and tucking his memories away so they wouldn't pain him, headed to find the woman.

He found her with the boy, and taking a liberty, touched her hair. She was lovelier up close. Devlin had a good eye. He only hoped Devlin wouldn't be hurt this time, and wondered how he could make certain he wouldn't.

When Kaitlin turned in her sleep, he shrank back, disappearing like a wisp into the shadows. Then after studying her, silently slipped away.

She saw a fleeting form in the darkness and thinking it a dream, closed her eyes.

*****

"I see you've been out," Devlin said softly.

With a hand to his chest, he turned to find Devlin sitting on the edge on his bed. He wanted to ask why he wasn't with his new bride, but knew full well why. "You look awful," he returned with a grin.

"Even in this light?" Devlin chuckled.

"I can see you," he assured him.

"You've gone to see my new bride?"

"She's lovely." He took a seat beside Devlin.

"She is at that. So why do I feel like I've made the biggest mistake of my life? I should have never listened to Eliot."

"I remember your biggest mistake," he said none too cautiously, pausing as Anna's face filled his mind. "This woman--"

"Kaitlin?"

"Kaitlin. She loves your son?"

Devlin rose with his sigh. "It would seem so."

"That is more than I can say for his mother. Kaitlin has been nothing but kind to him. Give her a chance and do the same for yourself and your son." *And give yourself a chance,* his heart thudded; he wasn't sure he was ready to listen.

Devlin raked his hand through his hair and seemed to study the ghostly shadows cast on the ceiling. He watched them dance too, they reminded him of another who'd been given a chance and she'd betrayed him.

"I don't know that I can?" Devlin said.

"You deserve it."

Devlin turned on him, his eyes hard. "No, you deserve it. If only..."

Devlin put words to the beating of his heart. His hopes. He rose and put a firm hand on Devlin's shoulder. "Don't. Don't go back. We both know the way the lot was cast."

"But it should have--"

"Never say it should have been you," he groaned. "You don't want this. I wouldn't want it for you."

Devlin shook his head sadly and laid his hand over the hand

clutching his shoulder. "No, of course not, but I long for the day when you can join me again."

"Don't waste your time, Dev." His lips tripped upwards, but held no joy. Time would never be a friend. "I'm content. My biggest hope and my greatest joy will come when I can see you are, too." After all they'd gone through to get to this point, any contentment was well deserved.

Devlin read the truth in his eyes and wondered if there would ever come a time when he could be content.

He doubted it.

Chapter Eight

Kaitlin, in a gown of summer white, free from the black of mourning, went in search of Devlin. Her husband. *The stranger.* He was busy in his study. Sensing her there, his head lifted. He smiled at her entrance, asked about her night. She told him she'd slept well then told him about her plans for the room. Delighted by them, and by her, or so his soft stare said, he listened avidly to everything she said. She wanted to sigh. Then he rose and came to where she stood. Taking her hands into his own, cradling them like priceless crystal, he leaned forward 'til his nose nearly grazed hers. He was so close she could feel his breath on her cheeks, her neck. The tender look in his dark gaze said he would kiss her. With a dreamy sigh she closed her eyes. Her lips parted with an anticipated breath.

"Oh, Kaitlin," he whispered, his arms enfolding her.

"Devlin," she groaned in return. His lips moved closer. Her lips ached to be touched by them. His lips parted. Then he started to serve her breakfast. Eggs. Bacon. Boy, did her dreams bounce. Vividly. Why she could practically smell the bacon. A scent so enticing, her stomach growled. So real drifting into her dream, she opened grainy eyes to find it. She shut them against the bright sun that filtered into the room with a moan.

"Morning, ma'am," came a cheery greeting.

Kaitlin's eyes fluttered open, closed against the light and fluttered open again. She'd been dreaming, about her husband nonetheless. A stranger. And she'd been enjoying it. She should be horrified, yet she wasn't. She wanted to dream some more. But she had company.

Slipping her arm from under Derrick, she sat up, rubbed her eyes, and searched the room for the speaker. With a couple of blinks, she focused in on Anita and the most ridiculous costume she'd seen a servant in to date. And she'd seen some pretty ridiculous costumes in her day -- two of them at the Clayborne Manor. If the light hadn't already done so, the outfit woke her up.

Surely Mr. Clayborne didn't require them to wear something so hideous every day. Perhaps it was Anita's choice.

"Good morning, Anita." Kaitlin raked a hand through her hair, pushing against pins she'd forgotten to remove, working out the rats that took up residence overnight. She tried not to comment on the voluminous pink and white striped outfit, complete with a horse's behind bustle, stiff white apron and poufy white hat Anita wore. She imagined how the others might look.

Dropping her gaze, Kaitlin studied the gleaming silver tray draped with lace, Anita held aloft. She licked her dry lips. Inhaling the heavenly aroma, she sighed deeply. "Is that bacon?"

"Was that your stomach I heard growling?" Anita teased then bit her lower lip and bowed her head as though she waited to be scolded for taking liberty with the new mistress. She probably expected to be rebuffed, if not discharged.

Kaitlin laughed and felt her face warm. What else had the maid been privy to? Had she talked in her sleep? "Loud was it? I didn't make it down to dinner last night. That will teach me." She felt Derrick's head as she spoke, and noticed the look of astonishment that rose on Anita's face. "Our young friend's fever broke." She felt relief then a pang of guilt when she realized she'd slept through the night without watching him like she'd promised. What if his fever had risen?

"Marla came up earlier and checked on him." Anita set the tray on the small table, her stiff uniform crackling like the newest *Harper's Bazaar* as she bent forward. "She said you were both sleeping like babies."

Kaitlin couldn't believe the starched servant's attire hadn't awakened her, couldn't believe she'd slept through it all.

"Speaking of babies." She hoped to change the subject, "How's Bradley? It is Saturday? Shouldn't you be home with him?" Dropping her legs over the side of the bed, she slipped to the floor and made her way toward the mouth-watering scent.

"Oh no, ma'am, but Bradley is well. I'll work my half day and be off."

"Shouldn't you be off today?"

"No, ma'am, tomorrow's my day." Lifting the lid of the tray, Anita set it aside. Kaitlin salivated over the breakfast of coffee, grits, eggs, bacon and toast. The tantalizing smells played havoc on her stomach.

"Goodness, there's enough to feed a horse," Kaitlin exclaimed as she lowered herself into a child-sized chair. "Is Mister Clayborne joining me?" She looked to the door with a mixture of hope and dread.

"Mr. Clayborne has already eaten. Margaret thought you might be hungry this morning," Anita explained as she set about dusting the room, her dress sounding with each tiny movement.

Okay, so it'd been more hope than dread. Kaitlin fought the building disappointment. "I doubt Derrick will eat any of this. Would you like to join me? Even if you don't care to eat, there's tea and I... I hate to eat alone." Anita eyed the door apprehensively. Kaitlin followed her stare and back again. "If anyone asks, I'll take full responsibility."

Anita laughed, albeit nervously, and took a chair. "I usually dine with the staff." She tucked her hands beneath her and sat straight in the chair, her gaze made continual trips to the door.

Kaitlin wanted to tell her it would be fine, it saddened her that no one, certainly never a mistress of the manor, or governess sat down with the staff. Did Devlin ever join them?

Kaitlin bowed her head, whispered a short prayer then began to fill her plate. She nibbled on the bacon as she did, trying not to ask Anita about her scarred face and trying not to gawk. "How old is your Bradley?

"Five. Carver is eight and Matilda is ten."

Kaitlin swallowed her bacon, and took a sip of her tea. "Sounds like a wonderful family. What do your children do while you work?" Kaitlin poured a cup of tea and held it out to Anita. Anita's squirmed in her chair then reached out. Her hand shook as she levered the cup to the table. Kaitlin held out the sugar bowl.

"Carver goes with his father and Tilly helps out in the Reinholdt's household. I used to pay a woman to watch after Bradley on the days my Ernie goes to the mill, but Ernie's wages were cut and we can't afford the luxury. Tilly watches him now."

The desire to ask if that was yet another cut they couldn't afford was on the tip of her tongue, Kaitlin squelched it. There were other ways in which to help. "You know it would do Derrick a world of good to have someone to play with from time to time. You could..."

Anita's head came up. "No, ma'am, I can't bring him here. I brought him once and Ernestine threatened to have me fired. I can't be fired."

Well, there was one reason why they didn't care for the woman, Kaitlin told herself recalling the frowns from the day before. She would have to give the woman the benefit of meeting her first before she decided for herself. After all, she had been instrumental in making her room so lovely had she not?

"She says the mister won't stand for it," Anita continued.

Strike two. Who was this maid to say whether or not Mr. Clayborne would like or dislike someone, and for that matter, what gave her the right to take over the household when Marla had been there longer? Marla should have the seniority.

"She says that the house has to remain neat, quiet and orderly. That's why she chose these uniforms. She says they wear them in the finest homes in the east. And abroad. Of course, she won't wear them herself," Anita went on to say, tearing off a piece of biscuit and nibbling it. Kaitlin felt her eyes bulge.

"Strike three," Kaitlin hissed under her breath.

"Ma'am?" Anita looked up, the biscuit at her lips.

"Nothing." Kaitlin took a deep breath to calm her nerves and stop the hair from rising on her neck. Hoping to throw off Anita's confused gaze, she smiled. "How long has Ernestine been on staff?"

Anita swallowed her food before answering. Her nose crinkled. "A year, if I recall."

Judging from her frown, it hadn't been a very good year. "A year and she's in charge of the household?"

Anita's shoulders hitched. "I can't say why, ma'am, but she helps Mr. Clayborne. She spends enough time with him she's privy to things we're not."

While Anita flicked a finger on her puffy sleeves, Kaitlin wondered about Ernestine and her relationship with Devlin. It sounded like much more than a secretarial position.

"You heard what he said yesterday, about your asking her if you need anything. Well, that's how it's been. Excuse me for saying this, but she's gotten uppity."

"Has she now?" Kaitlin said. Her eyes narrowed as she clutched her cup and studied the dark liquid. Her brows lifted as she angled a grin at Anita. "You know, I'm the mistress of the house now, which means I have the say so."

"Yes, ma'am." Anita seemed bewildered.

"My first directive is that you refrain from wearing those, and please excuse me for saying it so bluntly, but they are such hideous outfits."

Anita laughed brightly and flipped her skirt. "No offense taken, ma'am. They are hideous. Not having to starch this ugly frock will save us all a bit of time. Will you still require us to wear the green and white frocks?"

"Green and white?" Kaitlin croaked as a vivid picture of the short round cook, Margaret, dressed in such a uniform of green and white came to mind. Her stomach turned. "Neither the green and white nor the purple and white or whatever colors you may have. Let's go for something subtle, shall we? Perhaps what you were wearing before Ernestine?" She paused to roll her eyes.

"Secondly," her voice lowered and softened. "Your family is welcome here at any time. No now, I mean it. It would be my pleasure to watch Bradley on those days you need someone. That way Derrick will have a playmate."

"Ma'am, really I--"

"I mean it," she repeated, her voice firm behind a soft smile. "I won't be going to the home as often and Derrick does need the company. To make it easier on you, starting today you'll receive another dollar a week in wages. If that's not enough we'll make it two," Kaitlin added when Anita's mouth unhinged.

"No, ma'am, that's more than..." Anita fought back tears. "It's not necessary."

"It is to me. If you find someone to watch your boy, let me know. Until that time, he's welcome here."

"You're too kind, ma'am," Anita sniffed and caught a rolling tear. "I should return to my duties now."

"So soon?"

"There's much to do." She grimaced then rose and brushed her skirt, it sounded like she was wadding paper.

Kaitlin looked to Derrick. He was fast asleep. "When does Ernestine return?" Kaitlin asked, helping clear the plates.

Anita's head came up her mouth gaped. The cup in her hand shook as she set it on the tray. "Monday morning. But she's been known to pop in when the mood strikes her. I haven't seen her this morning... yet."

From her frown, Kaitlin wondered if Anita would be happy if Ernestine never returned.

"If she does arrive today, would you tell her I need to see her?" Kaitlin thought about it for a moment and changed her mind. "Actually, I should like to get settled in myself and clean up some. So if she does arrive, say nothing. You're busy enough. I'll search her out if and when I choose."

"Yes, ma'am." Anita picked up the tray and headed for the door.

Kaitlin walked with her. "Where might I find Mr. Clayborne?"

"He's out for a morning ride, ma'am. Should return in an hour or so."

Kaitlin frowned. She probably wouldn't have taken the ride, not with her legs, but an invitation would have been nice. "Well, that gives me time to clean up. I'll see you later, Anita. If not before you leave today then on Monday."

With Anita gone and Derrick sleeping, Kaitlin had nothing to do but change. She couldn't believe she'd slept in her clothes. She must look frightful with half of her hair still in pins and Anita hadn't said a word. She slipped into the room next to Derrick's to see how it looked in the light of day before seeing to her morning absolutions.

Opening the door wrested a sigh of delight. Daylight showed her new possibilities for decorating and cemented her desire to have the room. But she'd tread carefully. Give Mr. Clayborne a chance to get used to her in the household and the idea of giving Anita a raise. For which she had to talk to him. What if he said no?

Not allowing her mind to tarry on that thought, Kaitlin considered the room.

While Derrick rested, she'd clean it. No. She smiled slyly. She'd wait for Ernestine and make her clean it. How would she look in one of those silly uniforms scrubbing the floor? She scolded herself for her thoughts.

Before she did anything, she should talk with Devlin. It always returned to Devlin. What if he didn't want her cleaning the room? Maybe she wouldn't talk to him at all. Not about the room or the raise she'd promised Anita. She had funds of her own. If all else failed, she'd use them.

Washing up and choosing a simple black skirt and shirt to match, she dressed, checked on Derrick, who was fast asleep then went in search of her husband. *Her husband.* Her heart skipped a beat at the thought of seeing him again.

All the deep breathing in the world couldn't keep her heart from pounding when she met up with him. He looked better than the dream. The heat rose in her face at the reminder.

He sat behind his huge desk. One hand raked through his hair in frustration as the other drummed the desk. His head was bent over a stack of papers. With him unaware she was there, Kaitlin took the time to study him. She didn't get long, because almost as if he knew someone watched him, his head came up.

*****

His neck warmed, he started to smile but refrained. He was pleased to see her. Too pleased. He didn't like the feeling. She had dressed in that hideous black again and her hair was pulled up in a nice, neat, and right, as far as he was concerned, ghastly bun. Perhaps that was best, had she dressed more colorfully, with her hair loose and curling on her shoulders like yesterday, he would have no control over the heart that drummed steadily in his chest.

"Good Morning, Mrs. Franklin. I trust you slept well?" He stifled the memory of her sleeping before it took over his thoughts.

Kaitlin moved into the room. "Aren't..." She started only to stop. He wondered what was on her mind. Did it bother her that he didn't call her Mrs. Clayborne? "I slept wonderfully. I don't mean to bother you, but I wanted to thank you for the room. It's most thoughtful of you. The colors are divine. I appreciate it immensely."

Devlin found a smile, but hid it behind his hand. "I'm glad you're pleased." He didn't have the heart to tell her the room had been redone because it'd been worn and he was looking for a new governess. If it pleased her to think it was done for her, let her believe that.

He hated to admit he found enjoyment in her pleasure.

"Derrick is much better this morning. His fever broke. His cheeks have color again."

"That is good news." He wouldn't tell her that he'd looked in before dawn, only to find her there. He never entered the room.

She stood silently. It was awkward. If she waited for him to speak, he didn't have much to say. He was busy with his work. He needed to stay that way to keep his mind off her.

"I just wanted to let you know that. I can see you're busy so I'll not bother you any longer." Turning on her heels she headed for the door.

"Mrs. Franklin?" She turned. "You need to know that I will be traveling to Minneapolis on Tuesday. I will be busy until that time, but if you would care to join me for the evening meal, I would be pleased." It was on the tip of his tongue to tell her to wear something besides black.

"As long as Derrick is feeling better that would be fine, sir. I'm sure he'd enjoy seeing his father."

Devlin's eyes narrowed. "Derrick does not eat in the dining room. He prefers to eat in his room."

"Oh, I had no idea. I assumed... I hoped he might join us."

"If you prefer to eat with Derrick, I will let the staff know," Devlin said coolly and turned back to his papers.

"I never..." He bowed his head to the books and she stopped. "If you'll excuse me," she said dryly then took her leave as quickly as she could, leaving a dazed, bewildered and shamed man behind her.

Devlin slapped his palm to his forehead. Why had he treated her so? At least he hadn't mentioned her wardrobe like he wanted but he saw the anger and pain in her eyes. Hating himself for his callous response, he let her go. What would it have hurt to have his meal with his son? With her present, maybe the boy wouldn't seem so afraid. Maybe it would...

It's for the best, he told himself on a long sigh.

Who's best? The silence asked him.

Devlin wasn't about to try and answer.

Chapter Nine

Kaitlin wouldn't let his dismissal ruin her day. Nor would she let the fact that she hadn't discussed the room or a raise for Anita weigh on her. While Derrick rested, she donned her cape and took a turn about the manor.

Stopping in the barn, she got a closer look at the carriage. Sitting there, it didn't seem so foreboding. Perhaps it took on its other life when the black horses were added? But even they didn't seem so dark chomping on their oats in the stall.

"That stallion there is Lucifer, the other one is the Hellion."

Kaitlin turned quickly with a gasp to find Thomas' chest. Her eyes lifted. "Why such names?" No wonder she thought the coach so dark.

Thomas shrugged. "They ain't nothing like their names. Both are as gentle as kittens." He stepped into the stall and let the horses nuzzle on him to prove his point. He beckoned to her. She stood her ground.

She wasn't as tall as Thomas. "Next to those horses I'm a..." She bit her tongue before saying midget, but felt terrible for thinking the word considering the size of Thomas' parents. "Maybe another time."

Thomas chuckled. "I'll have to admit they are huge and they do look like their names." Kaitlin winced in answer. "Mr. Clayborne thought since some in town are commenting on his coach being evil, he'd give them more to talk about."

Kaitlin swallowed that tidbit of information with a grimace. Devlin had a strange sense of humor. For a private man, he liked to draw attention. Thomas at the reins only added to the draw.

"Funny thing is ole Cotton over there is meaner than these two put together." Thomas turned his attention to the horse in the stall past Hellion. A large hand rose in warning. "I don't even go into his stall."

Kaitlin followed his stare, her mouth felt like it would unhinge. The horse looked like it couldn't hold its oats let alone hold a temper. His brown coat was dull and shaggy. She swore she could see his bones through his hide.

"Don't let the look of him fool you," Thomas said, closing the gate on Lucifer's stall -- a task quickly and efficiently done, given the size of his hands. "He's one mean beast. Cur won't let you near him."

"Why keep him?" Kaitlin drew her eyes from Thomas' hands and met his eyes.

"He don't look like much, but he's fine stock. A Morgan," Thomas explained, which was neither here nor there to Kaitlin. She saw a horse, of the four-legged creature variety. "Mr. Clayborne found him on one of his rounds and brought him home. Someone's been mighty hard handed with'im. Mr. Clayborne thought he should have a chance. The new man

Pa hired claims to have a way with mistreated animals. One of the neighbors gave him a good reference, but we'll see." Thomas' tall body swayed with his shrug. "Either way it ought to be quite a show, 'cause that ole cuss ain't the welcoming type. Doubt anyone will be able to sit his back ever again." He tossed a hand full of oats over the rail. "You ride much?"

Kaitlin frowned. "It's been some time." She didn't mention that the last time cured her from wanting to ride ever again. She saw no need to sit a horse and get thrown again. In her condition, she doubted she could ride properly anyway.

"Don't frown so, I wasn't talking about Cotton here," Thomas jested, bringing a tentative smile to Kaitlin's lips. "Mr. Clayborne has fine horses for riding. You tell me or Pa and we'll get you one saddled up."

Again Kaitlin wondered about Henry. How in the world did he get a saddle on such a beast? "That's kind of you. But right now I'm partial to walking," Kaitlin assured him.

He shrugged. "Give it time and you might change your mind. Young Clayborne's taking lessons. You might join him?"

"I'm sure I'll be here with him." Kaitlin didn't diminish Thomas' smile by adding that she'd come to watch. Past that, who knew what would happen?

*****

Derrick was up and moving by evening time. He was weak, but able to keep food down. As they ate, Kaitlin wondered about Devlin in that large dining room, alone. She wondered about the horses. Why had Devlin named his favorite team such and why had he taken on the rogue? Who had the greater need in this large house?

Derrick who silently watched her? Who needed someone to love? The staff who carried problems of their own or Devlin who seemed so distant yet...

Don't forget your own need. She studied the boy with his head bent over the picture he drew. She felt like another rogue with her own secrets, who'd come to live at the manor.

Funny how well she already fit in.

*****

Sunday morning, after little sleep from a plague of dreams and legs that felt aflame, Kaitlin prepared to go to services.

It was a gloriously sunny, slightly brisk, day, so she decided to walk. She dressed Derrick warmly and headed for the door.

"Might I inquire where you're off to?" Devlin stood on the landing, resplendent in his morning attire, looking like the Lord of his domain. He looked down at her through narrowed eyes. He should know. She had a

Bible tucked under her arm.

"Derrick and I were going to church. Would you like to join us?"

"Mrs. Franklin, those who live at Clayborne Manor *do not* attend services. That includes those in my employ and most assuredly my wife and son."

She hadn't prepared for an argument. Kaitlin rubbed her arms to fend off a chill and she hadn't even opened the door. "But, I haven't missed a service yet. I hoped to go"

"Mrs. Franklin." His eyes were slits, which didn't hide the fire in them. When he stepped down off the landing, taking two whole steps she had the awful desire to run for safety. She stood frozen to her spot. Which was just as well, Derrick had wrapped himself around her leg so tightly, she couldn't move if she wanted. "I do not wish to argue this point."

She did. "Why? What harm is there in attending services? It is the Lord's day!"

"For some. Not for myself or my family. Is that understood? The rule stands whether I'm here or not," he added to clarify.

Kaitlin's mouth gaped. Had he read her mind? What could it possibly hurt for her to go to church? And how would he know when she was gone? She was prepared to argue until she got her way when she heard a still small voice tell her to obey. But, Lord, I wanted to...

I know where your heart is. He doesn't.

Even while he's gone? He'll never know...

I'll know. Remember my word is with you always.

Kaitlin smiled in understanding. "Mr. Clayborne, if you prefer that I don't attend services I will honor that request. Even if I don't agree." She blinked. "Since I won't be able to attend, might I have your permission to read the Holy Scriptures here? To myself and the boy?" *And anyone in the household who might be interested. Maybe even you someday.*

*****

Devlin was thunderstruck. He'd prepared for her stubbornness, not acquiescence. It'd been years since the scriptures were opened in his home. Years since he'd allowed the book past the door hinges. Years since he'd set a foot in the church, his wedding not included. He should leave things as they were. No need to cause a rift in something that ran so seemingly smooth.

So why was he willing to compromise?

For the hope he saw in her eyes? The fear he saw in his son's? Could this one small allowance be a stepping stone across the chasm between them? If so, he didn't want to miss the chance like he'd done the night before.

If only Kaitlin had chosen something besides the scripture.

Anna loved the scriptures, read them constantly. It did little good. Kate's desire to do the same made him question her motives. Would she use the scriptures as her excuse? Would she use them to try and mold his behavior or force him to be someone he no longer wanted to be? He wouldn't have it.

So why was he going to allow it?

"Fine, Mrs. Franklin. Read your scriptures. If they are disruptive to my household, I will put a stop to it." He turned on his heels. Kaitlin drew a deep breath. She coughed when he turned again. "Please don't ask me to join in your Bible readings. I do not care to hear them, and would ask you not to foist your beliefs on me as I no longer hold a belief in such." Give her time and she'll hang herself with them just like Anna did. He chuckled to himself.

Himself didn't find it funny.

*****

Stunned anew, Kaitlin watched him go. Askance, she turned her eyes to heaven and threw up her hand.

Trust me, Kate. My word does not return void.

"Yes, Lord," she whispered, and looked down to find Derrick staring at the ceiling.

"Well, young man, it seems as though our outing has been postponed." She hoped it wouldn't be indefinitely, because she missed the fellowship. She missed Reverend Marlow's sermons. But the Lord knew what he was doing. She had one person to read the scriptures with. That would have to be enough for now.

"Come along, sweetheart." Kaitlin finished hanging their coats. Grabbing Derrick's hand, she led him to the library, determined to get started right away. "We may not be able to go out, but we won't let that dampen our day. We'll start a roaring fire and see if we can find a story."

Dropping into an oversized chair, she pulled Derrick into her lap, and opened to Psalms.

"Psalms is one of my favorite books. I'll start here and then we'll read about a man who was swallowed by a big fish. All right? Good. This is written by a man named David. He became king of Israel. 'Be merciful to me, O God, be merciful to me. For my soul trusts in you. And in the shadow of your wings I will make my refuge. Until these calamities have passed by. I will cry out to God most high, to God who performs all things for me. He shall send me his love from heaven and save me.'"

*****

Devlin stood by the open door of his room listening to Kaitlin read the scriptures, hating himself his weakness. He should have told her no. Why didn't he tell her now? And why did he feel compelled to stand there and listen to what she had to say?

Dragging his hand through his hair, he drew a deep sigh, turned into his room, and slammed the door. He wasn't quick enough to miss the words.

"You were rather hard," he announced his presence. "She's not Anna."

Devlin labored on a sigh; he didn't want to discuss it. But he would never say so. Not to him. "Perhaps not, but I can't be certain what she'll do."

"I don't believe she'd ever turn against you."

Devlin shrugged. "I thought the same many times before and look where that got me. And you."

"I know you've been hurt." He sighed now. "We've all been hurt. But it has to stop sometime."

Devlin nodded. Yes it did. He wasn't ready to believe that time was now.

"How long will you be gone?"

"A couple of weeks. Longer, if the investigator found anything." Devlin crossed to the window. "Would you like to join us?"

"I'll sit this trip out." He was curious to see what Kaitlin would do next. If she was there to hurt Devlin or the boy, he would be the first to see her gone. He doubted that would ever be necessary. Besides Devlin would probably take Ernestine along. He had yet to make her acquaintance, doubted he really wanted to.

The woman moved into the home so meekly and within a month's time upended nearly everything. Things even Devlin seemed to take no notice of, or let pass without question.

But he took notice. And he kept watch.

Miss Ernestine had all but pushed her way in. Making herself indispensable to Devlin allowed her to spend a lot of time in company. But what did she want? Devlin? The wealth? Or more?

Chapter Ten

"See, Miss Kate. I told you there were ghosts," Bradley declared with a curt nod.

Kaitlin shook her head. But she'd heard the noise, and she followed the boys into the room to search for it. The search was crazy at best.

Save for some covered furnishings, the room was empty. At first glance it looked like a room full of ghosts, bringing the memories of all Greta said to the front of Kaitlin's thoughts. She nearly bolted when Derrick caught one of the dusty ghosts and lifted it. Gulping to clear her senses, she chided herself for being such a ninny. *Sheets on furniture*! And she'd allowed them to give her a fright.

Still, there had been a noise. It was an old house. The wind probably sounded in the halls. Where was the wind now?

She half expected the sheets on the furniture to start moving, and shook her head.

Swallowing her trepidation, Kaitlin smoothed the hair on her arms. "There are no ghosts," she said emphatically. "And the only monster dwelling here is getting ready to get you," she proclaimed with a growl. Raising her hands like claws, she started for them.

"Run, Derrick, run." Bradley -- nearly tripping over Derrick's heals -- squealed with delight, as Kaitlin gave chase. "Hurry, here she comes."

With Bradley giggling loud enough for them both, they darted round the ghostly furniture, out the door and started down the hall. They came to a screeching halt when Bradley ran into Ernestine.

"What is the meaning of this?" her bellow echoed the house. Craning his head, Derrick took one long look at the red-faced monster and ran. Bradley tried to escape, but Ernestine clamped down on his shoulder and pinned him to her side. "Anita. Anita. Come here, this instance."

Anita came to her side. "Ma'am?" She bowed her head.

Yanking the boy around, Ernestine turned to glare at Anita. Her body tensed. "What is the meaning of this? Why are you out of uniform?"

"I was..." Anita cowered.

"Why is this child here?" Ernestine interrupted, yanking the boy's shoulder. Bradley looked ready to cry, he stayed silent. "Answer me, Anita. I thought I told you your child wasn't allowed in this house. Nor are you to work without your uniform. And why was Derrick allowed to run through the halls in such a manner?"

"Perhaps I can answer that for you," Kaitlin said softly. Coming down the hall she moved to stand by Anita and take the woman's wrath. With her tawny hair and gaze, she might be considered pretty, but her scowl and deep-set eyes made her ugly.

"Who are you to answer me?" Ernestine replied cattily, her jaw jutted forth, her blond brows nearly formed one line as her eyes narrowed. "When did Mr. Clayborne hire you? You're not the new governess? If so, you're out of uniform, Mr. Clayborne will not tolerate it."

"I'm the one who gave Anita permission to bring her son."

"You have no right. Governesses must... Who are you?" Ernestine nostrils flared.

Kaitlin went on. "I am also the one who told Anita and the staff to get rid of their hideous outfits?"

"I asked your name?"

"My name is Mrs. Clayborne. Mrs. Devlin Clayborne." Kaitlin held her smile when Ernestine's milky white complexion turned a lighter shade of pale.

Ernestine let go of Bradley, who quickly ran to his mother. She stepped forward to Kaitlin, trying to scare her, Kaitlin supposed, but Kaitlin was too furious to be afraid. Ernestine eyed her skeptically. Her chest heaved.

"You can't be his wife. He was hiring a governess. He didn't mention anything about a wife."

"Does he keep you in such strict confidence?" Kaitlin replied, hoping to keep her face impassive, her emotions unreadable. "I assure you I am Mrs. Clayborne, and I would appreciate it if you relegate yourself to the job you were hired to do and leave the running of the home, my home, to me."

Ernestine frowned. Such loathing filled her eyes that Kaitlin decided she'd made an enemy. Right now, she didn't rightly care.

"Now if you will excuse us, we should like to get back to our fun, unless of course you wish to discuss this matter with Mr. Clayborne?"

Ernestine's pallor turned ghostly. "I see no reason to bother Devlin with this matter."

"Nor do I," Kaitlin returned, her jaw firm, her chin rose. "I would, however, suggest that in the future you address him in a manner befitting his station and yours. Have we an understanding?"

"Yes, Mrs. Clayborne," Ernestine offered through gritted teeth, her lips quivered with anger.

"Well then, Ernestine, you are excused." Kaitlin let her go, aware that her battle with Ernestine had just begun. But why? Oh Lord, give me strength. "And Anita," Kaitlin winked at her, "Bradley is welcome to stay if he wishes. If you don't mind?"

"I don't mind, Ma'am. Judging from his smile, he doesn't either."

"Good." Kaitlin caught a glimpse of Derrick peeking around the corner and held out her hands. "Then come along we have a whole house to explore."

*****

Ducking down the back stairs, he was ready to call it a day. He'd gotten too close earlier and scared himself enough that he decided to stay in his chambers for a time. It'd be far easier were he not so interested in the goings on upstairs. But when he heard the commotion in the hall, he had to check it out. It pleased him that Kaitlin stood up to Ernestine, he wanted to shout *Bravo,* but refrained.

He hated to return to the darkness. Still, with the way Kaitlin and the boys moved about the house, it would be best. He wondered how much longer he could stay hidden before they found him and whether he shouldn't show himself first.

*****

After finding treasure troves, and wonderful places to romp in, they returned to the nursery for luncheon. Stopping abruptly in the hall, Kaitlin grinned at the boys. "Before we eat would you like to see another wonderful treasure?"

"Oh yes," Bradley said breathlessly.

Fed by his new pal's excitement, Derrick smiled. His head bobbed in answer to his own curiosity.

"Well, let's see if she's here, shall we?" Kaitlin inched her way to the stairs. The boys followed, their heads scrunched to their shoulders with hesitant anticipation. When she reached the banister she put her fingers to her teeth and let go a shrill whistle. In seconds the hugest, blackest beast trotted up the stairs. The boys' eyes filled with wonder and fear. They inched their way back against the wall and stood there with mouths gaping.

Kaitlin rubbed the dog's ears and turned to the boys. The look on their faces amused her so she couldn't help but laugh. "I promise she won't bite." Kaitlin winked. "But if you don't come over here this instance and say hello to Lady, I might." Growling, she bared her claws and tickled them.

*****

Peals of laughter, uncommon at the manor, interrupted Earnestine and Devlin all morning. This new onslaught of unbridled joy filtering through the halls, pulled him to his feet. He opened the door to his study and took a deep breath as if to let the sounds seep into his office and his soul. He leaned against the doorjamb.

Ernestine, wanted to puke. She'd been taking notes without having gained his attention once all morning. She remained in her chair thinking of ways to get rid of the woman who'd not only ruined her day, but her life, by compounding her task. She knew what she was after, had been after it for the past year. She feared this new hitch would throw a wrench into her plans, and she treasured her plans. She meant to see them to fruition. She would have married Devlin to accomplish them. Now she had to alter her course.

She wanted to strangle someone. The thought was strangely pleasant in her state of mind.

Perhaps she'd strangle her mother? Her mother hadn't warned her of Devlin's plans. She said nothing about the woman who wormed her way into Devlin's home. Ernestine didn't understand her mother at all. Why did she want her here? She suspected it was for more than she admitted.

As soon as Devlin finished for the day, she would see to her mother. Taking care of the new Mrs. Clayborne would take a while longer. She found solace in the fact that the new Mrs. Clayborne didn't share the mister's bed. Nor would Mrs. Clayborne travel with them on the morrow.

She and Devlin would have two weeks together. Two weeks to turn the situation around. Ernestine considered the trip and hugged herself.

Perhaps she wouldn't kill her mother after all.

*****

Sitting at the long table, Devlin ate in solitude. Perkins alluded to the fact that the missus wouldn't mind if he joined her in the nursery. He'd gone so far to say she might welcome it. Devlin knew better. He wouldn't go where he wasn't wanted, and he would not put himself in the presence of his new wife. She was doing too much to his heart.

His stubborn resolve didn't keep him from traveling the hall under the cloak of darkness to see his son as he'd done every night he was home since Anna's leaving. Since his world crumbled.

It disappointed him that Kaitlin, who'd been there the past two nights, was not in the room. It was for the best. He frowned? Why did he have the desire to go find her?

Thankfully, he would be traveling for the next couple of weeks. He needed to get away from the woman, needed to strengthen the crumbling parameters of his heart. And he'd only been around her for three long days. So why did he feel like canceling the trip and letting Eliot handle things?

Trying to take his mind off Kaitlin, Devlin took a seat and watched his son sleep. The boy made him think of Kaitlin. He saw the smile Derrick wore for her, the trust in his eyes. The way he threw himself at her.

Devlin sighed. He had a desire to throw himself into Kate's arms. Would she let him? He hoped she'd return to the room.

Kissing his son's sweaty brow, he turned to leave and caught a glimpse of someone in the adjoining room. At first he thought a ghost sat in the window seat with her nose to the glass. When he heard her crying, she became all too real.

He stood in the shadows, wanted to go to her, console her. Had his callousness brought her tears? His cowardice stayed his feet. She wiped her eyes and climbed down from her seat. She walked about the room -- a vision with the moon as a backdrop.

She circled the room innumerous times. He'd watch her all night if he could, but when she started for Derrick's room, he took his leave.

She sat on the edge of Derrick's bed, massaging her legs, never knowing he'd been there.

*****

"You torment yourself," he replied when Devlin shut the door.

Devlin's hand flew to his chest. "Must you do that?"

"I rather enjoy it. Why torment yourself? Your new wife is a lovely woman. I'm not only talking about her face."

Devlin crossed his arms. "How can you tell? She hasn't been here that long."

"That's true. But the staff likes her. And your son is quite taken with her. As is Bradley. Children seemed to know better than we do."

"Yes, I know," Devlin gritted the words. If only he could be like those children. The years had tainted his trust. "I'm not ready. Besides this isn't really a marriage."

"Isn't it?" He laughed. "You stood before a preacher. Signed a license and brought her home. How can you say that?"

It's already realer than your first. Devlin blocked the thought.

"You know this is an arrangement. One I'm not sure will work. We signed a business contract. Plain and simple."

He cocked his head. "Contracts can be broken."

Devlin's lips twisted. "Not by me."

He laughed. "I wager you'll be the first to break it. It's nonsense anyway."

"I won't break it," Devlin informed him soundly.

"I would, gladly, if I were in you in your shoes." He sighed resignedly. "Since I'm not, I can only pray that you'll come to your senses." He rose and headed to the panel beside the bookcase.

"My senses are fine. Thank you. And I would..." Devlin stopped when he realized he conversed with an empty room. He smiled. "Perhaps your senses are out of order," he whispered to the darkness. All the more reason to get away and put them together again.

*****

She hoped to see him before he left the next morning, but made it downstairs just as the carriage pulled from the drive. She stood at the dining room window until the carriage departed.

"Will you be breakfasting, Ma'am?" Perkins asked, startling her.

She whirled like she'd been caught spying. The curtains fell from her hand. "That would be nice, if it's no trouble."

"No trouble, Ma'am." Perkins grinned and pulled a chair for her.

"Made a feast for Mr. Clayborne, but he didn't have much of an appetite this morning. And Miss Ernestine wasn't early enough to join him before they left."

Kaitlin stopped in mid sit and forced herself to take a breath. Despondent, she lowered herself the rest of the way. "Well, of course they... he'll be busy. He will need his secretary." She didn't believe herself for a moment. She uttered the words, but her heart and mind laid out a far more disappointing picture.

"Yes, Ma'am," Perkins agreed. "Will you require a coach to see your sister?"

Kaitlin shrugged. "Today? I hadn't planned..." Why see anyone? She'd only have to tell them her new husband couldn't bear to... Perkin's grin confused her. "Why?"

"With Misters Eliot and Devlin out of town, I thought you'd like to visit your sister." He winked. "She might enjoy the company."

So Devlin and Ernestine hadn't gone alone? Kaitlin smiled. "Perhaps I will take a trip to town." She sighed heavily and draped the napkin over her lap.

"Very well. Now let's see to your breakfast. The young sir won't sleep much longer."

Chapter Eleven

A morning in the dungeons -- the basement -- beneath the house, in the dank and dark, where they played as if they were captives in a castle, and the trio of woman and boys took sustenance in the kitchen. When the fare for luncheon was laid before them, Kaitlin could almost hear the boys wishing for the bread and water the prisoners might have received in the dungeons.

She was happy they hadn't stumbled onto anything or anyone. At least there'd been no strange sounds. No ghosts.

"What is this?" Bradley's nose scrunched as he plucked the steamed broccoli on his plate. Derrick grabbed up a small tree and waved it before his nose with the same look of distain.

"It's broccoli, young man. It's good for you," Margaret said flatly. She ladled a spoonful to Kaitlin's plate. The determined look on the little woman's face had Kaitlin ready to eat every bite.

Not so Bradley. He paid no attention to Margaret's face. He eyed the broccoli.

"Good for me?" Bradley's whole body crumpled. The tip of his tongue peaked out between his teeth. Groaning, he pushed at his plate.

Kaitlin studied the boys' glum faces and chuckled. She remembered a time when she wasn't much older than they, when she and Constance weren't so fond of broccoli either. And her brother, Graham, who loved the green weed, turned the ingesting of it into a game.

They were given a minute to eat as many florets as they could. The loser received two florets from the other's plates and lost his or her dessert.

Kaitlin played the game atrociously. Why she'd ever been stupid enough to agree to play it, she didn't know. It meant she had to eat broccoli, she learned to love it over the years. And she wasn't as fond of sweets as her sister and brother.

It was a silly game. Would it be silly to two little boys who eyed their broccoli like it might pop up and bite them? Bradley already tried to feed some to Lady. A floret peeked out from under the edge of his shoe.

"How would you like to play a game?"

They must have thought she meant outside, away from the broccoli, because when she explained that it involved the broccoli, Bradley moaned and Derrick held his stomach.

"That's a stupid game," Bradley assured her.

After she explained that winner's got the dessert, they warmed to it, hesitantly. She made it easier for them. "Since I was the last to lose, you can each put two of your trees on my plate." She smiled. "And you get to share my dessert."

Smiling over at Perkins, Margaret shook her head. The boys lifted the two largest florets from their plates and lay them on Kaitlin's, leaving them each with two to try and force down. Which after some gagging and coaxing, they finally did.

Once they'd had their dessert -- shortcake and strawberry preserves -- they helped clear the table and left to play.

"The meal was lovely." Kaitlin wiped her hands on a towel.

"Shall we set the table for this evening?" Perkins asked.

Kaitlin frowned. "I suppose th..." her voice died as she thought it over. The dining room was large, lonely. She wanted to join the staff in the kitchen. She enjoyed luncheons with them. Perhaps they didn't like her there. Given her station, was it improper to join them? "We should have it in the nursery this evening."

"You're welcome to join us here, Ma'am," Margaret said, flipping a clean cloth over the small island that served as their table.

Kaitlin caught herself studying the stool Margaret stood on and looked up. "I don't want to intrude?"

"Intrude all you want, Ma'am," Perkins assured her, "so long as we can intrude during one of your Bible readings?"

Kaitlin's eyes misted. She smiled like a dope. "Anytime."

"You're right, Lord," she whispered as she ran after the boys. "Your word will not return void."

*****

He grinned and turned to leave. Delighted, he stood in the shadows as they played. If only Devlin were there.

The boys came perilously close to finding his chambers, but were distracted by another arm of the darkened maze beneath the house.

The dog wasn't so easily deterred.

Lady slipped in without warning, nearly sending him into an apoplectic fit. A tempered beast, she gave no clues to his whereabouts. She would if she thought him a threat, he surmised. He would work at winning her over. He'd been extra quiet all morning so they wouldn't find him. Now, once again, he almost wished they had. He'd have welcomed them, welcomed the company.

Would they greet him as amicably? He doubted it. He'd seen too many run in horror from him to know better. He heard the stories they made up to explain his looks. Why foist himself on those who didn't want him around? Why try to live in a world where he wasn't accepted?

The last time he went out into the world, the last time he'd trusted, they nearly killed him.

He was better fit to entertain the ghosts.

He bowed his head. He told Devlin he was content to live as he did. But with Kaitlin's arrival to the manor, it became clear he wasn't content at all. He didn't want to hide in the shadows. He wanted a life like Devlin

-- freedom to walk in the sun, and visit with Derrick and the children. He wanted to be a part of a family.

What family would have him? Devlin wanted him. That wasn't enough anymore.

*****

With the master gone and Ernestine off the premises, the household fell into an easy routine. Kaitlin's winsome smile won over the staff. It helped that she ran her home with a firm but gentle hand.

During the day the house erupted with laughter and song. Bradley enjoyed himself so much, he told his sister and brother. Whenever they had time, they came to play, too. They uncovered treasures in musty rooms and in the stories Kaitlin wove as they played.

She not only played games but she taught the children the scriptures. She purchased paints and easels and, reminding them that God was a master painter, master craftsman, let them learn the beauty of color and artistry. They never knew what she'd have for them. Under her gentle tutelage, they studied music, art, history, reading and much more. She gave them a desire and stepped back to watch their appetites grow.

Evenings found Kaitlin and Derrick in the kitchen with Perkins, Marla, Margaret, Henry, and Thomas. Here they shared a meal, laughed over tales of the day, and appraised the pictures the children drew. Here they studied the scriptures and grew into a family.

"It will be a fine day when the mister realizes what he has in Miss Kaitlin." Margaret sighed. "The boy loves her dearly. Sometimes I think he wants to tell her."

"Did you see his eyes tonight when she cried over his drawing?" Marla turned wistful. She shook her head. "I thought I'd cry myself. The children love her."

"Do you think she'll get through to the mister?" Margaret flung the towel over her shoulder and dropped into a chair.

Perkins brows rose in consideration. "I think the mister has already gotten through to the missus and he doesn't even realize it. Neither does she," he added softly.

"You really think she cares?" Henry asked. "He hasn't even been here. They barely know each other."

"We barely knew each other," Margaret reminded him. "She must care for him."

Marla set down her cup. "Of course she does. She cares too much. I hope he doesn't hurt her."

"It's not like him to go around hurting people." Thomas rose to Devlin's defense.

Devlin never raised a hand or a voice to one of them. But he'd been curt with Miss Kaitlin and that displeased Perkins.

"If he does, I shall have to throw him over my knee like I did when he was a lad," Perkins teased. Teasing aside, he knew the time was coming, he just prayed Kaitlin would be strong enough to get through the mister's bitterness. Strong enough to find the man Perkins knew was lost underneath.

"Has she met him yet?" Margaret asked. The pots clanged as she handed them to Thomas to store.

"No, but they've gotten close." Perkins looked at his cup. "He's been trying to befriend the dog. I don't think it will be much longer until he makes his presence known."

"The sooner the better I say," Marla replied. "I love him dearly, but he throws me when he comes out from the walls like he does."

"They were close today," Perkins said soundly. "They heard him, they just don't know it."

"Bradley is certain there are ghosts in the manor," Henry replied.

"I still think there are." Thomas chuckled.

"It's unseemly if you ask me," Margaret declared, swatting her son.

Perkins looked up and cocked his head in understanding. "I'd like to see him come out again. But you remember what happened last time?"

The story about a vampire living in the county got started. It burgeoned from a rumor to near fact. There was a vampire who came out and stole children and animals. People began to lock up their families and livestock. A group of people even searched for him for a time. Thankfully the furor died, but not without heartache.

"Miss Kate would accept him, I know she would," Thomas proclaimed. "She's accepted us."

"Has she?" Margaret played the devil's advocate. "She accepts our looks that true, but she knows nothing of our pasts. Would she accept us so readily?"

"I think so," Thomas decided. "And she'd accept him."

"I agree," Perkins allowed, with a hand to the boy's shoulder. "But until he believes she will, until he's certain... he'll stay put. Just as we are."

Thomas grew tired of hiding. Miss Kaitlin had been nothing but kind to him. She looked at his over sized arms closely that first day, but she never belittled him. And she always had a smile for him. He would give her a chance, even if the mister wouldn't.

*****

Kaitlin heard the noise that night when she got up to stretch her legs. This time she couldn't blame the wind. The wind didn't play the piano. And it *was* the piano she heard. When she reached the observatory she found it empty, just as it had been a couple of days before.

Not one to believe in ghosts, no matter what the boys said, she settled her vivid imagination. If she could get her heart and nerves to comply with her head she'd fare better. When Lady slipped into the room she bolted from her bed and nearly screamed loud enough to wake the household before she caught herself.

"So you're the ghost of the manor," she told the dog. She began to relax at the notion when her mind had to go and remind her that Lady couldn't play the piano. "At least you're here now."

Lady's presence soothed her. Still, she pulled the covers to her neck, and begged the ghost to refrain from visiting.

Chapter Twelve

"Tell me about Devlin," Kaitlin urged her sister. "Why is he against the church? Why is he so angry? What happened in that house?" There were also the strange noises too, but to tell Constance about them meant she actually gave them credence.

Constance sighed and pushed down on the child who kicked from inside her womb. "I don't know the full story. I'm not sure that even Eliot does."

"What do you know? Do you know why he hates Reverend Marlow?"

"That I know. The first Mrs. Clayborne was taken with the good reverend's son."

Kaitlin gasped. "Why would Devlin hold that against the reverend?"

"Anna was active in church. Always reading her Bible, always praying. Devlin used to attend with her, only her life outside the church was far from Godly. When Devlin learned of her indiscretions, he held it against God and the church. Reverend Marlow included."

"That's so--"

"Human?" Constance grinned ruefully. "Eliot and I have tried to talk to him. Invite him to church. Show him we're not all playing a game. I want him to know God is the one he should turn to. It's a moot subject. Anna burned him with scriptures too many times. She told him to get his life straight, while hers fell apart. Kaitlin, he probably compares you to her."

"I'm sure he does," she said glumly. "He's probably waiting for me to go behind his back, and prove him right. That leaves out Sunday's Services."

"Why?"

"He told me I couldn't attend even when he was gone." Kaitlin stabbed a laugh. "That's all right, we've had our own study at the house. Perkins, Marla, Margaret, Henry and Thomas join us. Henry's eldest daughter and her family might come, too."

Constance smiled. When the Lord told her husband to send for Kaitlin, she'd been skeptical. She agreed, hesitantly. As far as she was concerned no one could break through the cloud of doom that Devlin erected around his home and his heart. But God was doing it and Kaitlin was the chosen vessel.

*****

Kaitlin, Derrick and Bradley sat in the room the children called the

Art Observatory, listening to Carver make mincemeat of Ludwig Van Beethoven's *Ode to Joy* from his Ninth Symphony. It was an easy rendition and Carver had prior music lessons, but hadn't practiced in months. He picked at the notes, hitting a few, missing many.

Kaitlin encouraged him to pick an easier selection, but the boy wouldn't be thwarted.

None laughed, that would have broken Carver's spirit. And the determined look on his face said he was giving it all he had. So they sat in silence, listening as if the great Beethoven himself graced them with his presence and gave heartfelt applause when Carver finished.

"Beautiful, Carv," Kaitlin said sincerely. Bradley got a devilish grin. Kaitlin didn't want him to tease his brother.

"Carver's coming along nicely. We must remember to encourage one another in love. Don't you play tomorrow, Bradley?" He graced her with a smile. Kaitlin mussed his hair. "Soon we will play the mistake game and see who wins. For now, I should like to show you boys what I've done with your paintings."

She led them past the partition to the place where their easels set in a circle, pulled back the sheet that covered a mound in the center, and showed them she'd framed their work.

"Golly." Carver bent to touch the handcrafted frame that held his painting of fruit. That's what he called it. Kaitlin called it *Abstract* art. "It's pretty like this," he said, getting a nod from Derrick and Bradley.

"No, the frame is so it can hang on the wall. The pictures were beautiful before," Kaitlin complimented. "We're going to hang them right there. For all to see."

"Right here?" Bradley jumped to touch the wall in question.

Kaitlin smiled. "And when we run out we'll move to the next wall and the next until the whole room is filled."

"Tilly's, too?" Bradley spun around.

"Tilly's, too," Kaitlin assured him. "Her paintings are wonderful."

"Golly," Carver said again. He looked back to the pictures. "Where are the ones of you, Miss Kaitlin?"

"Those have already been hung. Would you care to see?" Three heads bobbed in unison. "Then follow me."

She led them from the observatory and down the hall. Lady rose from her sprawl on the floor and fell in at her master's heel. "I've placed them where I see them day and night." She stopped in the hall between her room and Derrick's. Reaching for the handle, she turned back with a smile. "Come look."

Carver and Bradley moved for the door. Derrick froze to his spot.

"Derrick?" She reached for him. He slapped her hand away. Stunned, she tried to grab him. When her arms were tight around him, he kicked her. "Sweetheart, please what is it? Is it the room? Derrick? Answer me somehow."

*****

He answered the only way he could, by fighting her. He grunted. His body tightened as he fought to free himself. Clinging to her leg he lost sight of the light and people around him and remembered a night long ago when he'd last been in that room.

His mind returned him to that night. He recalled it in vivid colors of horror the only way a child could.

Cowering in the darkness, his back pressed to the corner of the wardrobe for protection, he listened to her cries, listened as the monster roared. Each time the monster raised its voice, he wanted to scream. Wanted to help. His courage waned, he was afraid to make a sound lest the monster hear him, too.

And know he wasn't supposed to be there.

He wanted to see the rainbow of glass bottles that lined her dressing table, the bottles that she'd forbid him to touch. But they smelt so pretty, and the colors drew him like a bee to nectar.

The scents still wafting through his senses sickened him now. Would they give him away?

His heart thudded, beating so loudly in his ears he knew the monster would surely find him. He covered it with his shaky hand so it wouldn't fly from his chest and give his hiding place away.

The scream blossomed in his throat, but he couldn't make a sound. Tears, like small rivers on his cheeks, he bowed his head to his knees to silence his sobs, and covering his ears with his arms, prayed for the crying beyond the door to stop.

The crying rang in his ears long after the room stood silent.

*****

"Derrick, Derrick," Kaitlin said louder, breaking through his manic pummeling. "Derrick, stop. Stop. You don't have to go in the room. I won't force you." His body went limp. "Oh Derrick, sweetheart, I'd never force you. You must know that." She cradled the wild-eyed boy to her chest. "Why are you so afraid of that room?" When she felt his tears on her neck, she started to cry. "I wished you could answer me."

"Mama said he doesn't like the room," Bradley answered from behind her.

Kaitlin looked up to see the boys. She'd forgotten they were there. "Why would your mother say that?"

Carver shrugged. "She said they don't take him in there. Miss Ernestine tries and the boy fights her every time. Mama said Ernestine said the boy was tetched. She said he finds ghosts where there ain't none."

"He kicked her last time she tried to take him in there," Bradley added.

He kicked Ernestine? Kaitlin wanted to cheer. She bit her lip. He'd kicked her, too. Her leg screamed. She hated to side with Ernestine, but felt she must on one count. "Miss Ernestine is right, there are no ghosts. On the other matter, she doesn't know what she's talking about." Kaitlin pulled Derrick closer. "He's not tetched." But she felt the pain of his frantic attack and that gave her pause.

He sat solemnly by the fire, wondering about Derrick's reaction. The commotion perplexed him. He didn't cotton to the idea of ghosts, but was Derrick tetched? He wouldn't believe it. Sitting there in the silence, remembering what had happened years before, something that Derrick lived through as well, he wondered if Kaitlin hadn't stumbled onto something important. How important, remained to be seen. If it dealt with what he believed, then things were beginning to unravel, and he had to be on his guard constantly.

So would Devlin, and Kaitlin. He would have to let them know.

Chapter Thirteen

After that incident, Kaitlin never tried to take the boy in her room again. She showed Bradley and Carver where their pictures were hung. But told them they would be moved that very day. They were surprised until she called Henry, Thomas and the new hand, Gerrard, to help move the furniture from her old room to the new one. Due to the fact that he was in a delicate situation with the horse, Gerrard opted out.

Kaitlin was of a mind to pull rank, but decided she'd make matters worse with Devlin if she pulled Gerrard from the duty Devlin gave him. She didn't need that on her head.

"It's quite a bit of work for two men."

"We've got strong willing backs," Henry assured her. "What would you have us do?"

"I haven't been sleeping too well." Which was the truth. She'd been up with her nightmare nearly every night and gone to walk in the moonlit room across the hall. At least there were no more noises in the night to add to her worries. "I've decided I would like the room with the windows," Kaitlin told Perkins in explanation. "After the fire, it's been hard to sleep in rooms without them. Perhaps I'll sleep better? You don't suppose Mr. Clayborne would mind?"

"Of course not, Ma'am," Perkins assured her, knowing someone who would. Ernestine wanted that room.

*****

"Derrick, would you like to come into my room now?" Kaitlin asked once the furniture had been swapped from one room to the other. He would go into the old room now, but not into the new room. One look and he froze like before.

What is it, Lord? Is he tetched like they say? What do I do now?

Take smaller steps

Smaller steps? Looking at the furniture, she was stumped. Lord, what... It hit her. Smaller steps. Henry and Thomas would love her, but she had to do for Derrick. Why? She didn't know.

"Henry, please don't think me awful, but I should like to move some furniture again," she told him after study that evening.

Henry who had his wife put liniment on his shoulders, groaned. Kaitlin knew they were exhausted. She could almost hear his silent complaint

"Whatever for?" Margaret replied, saying what her husband wouldn't.

Kaitlin glanced at Derrick and back. "I'm not sure the furniture is suited for the new room."

Henry scratched his chin. "I suppose the boy and I can help you until you get it to your liking. We have to finish our chores first."

Kaitlin's brows hitched. "Of course. I know it's a horrible bother, but I'm pleased you'll help."

Thomas chuckled. His laugh tickled Marla. They all knew that Henry didn't have much choice. The mistress of the manor needed furniture moved again, if he didn't help the mister would not be pleased. Kaitlin hoped they wouldn't see helping her as their duty forever

Taking the smaller steps took two days. After the morning study on Sunday, during which time Kaitlin asked for wisdom again on how to take these smaller steps, she asked the men to move the furniture from her room one piece at a time. Telling them, she wanted to get a feel for the way it should be decorated, so as not to draw attention to Derrick's problem. With each piece taken she would then invite the boy into her room. The boy would not be coaxed. Kaitlin grew disheartened.

Did I hear you wrong, Lord? Did I misunderstand?

Trust me, Kaitlin.

"Yes, Lord," she whispered, still disappointed. It should have been a boon to her dwindling senses that Gerrard finally came to help. The size of him, nearly six and a half feet, intimidated her, but his gaze caused her worry. He could be anywhere in the room and his dark gray eyes always found her. It didn't help that Derrick clung to her hip during the process. She wasn't sure if it was the furniture or Gerrard that scared him.

The men removed the chaise and Kaitlin asked Derrick to come into her room. He wouldn't budge. He stared past her like a great monster sat in the center of her room.

Kaitlin followed his eyes and saw Gerrard then she looked past him to the lone piece of furniture on the far wall and knew. She finally knew which piece of furniture held him at bay.

"Henry, you and Thomas leave the dresser please and take the wardrobe."

"Yes, Ma'am." With a sigh, Henry sat his end of the dresser down and went to the wardrobe.

Derrick backed up when the men carried the wardrobe to the open door. Kaitlin held out her hand and knew with certainty that he would take it and join her in the room. She turned toward the hall where the wardrobe now sat, he wouldn't move. Not until the offending piece of furniture was back in her old room would he pass that threshold again.

She had no idea why the wardrobe bothered him, but for his peace of mind, and hers, she wanted it out of the house. The men were going to love her. "Henry, I've decided that I would rather start this room with a clean slate. Could you possibly see that this furniture is moved to the storehouse as I will be purchasing new furnishings?"

"Yes, Ma'am." He sighed wearily, and started to move the furniture. Thomas and Gerrard, eying her like she was tetched, groaned, but said nothing.

"Don't worry about it all right now, Henry." Feeling badly for putting him through so much, Kaitlin laid a hand on his shoulder. "Sometime this week will be soon enough. Only the wardrobe needs to go now. Thank you, Henry. Gentlemen, I appreciate all you've done," she added to his helpers.

With the help of Gerrard -- who hoisted one end alone -- Henry and Thomas hefted the heavy wardrobe and made their way down the stairs. "The missus sure takes a long time to make up her mind," Henry whispered to Perkins after the wardrobe was placed securely in the shed. "I hope she doesn't want us to bring all back."

"She won't. Haven't you paid the least bit of attention?" Perkins grinned. Henry brows rose in confusion. "The missus wasn't having a hard time making up her mind. She did it for the boy. She found out about his fear of her room and wanted to know why."

"All be." Henry wiped his sleeve across his brow and worked a calloused hand through his hair. "Wonder why nobody thought to do that before?"

"Nobody cared to," Perkins said sadly. Not that he and the staff hadn't considered it, but the powers that be wouldn't be swayed to try. And Mr. Devlin stayed away too much and was too lost in himself and sorrow to notice.

"She did," Henry stated with a firm nod when Kaitlin with Derrick in her arms and Lady at her heels, descended the stairs.

"She sure did." Perkins smiled ruefully. He feared for whatever the young miss might uncover next. Would she be receptive to the secrets of the house?

Maybe it was time for some of them to be told?

*****

Worn from battling that blasted horse -- a bigger hassle than he wanted to tackle -- and a morning of moving furniture, Gerrard took a break. He sat in the corner of the barn considering what the missus had done and after some time, found he was none too pleased. He could put it off to addled female thinking, but that was too simple. She was up to something. What?

Then there was the boy. Why did he find the wardrobe so offensive? And why did he paste himself to Mrs. Clayborne's skirts every time he was close? If it were for the reasons he thought, he should be cautious.

She wouldn't like it, but given what he'd seen over the last couple days, it was imperative he make her understand.

From the rafters in the barn, he watched Gerrard. He took a chance coming out but something about Gerrard didn't sit right. He tried to remember where he'd last seen him, tried to place his features after he caught a glimpse of him in the hall that morning. He seemed to know his way around horses like he claimed, but something about him made him uneasy. What *that* might be, bothered him.

*****

Kaitlin sat up in bed unable to rest. Gerrard bothered her, but she didn't know why. He seemed nice enough. Helpful. Work went much faster with his strong arms. But every so often she'd caught him staring, with a look that sent a chill to her bones. After a morning in his company Derrick still shied from him. Whether from fright or because the man smelt strongly of horses and sweat, Kaitlin wasn't sure. Perhaps the fact that he looked like a mountain even when he sat caused her uneasiness. She doubted it.

He had a calm facade about him, but it sheltered an underlying anger that affected her unease.

If that wasn't enough, she heard noises again. She vanquished her fears long enough to crawl out of bed, tip-toe to the stairs and look to the ground floor, and realized she was quite alone, there had been no clicking of Lady's paws. A chill climbed her body. The darkness seemed to come alive the longer she stood there.

She bolted back to her bed, and started to get her heart to a calmer pace when she heard another noise. She realized she'd left her bedroom door open and unbolted. Whoever moved about the house had an open invitation to visit her. She backed until the headboard pressed her spine and with the covers to her nose, stared into the night.

Were she braver, she'd hunt for the source. Right now, she had no intention of being brave, no intention of being alone. Where had Lady gotten off to anyway? She'd been acting strangely as of late, spending long hours roaming at night. Did she sense the unease as well? Was it Gerrard? Or the ghosts?

"There are no such things as ghosts," Kaitlin chided herself for the umpteenth time. She searched for them as she jumped and ran to lock the door. She flew back to her bed in two strides. Shivering, she tucked her blanket round her knees, turned on her lamp and tried to read her book. She laid it down to listen for noises shortly thereafter, wishing Devlin was home.

For the life of her she wasn't sure why.

Chapter Fourteen

The morning dawned blanketed in crisp white snow. It crunched beneath Kaitlin's feet as she went to the barn to see to the carriage. She expected to see Gerrard and have her fears from the night before discounted. They grew stronger. Not only did he stare with those dark gray eyes, but Lady growled at him; would have nipped him if Kaitlin hadn't constrained her.

Gerrard laughed it off. "Been with Cotton since daybreak. Your dog probably caught the strong scent."

"Maybe," Kaitlin allowed. The stench was strong, but Kaitlin knew better. Lady acted that way when she didn't trust someone. Kaitlin wondered what the dog had sensed, but she wouldn't overlook it, nor discount her intuition ever again. Not until she had better reasons to do so and so far Gerrard offered her none.

She and Derrick took the coach to town and spent the day with Constance and Michael. She shared her feelings about Gerrard, hoping that her sister could give her some reason for them. Constance said she heard his references were good.

"I've never met the man myself and have no need to hire him. Devlin wouldn't hire him if he wasn't knowledgeable," Constance assured her.

That did little to calm Kaitlin's fears. She wasn't too sure of Devlin either, what could his acceptance of the man mean to her? *A lot,* she decided silently. She shrugged off the shiver on her spine. "His stare bothers me."

"Yes, but you've been far more conscious of people since the fire. Are you sure that's not what's happening?"

Kaitlin shrugged. It was true she'd had too many eyes on her in the past; the news hounds hunted her mercilessly. Maybe she gauged Gerrard by them. Maybe he wasn't staring at all, and she agonized for nothing. But Gerrard stared at Derrick as well and Derrick found a place behind her skirts every time the man was around. The reactions of dogs and children didn't lie. If only they could talk to her and tell her why.

"I doubt he's some reporter who's hunted you down," Constance replied, flipping the pages of her magazine. Kaitlin looked up wondering if her sister read her mind. Constance shot her a querying glance. "Is that what you think?"

"I don't know." Kaitlin groaned. "Perhaps it's just being in a strange house. Maybe that's got me wondering. I'm married to a stranger. And I'm actually beginning to believe the stories about the manor being haunted."

Constance looked up in surprise. "But you're always so level headed."

"Don't remind me. I've heard things, Con. I think I heard someone playing the piano the other night."

Constance shook her head in bewilderment. "Did you ask the staff if one of them might have been?" Kaitlin nodded. "And?"

"They were all in bed." Her lips curled. "Lady has been roaming the halls on a regular basis, but I don't for one minute believe she can play the piano. It was probably the wind."

"Others have heard things," Constance proclaimed.

Kaitlin felt her eyes might burst. She blinked. "Like what?"

"One governess quit after her first night proclaiming she'd seen a ghost moving about the halls. I've often wondered where she was off to herself -- trying to sneak into Devlin's room no doubt." She sighed heavily. "Oh, but I digress. Where was I?"

"Talking about noises, as I recall."

"Oh yes." Constance flipped another page. "A couple of years ago a rumor got started that there was a vampire with the whitest skin and the reddest eyes you've ever seen living there. He'd come out at night and hunt for blood. He liked the blood of children the best."

Kaitlin gulped. "What drivel. Did anyone actually get hurt?" she added solemnly once she'd considered Constance's words. Was that the monster Greta warned her about? The same one Constance had discounted? If something hadn't happened before, why was Constance sharing now?

"Nooo." Constance chuckled. "It was a silly rumor."

Kaitlin wasn't convinced.

Constance shook her head and tapped her book. "Someone probably saw a coyote or a wild animal hanging around and let their imagination run amuck. But now, the ghost is a differ--"

"Let's not get stuck on that," Kaitlin said quickly, her hairs rising. "I'm here for furniture not faerie tales."

"We could always discuss the governess." Constance grinned. Kaitlin shook her head vehemently. "Then furniture it is. What do you think of these?" she asked, pushing the catalog so Kaitlin could see it better.

Kaitlin looked closely, but the prior conversation weighed heavily on her mind.

By evening, with Con's help, the new room furnishings were ordered. It had been a lovely day, but the nagging fear camped in the back of her mind the whole of it. No matter how she tried to shake it, Kaitlin had qualms when the carriage returned for her that evening. Thankfully Thomas drove the team. Henry met them at the manor. Gerrard was nowhere in sight. She didn't know what she'd have said to him if he were there, or how she'd react if she heard sounds in the night. On either count, she didn't want to find out.

She laid there listening for them that night, and somewhere, though she tried not to, she dropped off to sleep.

When the cloaked form stepped into the room later and fixed the blankets about her she slept soundly.

*****

Kaitlin didn't want to use Devlin's funds to change what he'd redecorated, so she wired for her own funds. She hoped the new furniture would be in place before Devlin returned and his home wouldn't be in upheaval. Then she'd let him know how removing the old furniture eased things for Derrick. Maybe Devlin could give her some clues as to why it frightened the boy in the first place. Surely Devlin had to know. Was Derrick's fear the same thing that kept Devlin in his own tomb?

The furnishings arrived a couple day later on the train. With the staff's help and some from Constance the room was put in order before noon the next day.

Kaitlin studied the room with its fine new furnishing and took a long giddy sigh. "It's wonderful."

"I quite agree," Marla said, taking in the room.

"It's so bright and cheery. I couldn't have done it without you," Kaitlin gushed as she hugged Marla then her sister.

Constance chuckled. "Kate, you're the one who had the ideas. I helped pick the colors."

"You did much more than that," Kaitlin decided, watching Derrick who walked the room, awestruck. If only his father liked it as much. He had to.

"Devlin will like it," Constance assured her, practically reading her mind.

"I hope so." Kaitlin fluffed a pillow on the window seat.

"It is yours, Ma'am," Marla reminded her. "I doubt Mr. Clayborne will mind at all."

"Where are you going to put your ladders?" Constance asked, stepping to the window seat to sit by Derrick.

Kaitlin finger combed the pleats on the curtains as she considered Con's question. "I intend to put one in every room on the second floor that has a window. First, I have to get them made."

"Henry is a fine craftsman, dear," Marla replied. She looked about the room as if silently mulling something over and shook her head. She put her finger to her lip. "Ladders to the second story can be rather tall and bulky... Why would you want one in every room? Wouldn't they be in your way?"

"Not that kind of a ladder, Marla." Kaitlin worked the wrinkled form the bed linen and straightened. "These will be made out of knotted ropes and wood slats. They'll fold up into a small box that sits on the floor before the window." She took a long breath. "As to why, my first husband and child died in a fire. Had they a rope ladder, they might still be alive." She stepped to where Derrick and Constance sat, leaned her knee on the cushion and put her hand to the glass. "I'm frightened by the prospect of a fire. I don't want anyone else I love getting hurt."

"They really are quite handy," Constance went on to explain. "Eliot and I have one in each of our second story rooms now."

"Then ladders it will be," Marla chuckled. "I'll tell Henry to get with you right away."

Kaitlin turned to Derrick. "Once they're hung, we'll have your friends over so we can learn how to climb them. We'll pretend we're pirates. Does that sound like fun?"

Derrick eyes lit at the sound of pirates then his turned to the window. He looked to Constance, the window and back to Kaitlin. He seemed uncertain whether climbing the rope ladders sounded like fun or not. Then he bobbed his head.

"Good for you." Kaitlin laughed. Sitting beside him she drew him into her arms. "The ladders aren't so hard, sweetheart. In fact, they're rather fun."

"He'll get the hang of it." Constance grinned and rubbed her stomach. "We did."

Kaitlin recalled Constance's first climb down a ladder. After a couple rungs she stopped and hung there like a house ornament, so petrified Eliot nearly climbed up to get her. With a little coaxing and few deep breaths Constance started down again. If Constance could climb that rope, pregnant to boot, a daredevil little boy should have no problem. It was Devlin who concerned her. What would he say when he found a nice little box down by one of his windows?

Would he know that she put it there for his protection?

"Aren't you afraid the ghosts might try and climb the ropes?" Constance asked after the staff left the room.

"Bite your tongue," Kaitlin told her promptly.

The ghost stood in the closet wondering if he'd have the courage to try the ladders and whether someone else might be tempted to climb them.

He caught Gerrard out by the corner of the house, near one of the hidden doors. He couldn't say if Gerrard had used the door or whether he was out for a walk. He wanted to believe the later, but in frigid weather at midnight, it was hard. If Gerrard found the hidden passages, that posed a greater problem, a greater danger. If Gerrard knew about them, what was he using them to look for?

Chapter Fifteen

Thinking it the ideal way to skirt the subject of the room with Devlin, Kaitlin set up to have a nice meal in the dining room upon his arrival home. He would have a chance to relax and enjoy his meal then she would bring up the topic of the room.

It worked in principle.

Only when Devlin arrived home that evening, it was evident it wasn't to happen. He barely said one word to her before he called for Perkins to find him and Ernestine a meal. Together they walked into the solitude of his study and closed the door without another word, leaving her in the hall staring after them. But she'd seen Ernestine's smile.

She thought of the ladders then, of the strong, thick rope and how it would look around Ernestine's neck.

Not to be dissuaded, Kaitlin ate her dinner in the dining room. It was awfully hard to swallow the fine tasting fare with a lump in her throat. Every time a door opened, she hoped Devlin had come to join her. He never came. She played with her food and the wax from the candles then decided to go visit someone who might enjoy her company. And this he could accomplish far better than his father even while fast asleep.

Blowing out the candles, she turned for the doors, unaware the staff was heartbroken for her. Unaware that the ghost had seen. He was going to have words with the master of the house.

"I didn't even see her," Devlin gave as his excuse.

"Did you even go to the dining room? Did you even stop to consider that she might be waiting?"

"I didn't go anywhere but to the study. I was busy."

"Busy?" he growled. "Too busy to see to your wife?"

"Ernestine followed me. I wanted to find out why."

He swallowed the anger in his craw. "Are you sure?"

"Fairly. I went to meet the detective, she was supposed to stay and help Eliot with the brief, I swore I saw her. If it wasn't her then she has a twin in Minneapolis."

"Hmmm. She does have family there, doesn't she?"

"From what I gather. But I get the feeling she had other reasons for wanting to go. It's the why that bothers me."

"I know the feeling," he said with a heavy sigh.

Devlin met his eyes, his own questioning. "Did you find something out about Gerrard?"

"No, but I've seen him out near the house a couple of times. At ungodly hours. Near the passages."

Devlin's face registered concern. "Do you think he knows about them?"

"I think he's looking. I haven't caught him doing anything that would back up that theory though. Did you find out anymore? Did the investigator know--"

Devlin shrugged. "Nothing. And that bothers me. Gerrard's references are too pristine for my liking. I plan to stop by Orin's on my rounds tomorrow and see if he has any more to say."

And what about your wife, he wanted to ask, but held his tongue. It would work out in due time. It had to.

*****

The next day, Kaitlin hoped to meet with Devlin at breakfast and came down early expecting to find him. Only to learn he and Ernestine had taken a ride. Ernestine. The thought of the woman was such a catalyst she nearly flew up the stairs to her room. Thinking better of having a good stew, she went into the nursery.

Derrick was fast asleep so she took a seat by a window and stared out across the pond, across the field, wondering why she was there. All she had to do was look at the boy to know. She hugged her knees to herself and let herself cry.

How could the man marry her and bring his mistress into her house? Her home. Was it that? Yes, she admitted, it was becoming so. It infuriated her that Devlin would go against his word. It hurt. And she wasn't quite sure how to confront the issue.

How to confront any of the issues hanging over her head.

Kaitlin hated to admit it, but the storm clouds gathering in the distance gave her great satisfaction. They meant her and Derrick would have no visitors, but they could have fun despite the weather.

To see the icy rain frosting the pane, to know that Devlin and Ernestine were out in it, made it all the better. Maybe they'd catch pneumonia and... She checked her anger with a sigh. She didn't want anyone to die. Besides, the rain had turned to soft snow.

She loved the snow.

Remembered curling up beside Jean Marc by the fire and... *What if Devlin and Ernestine were held up in a cozy room in a like manner?* She gulped. She felt ill. She and Devlin might be married in name only, but she would never break the vows they took. Never.

Would he?

Lord, if she's his mistress I don't want to stay here. She told herself. *I've made such a mistake. Can't you just get me out of it? And let me go now? Her* eyes were drawn to the boy once more, causing her to rethink her thoughts. She was going nowhere and she knew it. Just as she knew that things would have to work out with Devlin. She'd made a vow after all.

But what had Devlin made? Did he really see their marriage as a contract, a convenience? Did he have a mistress? He wouldn't be so stupid as to fall for someone like Ernestine, would he? She snorted. It was highly unlikely.

She reassessed her feelings when they returned and Ernestine's laughter filtered through the house. Kaitlin's mind triumphantly took her down dark paths, painting pictures she couldn't bear to look at. She could see Devlin and Ernestine hugging and kissing and... She squeezed her eyes shut to erase the picture. Much to her chagrin, the thought remained.

Plopping into a chair, Kaitlin prepared to spend the evening watching Derrick sleep, but Devlin sent word that he'd like for her to join him for dinner. While she didn't want to, didn't want to face him after he'd spent the day with his lover, she still needed to discuss the room and his son. She had questions about Ernestine and the ghost.

There were far too many questions for her liking. They weighed heavily on her. She rolled her shoulders to alleviate her load and felt no lighter for her trouble. She would have to face them, one at a time, or she'd go insane. She needed to talk to Devlin.

She asked for the table in the dining room to be set again, hoping her husband, who asked to dine with her, would at least take the time to join her.

Dressing in a black silk gown, she made short work of her hair by twisting it into a firm knot -- secure as the one in her gut. Then she squared her shoulders and stepped into the hall.

Kaitlin thought of the man who waited below and found it hard to breathe. She thought to take the boy along with her, but he'd have to do with Marla's company for dinner yet another night. Gulping, she straightened her collar and headed down. She felt like she was headed for the gallows, dragging the hangman on her shoulders.

She looked over her shoulders to make sure he wasn't dangling there and swore she felt him. *Him or the ghost.* She chided herself for letting her imagination get the best of her and started off once more at a faster pace.

With a hesitant hand, she touched the knob to the dining room door. It was bad enough just thinking that Devlin would be there, worse, when she opened it and saw Ernestine. He was with his mistress, at the table she'd specifically hoped to share with him. Their heads bowed close together where they sat at the end of the table, they didn't even see her come in, which was fine as she was not staying. She would not sit through a meal with them. Backing out, she closed the door slowly and tried not to cry.

She left word with Perkins to tell Devlin that she didn't feel well and would be staying in her room for the remainder of the evening, which was close enough to the truth about now. If he wanted to see her, he could find her himself. Her legs were in need of a good massage and her head throbbed. She wouldn't add the pain that she felt in her gut, or her heart.

*****

Finished with his business, Devlin dismissed Ernestine. The way she eyed the table and him, he knew she hoped he'd invite her to stay, he said nothing. He let her go, wishing he wouldn't have to see her for the rest of the evening. Let her go, thinking he'd do well to get rid of her all together, but there were some things he needed to know, things she hid. He'd hired her for the purpose of uncovering them. She wasn't that great of secretary, but she would do while he had her in his employ. Let her deal with the paperwork. Let her look over the figures. Maybe she could shed some light on the discrepancies he'd found.

When the door closed behind her, he sat back to await Kaitlin. His *wife.* He was beginning to like the sound of that. He needed to apologize for the manner in which he'd treated her as of late. Yes, he'd been busy with this latest suit and concerned about Ernestine, but that was no excuse. And he wasn't quite sure how to handle it now.

He barely knew Kaitlin. He could remedy that he supposed and a part of him wanted to. He should have made more of an effort to get to know the woman. They were married after all. He should have done that before the vows were spoken. But he hadn't made any promises. It was clear from the onset that this marriage was an arrangement. Still, his mother had taught him better manners, and he needed to get to know Kaitlin on some level. At least for Derrick's sake.

"Derrick's sake," he said aloud. Who was he trying to fool? Kaitlin had been on his mind far too much for it to be just for Derrick's sake. Her blasted kiss had been on his lips, toying with his emotions. With his heart.

When the door opened, he looked up to see Kaitlin and found Perkins instead.

"Yes?"

Perkins took slow deliberate steps into the room. "The missus begs your pardon, sir, but she isn't well and has sent me to make her apologies." Devlin took a weighted breath. "Would you care to go ahead and eat?"

Devlin nodded. Perkins excused himself. Devlin ate in solitude. That's how he usually took his meal. Many times he supped in the chamber below so he wouldn't have to be alone. He could read the paper or look over some of his reports, he supposed. But he couldn't focus, the silence was deafening with whispers of Kaitlin. She was in the candle's dim glow. In the fine delicate china that had been placed. She should be there now. He was.

He wondered about her, caught himself trying to see her through the ceiling. Was she ill or doing what women time and eternal had been doing? Lying?

He chose lying and hated himself for it. But alone, he stewed on it.

The meal had been prepared with great care, and he had no appetite. Laying down his fork, he took a long drink of wine and joined Ernestine in the study to follow up on the books. When she showed him what caused the discrepancies, his belief about Kaitlin was cemented in stone.

He felt his gaze burn as he studied the books. Ernestine looked at him and turned her eyes but not before he saw the satisfaction there.

Devlin decided he didn't care if Kaitlin felt ill or not, he was going to see her.

Ernestine lay down her pencil and followed.

*****

Kaitlin worked up her courage to go down to supper again. If for nothing else, to let Devlin know that she wouldn't put up with him and his mistress cavorting in *her* home. When she stepped in the hall and found them, she came to a shuddering stop.

"Mrs. Franklin. It's nice to see you're doing much better." There was a cut in his tone, as if he wanted to yell but propriety kept him from it. He shut his eyes slowly, took a long breath before opening them. "Mrs. Franklin, I should like to discuss the books with you." The lines in Devlin's face seemed etched in stone.

"The books?"

"The books." He sighed and opened the ledger. "I see you've redecorated the room and that you've taken my suggestion to brighten your wardrobe." He scrutinized her with dark angry eyes and a scowl. "Which I hope you'll be wearing soon."

Kaitlin heard the underlying cut of her dress and tried to ignore it. She simply had to talk to him and getting into an argument would not allow that to happen. Lord help her, she wanted to strangle him. She took a deep breath and tried to remain peaceable.

For reasons beyond her, he was in an argumentative mood. What? Did he have a fight with his beloved? That warmed her.

"Granted, I take no exception to either. But, *Mrs. Franklin,* I am concerned that there are no expenditures for the room or the clothes in my books. Maybe you can tell me why?"

"Why?" She shrugged and met his eyes. "I secured the funds for both the redecorating and my clothes from my private accounts."

"You what?" He jerked as if he'd been slapped.

"I used my own money. It was my idea to change rooms. After you'd so generously decorated the other one, I couldn't bring myself to use your funds. As for my clothes. I saw nothing wrong with acquiring them with my own monies."

"Nothing wrong," he started and glared at her. Again he studied her dress through narrow assessing eyes.

Kaitlin put a hand to her collar, took a faltering step back. Her anger rose when she noticed Ernestine, standing behind Devlin, smiling. Kaitlin's warmth from a possible fight between Devlin and his mistress dissipated, her blood turned cold. Her gaze shot back to Devlin.

His obsidian eyes met her. He raised his jaw.

"How could you possibly think there would be nothing wrong?" Sarcasm thickened in his voice. "This is, after all, my home, and you are my wife. As long as you are my wife, you will use my monies for anything you require."

"What?"

"I want a list of your expenditures on my desk first thing in the morning. Then I will make out a draft so the money can be returned to your account." He met her eyes. "Have I made myself clear?"

"Clear enough," Kaitlin returned angrily. Her eyes misted. She turned to leave before they could see her cry.

"Mrs. Franklin. Mrs. Franklin. I'm not finished," Devlin called in a stern voice.

"I am," Kaitlin grinned to mock him and entering Derrick's room, slammed the door behind her.

Devlin started to follow and stopped. He turned on his heels and went to finish his work. "Come, Ernestine," he said gruffly. He didn't wait for her to follow. He knew she would. Just like a puppy.

*****

"You were rather hard on her, wouldn't you say?"

Devlin pushed the papers on his desk aside, his head came up. He didn't smile. "I wondered when you'd show up. If you've come to take me to task about my wife then I'd prefer you turn around right now. I took your advice to heart and waited in the dining room for her this evening and she feigned sickness."

"Are you sure it was feigned?"

Devlin turned hot eyes on him, but would not answer the question. "And she chose another room and redecorated it using her own money."

"Why should that bother you?" He shrugged and took a seat. "The room is quite lovely."

Devlin scowled.

He was well aware that Devlin hadn't even taken the time to look at it. "Why is it so awful that she used her money?"

"Because I'm her husband. I'm the one who should see to her needs."

"Humph," he returned now. "You haven't been here. She was only trying to make things better. Did you know your son was afraid to go into her other room?"

Devlin seemed surprised. He shrugged. "He's afraid of everything these days. Most of all me."

He ignored that last jab. "Yes, he's afraid. So she took the time to settle his fears. She's to be commended, not railed at."

"Perhaps I over did it?"

His brows came up. "Good of you to notice. What do you plan to do about it?"

"Maybe I'll send you to smooth things out?"

"And have her running for the hills?" he quipped in return.

"That might be for the best," Devlin said with a weary smile. He sighed. "Give me some time to take care of it. If I decide I can't handle it, we'll send you in."

He chuckled softly. From his standpoint, Kaitlin had Devlin checked. Deep inside he believed Devlin knew it too. Devlin didn't want Kaitlin to leave, he wanted to get to know her, but was a coward. They both were. But Kaitlin was making headway. How long would it take before she broke down Devlin's wall?

"Tell me about your visit with Orin? And Ernestine?"

Devlin's brows knit. "There's nothing to tell." He groaned. "I haven't learned anything more about Ernestine. And Orin assures me that Gerrard is everything his references claim."

"He seems pleasant enough, seems to know what he's doing--"

"But?" Devlin brows arched. "Have you caught him in the passages?"

"No. He hasn't been out the last couple of nights." He shook his head. "Something is wrong. I just can't put a finger on it. I feel as though I've seen him before."

"Is it him, perhaps?"

He shrugged. "He certainly has the build. But I didn't see him that night in the field. Remember? I'm not even sure if his name is Gerrard. This is all a gamble, Devlin." A *dangerous gamble,* he started to say, but he wasn't sure how dangerous it was.

"I know. I know." Devlin sighed heavily. If only Margaret had been closer, and wearing her glasses. If only, if only... If only he could find the answers he searched for. If only he could find his daughter. Then maybe he could rest. Then maybe he could begin to live his life again.

And strangely enough, after years of denial, he found he wanted to.

Chapter Sixteen

Crying as she did, Kaitlin barely slept. She'd spent time in prayer but her gut still felt hollow, her heart heavy. She'd crawled into bed wishing the Lord would make her disappear. And still couldn't rest. When the sun burst through the windows the next morning, she was already up pacing the floor. She'd been at it most of the night. Not only were her legs bothering her, but Devlin's reprimand was foremost on her mind.

The man had unmitigated gall. How could he take her to task over such menial things and do so in front of the staff? In front of Ernestine! And wasn't Ernestine just beaming at the sight. Why, Kaitlin was sorely tempted to march to his room and strangle him for his impropriety. She would too, if she wasn't so afraid she'd find him with Ernestine and have all her fears come true. Instead, she stewed the night away thinking of the best way to handle the stubborn mule.

Yes, I know I behaved awfully myself. But surely, surely he could have chosen a better time to bawl me out? He could have done so when his lover wasn't watching.

Kaitlin's whole body bristled with the thought. She'd merely used her money to redecorate a room, to make things nicer for Derrick. She thought Devlin would be pleased. He didn't even give her time to explain about the boy. No, he was only concerned that she didn't use his money.

It would serve him right if she went on a spending spree.

"Oooohhh. The gall of him." Her chest tight with anger, she turned on the floor and paced again. His idiotic concern about the money threatened to ruin her day and she wanted to have a lovely day. She and the children were going on an outing, had even planned to invite Devlin. That was out of the question. She could just strangle Devlin Clayborne's neck. "And Ernestine's," she growled, making another turn.

She would strangle neither one, nor would she let them ruin her day. Practically throwing on her clothes, she resolved to catch her *dear* husband before he could get away. To make a greater statement, she brought her dog along.

Stopping at Devlin's study door, she looked over her attire. If her husband didn't like last night's gown, this could throw him into an apoplectic fit. She rather liked the idea. She gave a quick rap then opened the door before anyone could answer.

*****

Devlin's head came up. His mouth soon gaped. He shook his head. She was dressed in jeans, an oversized shirt and vest and had tied a bandana about her neck. A large Stetson hung off her neck and lay on her back, haloing her hair, hair that fought against its bindings. She looked like no woman he'd ever seen. She was lovely. He stared from her to the beast, who sat looking almost as fierce by her leg, then back to Kaitlin. "Mrs. Franklin?"

At the sound of his voice Ernestine turned and scooted to one side of her chair. It didn't take long before her mouth was gaping. She covered her mouth to hide her smile. A cynical smile, as though she thought Kaitlin was an idiot. She let her eyes take in the whole picture, clear down to Kaitlin's worn boots and looked like she might laugh.

Kaitlin caught Ernestine stare and returned the favor. "If you'll excuse us please, I'd like to talk to Mr. Clayborne *alone,*" she said with a voice of authority.

Ernestine looked at Devlin before making any move, his nod told her to go. There was such fire in Kaitlin's eyes as Ernestine passed, Devlin wondered if his wife might not plant her boot on Ernestine's backside.

When the door closed, she turned back to him. Silence reigned supreme.

"Would you care to sit?" Devlin spoke first.

"No, I would not." Her tone was curt, her eyes fierce as they held his. She pressed her palms to her legs, her chest rose and fell with each breath.

"May I inquire as to what this is about?"

"No, you may not," she said firmly as she came to his desk. The dog never moved, but he felt its eyes. "But I will tell you just the same." He blinked at the sight of Kaitlin enraged and caught himself wanting to smile. This was how Eliot felt that afternoon trying to talk to her about the marriage.

"Well?" he asked.

"Well?" She took a deep breath. She fumbled in her vest pocket, pulled out some papers. "Here are the figures that you required." She dropped them on his desk. When he reached for them, she leaned in and covered his hand none too gently. "Let me finish by saying this." He met her eyes. "This may be a business arrangement, but I am still your wife. The next time you have anything to discuss with me, you can do it in a manner befitting my station. I might be obliged to listen. But if you ever take me to task or demean me in front of your... your... servant ever again, I won't hesitate to knock your aristocratic nose. Have I made myself clear?" she spat the words then turned for the door.

He rose, knocking the chair back. "Where are you going?"

She looked back over her shoulder. "Out," she said simply then opened the door and slammed it behind her.

Out? It was cold out there. Who in their right mind wanted to... he caught himself, he'd been out the day before in the rain and sleet, running from farm to farm checking on his holdings, meeting with clients. He'd come home covered in a blanket of snow. At least the sun was out today. Cold was not the excuse, he just wanted Kaitlin to come back.

She could yell at him all she wanted to.

When the door opened, he looked for Kaitlin. Eliot entered. "I met Kaitlin in the hall." He shivered. "Dare I ask what that was about?"

"No, but when you figure her out, will you let me know?" Devlin seemed bewildered as he turned to the window in time to see Kaitlin, her beast and Derrick head out the front door and cross the lawn of winter white. His head didn't turn until long after they had disappeared into the trees beyond.

Eliot could only smile. Yep, this was working nicely.

*****

He laughed so hard he nearly choked on his sandwich. He had to hand it to Kaitlin, she'd gotten Devlin's goat and he could hardly wait to rib him about it.

He took another bite of sandwich and wondered where she and the children were off to. He wanted to follow and see, but the sun shining on the snow hurt his eyes and body. He took a sip of his tea and hoped they wouldn't be gone long. The house was too quiet without them.

*****

"Is it okay to walk in there?" Carver asked when they were but a few yards out from the trees.

"Why wouldn't it be?" Kaitlin covered another length with long strides.

"Well," Carver paused to gulp. "They say a monster lived there."

"He killed little kids and ate 'em," Bradley added.

"Monsters?" Kaitlin stopped abruptly and turned. Her fellow hikers stopped. "Whatever are you talking about?" She had an idea.

"There's only one," Tilly clarified. "They called him the Monster of the Manor. He lived out here somewhere. He liked to roam the forest in the dark."

"You believe that?" Kaitlin asked.

"Uh huh." They nodded in unison even as Carver stated it clearly.

"Come now," Kaitlin argued, but couldn't help the tingle on her spine from reading their terrified eyes. She shook it off. "There's no monster." Or was there?

She remembered Constance's words. But it was only a rumor. A rumor too many people believed in.

"Yes, there was," Bradley said soundly.

"Pa said he used to come out when the moon was full, they said he drank the blood of animals and even some children," Carver said with his eyes on the trees beyond.

"He went after children and drank..." Kaitlin shook her head, it had to be nonsense.

Tilly's head bobbed. "Pa said the townsfolk were so scared they come out to get him. Ran him out of his cabin and into the forest. They tracked him half the night."

Kaitlin gulped now. "Was your father there?"

"Um hum," Carter said. The hair rose to attention on Kaitlin's arms.

"Pa said Mr. Clayborne killed the monster," Tilly added.

Kaitlin's brows furrowed. "Mr. Clayborne killed it... the monster?" Greta said something about him killing his brother. But... she blinked in bewilderment.

"Yep, Pa said he got him," Carver said proudly.

"Then what?" Kaitlin asked. *Did he burn at the stake*?

"He buried him," Tilly replied. "Told all the folks to go home, that they needn't be afraid of the creature anymore and he buried him."

"Where?" Kaitlin wondered aloud.

Tilly shrugged. "He didn't want anyone to know. Didn't want them to come back and dig him up."

"He wouldn't let the reporter take a picture or anything," Carver interjected. "He just covered him with his coat and told everyone to go home."

Kaitlin shook her head again. Devlin had killed a monster. The Monster of Clayborne Manor! Who was this monster? Where was this monster? She found herself checking the ground beneath her feet and sighed. Just another mystery waiting to be uncovered. The problem was getting anyone, namely a man named Devlin, to talk about it. He was tightlipped about himself and too vocal about her shortcomings.

Her lips twisted.

And the staff hadn't allowed her into their confidences completely. Yet.

If the children spoke the truth, as she believed they did, then the townsfolk might have some interesting things to add. However, opening that can of worms might not sit well with her new husband. Maybe Constance knew more. Kaitlin made a mental note to ask next time she was in town.

In the meantime, they had an outing to attend to. She wasn't going to let some long dead monster keep her from it.

With a deep sigh she turned to the children. "We can't let old tales keep us from our outing."

Bradley's lips quirked. "I don't know, he could still--"

"Now children, you say the townsfolk rooted him out. And that Mr. Clayborne made certain he would never hurt another soul." If indeed he hurt anyone. "Is that correct?"

Four heads nodded slowly.

"Then surely the forest is safe." Kaitlin shrugged. "There's nothing to be afraid of. Right?"

The children half smiled.

"Right?" she prodded again. "We aren't afraid, are we? There are five of us."

Bradley counted each one then pushed out his chest and nodded with firm determination. "I ain't afraid."

"Me neither," Carver replied not wanting to be out done. Being the eldest boy, he didn't have the luxury of being scared, but Kaitlin saw him tremble beneath his smile.

Tilly rolled her eyes. Heaving, she rubbed her arms. "Well, I am, but if you're going, so am I"

"That's the spirit." Kaitlin chuckled, clapping the girl's back. "And you, Derrick?"

He shrugged, looked from one person to the next, focused his eyes on the trees and took off walking toward them.

"I guess that's our answer." Tilly laughed as they fell in step behind him.

They walked on seemingly unafraid by their prior discussion. Although Kaitlin could see the trees held their attentions. She watched them herself. The moment she and the children stepped into the clearing, all eyes were drawn to the cottage. Everyone came to a halt and held their breaths.

"There it is?" Kaitlin said, studying the cottage from a safe distance. She would love to ask Devlin if it was his, should probably turn around and do so, but he'd probably bawl her out for getting anywhere near it then confine her and Derrick to the house. "Have you ever been here?" she asked Derrick.

He pondered it then shrugged.

"How about you?" She turned to the rest of the children. She wasn't about to ask if the monster once resided here, it would be futile to waste her breath when she already sensed that he did.

*****

"I've seen it before." Carver nodded slowly and gulped. His brother and Derrick looked at him, awed. Tilly scrunched her nose.

"Never been in though." Given the stories and his curiosity, he wanted to. "Me and my friends peeked in the window and went to the small shed at the back." He arched his chest for his audience. "But all traces of the monster were gone. If he'd been there to begin with." Carver shrugged nonchalantly, his audience watched him with silent awe.

Of course if they'd found anything they would have shed their skins.

No one had the courage to go in the cottage or the courage to admit they were afraid to do so. So they sat in the shed dreaming up stories, creating monsters in the shadows, until everyone was scared spitless. Going home, they had to walk closely, the lantern burning brightly. They applauded themselves for their courage, but they left as swiftly as their legs carried them and never returned.

Had Carver's father known, he would have tanned his backside. Still might. And here they were now, standing in the distance, staring at the cottage.

Carver wanted to run even now. But, beings that he was the oldest boy, he took a deep shuddering breath and grinned. "Ah, it ain't so scary," his voice squeaked slightly.

*****

"There are big footprints over here," Bradley exclaimed.

Kaitlin looked at the footprints in the snow and found herself looking for smaller Ernestine size prints, too. She shook her head. They could belong to anyone.

"Maybe they belong to Mr. Clayborne," Matilda offered, swallowing loudly. She gave credence to Kaitlin's fears.

"They could belong to anyone," Carver replied. "Maybe Henry or that guy Gerrard came out here."

Kaitlin hoped they didn't belong to Gerrard. She nearly headed home then shook off the thought. There were too many unknowns, and she was letting them scare her.

"But this is your dad's cottage, right?" Matilda asked Derrick. He shrugged

"I hope so, because monster or no, this is where we're going to have our lunch before we go on to see the foal." Kaitlin folded her arms stubbornly on her chest and grinned at their surprised faces. She acted courageous, but couldn't dispel the gnawing in her stomach. They should head home, but they needed a place to warm, the outing seemed like such a grand idea earlier in the week. Then she heard about the monster.

Monsters indeed. They would take a look around, eat their lunch and touch nothing. Surely the owner, which couldn't be a monster, wouldn't mind if they warmed themselves for a time? They wouldn't be long.

Then the monster could have his home back. She chided herself her idiotic thoughts and decided everything she said, the monster excluded, sounded good in principle. Until one factored in that she was with four very curious children. They would probably look around, monster or no. In truth, she was curious herself. Learning someone had been there recently made her curiosity worse.

It was on Clayborne land. Was this where Devlin and Ernestine had their trysts? Or was it the monster's haunt?

Taking hold of her wayward mind and Derrick and Bradley's hands, she marched toward the cottage.

Lunch went off without a hitch, no monsters interrupted their meal and everyone seemed to settle. After lunch, Kaitlin let herself meander round the cottage while she looked for clues to who might own it. She didn't know what she'd hoped to find, didn't know if she wanted to find anything. But someone had been there recently. She would not go thinking about monsters again, but the cupboards were too well stocked to think who'd been there would never return. She just hoped they didn't return and find her and the children.

With that in mind, she readied to go. She started to water down the ashes in the hearth, to clean any evidence of their being there and was sidetracked by the children who'd climbed up in the loft.

Mercy, but they had guts. She was tempted to remind them about the Clayborne monster, when Tilly invited her up.

"Come look at this," Tilly called, leaning over the rails.

Kaitlin's first instinct was to call them down. The second, and stronger, had her climbing the ladder to the loft to see what they'd uncovered.

"What is it?" she asked her head popping just above the landing. She didn't need their answer to know. The loft was filled with piles of sheet-covered furnishings. She slowly climbed the last few rungs. In the meager light, with dust floating in the scant rays of light, the sheets looked like ghosts. Kaitlin hoped their intrusion wouldn't wake them. The hairs on her neck rose. Were they invading what should lay dormant? They should go, should leave them sleeping. The children started to peel the sheets back and Kaitlin's curiosity won over.

There was a baby crib, a small dresser. Carver uncovered a rocking horse similar to the horses that ran in Derrick's nursery. Kaitlin stepped in for a closer look. Her brows furrowed as she touched the pink reins, and let her finger follow the D that had been carved into its saddle. She felt a strange foreboding as her hand skittered along the horse's rump. She looked at Derrick. He watched her so closely she had to pull her hand back.

What monster kept such treasures?

She started for Derrick.

"Look, pictures," Carter proclaimed flipping back a sheet with a snap.

"Golly," Tilly muttered as Carver moved the pictures aside one at a time so they could see the next.

They were portraits of a past time. Perhaps a time lost? Though she smiled, Kaitlin still found the hand of dread running her spine.

It clutched her about the neck when Carver uncovered the last. Why? She didn't know. But the picture of the small girl seemed to cry to her. No one said a word as they looked at it. Perhaps they'd felt the same hand. Or awe, but something had touched them so deeply they backed away.

Were they remembering the monster?

"Deanna," Tilly whispered, in fear and reverence.

No monster, just a small girl. Kaitlin wanted to know more about Deanna but Carver and Tilly were climbing down. Bradley looked for a moment longer, turned to Derrick with a sigh then followed his brother and sister.

Kaitlin turned to Derrick. He stood there, his body shivering, his mouth open, tears running down his face. He spoke words no one could hear. Kaitlin's only thought was to get him out of the house. They had found no monsters, they had resurrected ghosts and they were caught in

Derrick's eyes.

Chapter Seventeen

Devlin's mind strayed from work to the window. He hoped to see Kaitlin and Derrick returning. The cold should have forced them home, he decided, which was purely selfish because he wanted to see Kaitlin.

Her voice filled his thoughts. She was absolutely right. There was no reason for him to treat her in such a manner, not in front of a servant. Not ever. He hadn't been thinking and owed her an apology. He wouldn't blame her if she never talked to him again. But maybe that was for the best.

He wasn't a very good liar.

Knowing he fought a losing battle, he'd called an end to the meeting with Eliot and sent him home to Constance. He gave Ernestine the rest of the day off, sat down by the window in his office, and waited for his wife.

He started to pace when dusk began to fall and Kaitlin and Derrick weren't home. It grew dark early this time of year, but Devlin still worried.

Tried of waiting in the study, he went to his room to try and rest. He laid down certain he wouldn't' be able to do so only to wake up and find darkness had settled. He looked at the clock. Nine. How could he sleep so long? Had Kaitlin and Derrick returned? What if they'd been hurt? That thought, however erroneous, pulled him from the bed.

At the top of the stairs, Devlin heard the lull of music coming from the library. His steps, along with his racing heart slowed when he realized Kaitlin and Derrick were home.

He leaned against the banister. Was it his son or Kaitlin who played the tune so beautifully? He was tempted to find out, but fear kept him from joining them. He waited for them to come home, but he couldn't go to them. He was afraid to see the terror in his son's eyes. Afraid to see the compassion in Kaitlin's.

Making every effort not to face them, he'd become a shadow in his own home -- reduced to lurking in corners, listening to the sounds of life and happiness emanating from beyond closed doors. Doors he couldn't bring himself to open, doors that must remain shut to bar feelings he didn't want to admit.

No matter how he tried, Kaitlin's voice broke through the barricade in his heart. Her smile drew him. Thoughts of her compelled him to descend the stairs so he could be closer. But, he reminded himself as he began his descent, he couldn't get too close.

Stopping in the shadows beyond the open doors, he watched his wife. Was that what she was? He wasn't sure. He knew he shouldn't call her Mrs. Franklin but that always came out of his mouth. It felt most comfortable. And what did he feel for her? After Anna, did he really want to feel? Every fiber of his being screamed *yes.* After today, it probably didn't matter what he felt... she must hate him.

Whether she hated him or not, he was drawn to her. There she sat in an oversized chair, her legs tucked up beneath her, her eyes closed in calm. He could only feel. And it ached.

She listened to his son. *His son!* Dwarfed by the huge piano at which he sat, Derrick moved his fingers carefully over the keys -- playing a song better than most adults. His son seemed to want no part of him, but he continually turned his head to study the reaction of the woman in the chair.

Her eyes were closed, and her lashes lay softly against her white skin. Devlin remembered how her eyes flashed hot with anger that morning. Now she was a picture of serenity. Her features were soft against the dim light of the fire, and strikingly beautiful. She wore a wistful smile as she hummed softly with the music -- Chopin's Nocturne. Her fingers tapped gently on the arm of the chair as she mentally played along with his son. An invisible cord wrapped its way around Devlin, beckoning him to join them.

What harm would it do if he were to slip in and take the chair beside Kaitlin? Call for a cup of tea and relax in her company? Isn't that what families did? What they should do? He started toward them and stopped. He didn't want to break the spell, didn't want to see the smile fade on Kaitlin's face. What if she welcomed him? What if his son...?"

Stupid fool, he planted his feet. Wishing for things that couldn't be had him acting like a young pup -- daydreaming, desiring -- all because of some woman who probably couldn't care less that he was alive. It didn't matter. She was there to look after his son. *You don't care for her,* he told himself again.

She has no reason to care for you.

That didn't stop him from remembering the softness of her pliant lips beneath his on their wedding day. Would they be as pliant and warm if he kissed her now? They looked soft in the firelight. Would her body mold so beautifully against his? He shook his head. *You don't care for her.* But he wanted to hold her. He reminded himself of the reasons why he couldn't. Reminded himself what women were and what they did.

No one could ever really care for him. Love him.

His resolve strengthened, he felt the gentle bindings slip in waves around his feet. He was ready to march back to his room and let them be, relinquishing himself from having to look at her, having to want her. Want his son.

Freeing himself from temptation, he turned to leave. When Derrick hit a wrong chord and the music stopped abruptly, his attention returned to the library. To Kaitlin. Within the next few moments the walls that he'd just fortified to protect his heart from her crumbled and the silken chords began to weave their way round his soul once more.

*****

Kaitlin dozed peacefully until the music stopped. It took a moment to realize the room had gone silent. She opened her eyes to find Derrick seated at the grand piano, fearfully staring at her. She was dumbfounded. Was he thinking about the cottage? Should she try and talk to him? She'd tried already and he trembled each time. She didn't want to pursue it. But knew she must.

Why had she taken him to the cottage?

Slowly drawing her legs from beneath her, she dropped her feet to the floor and leaned forward, with her elbows on her knees, she rested against her hands. They would have to face it sooner or later. She begged for later after she learned more about the girl in the picture, but...

"Sweetheart? What is it?"

Derrick's eyes filled with tears, his mouth opened slightly as though he would answer. He said nothing. He took a deep ragged breath, pounded the keys and turned to face her again. Meeting his eyes once more, she saw all he needed to say.

The meaning of his unspoken words finally registered and Kaitlin wanted to cry. She was relieved it wasn't about the girl, but she wanted to find every music teacher and tutor and strangle their necks. Yes the child was talented, but how hard had they forced him to practice?

She fought the lump in her throat. He'd made a mistake and waited for punishment. So sure was he that he deserved this punishment, he even alerted her to his error.

"Derrick!" she exclaimed somewhat gruffly, shaking her head. His head whipped to face her. His mouth gaping, he froze. With a deep sigh she rose and joined him on the bench. Her heart wrenched when he slid away with a shiver. Bracing her hands on the edge of the bench, she smiled down at the boy. "Sooo, you made a mistake? Hmmm." Her brows furrowed. The boy nodded and slowly bowed his head.

*****

"Hmmm," Kaitlin grunted again and took a deep breath. "A mistake? Well, well, Mr. Clayborne," she paused. Devlin wondered what she'd do. Would he have to rescue his son from another overbearing instructor? He was a prodigy yes, but still a child. He was prepared to step from the shadows when she stopped him. "I think it's wonderful." She laughed mirthfully.

When Derrick met her eyes, the fear had been erased, replaced by bewilderment. He shook his head. His father stood silently in the hall shaking his head in like manner.

"It's only a mistake." Kaitlin turned on the bench and grabbed Derrick's hands into her own. "I was beginning to think you weren't human. Who taught you music? Drill instructors?" Derrick's mouth gaped further. He nodded. She giggled. "Oh, I know you're human. So am I. We're all human and we all make mistakes. I make them all the time. And I'm much older than six." Derrick's head shook vehemently. "Oh, yes and I play piano atrociously. Or so my music teacher always said." She tapped a finger to her cheek. "I see by the look on your face you doubt me. Perhaps I should demonstrate."

Facing the keys, she stretched her arms before her. Lacing them at the fingers, she pushed out. Her knuckles popped softly. Dropping her hands with fingers curled and splayed, hovering over the keys, she glanced at Derrick, gifting him with an impish grin.

"I'm no child prodigy, so you must promise not to laugh. Promise?" she said in a snooty fashion. Derrick grinned. "Good." She dropped her fingers to the keys, a C chord resounded. In seconds, she was lost in Beethoven's fifth pounding out the tune, her fingers dancing on the keys.

From his position in the hall, Devlin noted the way she attacked the keys. Her back hunched lightly, her arms and fingers flying, she played each note in dramatic fashion, hitting several wrong keys in the process. Wrong keys, Devlin knew full well she hit to prove to Derrick she played worse than he did. Wrong keys, Devlin knew she could play right when he'd heard her do so already.

Pressing his shoulder to the wall, Devlin leaned in to listen. He opened his heart even further to the endearing woman in the room with his son, who held him in awe.

Unaware of the rest of her audience, she played a few more measures then quit. "There you see," Kaitlin began, we all make mistakes." The way Derrick grinned, Devlin could almost hear him laughing. Kaitlin drew a deep breath. "Now that we've practiced, the fun begins."

His son's dark, dancing eyes lit with fascination and filled with questions.

"Yes fun. We get to play a game. Remember the game I told you and the boys we'd play?" Derrick's head bobbed. "We'll play it now. Constance and I played it all the time, to the chagrin of one Horace W. Gillwater -- our music teacher. He told Mother we thought the game up to spite him. You know what? He was right." She threw her head back and laughed softly. "And he was so easy to irritate. But I think most of it was hot air."

She giggled. "We christened him Fishface. His lips were always puckered. Anyway, the game is very simple. One of us plays while the other holds up from one to five fingers, changing them as often as he or she wants. The player has to play the song and make a mistake in each measure that the fingers indicate." She glanced at Derrick. His shoulder hitched. "Perhaps I could make the rules simpler? If you're playing and I hold up two fingers, you have to make a mistake every other measure. If I hold up three fingers, you must make a mistake every third measure and so on. Does that make sense?"

Derrick nodded his head slowly, still unsure.

"Clear as mud, huh? How 'bout I play and you hold up the fingers?

We'll use Trepak from Tchaikovsky's Nutcracker to keep our fingers moving somewhat rapidly. Ready?" Derrick nodded and held up three fingers. "See, you've already got the hang of it." She grinned and started to play.

The boy had the game down pat. He changed finger counts faster than she could keep up. From three to one, five to two, one to four and on and on. Breathless and laughing, she stopped and let him play while she sat back and held up her fingers.

When the music stopped, Kaitlin and Derrick fell into each other's arms. She laughed, he remained painfully silent.

Kaitlin pulled from the boy, she kissed his forehead and held him at arm's length. "You're a natural born player. Next time, we not only count out our mistakes but we change the speed of the music, too. It gets better each level. And just think you'll get to help teach your friends."

Devlin saw the wide toothed grin his son graced her with and felt the tears well in his eyes. He might be selfish, but he wanted that smile back.

"So what do we do now, young Clayborne? Should we have ourselves some cocoa?" Derrick shook his head. "You don't want your cocoa? What would you have us do?"

Derrick pulled out two sheets of music and laid them on the piano. He looked up at Kaitlin with a soft smile.

"Amazing Grace and Lorena... you have quite the taste. Which one first?" Derrick pointed to one. "Amazing Grace it is." Kaitlin positioned herself to play.

"A*mazing Grace how sweet the sound that saved a wretch like me. I once was lost but now am found was blind but now I see. Twas grace that taught my heart to sing, and grace my fears relieved. How precious did that grace appear the hour I first believed.*"

As Kaitlin sang with Derrick pressed to her arm, grinning up at her, mesmerized by the gentle tones of soprano, Devlin listened closer. While his son lingered in awe, something about her voice was hauntingly familiar. When he finally knew why, all the walls that had started to crumble sprang up stronger than before. The smile left Devlin's lips, replaced by an angry scowl.

Taking his leave, quickly, before he was angered further, he went to the kitchen and left word with Perkins that once his son was in bed he wanted to have a talk with Mrs. Franklin. Then he stormed out of the kitchen and went to his office to wait.

"What do you suppose that was about?" Margaret set down her coffee. "A minute ago, I saw him outside the library smiling at the missus and the boy. Now he's angry enough to kill."

"Can't say as I know." Perkins scratched one of the muttonchops hanging like winter wool on the sides of his face. "Can't say as I know at all."

"Well, if he were young, I'd be tempted to turn him over my knee," Margaret said, cocking her head sternly.

"I quite agree, Margaret, but he's not a boy anymore." Perkins sighed. No, Mister Clayborne was a man. A man who wouldn't admit he was lonely. A man who wouldn't admit he needed Kaitlin. Perkins just hoped the young miss wouldn't get such a sound verbal thrashing she'd leave. Because he rather liked her.

Chapter Eighteen

"Enter," he bade when he heard the light rap on the door.

Kaitlin pushed the door slowly and poked her head in. "Perkins said you wanted to see me?" she asked hesitantly, managing a half grin. She still cringed.

"Yes, I do." Devlin motioned for her. Even as he tried not to notice how beguiling she looked staring at him with her lips curved just so in a soft smile. "Sit down, Mrs. Franklin," he ordered, and felt a stab of regret when her smile went south. Better that way, he reminded himself. He jutted his chin and gave her what he hoped was a staid face.

Her sigh seemed to say *'Here we go again'* as she lowered her gaze. She took furtive glances about the room then settled in the chair across from him and folded her hands in her lap.

Her head came up. "Why did you need to see me at this hour?" He couldn't miss the coolness in her tone. "Couldn't this have waited until morning?"

"I regret to say, it couldn't," he assured her just as coolly. "You see I'm wondering if I should let you stay or send you away this very night."

"What?" She nearly came out of her chair. "What in heaven's name have I done? Was it because I threatened to pop your nose, or...?" She stopped. She seemed to hunt for the words. For the lie. She looked at him, looked as though she might cry. She shook her head. "Is it my Bible reading? You said I could read the scriptures. Derrick has joined me, but I haven't forced them on him or you. Or anyone in this household. Just what have I done?"

"You lie to me and have the gall to ask me what you've done? What kind of a game are you playing, Mrs. Franklin? Or should I say, Mrs. Dupree?" She reared her head back, her mouth unhinged. He heaved a hard sigh when he saw her reaction. "I see we understand each other."

She clasped her hands, they trembled. "I understand that you think you've uncovered another chink in my character," she shot back. "But I never lied to you."

"You never lied?" He nearly laughed. Nearly. "Then how is it I know you as Mrs. Franklin when your last name is Dupree. There's no use denying it. Granted, I never saw your face, but I had the privilege of hearing you sing while I was in Paris and I never forget a voice."

"I never denied being Mrs. Dupree. Had you asked, I would have told you. Franklin is my maiden name and Franklin was the name I preferred to be addressed by until we were married. So you see I never lied." She sighed deeply. "I realize I didn't change it legally so Dupree was still my name, but I have my reasons for not using it."

"Are you ashamed to be called Marchioness Dupree? Was your

husband such an awful man that you forego not only his name but the use of his title?" A brow crooked upwards in quiet contest.

"No!" The word came angrily. "How dare you even think it? My husband was the kindest, most wonderful man in the world. I loved him dearly."

"So much, you don't use his name?" His laugh mocked her.

She rose from her chair and faced him over his desk. When her eyes narrowed, boring into him, he was forced to lean back. Her courage surprised him. "What do you know of it? And what right to have to judge? Are you the one that has to live my life? I admit that I wear my name as a shroud. But not because I didn't love Jean Marc. You weren't there after he died. You don't know how painful it was. You didn't have to deal with reporters and the like. I was in no condition to have them anywhere near me. It was either use my maiden name and save my sanity or let them continue hounding me and pray they'd grow tired of the hunt."

Understanding rose. He knew how relentless reporters could be. How relentless people in general could be. They still questioned him about Anna and his daughter, still labored over the issue of a vampire and evil ghosts in his house.

His heart softened.

Her jaw clenched, she took another deep breath. Her chest heaved with anger. "How dare you sit there and call me a liar? All you had to do was look at our marriage certificate and you'd see the Dupree name. I never tried to hide it." She paused and pounded her fist on the desk. Awed by her passion he couldn't bring himself to say a word. He sat in stunned silence just as he had that morning. "And don't you dare say one word about my hiding behind my name. You who hide in this tomb you call a home. You who hide from your son--"

"Don't even start, Kaitlin." He was out of his chair. They were nearly nose to nose, offering dueling glares over the desk.

She gulped. "Why not? Just who's the liar here? I readily admit that I hide behind my name. Where have I lied? What are you willing to admit?" she challenged. "When you settle that in yourself then you can judge me. Now if you'll excuse me, I need to go." With a resonant sniff she whirled, opened the door and ran out, slamming it behind her. Slammed it so hard he felt his body quake as it reverberated through the house. He dropped back into his chair.

Opening his drawer, he pulled out the marriage certificate. The business contract. He prided himself on taking good care of business and yet he hadn't even looked at it since their wedding day. He took the opportunity now only because of Kaitlin. He didn't want it to convict her, even as he unfolded it, he knew it wouldn't. He wasn't prepared for the stab of guilt he received when he saw the truth written in her hand. Kaitlin hadn't lied at all. But once again, trying, as she said to put a chink in her character, he'd lied to himself. He compared her to Anna, waited for her to be Anna. Waited for her to despise him. He felt further remorse when he looked at her signature.

Kaitlin Michelle Dupree.

"Oh, dear Lord." He dropped his head to his hands with a groan. It didn't go nearly as smoothly as he thought it would. Never did. Why couldn't he see that Kaitlin wasn't Anna? It had been so easy to believe the worse of her. And now... Now after what he'd done last night, and this, she was probably upstairs packing to leave. He couldn't allow that, wouldn't allow it. He jumped from his seat and went after her with no idea what he was going to say.

"Have you come to see if I'm leaving?" She frowned when they nearly collided at the top of the stairs.

Her words disarmed him. "I... ah... No. Are you?" He studied her hands. There were no bags. That was a good sign.

She swayed in place. "I wouldn't leave Derrick without saying goodbye first. I was coming down to give you this." She held out a slip of paper, put it up to his face so he could see it.

He took it from her and stared from the page to her in bewilderment. There was an address written on it in big bold letters. "What is this?"

"I thought you'd like my father's address, that way you could write him and let him know his daughter is a liar and why you want me to leave," she said in a snotty manner. "After Derrick is up, I'll say my goodbyes and be on my way. Then your home will be rid of this sinful woman." Without so much as a bat of her eyes, she turned to leave again.

He grabbed her before she got too far and turned her around. "Look here, you little firebrand."

"Let go of me," she said calmly, fighting against his grip. Her green eyes flashed. "If you don't let me go, I can't pack. I wouldn't want to stay in your home any longer than necessary. Lord knows you can't have a liar..."

He covered her mouth with his hand. "Will you shut up? Please?" he added with a sheepish grin. "You're right. I got carried away. I..." He loosed his grip on her arm. "I don't want you to go. If you left, Derrick would never..." He wanted to say, 'speak to me again,' but that was already the case. His arms dropped to his sides. "Please stay. I was out of line. I beg your pardon for my outburst. I beg your pardon for taking you to task in front of the staff. I... Will you...?" How could he tell her he would miss her?

*****

"I accept your apology." she said before he could finish, although it might have been nice to let him grovel a while longer. "Now if you'll excuse me, I need to turn in." She wanted to talk to him about the cottage, but didn't want ruin the shaky truce they'd formed. They could talk about it another time. Now she had to go, she didn't want to, but her legs screamed for relief. If she didn't do something soon, she'd be screaming herself.

"Kaitlin, I'll be going out of town again, but when I return, might you consider spending some time with me?" She looked back to find his eyes almost pleading. "I feel we need to talk."

"I would like that. I think Derrick would as well," she said, with a touch of a grin. "Now I really should turn in. Goodnight, Devlin." She turned to go.

"Goodnight, Kaitlin," he whispered after her.

She closed the door to her room and leaned back against it, her heart rioting in her chest. Her legs ready to mutiny. She crossed to the window and looked out. Devlin was always leaving. Always running. Afraid to open up too far and let someone in. And how much could she push? How much did she want to? What did she want?

At least he said they would talk, but would that change between now and when he returned from his trip?

Massaging her thighs, she rested on her knees in the cushion seat of the window and pressed her head to the pane. The coolness soothed her brow. It had no affect on her heart or legs. "God, what do I do?"

She hated to admit it, but she was beginning to care for this man. It scared her. She dropped to her rear. What if she started to care too much? Would she be hurt again? Remembering her words and her tone stabbed her with regret. He would never return her feelings now.

"Have I ruined it with my big mouth?" She sighed, pressed her hand to the pane. "I don't know what came over me. I'm..." *What? Rash? Rude? Disrespectful*? "He had some of it coming." *Perhaps, but where was the love of God in that*? Had she hurt him and turned him against the things of the Lord further?

"Am I going to apologize?" she asked heaven. With a gulp knew she would. At least for throwing her father's address in his face and being so rude.

If she was going to have to face him, she'd have to do it with a clear mind. She needed to bathe her legs, but the pipes were frozen and she hated to bother the staff at such a late hour. Rising slowly, she decided to warm and carry her own water. Maybe walking would soothe her legs.

She was in tears by the time she started up with her third pail.

*****

From the shadows, Devlin watched her struggle with the pail. He heard her sobbing and came to see. He should help, but couldn't bring himself to face her. She was getting through his wall and it scared him. Terrified him. But he couldn't let her go on like this. She'd taken these late night trips before. But now she was crying. He wondered if he was the cause of her tears. Why was she hauling water for a bath at this hour? Why hadn't she called the servants?

When she stumbled on the stairs, he started from the shadows, wondering how much more of himself he'd lose just to look in her eyes again. He prepared to lose it. He wasn't sure if it was relief or regret that flooded him when Marla started up the stairs to help. Something said regret.

*****

"Here miss, I thought I heard you up and about. Let me help you with that." Marla grabbed the pail. She caught a glimpse of Mr. Clayborne in the shadows and held the question she'd been about to ask until they were in Kaitlin's room.

"Is it the legs again, miss?" She poured the water into the tub.

Kaitlin's eyes misted over again, with surprise and relief. "You know?"

Marla nodded.

"They're awful tonight. I hoped the walk would help but..."

"No need for excuses, Ma'am. Miss Constance told me." Marla smiled. "I was concerned that you never seemed to sleep and asked her why. I hope that doesn't upset you?"

"No." It was like a sigh. Tears moved along her cheek. "I'm glad you know. I'm rather weary. Usually I can handle it by taking a long bath and rubbing some oil on my legs. But with the pipes frozen, I haven't been able to bathe. And I didn't want to put anyone out."

"Ah miss, we wouldn't be put out to help you." Marla pushed the hair from Kaitlin's face. "It'd be our pleasure and duty."

Kaitlin sobbed harder. "I treasure your help. It won't be for too long though, my brother promised to come with something that should help. But that's a time off."

"Now, miss." Marla frowned. "I don't care how long it is. We are not put off to help. You've never been demanding and are always trying to help. Let us return the favor like we should."

Kaitlin found a smile. "It's evident I can't handle it alone."

"No, you can't." Marla chuckled. "Now slip on into that water while I fetch another pail."

"You sound like my mother." Kaitlin slipped into the tub. It was so warm and soothing on her legs, she was sleeping when Marla returned.

Checking the water over the next couple hours, keeping it tepid, Marla let Kaitlin rest. She woke Kaitlin around two to put her to bed then went to her own room, feeling tired but very much alive and grateful for the chance to have helped. Mr. Clayborne weighed on her mind. How did she get him out of the shadows and into the light that was Kaitlin?

Chapter Nineteen

"Don't say it." Devlin's hand came up as soon as he saw the dark form slip from the wardrobe.

"Don't say what?"

"You know," Devlin growled. "I know I'm an idiot. Heavens, she's crying and I have no idea what to do about it." He turned, his eyes filled with despair.

"Maybe it's the house that has her taking those long midnight walks?"

"Bite your tongue." Devlin sneered. "This house is not haunted."

"Of course it is." He laughed. "I ought to know, I'm the one haunting it."

"Has she heard you?"

"I believe so. She and the children almost found my chambers. At least the dog and I are getting along. Otherwise, your wife might have found me already."

"Maybe it's time she met you?"

"I'd like to stay out of sight for a while longer. You're new hand still bothers me." He waved his hand. "And before you ask, he hasn't done anything that I can see."

Devlin leaned in and rested on his elbows. "He was very personable when I went to check on the horse. Seems knowledgeable enough," he paused to reflect, "but he never looked me in the eye."

He nodded in understanding. The only person Gerrard seemed to have eyes for was Kaitlin, and when he looked at her they were dark.

Devlin shook his head. "Orin did recommend him. That should be enough, but I'm not too sure about Orin either."

"He's the one that's been undercutting you?"

"Yes. And he was Anna's friend." Devlin shook his head again.

He wondered if that was the main reason Devlin questioned the strength of Orin's reference? Others had undercut him. Orin wasn't the first. Probably wouldn't be the last.

"Maybe I'm looking for trouble where there isn't any," Devlin cut into his thoughts.

"With good reason where Gerrard and Orin are concerned." He crossed his legs. "I'll back you on that. But you've got to stop looking for it in your wife. She's a fine lady, Dev. Tell her the truth. She's nothing like Anna."

Devlin wanted to agree that Kaitlin wasn't anything like Anna. Fact was he did agree. His heart did. He was beginning to see and that scared him. He needed more time to think, to sort out his feelings. And being in this house near Kaitlin didn't help.

*****

Too wound to sleep, Kaitlin heard the muted tones of piano again. Lady breathed softly where she laid at her feet, she didn't seem as concerned as her master. Her master froze in her bed, barely breathing and listened. Beautiful music resonated from the walls. Surely a ghost couldn't play so wonderfully? So who?

Coward though she was, she donned her robe and went in search of the player. Opening the door, Lady slipped passed her into the dark. She started to call her back but didn't want to draw attention. She cowered in the shadows for a time then inched her way along the wall, her heart beat drowning the tones of the piano as it thudded in her chest and head.

Reaching the library, she listened at the door then taking a deep breath, stepped inside. Again it was empty. The muted tones played on. So clear were they, she moved closer to the piano and touched the bench just to see if anything was there.

It was cold. Kaitlin took a deep breath and laughed at her stupidity. She was a fool to think she'd find a ghost playing the piano. The keys weren't even moving. But the music played on.

Cowardice getting the better of her, she quietly retraced her steps to the door and started out. When she saw the shadow in the hall, she froze.

No ghost stood in the hall, but by her accounting it was worse. Ernestine moved through the house like a shadow. Why was she here at this hour? She followed her to see where she would go, wasn't sure whether to be relieved or further concerned when she saw her descend the stairs and leave quietly through the front door.

Without the proper clothes to follow her into the night, Kaitlin went into the dining room and tried to catch a glimpse of her from the window. The yard was empty. Ernestine had melted into the night.

Kaitlin rubbed her arms to stop the sliver of dread running her spine, chilling her bones, and realized the music had stopped. The silence, so foreboding, set her heart to racing. Scurrying as quietly as possible for the safety of her room, she closed the door behind herself and leaned back to catch her breath. And perhaps stop the ghost that might come through at any moment. With that thought in mind, the empty room only made her heart race more.

Had Devlin heard the music? She wondered if he'd mind if she came and sat with him for the evening. Was sorely tempted to, but lacked the courage to the walk the dark hall. Didn't have the courage to reach his room and learn he hadn't been alone.

She took a deep breath and tiptoed to Derrick's room. Even there she couldn't rest. She sat in one of the window bays staring into the darkness, seeing nothing. There was far too much on her mind. Far too many unanswered questions.

Far too many ghosts.

*****

Devlin heard the music and found it soothing. He knew the player. From the dull footsteps on the stairs, he knew Kaitlin was up again. He hoped she wasn't restless because of the song echoing through the house. He opened his door to find her racing up the stairs into her room. When he passed her door, he wanted to go inside and see if she was all right, wanted to know that she was okay. He wanted to tell her there were no ghosts.

Even though he felt them so strongly.

He stood quietly in the hall, a sentry at her door then turned to look in on his son. When he saw her at the window, he froze and pulled the door softly so she wouldn't know he was there.

"Go in." he said, setting Devlin's heart to racing.

Devlin gasped for air. "There's no need. I wanted to check on my son."

"And her?"

"And her," Devlin admitted solemnly, and turned down the hall, toward his room. He fell in step beside him. Devlin shook his head. "She heard you playing."

"I'll try not to play so loudly next time."

"Or at least close the door to your chamber." Devlin cuffed his shoulder. "I almost believe you wanted her to hear and hunt you down."

He laughed softly. "You're more right than you know. I think you want her to find you as well."

"I'm not lost and in hiding," Devlin quipped.

He only smiled. They were both in hiding, hoping to be found and they both knew it.

*****

To Kaitlin's delight, there'd been no more sounds in the night, and though she'd missed him that morning, Devlin had left a note reminding her that he wanted to talk with her when he returned. That was good news she decided, filling her plate with eggs and bacon. Maybe he was beginning to care for her? She was kidding herself, but it felt good to receive a note from her husband. It felt good to know they were beginning to talk.

It was short-lived when she considered Ernestine.

Ernestine hadn't joined him on this outing -- another small serving of jubilation -- but she still had a place in Devlin's life. A place Kaitlin wasn't sure about. Had she been coming from Devlin's room when she'd happened on her in the night? Kaitlin felt ill at the thought. She was in a quandary, and would have to find out soon? But how? There was nothing between her and this man, this stranger, she'd married. They'd exchanged vows. Vows she meant to keep. But what did they mean to Devlin? Was Ernestine part of those vows? Did she even have the right to ask? What would Devlin's answer be? Would he deny it or would he confirm her deepest fear?

She read his note again, thought about the meager bridge they were building between them, a bridge she didn't want to destroy by making accusations she wasn't sure of. She sighed. "Lord, what do I do? What do I do to reach him?"

What did she do with her feelings toward him? What were they? Knowing too well, she sighed again. What if she asked him and found out he cared for Ernestine? She would have to go? Would have to leave him and Derrick? Would have to be hurt all over again?

Her heaving sigh rattled her whole body.

And what of the ghost? "The person," she clarified. Did she really want to find out who played the music? Or just try and forget she'd heard a thing?

"Ignorance is bliss," she told herself, knowing the way her mind and heart were prone to wonder, it was far from it.

Kaitlin needed more information, but there was nothing she could do about it now. She would have to wait. In the meantime, there were other questions she needed answers to. For those she had an ally that wouldn't be offended if she asked.

*****

"Morning, Con."

"Katie, what are you doing here at this hour?" She peaked out the door. "I didn't hear the carriage." Nor did she see it now. She eyed her sister in bewilderment. "Did Thomas leave already?"

"No, we walked," Kaitlin explained. Closing the door, she helped Derrick out of his overcoat.

"Walked?" Constance was aghast. "It's freezing out there."

"Slightly brisk," Kaitlin mumbled as she peeled her gloves with her teeth. "Once we started walking, it warmed up quite nicely. Didn't it, Derrick?" She lifted the cap from his nodding head, his hair lifted and popped softly with static. He gifted her with a smile and rubbed his pink nose.

"Slightly brisk?" Constance couldn't believe her eyes or her ears. With a grunt she hung their over clothes on the coat tree by the door. "Are you trying to catch your death? The boy doesn't need to be exposed to such cold."

"Oh baaa. It's not that cold. Besides, my legs were on fire. I needed a walk. And Derrick wanted to play with Michael." She grinned softly. Derrick grinned too. Together they melted Con like butter.

"Well, off with you then. Michael's upstairs." She patted Derrick's behind to shoot him in the right direction. "I'll call you for chocolate soon.

Would you like that?"

Derrick stopped halfway up the stairs and turned back with a toothy grin. His head bobbed with delight.

It was all the answer Constance needed. But she wished for the words behind it. "He's a sweetheart."

"Ernestine thinks he's tetched," Kaitlin replied dryly, dropping in the nearest chair.

"Oh phssaw. What does that busy body know?" She lowered herself to the couch. "I wished Devlin would be rid of her."

Kaitlin sat in quiet contemplation, picking pieces of cat hair from the arm of her chair.

The frown on her face concerned Constance. "Why did you ask those questions? Do you believe he's tetched?"

Kaitlin's head came up. "No, I well... no, I don't think that. But there is something." She paused on a sigh, laced her fingers and stretched her arms over her head. "The children and I went for a romp in the woods yesterday. We were on our way to see the neighbor's new foal, when we found this cottage in a clearing about half a mile from the house, so we stopped to eat our lunch and warm up a bit. I'm pretty sure it belongs to Devlin. Funny, but I think it hadn't been that long since he'd been there."

She stopped and looked at the ceiling then shook her head and turned her attention to Constance.

"It was stocked with food. There was a nice sized wood pile, too. Anyway, we had our sandwiches then did some snooping."

Constance tensed. "Katie Michelle! Was that wise? You're sure the cottage belongs to Devlin?"

"Relatively," Kaitlin amended. "I'm fairly sure now." Constance settled some. "We found this stack of old paintings in the loft."

"Loft? You went into the loft?"

"Yes." Folding her legs beneath her, she planted her elbow on the arm of the chair and leaned on her hand. "We found some baby things and a stack of paintings, so we looked through them. There was a painting of a girl with the most exquisite green eyes and raven hair. She was dressed in a white gown with purple ribbons. She was lovely. I couldn't help studying her. Then I realized Derrick not only studied her, but he was crying. His whole body shook. I swore I could almost hear him." Her eyes fluttered shut with the memory then opened with her shiver. "He was so, oh, Con, I can't stand to see him like that. He was so quiet, but his heart filled his eyes."

Con's tears threatened. It was on the tip of her tongue to ask more about the painting when Kaitlin cleared her throat.

"Who's Deanna? Is that Anna's real name? Oh, Constance, I ached at the sight of the girl. Who is she to Derrick?"

Constance rubbed her arms. "Deanna, oh Deanna." Constance's voiced hitched as she whispered the name. "Deanna was Derrick's sister."

Kaitlin covered her gasp. Her eyes misted. "His sister?" She forced the words through the gaps between her fingers. "Oh, dear Lord. Dear Lord. Why didn't anyone tell me about her?"

Constance shrugged. "The mention of her name bothers Devlin. I've never seen the child. Others have said little about her. I think they stopped saying anything for fear it would hurt Devlin and Derrick."

"What happened to her? Where is she?" Kaitlin shivered

Con raked her hand through her hair. Exasperated, she pulled the pins from their mooring and let her hair fall from the prim bun. Shaking out her hair, she settled back and turned to Kate. "Deanna was Derrick's twin. They were three the last time anyone saw the girl. The last time anyone heard Derrick speak. Devlin looked for the girl, spent nearly a year hunting for her to the point of exhaustion and never found her. He still has an ear to the wind but..." Constance paused. The pause lengthened as she considered her words. "There's speculation that Derrick might know something about his sister's disappearance. But he isn't telling."

"What about the mother?"

"Anna?" Constance sighed. So rose the subject she didn't want to discuss. "Anna disappeared from the house two weeks before the girl. Some say she ran off with Reverend Marlowe's son. Others say Devlin ran her off. Still, some say he killed her and buried her on the grounds somewhere."

*****

Kaitlin fidgeted in her seat. Maybe Anna was the ghost? *Nonsense.* Her ghost was flesh and blood. She gulped nervously. "Margaret swears she saw Mrs. Clayborne after she'd left the house. That could coincide with Deanna's disappearance."

"I know. But not too many people believe her." Constance smiled forlornly and shook her head. "It was dark and Margaret can't see an inch past her nose without her spectacles."

"Where was Devlin? Wouldn't he know if his wife had returned?"

"Devlin had been called away to trial."

He was always being called away. Maybe he sensed the gho… Kaitlin shook her head so hard her neck kinked. *There are no ghosts.* She had to stop thinking like an idiot.

"So Deanna disappears and Derrick won't talk," her voice trailed off into silence. And Devlin's entombed in a mausoleum of pain and loss. "Con, did I tell you why I finally decided to change rooms?"

Con shrugged. "The windows as I recall."

"I did it for Derrick, too. I haven't been able to tell Devlin this, but I invited Derrick into my room, my old room. I'd hung the pictures that the children had drawn and wanted him to see. He wouldn't come in. In fact, he ran away. I went after him, but he fought me like a crazy person."

Con leaned forward in astonishment.

"I had a bruise on my shin where he kicked me," she paused and let her sister close her mouth. "Marla told me the room used to belong to Anna."

"I'm trying to recall." Constance sighed heavily. "I never really knew Anna. And I haven't had reason to discuss the room with Devlin or the staff. Heavens, I've been upstairs more since you've been there than any other time."

"It doesn't matter. What matters is I decided if the room scared him then I would move to the one across the hall, the one that adjoins his. But, once I had everything moved in, he was terrified of that room as well."

"What did you do?"

"I wanted to cry," Kaitlin said softly.

Constance nodded. "And after that?"

Kaitlin grinned. "The stable hands loved me, but I had them remove one piece of furniture at a time."

Constance's brows rose with her smile.

"When they removed the wardrobe, he came into my room."

"How utterly curious," Constance remarked. She leaned forward. "Are you sure it was the wardrobe?"

"I had it moved twice. When it was in the hall, he wouldn't go near it. Con, I know this sounds ludicrous, but what if he saw them use that wardrobe for something in connection with his sister and mother's disappearance? And it scared him so bad he won't talk. Or can't."

"Scared him so he won't talk," Constance repeated quietly as she considered it. She shrugged. "Did you check the wardrobe for anything?"

"I didn't find a thing."

"Maybe there was nothing to find. Maybe he saw something looking out of the..." Constance stopped and met her sister's eyes.

Kaitlin's senses put her hairs on end. Constance hit on something profound. "He hid in it! And he probably wasn't supposed to be in his mother's room. What could he have seen?"

Constance shrugged, and rubbed her arms. "Maybe we should have that hot chocolate now.

*****

Kaitlin stopped by the mercantile on her way home and looked over some material for new draperies. When she ran into Greta, she wasn't sure whether to smile or run.

"Well, young miss, it seems you're still with us. But then I hear Devlin hasn't been home too much. He hardly ever is. Must be hiding something," Greta commented with a wink as if Kaitlin should be privy to her secret meaning. She grinned in such a smug manner, Kaitlin wanted to knock the smile from her face. She prayed for patience. How she'd ever listened to the woman before she didn't know? "You haven't come to see the children, they miss you. And the boy, too," she said, looking across to

Derrick, who was busy studying the lemon drop jar.

When he turned her direction, Kaitlin noticed the way Greta backed closer to the shelves. She shrugged it off.

"We plan on coming soon," Kaitlin said in her defense. "I've been trying to settle."

"A hard thing to do in that house, I'm sure," Greta declared. Lifting a can from the shelf, she proceeded to study it. She set it down with a thump, and turned a skeptical eye to Kaitlin. "You haven't heard the ghost, have you?"

"The ghost?" Kaitlin blinked, invisible fingers ran down her spine.

"Yes, the ghost." Greta chuckled. "Not that I believe in such drivel, mind you. But others can sure tell a tale about it. You've heard of the ghost, haven't you, Farley?" she addressed the shop keep.

He shrugged. "'Spect most everyone has." He grinned at Kaitlin. "Can't say as I ever saw it. Nor do I cotton to the belief that there is one. Some people just like to make up stories," he added with a wink, letting his gaze drift to Greta before he rolled his eyes and sauntered away to help someone else.

"Of all the..." Greta sniffed then stabbed a laugh. She clutched another can and perused it. "As I said, I myself don't belief one iota of it. But enough people have mentioned the ghost I feel I should caution you." Another can hit the shelf with a thud, as she reached for another. "Some say it's the ghost of his dear departed wife. Others say it's the girl. But like Farley said, people do make up stories."

Kaitlin heard Farley grunt and glanced over to see him roll his eyes again. "I'm not one to believe in such stories either," Kaitlin replied.

"I was right about the freaks though, wasn't I?" Greta replied, baiting Kaitlin to turn.

"There are no freaks at Clayborne."

"No?" Greta frowned then chuckled. "It's rumored that four of the staff traveled with a side show. I hear they had billings and everything. Two were dwarfs, another an ogre, and the fourth they called Amphibian man."

"And anyone who spent their money to laugh and gawk at others and their misfortune is not worth spit." Kaitlin knelt and put the cans into their proper places.

Greta took a deep breath. "No, of course not, I wouldn't laugh or gawk. I might be mistaken, but I heard that one of them wanted to be gawked at. Touched even." she lowered her voice, "To put it delicately one was a... well, a--"

"What?" Kaitlin looked up she was bewildered. "What are you talking about?"

Greta whispered as if her constitution was slapped. "Why, a whore of course."

"Who..." Kaitlin couldn't bring herself to say it. "There are no prostitutes at the manor."

Greta sighed heavily and fanned herself. "No freaks, no whores. Well, that's good to know. All these rumors, what is a body to do?" She shook her head. "I suppose one should just ignore them, but I find -- speaking truthfully -- the thought of a ghost still scares me. That's why I caution you to be careful."

Kaitlin stood, her mouth gaping she stared at Greta. The woman just wouldn't quit. She wanted to say so much, but didn't want to lower herself to Greta's level. "Well then, I think you for the advice and if the ghost is around, I'll make certain to let him know you're asking after him. Perhaps send him along for a visit," Kaitlin added before she turned away. With a quick sigh, she turned again, and after catching Derrick's arm, left.

She walked out the door leaving the material for another day when Greta wasn't about. "Snooty ol' crow."

"Send him here first and I'll escort him there for ya," Farley called after her.

Kaitlin wanted to laugh but couldn't. She had a nagging feeling that Greta's words were closer to the truth than Kaitlin wanted to admit, but she offered them so cruelly.

Kaitlin didn't want to consider who Greta alluded to when she spoke of freaks and easy women. She had a good idea on one count. But it was none of her business.

She gathered Derrick's hand into her own, and took off down the street headed home. Home to her mausoleum. Home to the secrets. Home to her ghost.

Chapter Twenty

Kaitlin tried to settle her thoughts, but Greta's words followed her home and stayed with her from one day into the next. It would have been far easier to dismiss them had she not been curious already. She shared Greta's conversation about the ghost at the study that night and was reminded there were no ghosts.

"They ain't real, miss," Perkins said with a shake of his head. "You shouldn't listen to Greta."

"I know. I know." Kaitlin sighed. "But I have heard noises."

"It's an old house," Marla interjected.

"Yes, it is," Kaitlin agreed with a halfhearted smile.

"Besides, the good Lord ain't gonna let nothing happen to you," Margaret added. "Best to forget Greta's speculations. Woman's speculations don't amount to much no how."

"I know," Kaitlin said again. She did know, but she'd been guilty of trying to put faces with thoughts all evening. Who was the other freak, who was the prostitute? She hated herself. Prayed her mind would stop wondering uselessly. She needed to keep her nose in her own business and not worry so about ghosts. But all her prayers didn't remove the doubt from her mind. And all her faith couldn't stop her from bolting out of her bed and locking her door when she heard the floorboards creak outside her room.

Kaitlin barely slept, and when she did, she dreamed of side shows and brothels and ghosts. She arose with a dry mouth, grainy eyes, and a heavy heart. When she reached the kitchen for breakfast, it was clear in her mind what she needed to do.

She nearly chickened out when she saw the staff gathered there. Thankfully, Derrick was off with Tilly and the boys so there were no children to contend with. With a deep breath for courage, she encouraged them to sit.

"I have something I must tell you." She told them about her visit with Greta the day before. "So you see I must apologize. Whether or not the rumors are true, it's not my place to listen or carry them. Even in my own mind. I care deeply for each and every one of you. And would do nothing to hurt or demean you in any way. You must know that. So, if you will forgive me?"

"You have nothing to be forgiven for, Ma'am, you're not spreading any rumors." Thomas replied with an easy grin. "I was the ogre."

Margaret studied Kaitlin as though she waited for her jaw to drop. She shook her head when Kaitlin didn't seem shocked.

"I know that, Thomas," Kaitlin said. "But I shouldn't have listened to her. She was being cruel. She thinks little of any of you. But I care. And I don't like gossips." She patted Thomas' hand. "Whether you were in a show or not."

Margaret crawled up on a chair, and leaned on the table. "You know the dwarfs were Henry and me? But aren't you the least bit curious who amphibian man was or about the..."

"Now, mother, don't play the devil's advocate." Henry caught his wife's hand. "Weren't you the one who said it was time to get the secrets out? Weren't you saying you trusted, Miss Kaitlin?"

"Hush, old man," Margaret whispered. She tugged her hand from Henry's and met Kaitlin's eyes. "I do trust her, but it ain't my place to say."

"Margaret, I'm honored that you trust me." She looked to each person in turn. "I'm humbled if any of you do. Truly, I may be curious, but I don't need to know."

"That's exactly why I'm going to tell you," Perkins replied. Peeling his gloves, he held his hands out for Kaitlin to see. With a tear in her eye, Kaitlin took the webbed, six-fingered hand into her own. "And I have toes to match," he added soundly. Proudly.

Marla stepped forward. "You know about my glass eye. But I'm also deaf in one ear. I was kicked by a mule when I was younger. I wasn't in the sideshow, I was married to its proprietor. After he died, the Claybornes took us all in."

At that Kaitlin's mouth did drop. Not because Marla was any less in her eyes. But they had come so far together.

Anita took a long breath and gasped for more air. She peeked at Kaitlin and bowed her head. "I'm the whore," her voice wavered. Her tears slipped like tiny rivers on her cheeks. Kaitlin caressed Anita's shoulder. Margaret put an arm about Anita's shoulder and hugged her up.

She directed her gaze to Kaitlin over Anita's head. "She was put into the cribs when she was twelve, burned by acid when her she was thirteen because her madam found her keeping money back." She smiled ruefully. "She only wanted to leave. She finally did, but only after the madam nearly killed her. The Claybornes found her on the street in Minneapolis. Middle of winter it was and they brought her home."

Anita sobbed so hard now her body shuddered.

Kaitlin, crying herself, rose and put her arms about the woman. "Anita, I'm sorry for the life you had. And I'm so grateful the Claybornes brought you home, otherwise, I never would have met you. Any of you," she added softly, putting her hand to her heart.

Kaitlin was exhilarated and awed that her husband's family had opened their arms to so many. If only she could forge such a friendship with Devlin. But there were so many secrets between them. And God help her, she didn't know if she was ready to know them.

*****

"Reverend Marlow." Kaitlin's eyes lit with delight. "How lovely of you to stop by. Won't you come in?"

Looking passed her, he hesitated. *If Devlin was home? If...* He shook off the thought. For Kaitlin's sake, and his own, he wouldn't allow the ghosts of Clayborne Manor to stop him anymore. He would deal with Devlin if the matter arose, even looked forward to it.

"I'd love to." He grinned, pulled back his scarf and removed his hat. He looked down to find Derrick, bundled in his overcoat, watching. "Good day, young Clayborne."

Derrick grinned back, gave the reverend a nod then reached for his hat.

"Have I caught you at a bad time?"

"Oh no, Anita was taking the children out to make snowmen." She fixed Derrick's cap and sent him on his way. "Make a large one, darling. I'll come see it soon as I can." She waved him out the door then turned back to the Reverend. "What brings you out on a day like this?"

"I wanted to come by and see how you're faring. Wanted to let you know you're in our prayers." There was more he wanted to say. But wasn't sure how to start.

"Thank you." She led him to the parlor then once he was settled, took a chair and folded her hands into her lap. "I feel I should apologize. I miss service. I'd be there if I could but--"

"I know, child." Reverend Marlow smiled softly and reached out to pat her arm. "I'm aware of your husband's feelings. I don't hold it against you." He shook his head sadly. "I doubt I hold it against your husband."

"That's kind of you."

"But we do miss you. We'll keep praying for the day you can join us again."

"He does allow us to study the Bible here," Kaitlin declared.

"Praise the Lord." Reverend Marlow sighed. He knew the Bible hadn't been allowed at Clayborne Manor in years. To have Devlin allow it now answered his prayers. His heart uttered another silent praise to heaven. "It looks as if you're getting along fine."

"I am." Kaitlin bowed her head. She sighed heavily then looked up. "Actually, that's not all together true. Derrick and I get along swimmingly. But I don't really know the man I married. He seems so distant. Given the circumstances of our marriage that may sound absurd." She stabbed a laugh. "Just when I think we're making progress something else happens or he leaves."

"He is a very busy man," Reverend Marlow said simply.

She nodded. "But sometimes, ohhh. Sometimes I feel as if I'm making him angry. Making him leave. I think I could do better. Be a better witness." Reverend Marlow met her stare and held it. "I've been angry that I'm not allowed to join you in services. Angry, because Devlin doesn't seem to trust me and I haven't done anything. I just don't understand. What happened in this house? Do you know?"

"I wish I could give you all the answers. But I only know a little." He swallowed hard. Here was the opening he'd prayed for. Resolved not to let the chance pass, he went on to tell about his son and Anna Clayborne. "He'd come home from college for the summer. He was young and seemed deeply infatuated with her. Not that that's an excuse mind you, because he knew better. I saw how he watched her, but most men did. I guess, I told myself that my son would never cross the line. After all, hadn't I taught him the things of the Lord?

"I thoroughly believed he'd head back to school and forget all about Mrs. Clayborne. I allowed myself to be blinded. He began to talk about Anna, about how he cared for her, and how she needed him. She said they would travel. I didn't believe there was anyway a woman with everything she had would up and leave it. Not after she fought so hard to marry into it."

"She fought hard?"

The reverend nodded. "Anna's family faced financial ruin and Devlin became her escape. Had she not stepped in, your sister could have very well married the man. Constance is a beauty but Anna, well she knew how to turn heads."

Kaitlin blinked. "Meaning?"

"She was well-versed and rehearsed in using her womanly wiles. At first it seemed so innocently done. I'm not so sure now. Ted wasn't the only man drawn in. I found out later there were others who wanted to run away with her." Probably others he wasn't aware of. "But she chose Ted. For whatever reason, I'm not sure. When he finally decided to leave, Anna left with him. It's said she returned for her daughter. No one truly knows what happened. Not even Devlin, he was gone to the city at the time. Anna returned in a strange state of mind soon after the fact then disappeared sometime later. There was no girl with her, and no word from my son. Many questions were left unanswered. And many speculations have risen."

*****

Kaitlin shook her head, knowing full well what they speculated about, she'd wondered about the same things. After her talk with Constance, she'd been out to the wardrobe several times, and looked closer into the closets of the room she'd left.

And what of Anna? She'd returned only to mysteriously disappear again. *Was she dead? Had Devlin...* Her thoughts had her shaking her head again.

"I hope I'll hear from my son." Reverend Marlow's deep sigh caught Kaitlin's attention. Kaitlin saw the tears well his eyes. And knew how he must miss his son. Just as she missed Simone and Devlin missed Deanna. That insight made her want to weep for them all.

"I hope you do. I'm sorry I brought it all up."

The reverend brushed his coat and smiled. "I'm glad you did. I've been waiting for a chance to have my say. Devlin never cared to hear what I had to say. He was so angry. He could barely look at me much less talk to me."

"Didn't you tell the authorities?"

He nodded slowly. "They concluded that Anna ran away with my son, taking her daughter with them. And they're now living it up somewhere on the jewelry they stole from Devlin. Anna's later visitation was to find more."

"They stole jewelry?"

The reverend nodded again. "Some would say it was actually Anna's, but the staff says they don't recall Devlin giving her any of the family heirlooms, so she had to take them. No one, but Devlin and the authorities, are really sure what all they took. If anything."

Kaitlin was not about to ask Devlin what pieces were left. She wasn't that curious. Well she was, but there was no way she would ask. She was afraid to. She asked the reverend if he cared for a warm drink then sat back and considered her next step while he sipped some from his tea.

"I should be going," he said. He swallowed his cup full in another gulp and set the cup on the table. "I hadn't planned on staying quite so long." He rose.

"I didn't mean to keep you," Kaitlin apologized as she lifted from her chair.

"You didn't keep me. I enjoyed my visit." He grinned. "But I have a few more stops to make. I'm gathering donations for the Brewer family outside of Glencoe. Their house burned down. I was hoping maybe you'd have something to donate."

Kaitlin thought of the furniture in the shed. What she wouldn't give to have that menacing wardrobe gone. She nodded. "I think I might, but I'll have to check with Devlin first."

She slipped into her coat and followed him out, wondering how she would skirt this new issue with Devlin, when she had so many already. *Oh well, no need to let it ruin her afternoon,* she decided when she saw Anita and the boys in the distance.

She took off in a run to join them, paying no attention to the woman and man who stood watching just at the edge of the clearing.

*****

"She's snooping, I tell you." Gerrard sneered, at the woman across the field. "She was down at the cottage too. And that boy knows something."

"Keep your wits." She caressed his shoulder. "The boy won't say a word, he knows better. And she doesn't know a thing. If she did, our heads would be in the noose about now."

"We should be a little more cautious."

"We can't afford to wait," she retorted. "Have you found the passages

I spoke of?"

"I believe so. But I haven't been able to go inside. That blasted dog always manages to sneak up on me."

"Ignore the dog or kill it if you must, but get into those passages. That's what you're being paid to do." She pursed her lips. "With good money I might add."

He wondered if the money was good enough or if he would get his allotted part of the share. He chuckled to himself at that. As of now, he had a share of nothing. Was there really anything to find in that house?

"Just do your job," she said, cutting into his thoughts. "How are things going with the horse?"

His shoulders rose with his sigh. "I just as soon kill him, too. You did a job on him, blasted cur attacks at the slighted provocation."

She tilted her chin upward and blinked daintily. "Try not to provoke him. I had to make sure Devlin would take the horse on." She laughed softly. "Or else why go to the trouble to put the horse in his way at all?"

Chapter Twenty-One

Moving stealthily up and out the forward hatch, he closed it as quietly as he could and crouched by the fife railing. He looked up to watch the unfurled sails whip in the wind. Ah, he loved his ship. He could stare at the sails all day. His favorite spot was the crow's nest, high above it all. But he had no time for nostalgia. He turned and checked the forecastle and sighed with relief to find it empty. He prayed that meant he would have the time he needed. Taking a deep breath, he moved his way around the galley using the water casks and long boats as cover and made his way to the bilge pump where again, he crouched low and breathless, looking behind himself to see if the crew had come topside yet in search of him.

Staying close to the rigging and barrels along the deck, Black Bart, pirate of the high seas, scourge of the Barbary Coast, hoped to escape the snare of his mutinous crew and return to the minimal safety of his cabin where he hoped to find a fighting chance. He had just reached the stairs leading to the poop deck, and was just short of his quarters, and safety, when he took that one look back. And found himself surrounded. His heart racing, he knew all was nearly lost, but, even as he backed from the pistols and swords, keeping his back to the port bow and the sea, he prepared to battle.

"Throw down your sword, Bart," Phineas Bly demanded. "Are you rash enough to think you can take us? You are outnumbered."

"Outnumbered you say?" Bart shot back, looking at the men encircling him. Many were friends, or so he believed. Friends who had fought and pillaged beside him and who had later shared his ale. Friends he should be able to count on, and yet, he found no solace in their blood thirsty stares. He eyed his accursed crew. What a scurvy lot. His heart wrenched when his eyes landed on his midshipman. "Even you, Grimes? You who have sailed the seas with me for years? You who served my father before me? You would turn your back on me, your captain?"

Grimes grinned but said nothing in answer. Holding the tip of his sword to Bart's soft belly, he spoke his answer clear enough.

"Testy little toads, aren't we?" Bart commented with a grin. Flipping back his mane of curly black hair with a sniff, he set his feathered cap cockeyed on his head, causing a wave of guffaws and giggles to erupt from the pint-sized crew. "Who'll get you home? You'll be lost at sea without me to guide you."

Bly bit his bottom lip to stave his laughter, but still snorted indelicately. Once his laughter was somewhat under control, he turned to Bart. He'd masked his grin with a scowl, but he could do nothing about the laughter that threatened his voice. "I can shoot the moon, Bart."

Phineas Bly snickered. "So I say again, drop your sword. I'm captain of the Ironcross now."

"You? Ha!" Bart sniffed. "You dare take my ship from me? Stop this mutiny now, and I will spare your feeble excuse for a life."

"You are in no position to make demands." Bly grinned. He poked Bart with his sword. He stopped to straighten it before he stuck it to Bart's gut again. "The mutiny will stop as soon as you are cast into the briny deep."

"You would cast me off here? Here? Where the water grows angry? Here into the salty abyss? You would cast me to my death?" Bart asked incredulously. He took a cautious glance over his shoulder at the churning sea. "Humph. Surely after all I've done for you, you could take me back to Algiers?"

"All you've done for us?" Bly's laughter was sarcastic. "Why, you wouldn't think twice before throwing us in. You wouldn't give us the courtesy," he declared. "No, you will not go back to the coast. You will face the sea."

"Yes, take your chances with the sharks," a crew mate spat.

"See if you can get them to take you to Algiers," another piped up, causing Phineas to sneer.

Bart chuckled and planted his feet. "I will not relinquish my station without a fight," he declared, lifting his sword.

"Fool. Then you shall die fighting." Bly planted his feet and raised his sword. "Perhaps it's fitting. Your blood will draw the sharks."

"So be it," Bart proclaimed. Hoping to catch Bly unaware, he raised his sword and prepared to give a death blow, his plans were thwarted by the sound of a pistol. He looked down in wonderment. "Alas, I am shot." Letting his sword arm go limp, he dropped his weapon and grasped his chest. "Tell my mother not to weep for me," he added with a groan as he keeled and fell over the side of the ship.

"Die blackguard. Die," the crew chanted as they looked out over the sea. Their chanting stopped abruptly, they jumped from the deck and scattered.

At the silence, Kaitlin sat up from the blankets and pillows that served as the sea and looked around.

"What is this?" came a bellow behind her. She didn't have to turn to know who it was. She turned to face him with a smile. "Mr. Clayborne, you're back."

*****

Battling the cloth ocean, she tried to get herself out of the pile of linens with some decorum. She tripped, caught herself and stopped to fix her vest as if nothing was out of place. "When did you return?" she asked, finally meeting his gaze.

"That is of little concern," he said gruffly. It would only be for the day anyway. He'd stopped on his way through to the next county. "I asked you what *this* is?"

"This?" She looked around. "Oh, this. *This* is the sea." She made a wide sweep with her arms. "And this is the ship Ironcross." She pointed to the bed. "And the small group of children hiding in the utter most parts of this house are -- *were* -- the crew."

Devlin held his smile. "Are you aware that beds are for sleeping in?"

"Quite aware, sir." Kaitlin grinned and, unable to help herself, saluted. "But as you know, no one sleeps here." She thunked the dusty bed for effect. "And we did take our shoes off." Devlin glanced at her stocking feet and met her gaze again. She smiled apprehensively and scratched her wig. "We're going to clean up our mess. We were going to clean the whole room. But we found these lovely costumes and were sidetracked." She removed her dark curly wig and laid it on the bed. "It seemed a shame not to take advantage of them."

Hands clasped behind his back, Devlin stepped to the large windows and stared out in the mist. "My brother and I used to play here," his said softly, reverently.

"You and your brother? How wonderful."

"It was until I played alone." Devlin turned and saw the smile leave her face. What he wouldn't give to have the power to keep it there. "This room was his favorite place. We'd play for hours."

"I'm so sorry."

"There's no need. It was years ago."

"And yet you seem as pained by it now as if it were yesterday. How sad." Kaitlin picked up a load of blankets and dropped them on the huge bed.

"Why do you say that?"

Kaitlin stilled. "Can I speak frankly?" She toyed with the edge of a blanket then let it drop, and met his eyes.

Did she speak any other way?

"Yes," he said, although he wasn't sure he wanted to hear. She had a way of stripping his defenses with her frankness.

*****

"You've lost a lot, Devlin, your parents, your brother and much more. But you're alive and you have so much. A home, a bright, sunny child," she paused and thought of the child. A child she'd been trying to reunite with his father, trying to assure of his father's love. Would she have to start over again? She caught herself. "And you have a name," she paused again and chose her words. "I find it sad that you should still have life, life that those you love would want you to live and yet you hide yourself off in this tomb. I wonder. Who died the greater death?" She could tell by the flash in his eyes that she'd hit a nerve.

It hurt her to see.

She expected him to reply, prepared herself for the bellow, but he stood there shrouded by an eerie silence, staring at her. He looked like his son and she had an overwhelming desire to run to him and cradle him in her arms. Unsure what to do, she stood her ground. His eyes sullen, he turned back to the window. The silence passed awkwardly between them.

"If you'll excuse me, I must find my wayward crew," she said softly after a few moments.

*****

He watched her reflection in the glass as she backed her way to the door with halting steps. He wanted to tell her to stay. Beg her to understand him, but he let her go -- the words he wanted to say remained lodged in his throat. "Kaitlin." He barely whispered the name, hoping she'd somehow hear it and return. He remained alone.

Sitting on the edge of the bed, he stared at the room. Awash with memories, he covered his face with his hands and allowed himself to feel, allowed the words Kaitlin had said to enter his body as a tiny seed of hope and take hold in a heart that had been dying behind a wall of despair.

Eyeing the door, he wondered if he really could live again. If so, could he trust Kaitlin to care for his wounded spirit? He told himself that it didn't really matter if she did or not, but knew with his whole heart, her feelings mattered. Lord, it ached to be vulnerable, to care. Whether he admitted it or not, whether he wanted it or not, he cared for Kaitlin.

The stranger. His wife.

*****

"You should go after her," he announced his presence as he stepped from behind the wardrobe.

Devlin turned. "So you are there."

Positioning his cloak, he sat down by the window and felt the warmth. Wished he could allow himself to feel more. "Why do you sit here moping? Go join her."

"I can't."

Devlin sounded so forlorn, he wanted to weep. Being in this room, this room he loved, made it worse. "But you can," he argued. "Tell her your secret. Tell her your fears."

"Don't you think I want to?" Devlin returned angrily.

"Then do it."

"Do it?" Devlin groaned. "And have her look at me with contempt? She'd leave within the week and I couldn't bare it."

"So, you do have feelings for her? I thought as much after the way you were sneaking about the hall outside her room the other night."

Devlin rose angrily and stared out the window. He slammed the pane. "All right, I admit it. I want to tell her, but I-I--"

"Don't want to be hurt again," he finished. "Land sakes, man, but we are a pair, aren't we?" Devlin sat down with a sigh and tried to smile. He put a gnarled hand on Devlin's knee. "Go to her, Dev. Tell her."

Devlin rose as if stunned and began to pace. "I'm busy."

"Always busy."

"I don't see you rushing to make her acquaintance."

"I would join them, if I could."

Devlin stopped. Met his eyes. "I wouldn't stop you from keeping company with her." His companion doubted that was because of his great trust for Kate. It was more his trust for him. Besides, Devlin knew there was little he would or could do anyway. "Have you tried?"

"Past playing the piano and hoping they'll find me. I'm afraid to." He sighed, then laughed. His cloak billowed softly as he raised his hands and dropped them. "My feet long to take flight, but..."

Devlin stared at his own feet. "You're right, we're a sorry lot," he mumbled. His head came up. "I can introduce you?"

Again he read the unspoken trust in Devlin's eyes. He rose. Devlin might trust him, but did Kaitlin? "I'm not ready to face the fear I know I'll see in her eyes. In the children's eyes."

Devlin placed his hand on his shoulder. "I understand. Perhaps things are better left untested."

"Perhaps."

They parted knowing it wasn't.

He took his leave down the darkened stairs to the loneliness of his chamber, cursing the night around him. It had taken residence in his heart for too long.

*****

The wardrobe closed and Devlin thought of the self-imposed night he dwelled in. He wanted to climb out of. But was he ready?

When he heard the laughter in the hall, he wanted to run join them, but, reminded of his work, he went to his study instead. He managed to get little done with the laughter assaulting his senses. All he could see was Kaitlin. And his son.

When the knock sounded, he let himself hope it was Kaitlin. It was time for Derrick's nap, maybe she'd come to see him.

He managed to hold to his frown when Ernestine stepped in.

"So you are back." She smiled pleasantly. "I hope your trip went well," she added as she took the chair across from him.

He'd accomplished what he'd wanted to. "It did."

"Have you much work to do?" she asked, eyeing him and the paperwork before him.

"Nothing I can't manage."

She started to frown then caught herself and flipped a tendril of hair.

"Well then, I'm free to help the ladies at the home. They're putting together some goods for that family in Glencoe."

"Family in Glencoe?"

"Oh, of course, you've just returned." She grinned and tilted her head in a coquettish manner. "Well, this poor family in Glencoe, the Brewers, I believe, ran into a bit of hard luck. Reverend Marlow has been collecting some necessities to meet their needs. I'm surprised your wife didn't mention his visit."

That stabbed his attention. He met Ernestine's gaze. "Reverend Marlow was here?"

Ernestine smiled. "He and your wife spent a quiet afternoon together, probably discussing the Brewers."

"Really?" He gulped, his blood coursed through him. "I'm sure I'll be hearing about it soon. Now if you'll excuse me, I really should get back to work."

"Of course." Ernestine lowered her eyelids amicably. "Let me know if you need help. I'll be down at the church. If I see your wife, I'll let her know you're home," having said what she came to say. Ernestine turned, her smile threatened to take up her entire face.

Devlin started to tell her that Kaitlin knew he was home. But what did it matter? All he could think about now was that she'd spent the afternoon with the reverend and was now helping him. Had she gone to the church against his wishes? Was she visiting him for other reasons? From the sounds of it, she planned to go see him now.

He jumped from his chair and went looking for his wife. He found her by the front door, slipping into her coat. He needed no explanation.

"Why was Reverend Marlow here without my being notified?" Why did you go to the church against my wishes?" He stopped himself before bluntly asking her if she was being unfaithful to him.

Kaitlin's nose crinkled. "What are you talking about?"

He stepped closer. "What I'm talking about is why you went to church against my wishes and why must I always be informed of the goings on in this house from the staff instead of my wife?"

Kaitlin's brow's hit her hair line. "Just what did the staff say?"

"I'm told that Reverend Marlow came for a visit. I'm told you're heading there now, to the church, to help him." *To see him.*

"You've been misinformed," Kaitlin said simply. "Reverend Marlow came to visit. He wanted to tell me about a family in Glencoe who was burned out. Wanted to let me know I've been missed at services. But I haven't broken my promise to you. Nor will I. I told Reverend Marlow that there might be some things I could donate, but I needed to talk to you first. But you're never home. And when you are, you find fault with everything I say." She huffed a breath. "The nearest thing we've had to a conversation happened this very afternoon, and briefly before you left. As for where I'm headed now... had you asked me I would have told you. I asked Henry to bring the carriage around so that Derrick and I might accompany Anita's children home."

Devlin turned to find the children standing in the doorway to the kitchen behind him. "I'm sorry, Kate."

"Perhaps you are," she allowed. "Now if you'll excuse me, I promised Anita I'd have her children home in due time."

"When will you be back?"

"She's invited us for dinner." Kaitlin stopped and twisted her lips. "You're welcome to join us or we could do it another time and..."

"I can't," he said quickly, surprised by her invitation. "There's no need to change your plans. I hadn't planned to be here." Except he wanted to see her, see how he would handle being around her. "I have some work to finish before I leave again in the morning."

"You're leaving again?" She seemed disappointed. Even after he railed at her.

"Yes. I only stopped on my way through."

"When might we expect you back?"

"I can't say." He could say a week or a couple days, but all he wanted to do was get away from those eyes and the way they made him feel. He'd hurt her and he couldn't bear it. "Enjoy your visit. Perhaps I'll see you when you return."

"Yes, perhaps."

*****

Her head was bent as she walked toward the carriage. Had he allowed himself to walk with her, he would have seen the tears she desperately tried to hide.

Devlin wasn't up when she returned later that evening. She didn't expect him to be. As long as he didn't trust her and yelled at her nearly every time they were together, she didn't want him to be. Her mind didn't believe that lie. In truth, she'd hoped to find him up. She hoped for a chance to talk to him, to break through the wall around him. To banish the ghosts that walked with him. But the house was an empty, silent tomb.

Unfortunately, she was growing accustomed to it.

No, that was a bigger lie than the first.

*****

Devlin was up when she came home, but didn't allow himself to come out of hiding. He'd broken his resolve by coming home. He had to remain strong to protect his wounded heart. Had to control the urge to get closer to her, take her in his arms and see if she was as soft and gentle as she sounded. As soft as she felt in his arms on their wedding day.

Accustomed to the silence and the ghost, he stayed in the shadows. He went to the chambers below.

He touched his cloak, wrapped it about his shoulders then pulled it off and threw it over the chair. With a groan, he ripped it from the chair and marched to the fire.

"We'll only be forced to get you another," Devlin said softly, causing him to stop. He turned. Devlin saw the glistening of his eyes.

He clutched his cape to his chest. "I'm going crazy."

"Maybe it's time to go to the cabin again? We haven't been together in some time."

He shook his head and dropped his cape to the chair. "There has to be more to life."

"You can give her a chance," Devlin said, feeling rather stupid about his choice of words when he wasn't giving her a chance either.

He shook his head. "Why, so she can see how hideous I am? So I can come back to my tomb?" He dropped into the chair, rested his elbow on the arm and cradled his chin. "I'm tired of the darkness."

"But it keeps you alive. It keeps you safe."

"Does it?" He gulped. "For what, to crawl like a slug in the recesses of life?"

Devlin bowed his head. "You're not a slug."

"I'm worse. What I don't understand is why you hide? You have a chance to live again, and yet, you prefer the darkness. You entomb yourself. I know you've been hurt. But watching you hide away, makes me hate myself more."

"Why?" Devlin asked. He lifted his head.

"Because I feel like part of the reason you hide away is to protect me." He groaned. "You should have never agreed to keep me on. You don't have to be saddled with me. I--."

"I'm not saddled. I happen to care a great deal about you. You are a blessing."

"And *your* family?"

"My children are the only things that Anna gave me I can call blessings."

"Then take part in them. Deanna may be gone, but Derrick needs you."

"You sound like Kaitlin."

"Then listen to her. She'll be a blessing, if you'll give her the chance. I think she'll gift you with much, much more."

"I'll be leaving again in the morning," Devlin said, arresting his attention.

"Why did you come home?"

"Because I'm not as content with the situation as I seem?" Devlin rubbed the back of his neck. "Perhaps I'm trying to find a way out of my tomb? And I'm not quite sure where to begin."

"Kaitlin would help you," he said assuredly.

"Maybe." And that was his greatest fear.

Chapter Twenty-Two

One week and still no sign of Devlin. Kaitlin feared he'd never come home. She wondered what she had done to run him off. To top it off, Ernestine wasn't around either. Had she gone with Devlin?

The winter so prevalent outside, moved into her heart.

"Oh, Lord, I've made a complete mess of everything."

"No, you haven't," came the reply.

Kaitlin spun around. She managed to breathe when she saw it wasn't the ghost. "Marla?"

"Miss." Marla set down the tray she carried. "Margaret thought you might like some of this hot bread. I thought you could use some tea."

"That sounds wonderful," Kaitlin replied, though she was in no mood to eat. "I'll go see if Derrick is up from his nap yet, and--"

"No, you won't," Marla said firmly. "First, you sit here and give an ole woman a listen." Kaitlin took a seat on the edge of her bed, put her elbows to her knees and slouched with her chin in her palms. She felt weighted by the world.

Marla sat down beside her. "It's probably not my place and you can tell me to go if you have a mind to. But you've got to know a few things. Things I should have told you long ago. First of all, you haven't ruined anything. This house has never been so alive. Not even when Anna lived here. In fact, the last time joy filled this house Devlin's folks still resided here. And it was Devlin and his brother making the ruckus. But Devlin has forgotten how to laugh. He's forgotten how to live."

Marla's voice broke, "Don't you go thinking you've run him off. He's spent more time at home since you arrived than at any time since his parent's death."

"What?" Kaitlin straightened and swiped at her eyes. She couldn't believe it.

"It's true," Marla said. "He has an apartment outside the Twin Cities where he spent most of his time. For us to see him a week or two out of the year wasn't uncommon." Marla put her hand on Kate's knee. "I hear you crying. I hear you praying because you think you're a failure, but I want you to know you're not. You're breaking through. But you've got to understand that Devlin has lost so much. And Devlin was betrayed."

"By Anna?"

Marla drew a long breath and dropped her hands on her knees. "Yet, he thinks he failed her in marriage. He thinks he failed his son. He bears the burden of his lost daughter. He thinks he's the one who isn't good enough to be part of this house. This home anymore. He's the one who hides in the shadows unsure of how to join in."

"Do you really think so?" Tears rolled down Kaitlin's cheeks.

"I know so." Marla caressed her cheek and caught a tear. "Don't give up, Kate. You keep praying and you keep trying. Devlin doesn't realize it, but he needs you more than his son does. That's hard for a man who believes he should handle things. The one who should have handled them before and didn't. Do you understand?"

Kaitlin nodded her head. Perhaps she did. That's why she told Devlin what she had about his brother earlier that afternoon. That seemed too long ago?

"You care for him, don't you?"

Kaitlin stabbed a laugh. "How could you tell?"

"It's in your eyes, miss. It's in your eyes." Marla caught her in a hug. "Now I suggest you enjoy that bread while it's still warm or Margaret will have my hide."

*****

Devlin stood at the window and looked out into the mist -- another lonely night in a lonely hotel. He couldn't even go to his apartment. He didn't want to. He wanted to go home. He thought of Kaitlin. Little kept him from returning to her, little, but himself and the ghosts attacking his senses.

Their voices were strong tonight. He raked his hand through his hair, tried to eradicate the sounds, they remained -- Deanna's, the strongest of all. He had failed his daughter and his son. By rights Derrick should never talk to him again. Had he been there, had he... his heart heavy, he gulped back the tears. He was a blasted coward. But he could remember, only too well, the look in his son's eyes when he returned home that night after Deanna's disappearance. His son gave him the same sullen look now. Would it ever change? Would he ever have his son's smile, his son's love again?

Did he, having failed with the boy's mother, deserve it?

If he could find his daughter, he might, but his chances of finding her dimmed. Still, he held on. Still, he searched. He could almost hear her calling to him now.

With a groan, borne from the depths of his sorrow, he pressed his forehead to the pane and searched for her in the mist.

*****

He faded into the shadows in the library and watched. He could announce his presence and confront her, but stood quietly instead. She toyed with the books on the shelf, pulling them quietly, and opening them. Her groans grew stronger each time she put one back.

He had a good idea what she searched for. She would never find it. He'd hid what she wanted too well. He smiled. At least now they had the evidence they needed. He'd follow her and see where else she led him.

Kaitlin froze at the top of the landing and held her breath. With a hand to Lady's head, she kept her in place. Ernestine was in the house again. And Devlin wasn't even home. "Good girl." She patted the dog. If Lady hadn't whined, she would never know. She started to confront Ernestine when another shadow, dressed in a dark cloak formed out of the darkness as if born from the night, and proceeded to follow Ernestine.

The hairs on her arm stood on end. She'd found her ghost -- a man, a large man, by the look of him. Was he the one Ernestine had come to see? By the way he hid in the shadows, Kaitlin doubted it. So who was he?

The thump of Lady's tail on the floor, stymied her. She put a hand to the dog's head again and quietly commanded her to stay.

She could do nothing to muffle her gasp when she looked up to find him watching her. She could run, she supposed, but where? And blast it all, her dog, her trusty dog had disobeyed her command and headed down the stairs toward him.

Kaitlin's mouth gaped when he took a step in her direction. She expected to die at any moment, and nearly fainted when he bent to pet the dog's head. She felt his eyes on her when he straightened. She took a deep breath as if to speak when he put his finger to the lips hidden beneath the hood of his cape, and with his cape unfurling behind him turned and followed Ernestine into the night. Catching her wits, she called for Lady to heel, and was pleased to see the beast obey.

Her heart pounded in her head when she crawled into bed beside Derrick. Kaitlin covered her heart, she wished she'd never gotten up to stretch her legs, wished she'd never... "Lord, is he going to come back and kill me now?"

"Idiot," she chided herself after a moment. If he'd wanted to harm her, he'd have done so already. "Don't try to appease me now," she told her dog when Lady crawled up to lay at her feet. She should be happy that the dog heeded her command and came when she called. "But you were friendly with him. Who's the ghost?" she asked the dog and groaned aloud when there came no reply. "Oh, it doesn't matter." But it did matter. She sighed heavily and pulled her blanket to her neck.

"Devlin, where are you?" she whispered to the darkness. She prayed that he'd return home soon. Because she wanted some answers. And she wanted them yesterday.

*****

Wary, Kaitlin rose before the sun. She'd lain awake watching the shadows on the wall. Believing everyone was the '*ghost*' come to get her. She finally rested but only after she'd prayed a verse over and over again.

She wanted to hunt for her cloaked intruder, and would have if she could get the children to join her. They'd taken a turn on the rope ladder to Derrick's room, and were contentedly drawing and reading now. They kept her busy, but never busy enough to keep her mind off the figure in the shadows.

"So who's Nehemiah?" Carver asked.

"Perkins said he was as tall as my knee," Bradley informed them with a disbelieving, albeit unsure grin.

Kaitlin snorted. "I don't think he's as short as that. But in answer to your question, he was commissioned by the king to rebuild the walls of Jerusalem."

Carver shrugged. "That ain't so much. Mr. Clayborne's dad and them built this." He let his arms fly above his head in a swirling motion to encompass the room.

"Yes, they did?" Kaitlin agreed. "But did they have to hold a weapon in one hand and a tool for building in the other in case they were attacked?"

"Pa said they had to fight Indians," Bradley said with a jut of his chin, his eyes nearly popping their moorings.

"Really?" Kaitlin was astonished. Derrick grinned as his head bobbed. "Hmm. Well, maybe he's more like Nehemiah than we know. Do you think God told Mr. Clayborne's father to build this house?"

"Pa said they built it to protect the people in the county," Carver proclaimed. "Reverend Marlow told us once, that Mr. Clayborne felt God wanted him to build it. And you know what?"

"Nooo... what?" Kaitlin asked deeply interested.

"It must have been God's plan, because this was one of the houses that people came to when the Indians attacked and killed all those people. And no one died here."

"My pa hid here," Bradley interjected.

"He did?" Kaitlin blinked.

"Yeah," Carver answered. "He said they fed everyone and set guards so people wouldn't be afraid. And they had services and prayer and everything."

Kaitlin gulped. "Then they were very much like Nehemiah." *When had things changed so drastically that Devlin wouldn't allow even a Bible in the home?* "Would you like to hear more about Nehemiah then?"

"Yeah," Bradley declared. Carver and Derrick just nodded. But their nods were so adamant she had little doubt they wanted to hear more.

Kaitlin started to read, when Perkins came into the nursery. "Miss. I'm sorry to bother you, but I've been asked by Anita if you would come to the kitchen."

"Why, of course." She rose from her spot on the floor. From the look on his face the matter was of extreme importance. She handed her Bible to Perkins. "Would you mind finishing this for me?"

"Would love to, Ma'am." Perkins grinned.

*****

"My heavens, what happened?" Kaitlin exclaimed when she reached the kitchen and saw Tilly laid out on the table, her back welted and bleeding. Mouth gaping, Kaitlin stepped forward for a better look. "Who would do this to a child?"

Thoughts of the '*ghost*' were pushed to the hinder most parts of her mind.

"Mrs. Reinholdt." Margaret scowled as she and Anita and Marta tended the girl's wounds.

"Why?" Kaitlin's eyes filled with tears.

Anita looked up, her eyes red with tears, fear filling their depths. "Tilly said she ruined her luncheon," she managed before she her voice broke. She bowed to the tears. Kaitlin put an arm about her shoulder.

"Luncheon, smuncheon," Margaret growled. "She spilt a tray."

"A tray?" Kaitlin asked in bewilderment. "A *tray*?"

"Mrs. Reinholdt had her friends over today and Tilly tripped and spilt the tray she carried in front of them," Marta explained what Tilly had managed to tell them before she fainted. "Mrs. Reinholdt was so angry her gathering was ruined, she beat the poor child once everyone was gone and sent her on her way."

"Poor child arrived on the doorstep a little bit ago, barely able to stand," Margaret added.

"Of all the..." Kaitlin's arm tightened about Anita. "Oh, Anita, I'm sorry."

"It's okay, Ma'am," Anita said softly.

"No! No it's not," Kaitlin assured her soundly. "This could never be okay. I think it's time I called on Mrs. Reinholdt."

"No, Ma'am, please." Anita looked up, pleading. "She'll only hurt her again. She's done this before. I tried to talk to her, but she wouldn't listen to me. I don't want Matilda hurt."

"She won't be," Kaitlin said firmly. "Trust me. I'll make sure of it."

Chapter Twenty-Three

"Mrs. Clayborne. Do come in, come in," Mrs. Reinholdt gushed. Her smile practically merged with her eyes. Kaitlin moved into the hall and allowed the butler to take her coat. Then followed Mrs. Reinholdt into the parlor where her daughter sat fumbling with her needlepoint. "Louisa, say hello to Mrs. Clayborne. "Louisa gave a curt nod, but made no move to acknowledge Kaitlin in any other manner.

Mrs. Reinholdt's lips pursed at her daughter's lack of decorum, but she said nothing. She motioned Kaitlin to the chair. "Do have a seat. Could I offer you a cup of tea or...?" When Kate shook her head, Mrs. Reinholdt took her seat. "I am so happy that you've come for a visit. I've hoped you would for some time now. I've been meaning to stop and see you."

"It seems I should have come sooner. As it stands, this isn't a social call."

The tone in Kaitlin's voice got Louisa's attention, her hands idled, her needlepoint dropped to her knees. Mrs. Reinholdt seemed perplexed. "Not a social call? Might I ask what brings you to my home?"

"I've come to discuss Matilda."

Louisa looked at her mother. Mrs. Reinholdt met Kaitlin's eyes. "Matilda? Whatever for?"

"I've come to talk to you about the condition of her back."

Mrs. Reinholdt sniffed. "Then you've done so needlessly, it's none of your concern. Now if that's--" She started to rise then settled when she noticed Kaitlin remained in her chair.

"But it is my concern. That child was beaten."

"Beaten?" Mrs. Reinholdt was flabbergasted. "No, only disciplined for her shoddy work. While I was entertaining, I might add. As she is my servant, I have the right to discipline as I see fit."

"I disagree," Kaitlin said, her stare as stern as her voice. "You see not only did she arrive on my doorstep bleeding and near unconscious, but she was freezing because she was forced to walk the distant in her condition. And that, ma'am, is my concern." Mrs. Reinholdt opened her mouth. Kaitlin wouldn't allow her to speak. "So I've come to warn you that Matilda is as much in my employ as she is yours and if you ever touch her that way again, I'll gladly cane you myself." She ignored Mrs. Reinholdt's gasp. "Furthermore, if you don't agree to my terms, I just might."

Louisa mouth dropped open much like her mother's. Mrs. Reinholdt began to sputter, "Of all the... I've never been so appalled in my life and in my home nonetheless. You have no right to tell me how to discipline my servants. I must ask you to leave." She started to rise again.

"Oh, but I do, and I will," Kaitlin said firmly. Mrs. Reinholdt took her chair once more. "You may think you have the right to discipline your servants, but you don't. And if you see fit to argue with me, rest assured that I will speak to my husband about some kind of legal recourse in this matter. It's either that, or you work things out with me."

"With you? Why I'd rather--"

"It is your decision, of course," Kaitlin interrupted. She would not, could not waver. "But as I said, I'll talk to my husband and with his help, I'll make sure you won't be able to use his lands anymore, or have him to deal with come harvest. Have I made myself clear?"

Mrs. Reinholdt gulped. Kaitlin had made herself perfectly clear. So clear, Mrs. Reinholdt trembled. "What are your terms?"

"They're not so bad." Kaitlin grinned with satisfaction. "Matilda will be in residence at my house. You will come each day to tend her until she's healed."

"Well, I..." The harumph didn't escape, but Kaitlin read it in the woman's eyes.

"You alone, Mrs. Reinholdt," Kaitlin reiterated her terms. "Of course Anita will be there for her daughter, but make no mistake, you will tend to the child." Mrs. Reinholdt took a heavy breath. Louisa smirked. "And just so we know you won't be tempted to hurt the child again, or tempted to shirk your duties, Louisa will stay with me. She will reside with me for one whole week, and tend to the girl when you return home each day."

Appalled, Louisa was out of her chair, throwing herself in her mother's lap. "No, Mother, I can't. Please don't send me."

"I'd say she doesn't have much choice," Kaitlin replied to the girl.

"But why?" Louisa started to pout. "I didn't beat the stupid girl. She spilt the tray not me."

Stupid girl. Kaitlin took a deep breath. "No, perhaps you didn't. But as it stands, with Tilly down, I am in need of someone to take her place. And if you're with me, your mother might think twice about the care she gives Matilda. Because she will have no idea what I might do to you."

"No, Mother, she's going to beat me," Louisa cried, and clung to her mother's neck.

"You won't beat her?" For the first time Mrs. Reinholdt showed a modicum of concern for someone else. Perhaps she was worth redemption?

Kaitlin shrugged. She gave her a hard look. "That's entirely up to you. Of course, if I follow your mind set, then I have every right to discipline her as I see fit. She'll just have to make sure she serves me well. And tends to Tilly with the utmost care."

"But, *Mother*, I've never served a day in my life. I don't want to look after Tilly."

"You have no choice, darling, you must do as Mrs. Clayborne asks," her mother said simply.

Louisa's response was to push off her mother's lap and stand before her in a defiant manner. "I hate you. I will not be someone's servant. It's demeaning," she yelled, and turned to run away.

Kaitlin grabbed her arm before she could go, startling both Louisa and her mother.

"Don't you dare hit me," Louisa screamed. The imp had the audacity to try and kick Kaitlin. While her mother stood and watched, whispering, "please no, please no." Kaitlin quickly swiped Louisa's other leg from beneath her when she tried again, dropping the girl to the floor.

Louisa's started to wail and her mother finally stepped in. "Please don't hurt her," she said, enveloping her daughter in her arms, shielding her.

"I wasn't going to," Kaitlin said soundly, rolling her eyes. "I was merely going to tell her to apologize for speaking to her mother in such a manner. And have her go pack her bags."

Nonplused, Mrs. Reinholdt had nothing to say. She helped her daughter from the floor then sent her to get her things.

*****

They rode home in silence as Louisa stewed. From her corner of the carriage, she skewered Kaitlin with her stare like Kaitlin was the devil incarnate. Kaitlin held the smile that threatened to break free. Louisa had it all wrong, she would never beat her. She hoped both the Reinholdt women would learn a lesson in compassion once this was over with.

It appalled her that those with so much could treat people so inhumanly. And believe their wealth gave them the right to do so.

Kaitlin reminded the girl to grab her bag once they reached the manor then had to keep her from trying to foist it off on Perkins when he met them at the door.

"No, Louisa, you will carry your own bag." Louisa started to pout then probably giving her circumstance some consideration, decided to hold her tongue. "But do sit it down while you remove your coat," Kaitlin suggested when she saw the girl back against the wall, clutching her bag like a shield before her.

"Well, here they are, ma'am," Perkins said, announcing Anita, Margaret, and Marla's arrival in the hall. Henry came in from the servant's quarters carrying Tilly.

Kaitlin finished hanging her coat and went to check on Tilly. "It's all taken care of." She noticed Louisa's face had paled at the sight of Tilly. Perhaps the child had a heart after all.

"Are you sure it will be all right?" Anita asked, openly worried.

"It will be," Kaitlin assured her. "Mrs. Reinholdt will arrive in the morning to see to her."

"What if she doesn't do...?" Marla started to ask.

"Then I'll see to it she does." Kaitlin glanced over at Louisa then back to the women circling her. "I guarantee she'll do what we've agreed to. In the meantime, put Tilly in my bed, and set a roll for Louisa. She'll be staying with her in the evenings. But first, see to it Louisa is comfortable and fed."

"Yes, ma'am," the staff said together.

"Come along, dear." Marla reached out.

"But I..." Louisa hesitated and looked over at Mrs. Clayborne, unsure what to think, who to follow or trust.

"Do go on, Louisa," Kaitlin said softly.

"You're not my mother." Louisa scowled.

"And praise God for that," Margaret muttered.

Kaitlin smiled at the cook then met Louisa's fiery glare. "I never claimed to be. But you will be staying with me for the week and you will mind."

"And if I don't?" Louisa said snidely.

"That remains to be seen," Kaitlin returned. "But mark my words, if we have any further outburst from you, you won't enjoy the consequences. Now off with you."

At the threat of discipline, Louisa scurried to catch up with Marla. She glanced over her shoulder then fell into step behind Marla without further comment. Kaitlin couldn't help notice the way Louisa's eyes traveled round the house, in awe, as she climbed the stairs or the way they'd traveled to the open door of the study where the piano sat in plain view.

*****

Louisa stared at her plate and tried to ignore the servants and boy across the table, he made no attempt to hide his curious stare. She knew who he was, everyone knew Derrick. Everyone knew he was tetched, which explained his piercing eyes. But why was he in the kitchen eating with the servants? Was his new mama disciplining him? She bit off a piece of bread and chewed it slowly to keep herself from asking. She about choked on it when Kaitlin came in, made herself a plate and took a seat by Derrick.

She put her arm about the boy and drew him to her in a warm hug then turned to Louisa. "Is your meal satisfactory?"

Louisa met her eyes and was hard pressed not to see the tenderness in the vivid emerald stare. "It's fine," she allowed herself to say. Wondering how the woman could seem so kind when she just knew Mrs. Clayborne had brought her here to beat her.

"Good. We can't allow you to go hungry." Kaitlin chuckled and bowed her head to Derrick's. "Can we, young sir?" The boy shook his head and smiled, throwing Louisa all the more. The smile he gave Kaitlin was as endearing as was the one she returned. There was no fear or contempt in it, but what did a tetched boy know?

What did Louisa know?

She was pretty sure they didn't feed her out of kindness. No, they couldn't let her go hungry, she had too much work to do. She frowned and ripped off another hunk of bread.

*****

Kaitlin's smile waned as she studied the girl. She hated to frighten her, but she couldn't allow Mrs. Reinholdt to get away with her treatment of Tilly. Nor could she allow Louisa to think it was right. If all went well, Louisa's view of her would change.

If all went well?

Finishing their meal, Kaitlin was of a mind to believe nothing could go well. Louisa was a handful -- a spiteful, pampered brat, asking for a firm hand on her backside.

"I will not be treated like a servant. You can treat the boy that way all you want. Make him eat with the servants. He's tetched he doesn't care. But I have my wits and I am a gentleman's daughter," she railed brazenly.

"As am I," Kaitlin returned softly, even though she wanted to scream. "Derrick and I eat with the servants because we want to. We enjoy our time with them. The boy isn't tetched, he just loves his servants."

Louisa's mouth gaped in disbelief. "Surely you--"

"What?" Kaitlin interrupted. "Surely a woman of my station would eat in the dining room?" Louisa's head bobbed. "It's big and cold and lonely in that dining room. The kitchen is warm and we have pleasant company. Derrick and I find it suits our needs perfectly." Derrick's head bobbed now. "They're kind to allow us to join them."

Louisa studied the staff with a sneer then met Kaitlin's eyes again. "I think I'm ready to retire now."

"I'll take you to your room, but you won't be retiring yet," Kaitlin replied. "Remember you are here to help with Tilly."

Louisa opened her mouth to comment then shut it. She crossed her arms high on her chest in open defiance. She probably figured Tilly got what she deserved. Kaitlin found that thought disheartening. She hoped Louisa's mindset would change once she saw Tilly's wounds.

When they reached the room and Louisa took her first good look at Tilly's back, her petulance turned to shame. She stared at Tilly's back. It was raw in places and oozing blood. Sickened, she turned from the sight and caught her stomach. Kaitlin asked Marta to put Derrick to bed while she went to help Louisa who was pale as a ghost and fighting for air.

"Take a seat, miss," Anita said with a frown. Louisa stood there.

Kaitlin put her arm about Louisa's shoulder and led her to the divan. "Sweetheart, take a seat and put your head to your knees."

The movement brought Louisa from her stunned state and caused her to look at Tilly again. With a whimper she leaned into Kaitlin's side, her tears spilled with her hiccups and gasps. "Please, miss, I can't do this, she's so... she's bleeding." She started to hyperventilate.

Kaitlin got her seated and made her put her head to her knees. When she could breathe again, Louisa cried. She looked up, the tears rolling down her cheeks. "I didn't know it was so bad. I didn't know." Having said thus, she covered her face.

"Ah, sweetheart," Kaitlin gentled. Pulling the girl to her chest, she embraced her gently. "I don't even think your mother realizes what she's done." She would on the morrow though.

"I don't want to look," Louisa cried, pressing her face to Kaitlin's shoulder. "Please, don't make me look at it."

"All right." Kaitlin sighed. She wouldn't force her. "But I still need your help."

Louisa looked up. Swiping her hand beneath her nose, she posed a question with her eyes.

Kaitlin inclined her head. "Tilly likes to be read to. While she's cooped up in the bed I hoped you might be a companion for her."

Louisa's eyes filled with relief. "That's what you want me to do?"

Kaitlin nodded. "She's been reading *Little Woman*. Do you suppose you could sit with her for a spell and read to her?"

Louisa blinked her tears. "Louisa May Alcott's *Little Woman* is one my favorite books. I like Jules Verne as well. But I thought you would--"

"Beat you if you didn't take care of her back?" Kaitlin finished for her.

"Yes," Louisa said somewhat hesitantly.

Kaitlin held her at arm's length. "Louisa, I've never beaten a soul and I don't expect to start now. But like I said, I won't put up with selfish outbursts nor will I allow your mother to get away without seeing what she did." She drew a long sigh, and wiped a tear from Louisa's cheek. "Tilly needs a friend right now. I'd love it if you would be that for her. I know she's a servant. But she's a special young lady. And I believe you need a friend just like she does."

*****

He stood in the shelter of darkness, listening as Louisa read to Tilly. He wanted to step out from his ebony shroud and sit at the reader's feet. But he didn't want to wake up the household with screaming.

Screaming. He put his hands to his face and remembered the last time he tried to befriend someone. He put his hands to his face and wept softly, his shoulders rocked with his sorrow.

Watching from the shadows had been so easy before. Now it threatened to kill him. He could feel it, like poison in his bones.

Chapter Twenty-Four

Kaitlin woke with her stomach in knots, praying that Mrs. Reinholdt would take to Tilly as her daughter had. Praying that she wouldn't throw a wrench into the changes made in the girl's heart. And for the first time in hours, she thought of the '*ghost*' as well.

Strangely, to do so didn't feel her with trepidation as it had before. She decided since Devlin wasn't home to give her answers and the staff would say nothing, since it was breaking confidences, she would find her '*ghost*' and confront him instead. First she had Mrs. Reinholdt to contend with.

Mrs. Reinholdt arrived promptly at eight. Kaitlin met her in the hall and proceeded to tell her how her daughter was and let her know that they were just beginning to change the bandages from the night before. She didn't cringe or let on to anyone, namely her '*ghost*' that she knew he probably watched. She even managed a smile for Mrs. Reinholdt, who seemed shocked, but said nothing.

*****

Mrs. Olga Reinholdt was stingy with her words, curt with her nods and bristling as she mounted the stairs with a sniff. Her haughty demeanor changed the moment she stepped into Kaitlin's room.

Her daughter read softly to the girl laid out in the bed. She hadn't seen Louisa that peaceful in years. When Louisa looked up and gave Kaitlin a smile, such a soft smile, her heart cried. Her daughter hadn't graced her with such in some time. It nearly tore her heart out to see it given to another now. But she wouldn't let her defenses fall. Not here, in the presence of servants and strangers.

The girl on the bed broke her defenses, stripped them from her. Broke her heart. Or perhaps it reminded her of the little bit of one she still had.

"We were just getting ready to change the bandages," Margaret replied to the silence, taking Olga Reinholdt's attention from the girl, reminding her that others were in the room. She met Anita's eyes and wanted to crawl away in shame. The woman had every right to be angry, to take a cane and beat her senseless. She almost wished she would. Then she wouldn't have to see the hurt in another mother's eyes. She wouldn't have to be reminded that she was so very lacking.

Margaret backed away, allowing Olga the space by the girl. The space to do what she must. She stepped to the bed and put out a tentative hand. Up close her defenses failed completely.

"I am so sorry," she uttered softly. Then went to work tending to what she'd broken.

*****

He melted into the shadows along the study wall. Woman was getting bolder, her visitations more frequent. He had to give her credit, she was good at what she was doing, and quiet as she moved through the house like a whisper. She'd taken to wearing a cloak -- much like his -- to hide behind. Had he not caught her before, he might wonder who hid beneath the flows of material.

With everyone busily tending Tilly, they would never know she was there.

Again he wanted to stop her, jump from the shadows and give her a fright. But she had threatened no one and he rather liked the chase. As exhilarating as it was, he knew he couldn't prolong his wait much longer or allow her to continue searching the house indefinitely. She might stumble on something. She might stumble on him.

As it was, tonight, he hoped to follow her home and learn who her accomplices, if any, might be. When she turned for the door, he gave her a moment and followed.

*****

Kaitlin bolted from her bed, her heart hammering in her head. She heard a thump. She took a deep breath and relaxed when she saw the sun fingering its way through the curtains, and Derrick quietly playing with Lady at the foot of her bed. He tossed the bone and sat back to watch the dog clamber across the floor, catch the bone in her teeth, and promptly trot back to the boy to drop it by his folded legs.

Hence the thump.

Kaitlin stretched and watched them in quiet play. Words weren't necessary, understanding was in their eyes, the toss of the bone. Were her silent actions and the quiet hope in her eyes getting through as well? Marla said as much. Still she wondered, wanted more. How long should she keep her silence? How long before she had to speak? She decided the time was already past. She thought of Greta again, and realized she'd waited much too long to get her house in order.

Yes, she was getting through to Derrick, and the staff, and her '*ghost*' seemed to be coming around, but Devlin was distant. But, her thoughts reminded, there was another who'd she'd allowed to stay entombed in her sorrow far too long. She kicked her legs off the side of the bed and decided now was the time to remedy that as well.

*****

"Come lay beside me, darling," he practically cooed as he reached out his hand.

She turned with a sniff. "Darling, now, you know I'd love that more than anything. But your wife is waiting. You've been gone a long time. She'll be wondering where you are."

"So, let her." He shrugged. "I want to spend time with you."

"I know, I know." She sighed and pulled up her hair to twist it. "But you have to go home." She moved to sit beside him on the bed, and with a pat to his thigh, leaned over to kiss his shoulder. "Soon we'll have all the time in the world together." His arms encircled her, hoping to tempt her to stay. She pulled away. "But not now. Other matters have to be attended to first."

He groaned as she walked away and slipped into her dressing gown. He knew what those other matters were without her going into detail. They were all they talked about. They were all consuming. As she slowly brushed her hair, he thought of other things more interesting for consumption. He'd thought about it for years it seemed. He sighed. Soon wasn't good enough. He had to urge the moments along. Though he hated to admit she was right, she was, he needed to be home. His wife was beginning to concern him. She wasn't as content as she'd been, but, perhaps, he could spend some time with her and soothe her doubts. If that didn't work maybe a sound thrashing would settle her.

Either way he still had to go home.

"Don't frown so, darling," she said when she caught his reflection in the mirror. "You know I want you to stay. I want nothing more in the wide world." *And to see a completion of their plans*, she told herself. For that she needed him home to see that nothing or no one got in her way.

*****

"Olga." Kaitlin smiled as she stepped into the room carrying a tray laden with coffee and scones. It was Mrs. Reinholdt's third day there. She hadn't left the girl's side at all, had gotten little rest with her brief naps. Much had changed, Tilly was coming around nicely, and Kaitlin was pleased, but the softening of Olga pleased her most. "I hoped you might join me for tea?"

Olga looked up, hesitant. "But I..."

"She's resting, Olga." Kaitlin smiled. "I'm sure Louisa won't mind staying with her."

Olga saw her daughter sitting there. She'd been so engrossed in caring for Tilly, it was the first time she'd noticed her child that afternoon. The first time she'd truly noticed her in days. Perhaps years?

What a beautiful girl.

Her daughter smiled. "I can do it, Mama." Olga suspected Louisa hoped she'd leaved so she and Tilly could be alone. Louisa looked forward to those times. Olga could see them as they talked about what they were reading, and shared secret dreams. Louisa didn't even mind dabbing Tilly's back anymore. She wanted to be there for her friend. Her new and very dear friend.

Olga was pleasantly shocked. Where had the young woman before her come from? No, where had she been for so long? To that end, where had she -- Olga -- been all this time? Her mother used to say she was the kindest most compassion soul she knew.

She'd been lost in a shell. A shell that Orin's heavy hand forced her to crawl into. Olga hated that she'd lost herself and in the process, nearly lost her daughter. It would not be so anymore. Never again would she stand silently as he lifted his hand and harsh words to her. Never again would she shut her daughter out.

"You're a fine young woman, Louisa, and I thank you for the offer, but I really should tend to Tilly." She ran a hand along the puffiness beneath her eyes.

"Mama, you need to rest." Louisa said softly, laying a gentle hand on her mother's shoulder.

Olga was reduced to tears. She pulled her daughter into her arms. "But I'm the one who did this to her. To a child. Oh, Louisa, I've been so..."

"Hush, Mama," Louisa said softly, sounding older than her years. "We've both done things. We've both..." She couldn't finish. "Oh, Mama, I've been awful to you and, Mama, I love you."

*****

Kaitlin smiled and blinked her tears. She wondered if it wouldn't be best to leave them for a time. "You've been tending to her for three days now, Olga." She picked up her tray. And hoping not to sound too bossy said, "I'm going to require you to take a break and join me in the parlor at one."

She wasn't sure Olga heard her, but she left anyway. Left so mother and daughter could get reacquainted. And wondered when she might have the chance to leave a certain father and son to do the same thing.

*****

Olga and Louisa, returned home once Tilly was able to get out of bed. But they visited often and started to join the studies in the kitchen. Louisa spent long hours with her new friends. Joining in the romps and lessons as often as she could, she lived the childhood she had missed, and even took up her music again.

One of Kaitlin and Olga's greatest pleasures was to take tea in the study and listen to the children play the piano.

"I thought I'd never hear her play again." Olga sighed when her daughter finished her piece. Not since Orin had broken the piano in a fit of rage had she heard her play. She realized now how much she missed it. Knowing her daughter's talent and love of music Olga purchased another piano. Her daughter wouldn't touch it. "Thank you so much for giving me my daughter back. And for helping me find myself."

Kaitlin patted her hand. "Olga, I'm pleased things are mending between you. I'm so sorry I was heavy handed with you both."

"I think you had to be," Olga said. "Thankfully your hand was tender, too. I was so blinded I didn't care to see. Things are much better." She sighed again. If only she could mend things between her husband and herself. If only she could find the man she'd married years ago. He rarely touched her now. And when he did he used an iron fist. She searched for excuses for his behavior, grew weary of hunting for them.

Was he wrapped up beneath a shroud of anger and bitterness just as she'd been? Wrapped up trying to find the pot of gold at the rainbows end? She wondered if her husband could be found at all. If so, she prayed for the way to reach him, even as she wondered if she really wanted to.

*****

Kaitlin thought of those she needed to reach: Devlin, who had yet to return home, and Derrick, who grew more dear to her each day. She believed he would talk soon, and prayed for that. And then there was her '*ghost.*' It was high time she found him.

Quietly biding her time, she began to look for him. She sensed his presence now. Caught a glimpse of his cloak in the wardrobe where he watched as Louisa read to the children. Was he aware that she saw him? She believed he was. She wanted to invite him into the light, but held her tongue, hoping he'd realize she wasn't afraid of him and come out himself. She didn't want to call to him and have him slip into the darkness before she found the necessary path to follow him.

To gain his trust, she began leaving a tray for his luncheon and books for him to read. She wasn't sure whether to be happy or sad when she found the tray returned empty, and the books gone.

Coming to the manor, the tomb, she never thought it was the living she'd have to rescue. She prayed for the means and the patience to do so, before she became entombed as well. Though she tried to be patient, her impatience with an ever-absent husband and a '*ghost,*' grew. She feared she wouldn't reach either one.

Until one day she found a note on her pillow with the words 'thank you' scrawled on the page. That held her impatience for a time. But not for long.

Then the next evening, to her surprise, the wardrobe was left open when he returned the tray. Maybe his impatience gnawed at him as well. She decided to follow the path he left for her and find out. A dim lantern lit the way down a spiral staircase and led her to the basement of the house. Then cast the direction to an open door. Holding her breath, she clutched her robe and inched along the warm corridor. When she came to the open door, she peeked into a room lit by firelight. An easy chair faced the hearth, a trunk set at the end of a large four-poster bed. The wardrobe in the corner seemed to stand as a sentinel over the lone figure sitting at the table, the fire glowing behind him.

"So you've found me," he said without turning when she stepped into his chamber.

"Because you wanted me to," she said softly, staying in her place. She didn't feel the faintest bit of abandonment when Lady drew to his side. He stroked Lady's back with a gnarled hand. "Does Devlin know you're here?"

"Yes," he answered softly.

She barely heard him over the beating of her heart. "Who are you? Why do you hide?"

He turned slowly, his face beneath his cloak. "Are you sure you want to know the answer?"

"Yes." She took a small step to show her resolve. "You wanted me to know, otherwise you wouldn't have left the trail for me."

He laughed softly. "True, true." His head bobbed beneath the cape. "But before I answer you, you must promise you won't run from here when you get what you desire?"

"I promise," she whispered, her heart thundering in her head.

Slowly he pulled back his cape from his head, and stood there, head bent. Trembling. Why? Surely he couldn't be as scared as she was.

Kaitlin raised her lamp and found her answer. With a shaky hand, she wiped her tears and moved forward to study him. A ghost stood before her with skin as pale and translucent as winter snow. With eyes nearly red as the fire. And hair the color of ermine.

He stood silently, barely breathing as she looked him over. "Aren't you afraid of me?" His voice was harsh with tears.

"Not anymore." She touched her hand to his hair. It was as soft as silk. "I only wondered why you hide in the darkness."

"Now, you can see." He stepped away from her hand. Pulling off his cloak, he laid it over the chair. She saw his twisted body and the lump of muscle and skin that grew on his back and distorted his shirt.

She started to touch his deformed shoulder then dropped her hand to her side. "What is your name?"

"Eldon. Eldon Andrew Clayborne."

Chapter Twenty-Five

Devlin's brother! Kaitlin couldn't believe it. Devlin's brother, who was thought to be long dead, was the ghost of Clayborne Manor. Devlin's brother was the vampire who walked the hills at night.

"I apologize, but I heard you were dead."

"No." He heaved a breath and drawing his cape from the chair, he sat down and held it to his stomach. "But at least the ruse is still working."

She lowered herself into the empty chair. "Ruse?"

He raised his arms. "I've been cursed with the same ailment as my father before me, a disease with no known name or cure." He dropped his hands to the table. "I crawled into this darkness to search for a cure."

"Did you find one?"

The darkness is my remedy." He sighed and tapped a gnarled finger on the table. He met her gaze. "And you know why I hide. It's safer this way. Devlin shot and killed the monster so people would stop looking and I could live a somewhat normal existence."

He folded his hands together and closed his eyes as if saying a silent prayer.

This was a somewhat normal existence? Fear kept him entombed.

And Devlin protected him. Another lost soul had found shelter under her husband's wing. Who sheltered Devlin?

Kaitlin looked about the chamber. It had all the comforts a body could want, but none of the comforts it took to maintain a spirit. "So, Devlin comes to see you when he's home?"

"As often as he can," Eldon replied meeting her gaze. "Other times I go with him."

"Will he have this...?" Her hands fluttered as she searched for the word. "Ailment. I mean if it's hereditary, will...?"

"He won't get it," Eldon finished her thought. "Devlin isn't really my brother. He was adopted as a child."

Kaitlin frowned. She'd thought the fear of his getting the disease was what kept him from her.

"Why do you look that way?"

Her frown intensified. She shook her head. "This will sound awful and it's not meant to offend, but I hoped that it might be Devlin's fear of this ailment that kept him from--"

"Opening up to you," he finished again and smiled. "No, there are other secrets, secrets which I cannot tell. I wouldn't betray his trust."

"I'm not asking you to." Her shoulders slumped, her lips twisted. She stared forlornly at the walls. "I just wished he'd tell me. I wished someone would."

"Perhaps you've only to ask him?"

"I might if he were ever home."

"He's coming home," Eldon said softly. Home to a place where his heart could settle, home where he could love and live again. He just hoped it wouldn't be too much longer before he arrived.

*****

"How was your sister?" Olga asked her husband who lay by her side, distant as ever. She wanted to touch him, yet her arms stayed close at her sides.

He drew long on his cigar before he tamped it out. "The doctors say she's coming around. I wasn't allowed to visit as long as I hoped to."

"I'm sorry," she said softly and put a tentative hand to his shoulder. She felt him tense under her hand, and pulled back. "I could visit with her if you like?"

"There is no need for you to be sorry," he replied a little too firmly for her taste. "And the last time you tried to visit her she was uncontrollable for days. It's better I go alone."

Which he did the first of every month. Faithfully. There were times she wished he'd just stay there. But he was her husband. She had vowed to love him and stay with him. It became increasingly harder to do. His sister was just another wedge between them.

Shutting her eyes, she thought of how life might be if her first husband, Louisa's father, her true love, was still alive. She missed him terribly. But her father wouldn't hear of her living alone, wouldn't hear of a woman taking care of the family estates. He'd all but pushed her into Orin's waiting arms. What would he say now if he were alive to see the mockery of their marriage? He'd probably tell her a woman's place was with her husband no matter what he did. She sighed heavily. Perhaps that's why she wished she was dead?

The only bright spot in her life now was Louisa, her only concern Louisa's welfare. And of course, there was Kaitlin who'd opened her eyes to the downward spiral she was in. Depressed, she'd sat back and allowed her life to deteriorate. Allowed the abuse. Even joined in it. She turned to see her husband's silhouette in the moonlight, and upon his breath, promised she would never allow herself to be in that spiral again.

*****

"Morning, boy." Gerrard stepped from the stall and closed the gate.

Derrick froze in his spot, studied the hay on the stall floor. He wanted to find Kaitlin. He hadn't planned on finding him.

"Shouldn't you be staying by your new mother skirts about now? Or are you out treasure hunting?" Gerrard laughed and fixed his suspenders. Derrick looked up. "What kid? No answer? Cat got your tongue?"

Gerrard's eyes held no sign of the laugh he proffered. Derrick shied in fear. Gerrard grinned, but his grin held an edge that had Derrick searching for a way out.

"Now boy, no need for that. I'm not going to hurt you. Well, not unless you somehow manage to get in my way while I'm in there," he added easily, pointing to Cotton. His eyes darkened when he met Derrick's again. "You don't want to go in there, do you? I doubt there's any treasure there. Or is there?" When he stepped closer, Derrick gulped so hard his Adam's apple bobbed, he stepped back. "Nah, ain't no treasure in there. 'Cept the horse. He ain't so bad, boy. Just can't be provoked. Myself neither, if you catch my drift?" he added calmly.

Derrick didn't like this hand, neither did Kaitlin or her dog and that was enough encouragement for him to dislike him all the more. He'd heard enough talk about the treasure of the manor and decided that's what the man was really talking about, but he didn't want to stay another minute in his presence to find out for sure. He turned and started to run, and found himself planted against Kaitlin's skirts. He wrapped his arms around her legs and held on tight.

*****

"What's going on?" Kaitlin asked, meeting Gerrard's deep stare.

He shrugged. "I was telling him about the horse, reminding him how dangerous it would be if he decided to visit the ole cur. He must have gotten spooked is all. I apologize if he did. I just wanted to caution him."

Kaitlin believed none of it. More had happened, and neither one was telling. But Derrick's eyes said enough. "I'm sure he won't be visiting Cotton anytime soon," she said with an even voice, surprising herself. She broke from Gerrard's stare and looked at the boy. "Didn't Marla tell you I would be back soon?" Derrick nodded slowly. "Then what are you--"

She was interrupted when Marla came running breathlessly into the barn. "Oh, there he is." She took a long sigh. "I'm sorry, Ma'am, he come looking for you when I turned my head."

"It's all right, Marla." Kaitlin smiled. But it wasn't all right. As long as Gerrard remained in residence she doubted it would be.

*****

"Are you sure Orin didn't have any problems with him?" Kaitlin asked Olga about Gerrard later that day.

Olga shrugged. "I'm not the best one to answer that. I didn't even know Orin had hired him." She frowned apologetically. "I've left all the business matters to Orin." That was going to change now. Her father might have felt a woman didn't have the brains to run his business, but he also didn't want his holdings squandered. The accounts were in her name and she was going to start having her say in matters, whether her husband liked it or not. She laughed nervously at the thought. "I've only learned this morning that we have three horses beginning to foal."

That was something else she'd use to delight in. The horses. She hadn't been to the stables since her father's passing. Her trip there this morning, with her daughter in tow, had been a boon to her resolve.

Kaitlin studied her friend. "Don't be too hard on yourself. I'm not even sure how many horses the manor stables. Or how much land Devlin owns."

Olga's brows knit with that proclamation. Then she started to laugh.

"What?" Kaitlin asked in bewilderment. "What is so funny?"

"I'm remembering the day we met. I wouldn't have known you had no knowledge of your husband's holdings. You'd seemed pretty sure that Orin ran his herd on Devlin's land."

Kaitlin grimaced. "I'm still not altogether sure."

"If it's any consolation, neither am I. Given the turnout, I think it was best for both of us to be in the dark at the time." Olga tapped her cup with her fingernail. "Next time I won't be so easy to cajole."

Kaitlin met Olga's eyes and smiled. "I doubt there'll be a next time?"

"I certainly hope not." She laid her hand on Kaitlin's arm, and reveled in their new friendship.

"How was your husband's visit with his sister?"

Olga shrugged. "Same as always, I suppose. He doesn't say much about his visits with her. Less, each time he goes."

"It must be terrible knowing your family member is confined to such a place?" Kaitlin commented.

"It weighs on him heavily," Olga agreed. She just wished it didn't weigh quite so heavily. Because each time he went north, he returned to her a greater stranger.

*****

"Now, children, remember what I said," she reminded softly. *Please, let them remember,* she whispered heavenward. Eldon was taking a big step coming to visit with them and she didn't want him hurt.

"We remember," Bradley informed her.

Derrick nodded.

Carver shrugged. "I don't see what the big deal is all about. It's just Derrick's uncle."

"Do you remember him?" Tilly asked Derrick.

Derrick shrugged, and shook his head.

"He was very little the last time he saw his uncle," Kaitlin explained, quietly hoping Eldon's presence would help draw the boy out of his shell. And quietly fearing it might push him further in.

"Does he look like Mr. Clayborne?" Louisa asked with a quirky grin.

"No, remember I told you there is no resemblance. And he--"

"Has an ailment that might scare us," Carver finished. "When's he gonna be here?" he asked with all the patience of a child on Christmas morning.

"Soon," Kaitlin answered, trying to sound sure of herself. She had a feeling he might not show. She wouldn't blame him.

Relief and trepidation flooded her when she heard the closet door creak. She whispered a prayer and crossed her fingers.

*****

Eldon had combed his hair then fixed his cloak about his neck, and resisted the temptation to throw it over his head.

What was he doing? Why had he agreed to join Kaitlin and the children for lunch? It was pure insanity -- born of loneliness and the need for acceptance. Yes, Kaitlin had accepted him, and she meant well to ask him to meet the children. Didn't she realize that the look of him frightened most people?

Heavens, he still gasped when he looked in the mirror.

He could stay put, he supposed, but then she'd come looking for him. He'd promised to join them or at least try. Figuring it'd end terribly he'd already asked Perkins to prepare him a tray.

Pushing back his ermine hair one last time, and squaring his shoulders, he headed for the stairs.

Eldon stepped into the room, and looked from one gaping mouth to another. There was no fear, only astonishment. He looked at his nephew and then he saw... What? The boy was crying and looked at him so intently, he wasn't sure what to think.

Maybe he shouldn't have come.

"Look, Miss Kate, he's white as a sheet," Bradley blurted, giving credence to Eldon's fears.

"Bradley, now that's not nice," his sister reprimanded before Kaitlin had a chance.

Humiliated, Eldon turned for the closet, only to stop when Derrick cried out. He whirled around.

"Derrick, you spoke. What did you say?" Kaitlin asked, dropping to her knees beside him, her skirt brushed the dusty floor. "Derrick, please what did you say? Say it again."

Derrick smiled and blinked back a tear. "Horse," he whispered as if the sound of his voice hurt his ears. His lips trembled. There was a collective gasp from the other children.

Eldon crossed the room and knelt before the boy. "You remember me?" Derrick nodded. "What do you remember, boy?"

"Horse," Derrick said again, then bowed his head against Kaitlin's shoulder.

"Horse?" Kaitlin met Eldon's eyes, her own eyes questioning. "He was in the stable this morning."

Eldon blinked back his tears and shook his head. "I made the carousel horses."

*****

Horse. Kaitlin touched the steeds now, and said it over and over again in her head. She wanted to hear it again. But Derrick hadn't said another word.

Eldon stayed on with the children that afternoon. Answering their questions and joining in a time of play. He soon realized that Bradley was apt to say anything that came into his head, and it wasn't meant to be rude. The boy wanted to know things and unlike the others, wasn't afraid, to ask. He just didn't understand the meaning of offend or fear. Or tact.

"Can you see good with those eyes?"

"As good, if not better than you. Only the light hurts them."

Bradley took a moment to consider that then ventured into another thought. "Does your skin feel the same as mine?"

"Touch it and see."

"Why is your hair that color?"

"It's part of my ailment."

"Can I get it?"

"No, only my children can."

"You gonna have kids?"

"No." There was sadness in that single word.

"How come your hands are twisted?"

"I burned them badly by going out into the sun too long."

"Do those hurt?" He touched the scars on Eldon's cheek.

"No."

"Are you the vampire?"

"Bradley now..." Kaitlin began.

Eldon raised his hand to silence her. "That's one of the names I've been called. But I'm not one. I don't drink blood and I don't chase small children into the night." He growled playfully at Bradley then sobered. "Inside, I'm just like you. See these blue lines? They're my veins. You have them, too."

Bradley checked his arm and looked up with eyes dancing. "I don't think you're no old vampire anyway. You're nice. My dad always tells me stop asking so many questions. But you didn't mind at all."

Eldon smiled. He wouldn't go so far as to say that, but he was warmed by the sentiment just the same and warmed by the knowledge that he'd spent time with others and had been accepted.

It was time Devlin realized he'd be accepted as well.

Chapter Twenty-Six

"Bradley, you have to stop moving," Louisa scolded she mixed colors of paint on her palette and ran the brush on the canvas with a laugh.

"I'm tired." Bradley swiped at his hair and nearly fell off the stool.

"You've only been sitting for ten minutes. If that." Tilly chuckled.

The boy's lips puckered when he looked over at Kaitlin. She noticed the red paint at the corner of his lips. Would he ever stop chewing on the end of the brush? Would he ever sit still? At the moment it was rather doubtful. "Am I gonna have to sit here as long as Louisa? Can't we just use a bowl of fruit? Or Lady?" He eyed the dog where she lay at Kaitlin's feet. "See, she's already sitting."

"Come on, Bradley, you don't..." Louisa went silent. Her eyes fixed on the door. Her gaping mouth snapped shut. "He could be our model," she spoke loudly on a sigh and blushed profusely.

"Mr. Clayborne." Kaitlin lay down her brush and started to rise.

Devlin lifted his hand to stop her as he entered the room. He studied her with a smile. "Don't get up on my account. I don't mean to intrude. I wanted to let you know I was home. I wondered if we might have the chance to talk once you're finished."

Kaitlin gulped and nodded. But, Lord help her, she was frightened about what he wanted to talk about. "You're welcome to join us if you'd like."

"Oh no, no." He chuckled. "You might try to get me in that chair." Kaitlin felt her heart flip. Not only did he have a beautiful smile, which caused him to be all the more handsome, but... How long had he been listening? "I have some things that need attending. I'll meet you in my study as soon as you can join me." Kaitlin nodded again. "Good. Good day, children," he added and started to turn.

He stopped when Derrick peeked out from behind his easel and smiled. Kaitlin thought he might go to his son, but he turned and missed his son's frown and the sigh that escaped Louisa's open mouth.

"So, the traveler has returned?" Eldon said as he entered the room, causing Kaitlin's heart to riot again.

"Must you do that?" She clutched her chest, she looked down and realized she held her brush and now had a blue splotch over her heart. She thought her heart was trying to get out.

He laughed. "I rather like to show up unannounced." Kaitlin shot him a playful sneer. Eldon smiled brilliantly. "I only thought to grace you with my presence, but if you don't want me to sit for you then I can go?"

"Nooo." Bradley jumped from his chair, and with a mad dash caught Eldon's hand before he could retreat.

"I guess that settles it." Eldon met Kaitlin's eyes. "Unless of course you don't...?"

Her lips twisted with her laugh. She rolled her eyes. "Of course we want you to stay." His presence had been most welcome the past few days, why would it change now? "And we want you to sit for us."

"Good," he said, plopping down on the stool. His grin turned mischievous. "You do have enough white paint?"

Kaitlin's mouth unhinged. It shut when she heard the laughter around her. "I don't know if it's white enough," she said smugly as she lifted her brush.

Shortly thereafter, Eldon began to form on her easel, but all Kaitlin could think about was the man who waited downstairs. She prayed her meeting with him would go as amicably as the one with Eldon did now. She prayed one day Devlin would sit on that stool. Smiling as calmly as his brother.

*****

"Please, take a seat."

"I prefer to stand."

"I prefer you sit."

"But I..."

"Kaitlin, please, sit down."

Frowning, she slowly took a seat. It pained her to do so. Her legs were tight and in need of a massage. She hoped to retire to her room for a warm bath and a quick nap once the children were gone. But Devlin had decided to return home.

Her back straight, she tried to sit still. Tried to remain in her chair though the skin on her legs felt so taut it might snap. Pushing her hands into her lap, she all but held herself in her seat.

She couldn't keep from fidgeting. At least he was busy with paperwork. But his reason for wanting to talk to her plagued her through the duration of the art sitting. "Why did you wish to see me?" she asked in a high voice.

His head snapped up. He wore a frown. Was he angry? She should be angry, he'd made her sit. She should tell him... *Quit being belligerent.*

He shook his head and took a moment to clear his papers to one side of his desk.

She used the time to catch her breath and stretch her legs, resisting the temptation to hike her skirt and massage them. She studied her lap and willed her legs to stop hurting.

"Kaitlin? Kaitlin?"

Her head came up. "Yes, sir."

He studied her pensively. "Are you all right?"

She gulped. "Yes, sir."

He flinched slightly, opened his mouth as if to speak and shut it for a moment. "Good. Kaitlin, I would like to know why, upon my return today, I should hear your name being bandied about town?"

"Bandied? I don't know." She shrugged, and concerned about her legs, paid little attention to the conversation at hand. She bit the inside of her cheek to keep from screaming, especially while he watched her.

She could feel his eyes on her as strongly as if he caressed her.

"You have no idea?"

She shrugged again after a moment.

"Have you ever met Orin Reinholdt?"

"No." She met his gaze.

"You're sure?"

She nodded. He frowned like he didn't believe her. He should. She'd never met the man.

"Why would a man you've never met wish to malign you? Are you sure you haven't had dealings with Mr. Reinholdt?"

"Positive," she said soundly. "Reinholdt is a common enough name, but I've never met Orin. The only Reinholdt I've had dealings with of late is Olga Reinholdt."

"Orin's wife?"

Her lips twisted with her frown, she grimaced and stared at her hands. Her dealings with him had been in a rather round about way. She hadn't thought how Orin might react to her dealings with his wife and Olga hadn't let on.

As if trying to gauge her, Devlin rose and sat on the edge of the desk and looked down at her. "What did you say to Olga that would anger Orin?"

Kaitlin looked up to find him scowling. The expression was nothing new. It was the coal dark eyes, so stormy and yet, aflame, that threw her heart a kilter. She did love this man. But did he have to look so formidable? Exactly how he wanted to look no doubt.

"Well?"

She gnawed her lip. She needed him back in his seat, behind the secure partition of his desk. "The explanation could take some time. If you'll take your chair, I'll gladly clear matters for you."

"I'd prefer to..."

"Positioned as I am, my neck hurts," she said quickly, making every effort to lean her head back as far as she could.

He studied her and grimaced. Did he see that her head was craned back, her legs were stretched outwards and her hands pressed inwards on her abdomen? He shivered and walking round his desk, calmly took his seat.

"So?" With elbows propped on the table, he eyed her over steepled fingers.

"Up until two weeks ago... I'd never met Mrs. Reinholdt and would have gone on just as blissfully not knowing her were it not for Tilly."

"Tilly?"

"Matilda. Anita's daughter. She works in the Reinholdt home every day from seven until noon or one. She usually goes home directly after her duties are complete, but two weeks ago, on Monday, she came here instead." Her story compounded her pain, tears rose in her eyes. She chewed on her lips for a time then continued.

"She was crying. She could barely walk. She collapsed on the back porch. When her coat was removed, they found her back was bleeding." Kaitlin's eyes swam with tears at the memory. Now things were amicable between her and Olga. Or so she hoped. Would Orin throw a wrench into their friendship?

Devlin lowered his hands to his desk. His eyes were sullen. "What happened, Kaitlin? Was she rap--"

"Oh, no." Kaitlin shook her head. She sniffed. "She'd been beaten by her employer."

"Mrs. Reinholdt? Why?"

Kaitlin swiped at her eyes. "Tilly was serving Mrs. Reinholdt. She stumbled on the edge of the carpet and before she could catch herself, she fell. She toppled the tray she carried, spilling its contents. It could have been cleaned up, but she fell while Mrs. Reinholdt entertained guests and broke an expensive sugar bowl in the process."

Kaitlin's blood surged. "Mrs. Reinholdt told her to clear the mess. Then after her guests were gone, she took a cane to Tilly's back."

Kaitlin met Devlin's eyes. Was the frown furrowing his features meant for her or Mrs. Reinholdt? She looked toward the clock watching him out of the corner of her eye. "I was so infuriated I went directly to the Reinholdt's home to have it out with Olga."

Devlin's brows rose. He covered his mouth with his hand. "Go on."

Kaitlin met his eyes again. They didn't seem so dark now. "When I introduced myself, she smiled. She thought I'd come to visit, hoped I'd have tea with her. I assured her that I was not there to socialize. I told her in no uncertain terms that I should like to discuss Tilly. She said it was none of my concern." She took a deep breath and jutted her chin. "I said it was my concern and if she ever touched Tilly or anyone like that again, I'd cane her myself."

"You told her that?" Devlin seemed to choke out the words.

"I surely did," Kaitlin assured him soundly. Angered by the story, she all but forgot her legs.

"How did she take it?" His eyes filled with curiosity.

Kaitlin bowed her head then looked up with a frown. "Not very well. She told me she had every right to discipline those in her employ as she saw fit. I told her she may think that, it was her choice, but if she maintained that right then I would maintain mine as well. And if she didn't choose my terms, I told her I would talk to you about some kind of legal recourse." She cringed. "I told her I would see to it that they would not be allowed to use your lands or rely on your business dealings." She bit her lip and lowered her head, waiting for him to start bellowing.

"Did you now? And did threatening in such a manner have the effect you were hoping to achieve?"

Kaitlin looked up apprehensively, her lips twisted. "Mrs. Reinholdt was petrified."

Devlin's brows quirked then knit together. It looked as if he wasn't pleased knowing she'd used him as a threat. Then his features seemed to soften. She didn't know how to read him. If only he could be proud of her. Even back her now.

"What were your terms?"

"My terms?" She grimaced, certain he'd be displeased. "I told Mrs. Reinholdt that Tilly would be staying at our house, but she had to come tend her. No servants would be allowed to attend the girl only Olga." Devlin's smile was so bemused, Kaitlin had to roll her eyes.

"How could you be sure she would do it and not harm the girl?"

"I brought her daughter, Louisa, home with me. I told Mrs. Reinholdt if she did anything to mistreat Tilly, in any way, her daughter would pay?"

"And she agreed!"

"She somewhat had to," Kaitlin muttered.

Devlin's smile was so broad and uncommon, Kaitlin could only stare. He smiled twice already. It made his handsome features even more so. "What did Louisa think of this?"

She tapped a finger to the flutter in her chest. "She thought I was going to beat her. She soon learned otherwise. I think she's quite happy with the turnout."

"How so?"

"Well, she joins us in the afternoon now, quite frequently." Kaitlin grinned. "She was in the observatory today. She wanted you to be our model."

Devlin took a deep breath. "I guess there's no question that things are working out. Still, I'll have to talk to Orin and let him know I don't care for him maligning my wife."

"That's kind of you. But as I said, things have worked out." Kaitlin felt her tears coming again.

"Be aware, I would have helped you take legal recourse. Still can. You've only to ask."

"I doubt it will be necessary." She started to rise. "But I appreciate knowing that you'd help. Well, I better..."

He rose from his chair and came quickly to her side. So quickly her heart hit her throat. "Kate, we spoke about having dinner and taking some time to talk. I wonder if we might start this evening."

She gnawed her lips. "I'd love to, I really would, but I've made other plans. You are welcome to join me. I'm sure my companion won't mind." When she saw his frown she thought to tell him Derrick was her companion but she was afraid he wouldn't come.

"I wouldn't want to intrude."

Kaitlin considered what was going on in his mind. Did he wonder about her companion? Probably thought the worst, given the frown he wore. Had he been home, he'd know the truth. He'd know she wouldn't have turned to anyone else.

He raked his hand through his hair and clutched it tightly.

"Devlin, you wouldn't be intruding. If you'd like to join us, meet us in the front hall by seven and we'll go together."

"I doubt I'll show." His smile sobered, his voice went low. "I'll probably be busy. We can do it another time."

"I hope you're not too busy," she said softly. "We'll wait for you, in case you change your mind," she added then turned to go before he could make another excuse.

Chapter Twenty-Seven

He'd let her go, believing he'd already lost his chance with her. Believing he wasn't worth her time anyway so it was for the best. Still, the thought of her with someone else when she was his wife, grated on his emotions.

He intended to be busy, but because of Kaitlin, he couldn't accomplish a thing. The woman was on his mind far too much these days, and, were he honest, on his heart. If nothing else, he would like to get a look at this companion. Perhaps, if the mere mention of his name could scare Mrs. Reinholdt, the look of him would petrify. He could use that to his advantage and scare this interloper away.

Devlin slowly descended the stairs, listening for Kaitlin and her companion as he came. So sure was he that he wasn't going to join them, he spent the afternoon thinking about what he would say, and had dressed impeccably in a dinner jacket complete with ascot and tails. He hoped the look of him would leave his wife and her companion speechless.

When he entered the hall, he was the one left speechless.

Not only was Kaitlin there, but she was dressed in a gossamer silver gown, which succeeded in taking his breath away. He nearly groaned aloud when she covered it with her shawl. Derrick was there with her, dressed very much like a young gentleman prepared for an outing. Was she going out, dressed like that and taking his son? He wouldn't allow it.

"Are you planning to take my son with you?" He sounded his presence with a growl once he'd found his voice.

Kaitlin spun to face him with a smile that bore no hint of guilt. "You've decided to join us."

He met her eyes in bewilderment.

She studied him with a soft smile on her face. Didn't she hear him? He wasn't playing. She seemed almost pleased to see him, pleased with his appearance. The truth was probably more that she was happy he'd taken the bait. She'd used his curiosity against him. And... why did she smile so softly? She slipped Derrick into his coat.

Devlin was thrown by her smile, but he wouldn't be beguiled. "You don't honestly think I'm going to let my son join you this evening?"

Kaitlin turned, her grin turned impish. "Of course I do. Or I hope so," she amended swiftly. "He is my escort after all."

"I won't allow..." he paused, her words finally sinking in, "Your escort? And where do you plan to take a child of his age?"

Kaitlin's brows rose. Her lips twisted in amusement. "You'll have to join us and see. Won't he, young man?" She turned and asked Derrick. "You don't mind if your father comes along?"

Devlin expected an emphatic No. He was astonished when his son, nodded his agreement -- furthermore, when his son smiled up at him. Another smile in so short of time from his son. What was going on here? Didn't the boy remember that he'd failed him? Didn't he remember his sister?

Kaitlin seemed pleased by the dumbfounded look on his face. Perhaps the evening would be okay after all.

"Lord, let it be," she said in a whisper.

"What?"

"Oh, nothing," she said happily. "Let's be off then."

Devlin didn't press for further explanation. He turned for the door, was bewildered when Kaitlin took Derrick's hand and turned to go down the hall. They marched a couple steps and stopped. Smiling she looked over her shoulder and giving her husband a look that nearly melted his heart, she crooked her arm. "Are you coming?"

Devlin slipped his arm through hers and let himself be led along. It was good she led the way, as he was too busy trying to figure it all out. Trying to figure her out. She never failed to amaze him.

Several questions ran through his mind as they turned onto the west wing and headed for the solarium. Several more arose when they stopped at the doors.

Derrick tapped softly. Devlin turned to Kaitlin. She must have read the questions in his eyes, because she answered with a smile that said, 'trust me'.

He could do nothing else at this point. And it scared him. Scared him, because he wanted to trust her. Scared him, because for some strange reason, he did.

When the door opened, they were met by the smug face of a boy. He was dressed in a large white shirt, with an oversized jacket and black slacks. The whole ensemble swallowed him whole. It sagged at his ankles like someone had taken waves of material and wrapped it around his body. Devlin noticed the outfit as one his father used to wear, one that had come from the box in the play room. He and his brother had worn it many times.

"Good evening," the boy said, pulling Devlin from his reverie. The boy's brows furrowed in concentration as he worked to keep his voice low, and Devlin found the workings of a smile. "May I take your coats?" the boy added. Then he coughed.

Once he had his breath again, the boy looked up, red of face, trying not to laugh and break his sober countenance, and bade them to follow.

With a bemused grin, Devlin followed. Once the boy had them seated at the lone table in the middle of the room, set with fine china and candles, he took a deep breath and allowed himself to smile.

"How am I doing, Miss Kate?"

"Beautifully, Carver," Kaitlin said simply.

The boy's chest swelled with pleasure before he cleared his throat and took his smug look again.

"Here are your menus." He slapped them on the table before each of them. "Your waitress will be with you shortly."

Devlin had to smile when he heard Carver's voice squeak. He looked at Kaitlin.

"It's pretend restaurant night." Her eyes danced merrily. "Louisa is our chef this evening. Oh, it's okay." She chuckled when Devlin's mouth gaped. "She won't poison us. But you can only order the Sausage and Sauerkraut."

Devlin's lips quirked. Kaitlin chuckled again. He was warmed by the sound of her laugh. Warmed by the light in her eyes. Warmed when she laid her hand atop his. It took all he had not to take her hand into his own. Not to pull her into his arms and kiss her as he suddenly had the desire to do. Instead he let himself get mesmerized by the tenderness in her eyes.

"Louisa's sausage and sauerkraut is actually pretty good. You'll be surprised."

Surprised! Devlin's brows hitched. He didn't have to wait to be surprised, he was already.

She patted his hand. "Oh, and since it's German night, you must order your meal in German." She took a deep breath. "I was supposed to greet the maître d' in German, but my German is atrocious."

Devlin dropped his gaze to where her hand lay on his. He didn't even care that she wore the mittens, hadn't even noticed them until now. All he cared about was the woman beside him and the serenity he felt in her presence. Lord help him, but he didn't want to lose it.

"I suppose I can manage some German." He looked up with a smile, hoping Kaitlin would see. As long as her hand was on his, he'd speak any language she wanted.

He hid his frown when she lifted her menu to peruse it, removing her hand from his, allowing it to chill. He stared at the menu she hid behind. She was right there and yet, he was near breathless to see her again. He caught himself staring and looked down at his son.

*****

Kaitlin hid behind her menu, her shroud, trying to catch her breath. All she wanted to do was stare at her husband. But her face was heated, so she studied her menu and fought to keep her eyes from wandering to Devlin. When she could read no more she turned her attention to Derrick and was struck by the similarities between father and son.

Derrick would be a lady killer when he grew up, Kaitlin was certain. All one had to do was look at his father to know. And Kaitlin eyes, heaven help them, were intent on looking.

Her heart thundered in her chest when she realized he looked back.

Kaitlin was never so happy to see anyone as she was to see Tilly, their waitress for the evening. Not only was it an excuse to tear her eyes away from Devlin, but the girl looked so much better, Kaitlin felt the tears well in her eyes.

Devlin studied the girl then met his wife's gaze. "Those look familiar?" he said of the clothes Tilly wore.

"They were in the trunk. Maybe they're your mother's."

He nodded slowly as if he recalled the gown. Then he turned his attention to Tilly. "Good evening, Tilly," he said with a soft grin. "I'm glad to see you're up and about."

Kaitlin was warmed by his words.

"Sir, thank you, sir." Tilly curtsied and turned beet red.

Kaitlin covered her grin. She knew exactly how Tilly felt under Devlin's gaze. He would be the topic of conversation in the kitchen once Tilly was able to get back and tell Louisa. Perhaps that explained her stammering when she tried to take their order?

Kaitlin thought to remind Tilly that it was easier to write when one looked at the paper, but she had her own problems. How did she order, even speak, with Devlin there?

Did the man know what a hazard he was?

Kaitlin took a deep breath and made her order.

Devlin laughed. "You're right, your German is atrocious," he replied after hearing her annihilate the language. "Why don't I order?" he suggested then proceeded to do so with such flawless diction, Kaitlin wondered if he'd been talking German since birth.

"Why, Mr. Clayborne, you are a man of mystery."

Too many mysteries.

"Is that good or bad?" He winked.

"I'd say it's good," she said then turned to study the room so she wouldn't have to look in those deep dark and very beautiful eyes.

*****

"So, the children put this whole thing together," Devlin commented once the meal was over. The conversation had been such he didn't want it to end. He learned more about his son and new wife in those brief moments then in all the time she'd been there. He rather liked what he'd learned. Liked sitting down for a meal with his son and not being pierced with frightened glances. He much preferred the smile.

"They really enjoy it." Kaitlin's sigh was so satisfied Devlin could only -- for the umpteenth time that evening -- stare.

"They've done a fine job."

"Yes, they have," she echoed dreamily. She blinked and set to wiping Derrick's cheeks.

Devlin wanted to scream, or, at the least, be his son for the remainder of the evening. Then she could pamper and care for him. He wouldn't be put out if she dabbed his cheeks with her napkin. Or stroked his hair back from his face.

He caught himself before he sighed.

"Oh." Kaitlin nearly unseated herself, startling her table companions. "I've been remiss. We can't forget to thank the chef and her helper for their hard work and tell them how much we enjoyed our meal." She called Carver, who stood at his post by the doors and asked him to let the chef know they would appreciate an audience.

The chef, a tall lanky girl, with fiery red hair that frizzed about her freckled face, stepped up to the table, grinning and fidgeting. She clutched her oversized shirt and heaved a sigh. Devlin remembered her from earlier and smiled. A hazard to poor Louisa. When her gaze fell on Mr. Clayborne, her breathing turned laborious and her face blossomed to a rich pink. The hue deepened as Kaitlin complimented her on the meal.

The sausage, or bratwurst, had been tough, the sauerkraut burnt, but Kaitlin said nothing of this. No, by the time she was done, Louisa beamed with pride.

Had he not eaten the evening fare, Devlin could well believe that he was in the presence of a world-renowned chef. "You did an excellent job," he added, sending Louisa into near apoplexy. She fanned herself. Evidently the blush permeating the young girl's cheeks had little to do with the compliments and more to do with him.

When Louisa tripped away on waves on euphoria, Kaitlin turned to Devlin's with a mischievous grin. "Now for the chef's helper."

Devlin was out of his chair as soon as his brother entered the room. "How did you...? When?"

"No questions tonight. Just compliment me and let's get on with it." Eldon grinned as his brother hugged him up. He pushed back. "Tilly is waiting to entertain us. I fear Miss Louisa and Miss Tilly have such crushes on you, you'll have to ask them to dance and make this an evening to remember."

"Would you mind?" Kaitlin added, her eyes glistening with light and tears.

Devlin shook his head. "As long as you promise to save a dance for me?"

The heat rose unbidden on Kaitlin's cheeks. She bowed her head slightly, looking at him through hooded eyes. "I'd like that." Her head came up. "As long as my escort doesn't mind?" She turned to Derrick.

"Son?" Devlin let his gaze fall to the boy.

His grin was all the answer Devlin and Kaitlin needed.

Devlin took a couple of turns on the floor with Louisa then a couple with Tilly while Louisa played the piano. But his eyes returned to Kaitlin, watching as she danced with Eldon, Carver, and Derrick.

He was at first envious of the way Eldon held her in his arms. Envious that his brother and his wife had become friends. He remembered Anna then, how she'd betrayed him, and felt himself growing angry. Then he realized the way Kaitlin's gaze kept finding his across the room. He noted the way she talked with Eldon and how she wasn't afraid to touch him. Even Louisa and Tilly laughed as they passed in his arms.

Kaitlin had accomplished much in his absence. He was sorry he hadn't been there.

He noted the gentle way she helped the boys, never seeming to mind if their feet crushed hers. Kaitlin danced past with Derrick high in her arms, her smile said she enjoyed herself. And Devlin enjoyed watching. All he wanted to do was hold her in his arms. When she switched to dance with Carver, he made his move.

"Mind if I cut in?" He tapped Carver on the shoulder.

Carver stepped back with a, "No, sir," and Devlin pulled his wife into his arms.

"I thought I'd come save your feet. I know how Eldon dances," he quipped as much for her as Eldon who watched the proceedings like a mother hen.

*****

Kaitlin laughed. "How utterly kind of you. I'll probably have to soak them."

"I'll be glad to draw the water," Devlin said softly, causing Kaitlin to wonder if he was jesting or not. When she met his eyes, she had her answer. He grinned. "Seems I've been remiss, Kate." She blinked. "I've yet to compliment you on how lovely you look this evening."

Kaitlin wanted to melt in his arms. She took a deep breath. "Then you must thank Constance, this gown belongs to her." Once she realized what she'd said and how flippant she'd sounded, she blushed all the more.

Devlin winked. "Then I'll be sure to thank her." His embrace tightened. "You've unmanned me, Kate," he whispered.

She blinked again. Had she heard him right?

"You've turned my house upside down. In a wonderful way," he added quickly. "Eldon hasn't been out in years, and Derrick is... happy. He doesn't seem so frightened. Thank you, Kate." He laid a light kiss on her cheek.

And you? She wanted to ask. If she could just meet his eyes. She put her head to his shoulder instead and let herself get lost in the evening. Would they ever have another?

Warm and secure in his arms, she prayed they would. Prayed the night would never end. But it did. The clock struck ten, sounding the end to their evening all too soon.

She lifted her head from his shoulder. "I'm sorry to call an end to this. I've truly enjoyed myself. But I promised Anita and Olga to have their children home at a decent hour. I'm afraid it's quickly becoming indecent."

"I understand." He released her slightly. Chilled, she wanted to feel his arms around her again. "Can't have their mothers upset with us. They wouldn't be allowed to visit as much then." He took a deep breath. "I am feeling rather tired myself." Kaitlin wanted to frown. Was he going to excuse himself and disappear again?

Please, Lord, not now. Her eyes drifted heavenward and back to find his gaze still upon her.

"I'll just get my coat and join you," he said. She blinked. "That is of course, if you don't mind my company?" Catching a strand of her hair in his fingers, he awaited her response.

She felt herself blushing. "I'd love your company. Eldon will be seeing the children home. I was only going to tuck Derrick in."

"Then my help is still needed." He grinned and let his gaze drift across to where his son was face down on the table, sleeping soundly, using his stacked arms as a pillow.

*****

"When did you find Eldon?" Laying his son down on the bed, Devlin pulled the boy's shoes

"I wouldn't have found him, if he hadn't let me." Devlin looked up. Kaitlin set the shoes on the shelf. "He left the wardrobe open for me."

Devlin's brows rose. "You weren't frightened?"

Kaitlin sighed. "Honestly, I was terrified. Only because I feared he wouldn't accept me." She sighed again. "But I'm glad we finally met. I rest easier knowing he's here." *Especially when you're not*, she wanted to add. "He's been wonderful with the children."

"Eldon had always been friendly with the children."

"You were wonderful yourself," Kaitlin replied softly. "Louisa and Tilly will never forget this evening."

"Nor will I," Devlin said. When Kaitlin found his eyes on her, she knew he spoke of more than the children. He tucked the covers round his son and laid a kiss on the boy's brow. When he rose, her heart nearly stopped then thudded heavily in her chest. She stood quietly, her body trembling as he crossed to her.

Kaitlin," he whispered. Desire laced his gaze before he drew her into his arms. "Kaitlin. Darling, Kaitlin." he said, before his lips touched hers.

Chapter Twenty-Eight

Kaitlin awoke with Devlin on her mind and the taste of him on her lips. Just to recall the feel of his arms about her made her heady. He could have gone on kissing her and she wouldn't have minded. Gentleman that he was, he held her for time then with another kiss that fingered its way to her toes, he said goodnight and slipped away. The promise of more hung between them. She clutched that promise now as she pressed her fingers to her lips, and stretched like a cat in the sun. What would he say when he saw her this morning?

Would the magic still be there? Would the desire be in his eyes as strongly as it had been the night before? Would he pull her into his arms again? Her heart flipped at the thought.

Euphoric from the wonderment of the night, she dressed then practically floated to the door. No sooner had she stepped into the hall, her euphoria died. Her feet were grounded and planted to the floor when she saw Ernestine coming from Devlin's room. At such an early hour? Thinking she knew why she'd be in Devlin's room, Kaitlin stifled the desire to scream, to cry and tried to melt back into the wood work. Ernestine saw her.

"Good morning, Mrs. Clayborne," she said in a sickeningly cheery voice that grated on Kaitlin's already irritated nerves.

Kaitlin wanted to slap the Cheshire cat smile from her face. Her lips trembled. "Might I inquire what you're doing here at this hour?" *Coming from my husband's room.*

Ernestine beamed with her sigh. She touched her gown at the neck. "I was headed down to get Devlin's -- Mr. Clayborne's -- breakfast. He isn't feeling well."

Kaitlin could just bet he wasn't! After spending the evening with Ernestine, who would? No wonder he hadn't stayed with her. He wasn't being a gentleman at all; he wanted to get to his lover. His kisses were only to appease her. She took another deep breath. "So, he isn't feeling well?"

He'd feel worse when she got through with him.

"No, he's a bit under the weather today." Showing no bit of fear or shame, Ernestine stepped to the stairs. "I really should get his breakfast. I assured him I wouldn't be gone long."

Her blatant disregard made Kaitlin bristle all the more, she stopped her. "Don't bother. I'm sure you've done more than enough. I'll see to Devlin now." Ernestine's eyes flashed, her nostrils flared, she opened her mouth, then shut it. Kaitlin mustered a smile. "Oh, and since he isn't feeling well, why don't you plan on taking the day off. Spend some free time for yourself. In fact, go ahead and take the weekend. I doubt he'll be doing any work today."

"But I -- the whole weekend?"

"The whole weekend. Do go on, Ernestine. I can take care of my husband," Kaitlin said coolly, her fluttering hands directing the way to the stairs and on to the door.

"I'm sure you can," Ernestine said, somewhat dryly. She sniffed as she stepped around her tentatively at first, then she smiled boldly. "I'll be off then. I have some private matters to attend to anyway. I hope Dev-- Mr. Clayborne won't be upset when I don't return. You will tell him why I'm gone?"

Fuming inwardly, wanting to dismiss her and tell her never to show her ugly face there again, Kaitlin watched her go down the stairs. She didn't miss the venomous smile on Ernestine's face. But she would not allow herself to show her feelings to Ernestine. She would not let her know how she hurt. When she felt she could breathe again, she tromped down the stairs thinking of every way she could murder her husband.

It was high time the devil got his due. Play with her senses... why she'd show him.

*****

Kaitlin quietly relieved herself of her burden, marched to the nearest window and pushed back the curtains, using just a dash of dramatics to accomplish her task. Devlin had to be blind or dead not to notice when she practically pulled the rod from the wall. The light that filtered through the opened drapes nearly blinded him.

"There we go. Isn't that lovely?" she asked, all too cheerfully, spinning around to smile at him.

"Shut the blasted curtains," he growled and flipped an arm over his eyes.

"Oh, now, it's such a beautiful day." She made her way around the room opening each and every curtain, allowing the sunshine to spill into every nook and cranny of the room. "It doesn't look like a tomb anymore." She sighed and pulled the last curtain.

His arm flopped back against the bed. Strengthened by anger, Devlin sat up glaring at her. "Shut the curtains," he repeated his directive in a lower, more menacing manner.

She spun around with her hands planted firmly on her hips and smiled. "You shouldn't worry, Mr. Clayborne. It looks as though you don't turn to ash in the sunlight anyway. You feared for nothing."

"Get out of my room." Each word sounded like its own distinctive bellow. He would love nothing better than to get up and throw her down the hall about now, but he was too weak to move. She knew he was ill. That, no doubt, was why she felt she could torment him. What he couldn't understand was the anger. She'd been so docile when he left her last night. She'd have done anything for him. He wanted that woman back.

"I'm not going anywhere," With a quirky grin she stood there baiting him. Again he wondered what had become of the quiet gentle angel he'd been dreaming of. And just who was the aberration before him? He swore he saw horns.

Her eyes flashed. "Not until I have a word with you."

"Ohhh," he groaned and lay back against the pillow. This, he did not need. He wondered what had set her off. They had parted on such amicable terms. His put his arm over his head again. "I'm in no mood, Mrs. Franklin. Now go away."

*****

Mrs. Franklin indeed. That wasn't what he'd called her last night. Had it only been a dream? She felt her body tense as taut as a bow. By the time she made her way to his side of the bed she felt like it would snap.

"Look here, Mr. Clayborne. We will discuss this. I'm already the talk of the town. I will not be the village idiot. Do you hear me?" She grabbed his arm. The heat beneath her fingers stopped her. She gasped; her anger melted into contrition. "Oh, dear Lord, you're running a fever. I'm so sorry. Truly I am. Can you... do you need...?" She stood there like an idiot, her thoughts tripping over each other.

"Just let me rest," came the tired response. He lifted his arm and stared at her. "Let me rest. Perkins will see to me."

"Yes. Yes, rest that's what you need," Kaitlin whispered as she backed her way toward the door, away from his glazed eyes.

Slipping from the room, she felt like crying. Why did she go to his room ranting and raving like a crazed, jealous, lunatic with him so sick? How in the world was she going to explain the fact that not wanting the servants to hear how she was going to let him have it, she'd given them the weekend off? Perhaps if she nursed him over the next few days, he might be more agreeable to what she needed to say. But what exactly did she need to say?

Perhaps, he would forget the morning's debacle. Maybe in his weak condition, he hadn't heard her.

"Fat chance that," she muttered. Trudging to the kitchen to prepare him some broth, which would better suit his stomach than the meal she'd carried up already, she hoped he would forget.

Unfortunately, things didn't go all too well the next turn around either.

She planned to take care of him, but the man was stubborn -- even while sick. He didn't want her help. Evidently he wasn't sick enough for her earlier outburst to go unnoticed. She wanted to kick herself.

"Just go, Mrs. Franklin and send Perkins up. He's seen to me for years, he can very well see to me now." Weary, he closed his eyes. She wanted to scream.

She thought of getting Eldon and letting him deal with his stubborn cuss of a brother, but decided she wanted no one else to care for him. But her. Nearing his side of the bed, she crossed her arms to keep from strangling him. "I can't send Perkins up." Leaning over him, she waited until his eyes opened. "He's not here."

She straightened and went to work unbuttoning the cuffs of her blouse. Better that than meet his eyes, she reasoned. She took a deep breath. "I gave the staff the weekend off. With pay, of course." She stuck that in quickly, hoping to calm him. By the groan, it hadn't served its purpose. "And Derrick has gone to stay with Constance. That way I can tend to you."

Dropping her arms, letting them glide down her skirt, she met his hard gaze. She was going to have to be just as stubborn. Squaring her shoulders, she swallowed hard. "You're stuck with me. It's my help or naught," she said smugly.

"I'll take naught." He took a deep breath. "Close your mouth, Kaitlin." He looked about to laugh when she snapped her mouth shut. "I will not have my personal matters attended to by some woman."

"Some woman or just me?" she shot back. He looked confused. She waited for him to ask for Ernestine, and prepared to strangle him whether ill or not.

"No woman, Kaitlin," he moaned, surprising her. "If Perkins isn't here then I'll see to myself. Now go away." Raising a weak hand, he shooed her from his presence, like he was flicking a fly. Did he really think she'd obey? He should know better.

"No, I'm going to help you. You're too weak." She pushed back her sleeves and began straightening his covers. "I'll see to your meals and your bath and... I'm sure it will be no trouble to empty a bedpan or two."

His eyes flashed with shock. "Irritable woman," he mumbled. "Must you be so stubborn? I told you, I'll see to myself. Now go away so I can rest," his new directive sounded rather like a plea. His eyes fluttered shut.

"Fine, Mr. Clayborne." Kaitlin grinned when he opened his eyes. "I'll go, but only if you prove to me you can handle it."

"Whaaat?"

"Prove to me that you'll be all right alone. All you have to do is walk to the door. Do that and I'll leave." Having laid the challenge before him, she stepped back and waited.

He studied her through hooded eyes, sighed heavily and threw back the blankets. The way he fought them, they looked like they were weighted. She turned her head as he fixed his night shirt. When she looked back, he was sitting up. His legs dangled over the edge of the bed as he tried to stay aright.

"Once I go to the door you'll leave?" he asked, breathing as if the movement had taxed him. He sat there as though his rear were anchored to the bed.

"I promise. You make it to the door and I'll leave you to fare for yourself."

"Fine." Another deep breath and he stood, reeling like a drunkard. She bit her bottom lip to stave off her laughter. He was determined, but one step from the bed and he proved to himself and her, what they already knew. He was too weak. Devlin blinked and fought to keep his eyes open. Then his chin lowered until it hovered his chest. When his knees buckled, Kaitlin was there to catch him. It took all her strength to keep him from falling and taking her with him.

"Seems we're stuck with each other." She guided him back to bed, helped him get settled, and tucked the blankets around him.

"I just want to rest," he told her feebly, his eyes fluttered shut.

"Good, we finally agree. I'll stay," she chirped.

*****

Opening his eyes he thought to protest, but her cool hand on his brow disassembled his already fragmented thoughts. One look at Kaitlin and he knew it was futile to put them back together. His angel had returned.

"Just as I thought. Your fever is higher." Her fingers made a gentle sweep across his head and pushed back his hair. "I'm sorry for my rudeness earlier." He heard her whisper. He wasn't about to ask her what she'd been about ranting as she did. He'd wait until he possessed the wherewithal for battle. For now the demon was gone. An angel sat in her place. He liked the angel.

She turned to fetch the cloth from the bowl of water that sat on the nightstand then took a seat on the edge of the bed to care for him. One hand returned to stroke his hair, the other, holding the cloth, dabbed a cool trail from his face to his neck.

"You go ahead and sleep," she said when she saw he was still watching. With her thumbs she gently stroked his lids so he'd have to comply.

He fought sleep, but she started humming a lullaby and it wasn't long before he succumbed to the gentle assault.

*****

When his breathing deepened, Kaitlin wrung the excess water from the cloth and laid it back on his forehead. She felt guilty at her treatment of him. "I'm sorry, Lord. I really am. I spoke in haste. In anger."

She'd been upset and he'd been stubborn, but that gave her no cause to treat him so rudely. She would have to tell him why she'd been angry, but now... she wondered if he'd listen to her apology. If he'd forgive her?

She pressed her lips to his forehead. "Sleep well, Devlin."

Chapter Twenty-Nine

Devlin woke to darkness. His body ached, he felt afire. He put a shaky hand to his head to feel the flames and found a damp cloth instead. It was warm. Looking around through the haze that blanketed his vision, he caught a faint glimpse of a woman lying on the floor beside his bed, wrapped in veils of moonlight, sleeping.

He assured himself it was only a dream brought on by the fever that wracked his body, but that didn't stop him from reaching out to touch her. It didn't stop him from letting his fingers glide through her hair. He closed his eyes with a sigh at the softness of the silken tendrils and soon was sleeping again.

"Kaitlin, darling," he whispered as he pulled her toward him. "I want you, Kaitlin. I want this to be a real marriage. Do you understand me, darling?" When his fingers nestled in her hair, she felt a shiver run down her spine. "Love me, Kate. Love me and be my wife."

His lips were closing on her when she heard coughing.

Sitting up, Kaitlin checked the fire. It burned low; she would have to stoke it soon. Running a hand through her hair, she checked her patient. He was on his side with his arm hanging over the bed, his cloth had fallen on her. She plucked it from her shoulder and rose to care for him. Rinsing the cloth in the bowl of water, she thought about her dream, and had to laugh -- which she did quietly, so as not to wake Devlin. She couldn't bear to have his angry eyes on her. After the way she'd treated him, she wouldn't be surprised if he sent her packing once he recouped. The thought bothered her.

Surely he wouldn't send her away from Derrick? From Eldon? From him? Her gut wrenched. "Would you?" she whispered, and let her finger run along his cheek. Taking the cloth, she began to bathe his body again. "Oh, if only we..." She shut her mouth before saying more. Who was she to think he'd ever want her? *Not in a million years,* she assured herself. *You've got to stop with the dreams.* But with her hand on his warm body it was easy to dream. Easy to want.

With the memory of their dance and the kiss to follow, it was harder still.

He looked so peaceful laying there, his dark brows casting a shadow on his dark skin, his ebony hair wavy against his cheeks and on his neck. *Peaceful and soft.* She let her fingers glide through his hair and down along his neck. *You are a softy, aren't you?* Yet, even in his silence, she felt the shadow that hung over him.

She heard it in the cries from fever-loosened lips. She tried to make sense of his words, but learned only enough to know that Devlin ached from the secrets he held. Most of that ache was found in one name. Anna.

He cried her name in the darkness. Yelled at her in the daylight, but said little to alleviate Kaitlin's growing curiosity.

Kaitlin wondered about Devlin's first wife. What had happened to build such a wall? Could she break it down, for Derrick's sake? *Perhaps yours, too,* she smiled at her patient then chided herself for thinking so. She let some cool water drip to Devlin's lips; they glistened in the firelight. She remembered how they'd felt on hers and fighting the urge to kiss them, stroked her thumb gently across them instead.

Leaning forward, she pressed her lips to his cheek and whispered a short prayer. Her prayer over, she bade him to get better. "You will, won't you?" she sighed. "Derrick needs you." *I need you.*

With another kiss to his cheek, she sat up and laid the back of her hand to his head, tsking at the fever beneath her touch. "You have to get better."

Positioning the cloth on his head once more, she went to stoke the fire then lay down on the floor beside his bed and slept. Unaware that he was awake and listening.

For the next couple days Devlin was in and out. He saw her face over him, felt her hands on his skin. Heard her prayers. He reveled in the feel of her arms about him as she bathed his body. Reveled in the sound of her voice as she calmed him with her words or singing. There were times he felt it all a waking dream, but so wonderful was the dream, he didn't want it to end. He knew it would.

Kaitlin spent little time from him the first couple of days. Only long enough to change his water, warm his broth and see to private matters for herself. By the evening of the second day, she looked more disheveled than he. She hadn't changed her gown, nor had she combed her hair, her only concern was Devlin.

She was bound and determined to see him well. After reading to him from the scriptures as she bathed him -- all the while hoping he wouldn't wake up and yell at her -- she woke him and forced some liquids down him. She was pleased to get a fare amount down him. Her pleasure ended when it came back up. She had to take a bath herself. It was her own fault. She'd made him eat.

Now that she knew the broth had a tendency to return, Kaitlin wouldn't require him to eat so great an amount. Nor would she sleep on the floor beside his bed. She moved a pail there and prepared to sleep in the chair, when she was reminded of Eldon. She was exhausted, but she couldn't help wondering why he hadn't come to visit her.

With Devlin sleeping soundly, she slipped from his room and sought the corridor through the wardrobe in her room. Taking the passage seemed eerie to her, it didn't help that her tired mind readily plagued her with fears. It was only the dark, which her little candle didn't light enough for her.

There are no ghosts. She nearly shed her skin when she heard the groan and about bolted back up the passage. Curiosity piqued, she stayed her course.

With a tentative hand Kaitlin knocked on Eldon's door, there was no answer. When she opened it, she found Eldon bent over a pail, clinging to it for dear life, heaving. He barely had the strength to lift his head when she came to his side.

"Why didn't you tell me you were sick?" she scolded him, gently.

He glanced up giving her a closer looked at his glazed eyes before he bent and heaved again. She held his head, studying the wall so she wouldn't be tempted to join him over the pail. Then helped him to bed where she wiped the spittle from his lips and ran cool water over his fevered brow.

When he seemed like he might rest, she pulled a chair and sat down.

His eyes fluttered open. "I'm all right, Kate. Go back to Devlin."

So he did know Devlin was sick. He must have come up and she hadn't seen him. "Why didn't you tell me you were sick? You're as stubborn as your brother." She swept the cloth through his ermine hair. It was a tossup as to which brother was the most obstinate.

Both were strong, independent males who hated being cared for, hating being weak -- especially in front of a female. As with Devlin, she didn't listen to Eldon's protests. Although her body wished she would.

After trudging the stairs her third time and spending waking hours with Devlin, her body screamed. She dropped into the chair across from Devlin and tried to sleep. She was given little, if any time.

Dragging herself down the stairs to check on Eldon, she scolded herself for her stupidity. If she hadn't sent the staff away, they'd be there now to help.

"You just had to send them away," she whined to the darkness. And almost believed she could hear it laughing at her. Eldon did make her trip somewhat easier by telling her about the hidden door in the wardrobe of Devlin's room.

"If you insist on coming, use the shorter route," he'd grumbled then proceeded to push her away as he leapt for the bucket. He managed to catch her with vomit in passing. She wiped the excess from her skirts and told herself to live with the smell as she lacked the strength to draw a bath, no matter how she might need it.

By the morning of the third day, the toll was immense on her body. Muscles she never thought she had, ached. At least the staff would be back the following day -- she'd rest then. Devlin would rest better with Perkins attending him. They could even move Eldon in with Devlin so Perkins wouldn't have to run between them and she could go to sleep for the next three days.

She'd already tried to move Eldon, thinking it would help alleviate her exhaustion, but his legs were like limp noodles and she didn't have the strength to hold him. She put him back to bed and let Lady drag her back up the passage. Where she fed the fire and dropped into the chair, she was practically asleep before she touched the cushion.

*****

Devlin awoke. His head felt detached from his body, he put a hand to his head to see that all was connected. His body felt clammy. His hair, sticky. His throat parched. Looking around his room, he caught a glimpse of a woman sitting in his oversized chair, reading. The fire's lazy glow served as her backdrop. Kaitlin. He smiled. It hadn't been a crazy dream after all.

"Mrs. Franklin," he whispered, and groaned at the sound of it in his ears.

Her head came up. She smiled brightly. But he could tell she was tired. "So, you're awake again." Closing her book, she laid it on the arm of the chair, and drew to his side. She took a seat on the edge of the bed, and felt his head. "Well, it's down from earlier. I think it's broken." She dipped the cloth in the bowl of water and dabbed his face and neck.

She met his gaze. "Would you like to try and eat?" He shook his head. "You will need to drink something." She laid the rag on his head and reached for a glass of water. "Here, try this," she said softly. She put an arm behind his head, helped him lean forward.

With her help, he got the glass to his lips and managed a sip then laid back. Closing his eyes, he took a moment to catch his breath, while she dabbed the cloth on his skin.

"What were you reading?"

"Nothing really." She grimaced as if she were afraid to tell him she was reading the Bible. Afraid she'd upset him. He caught her hand beneath his and met her startled eyes.

"What was it, Kaitlin?"

She inched away before answering. "I was reading in Psalms."

"Psalms." She tensed like she waited for his bellow. He smiled. "Is that what you were reading to me?"

Her eyes wide with surprise, she met his gaze again. "Yes," she practically squeaked. "I didn't mean anyth--"

"Would you read to me now?" he inquired. Her mouth gaped. "Please?" He squeezed her hand. Her head bobbed ever so slowly. "Good," he whispered. Giving her a grin he hoped she couldn't deny. She didn't look at him.

When his hand freed her, she rose and crossed the room in a half-daze to retrieve her Bible. When she leaned forward to grab it from the arm, she became all too aware of her nightgown. Burning red with mortification, she grabbed the blanket from the chair and wrapped it around her shoulders, but not before he realized what she'd done.

*****

Hoping the fire would account for the flame on her cheeks, she went to the fireplace and added another log before returning to his side.

His bed. The flame rose higher in her cheeks. Why in heaven's name did that bother her now? She'd sat on his bed for the last two days. Hadn't he been in it? *Of course he had,* she calmly assured herself. So why did she find little assurance in that? Why did the sight of him awake and sitting there with the blanket draped over his middle, cause her heart to flutter irreverently?

"Are you all right?" he asked.

She drew to the bed and stopped.

"Ah huh." She wouldn't tell him what the sight of him did to her. "Are you?" she managed. "Are you cold? It is a little chilly tonight. I should get you a shirt." She laid her Bible down and made a beeline to his dresser.

To his credit, he didn't burst out laughing when she returned and without so much as a word helped him slip into it.

"There," she said when he was all covered. She refrained from patting his head. "That should keep you from catching a chill. Now I'll just get the chair and slide it over here."

"There's no need to get the chair. Sit here beside me." Sliding over, he patted the empty spot. Again his eyes sparkled, he looked ready to laugh. "Well?"

"Ah..." Her frown deepened as she took a seat on the edge of the bed, her back rigid. Her eyes glued to the Bible.

"This would be more comfortable, Kaitlin." He plumped a pillow for her to lean on, and seemed surprised when she moved slowly onto the bed. She primly tucked her gown around her legs and shrank beneath her blanket. He sank into his covers and turned on his side, his back to her. That did little to help her relax.

*****

It said a lot for his will power when he wanted to face her. Touch her. The way she looked with her hair disheveled and laying over her shoulders was more than he felt he could bear. He kept his back turned.

He heard her deep intake and sighed.

"I'll be reading from Psalm fifty-four," she said after a long silence and another deep breath. "Don't think you'll hurt my feelings any if you decide to sleep again." He could almost hear her hoping he would, and bit his bottom lip to stave his laughter. He sobered quickly, when the bed gave beneath her weight as she moved. It took every ounce of his strength not to turn, every ounce not to draw the woman into his arms and feel her lips against his.

At the sound of her voice the desire grew, and yet, strangely, while the desire for her remained, the desire to listen to the words she spoke grew stronger.

"Save me O God, by thy name, and judge me by thy strength. Hear my prayer, O God: give ear to the words of my mouth. For strangers are risen up against me, and oppressors seek after my soul. They have not set God before them. Selah." She paused, coughed and continued. "Behold God is my helper. The Lord is with them that uphold my soul. He shall reward evil unto mine enemies; cut them off in thy truth. I will freely sacrifice unto thee: I will praise thy name O Lord for it is good. For he hath delivered me out of all trouble: and mine eyes hath seen his desire upon mine enemies."

She continued into Psalm fifty-five. Her voice seemed distant as he considered what she read. He thought of his enemies and wondered if it wasn't time to lay the anger he'd been harboring for them at the Lord's feet. But in the next breath, he wondered if God would really care if he did. Did God care enough about him to answer his prayers? If so, why had his first marriage failed so miserably? Why had He taken Deanna away? Why did his own son shy from him? And why had a woman like Kaitlin become his wife? Why did she care for a child that was not even her own? Why had she taken care of him and why was she, even now, lying next to him? Could a woman truly be trusted?

He hated himself for letting that thought have free reign.

With the desire for her still on his lips and the questions burning in his mind, he turned. She was sleeping.

"Kaitlin," he whispered as he moved the Bible she nestled against her chest and drew her into his arms. She snuggled against his warmth. In that instance, he saw the hands that she kept so deftly covered with her gloves and saw what his son lovingly held and kissed. Following the example of his son, he felt compelled to do the same. His heart broke as he touched the scars to his lips. Broke to know that he knew nothing about the woman he called his wife.

With her warm against him, her breath falling on his neck, he felt the wall that had been breaking since he married her crumble further. He knew beyond the shadow of a doubt he was falling in love with his wife, falling in love with a woman who had given of herself and brought joy to his home. He was falling in love with a stranger whom he felt like he'd known forever. Would she feel the same? Could she love him back? Love him like she did his son? Or would she be like... He couldn't bring himself to say her name, didn't want her memory to touch the moment, a moment filled with Kaitlin.

Pieces of Anna remained in the unanswered questions. In the unspoken secrets that would have heavy bearing on the relationship he wanted with the woman in his arms. What would she say when she learned them?

"What will you do with my heart, Kate?" he whispered, kissing her hair.

Chapter Thirty

Kaitlin rose to warmth all around her. She snuggled against it, drew a deep breath and made the mistake of opening her eyes. "Oh my heavens."

Not only had she been resting comfortably. Too comfortably in Devlin's bed, in his arms, but she'd forgotten about her other patient all together. Some nurse she was.

Mortified, she felt her body heat from head to toe. She felt herself turning crimson. If Devlin woke and found her like this, he'd probably think no better of her than the other women who'd come to his home proclaiming to be there for the boy. *But they were governesses. Weren't they? She was his wife. Right?* She wasn't prepared to stay and find out if there was truly a difference in Devlin's eyes. She maneuvered out of his arms inch by inch -- a task that would be easier if he didn't hold her so tightly -- slithered off his bed and gathering her blanket and Bible, tiptoed to his door.

"Where are you going?"

She froze in place with her hand on the knob, tempted to open it and run.

"Kaitlin?"

She turned slowly. "Derrick is back. I should see to him."

"Ah." He closed his eyes for a moment. She reached for the door. "Before you go, perhaps you could tell me what that was all about the other morning?"

Her lips twisted in disappointed. *You just couldn't make him forget, could you?*

"What exactly did you mean by the village idiot? Kaitlin?"

She didn't want to discuss this right now. Ever. Okay, someday, but not now. She pulled her blanket to her neck and clutched it. "I just wanted... I realize..."

"Kaitlin." He rose in his bed.

Why did he have to use that menacing tone? And those eyes?

"Well, I... everyone knows about the circumstances of our marriage. I'm the laughing stock in town. I can handle that. But I would appreciate it, if in the future when you have need for female companionship, that you would not bring her into the home you said would be mine."

He blinked and shook his head in confusion. "What are you talking about? I don't have any female companions. Where did you get that I--"

"Ernestine was coming from your room the other morning. She was... ohhh." Her lips puckered. "Had I known you were ill, I wouldn't have brought it up in such a manner. Forgive me," she whispered and made her escape.

Leaving a terribly confused, but positively happy man behind.

She had come to take him to task about his relationship with Ernestine, and there was none. She was jealous. Pulling the pillow where she'd laid her head into his arms, he smiled, and wondered why she had such a foolish notion about Ernestine. And decided, even if he had to bolt the door so Kaitlin couldn't slip out, they would finish the conversation.

Maybe he'd find the opportunity to kiss her again. His heady thoughts lulled him to sleep.

*****

Kaitlin said her piece and confronted him about Ernestine; she swore she heard a death dirge as she trudged down the stairs. Now that the affair was in the open, he'd probably call for her to leave and she couldn't bear it. Unwilling to make that happen any sooner than necessary, she sent Perkins, who had returned, up to care for Devlin while she went to check on Eldon. She found him sleeping peacefully then went to get Derrick and spend what time she had left with him. If his father wanted to be rid of her, he'd have to come tell her himself. She would not return to that room to give him the opportunity.

*****

The day was half gone and Devlin was stymied. Why hadn't Kaitlin come back? Yes he felt better, and yes, Perkins had returned, but he wanted to see her. Wanted to explain that he and Ernestine were not having an affair. To that end, he stubbornly refused to waste another moment in bed.

By the time he'd crossed his room to get his robe and made it to his door, he was exhausted. He stopped to catch his breath. He should climb right back in bed. But he was a fool. A fool for Kaitlin, he admitted with a sigh.

Using the banister to keep himself aright, he moved his shaky body down the corridor toward Kaitlin's room. He'd been sick and he was tired, but thinking of Kaitlin made him felt very much alive.

"Sir, you shouldn't be up," Perkins dogged him to return to his bed. "Sir, please, let me help you."

Devlin would not be helped. He didn't want to return to the cold tomb he'd fought so hard to get away from. "Perkins, unhand me." Perkins heeded the tone of the mister's voice and stepped back. "If you must help me, tell me where I can find my wife."

Perkins was dumbfounded. "Your wife, sir...? Oh, your wife." His smile was doltish. Devlin had never addressed Kaitlin as such. "She slept most the morning, but she and the children are playing in the snow right now. If you'll return to your room, I'll tell her you want to see her when she returns."

Devlin groaned. "I want to see her now."

"I'll call her right away, sir."

"No," Devlin said firmly, weakly. "Just tell me where they're playing."

"The north yard, sir. Below the nursery. But it's much too cold for you to--"

"Thank you, Perkins." Devlin clutched the rail and started down the hall. He stopped when he noticed his butler standing there. "That will be all, Perkins," he dismissed him when he came alongside to help. His lips twisting, his brows arched, Perkins took his leave.

Devlin continued down the hall, using the walls and rail for support -- it stretched like an eternity before him. He finally reached the room, thought to go in then took the next door instead and found himself in Kaitlin's room. His wife's room.

He hadn't set one foot in the room since the day he'd confronted her about the finances. Even then he'd never taken the time to look at what she'd done. He'd never taken the time to appreciate anything she'd done since her arrival.

Some kind of husband he was.

He let his gaze sweep the room and took the time now. He came away amazed at how elegant, simple and inviting the decor was. A picture of Kaitlin.

Taking a seat, he promised himself he would tell her what a lovely job she'd done, and take more time to study it, but for now he wanted nothing more than to look at her.

"Now, Derrick, surely you don't mean to throw that at me?" Kaitlin gave him a forlorn expression but couldn't keep from smiling at the boy with the fiendish grin. A grin that said he'd made no mistake targeting her. His hand yielding a large snowball, he stepped forward.

"Derrick, I warned you." She grinned mischievously and held up a much larger snowball.

"Ah, she ain't gonna do nothing," Carver assured his friend. "She's a girl, they can't throw."

"Oh yeah," Tilly exclaimed, letting her snowball fly. It caught her brother on his bare neck. He squealed like a pig and dropped behind the snow walls of the boy's fort. The girl's had no time to drop behind their cover when the snow started to fly.

Snowballs flew fast and furious for the next few moments, while Devlin watched from his perch. Soon with the battle waged and their energy waning, the combatants began to drop in the snow. Devlin listened to the peals of laughter as they made angels, but that stopped all too abruptly when his son stood and, for reasons beyond him or anyone else, began to cry.

When Kaitlin came to his side and walked him passed the girl's fort Devlin saw why his son was so sorrowful. In their glee they had broken a snow statue. But why did it bother his son so? He pushed open the window to hear better.

"It's okay, sweetheart." Kaitlin used the tail of her coat and dried his eyes. "We can build another." Derrick shook his head. "Oh, darling, yes we can." She touched the broken statue. "Do you believe in miracles?" she asked the children.

"Miracles?" Bradley shrugged.

"Yes, miracles," Kaitlin said again. She bent and picked up some snow and began to pat it into a ball. When it formed, she held it up to the children. "This is a snow seed."

"Ah, that's a snowball," Carver assured her with a flap of his gloved hand.

"No, this is a snow seed," Kaitlin returned and proceeded to place it on the broken statue. "If we plant it properly we might have a whole statue tomorrow."

Carver chuckled. "Nah, that can't grow a statue."

"I think it can," Tilly said softly.

"It's just a snowball," Carver argued.

"Have you ever seen the seed of a flower?" Kaitlin asked.

Carver shrugged. "Yeah, but they got to have water and sunlight to grow."

"We have water all around us," Kaitlin replied. "And the sun comes from our believing. That's the warmth this seed needs to grow. And each time a seed grows it's a miracle."

"Really?" Bradley whispered now. He reached out and touched the seed where it lay on the broken statue. Derrick touched it as well. Then they both looked up at Kaitlin.

"I believe," Louisa said, coming to lay her hand on the statue.

"Me, too," Tilly said, reaching out.

Kaitlin turned to Carver. His nose crinkled. "Will it be the same statue?" he asked, his skepticism waning.

"I don't know," Kaitlin replied with a smile. "Each seed is different. Unique. Just as each of you are. Just like each snowflake. What do you say, Carver? Are you willing to believe?"

Carver's shoulders hitched. "I don't know." He reached out to touch the snowball. "Hey, it's kind of warm."

Devlin knew there was no such thing as snow seeds, but that didn't stop him from wanting to touch the statue. He stared at the statue long after they were gone. And for a moment, just for a moment, he thought he saw it glowing. With a chuckle and a shake of his head he shut the window.

He was tired, but the sounds rising from the kitchen below pulled him to the stairs.

*****

The kitchen bustled with warmth and laughter. Margaret had cookies and chocolate for the rosy faced troops sitting around the island, giggling about the battle they had waged.

"I caught Miss Kate right here." Carver laughed and touched his collar.

"Yeah, but I got you right in the face," Louisa said, proudly. Carver's frown set Perkins to laughing.

"Who did you get, ma'am?" Marla asked.

Kaitlin smiled sheepishly. "My aim is atrocious. The girls made me the official snowball maker and they threw them."

Perkins laughed so hard, he nearly choked on his cocoa.

"It's not so bad," Kaitlin said then sighed. "Louisa has promised to give me lessons so I'll be ready for our next battle. By the time winter's over I should be able to hit the side of the house."

Perkins choked this time.

"Look! Chocolate is coming out his nose," Bradley cried with delight. And everyone roared. Derrick's shoulders lifted with his need to laugh.

Kaitlin waited for it to break free. Yearned for it.

"Can you teach me how to make chocolate come out my nose?" Bradley's asked Perkins. Derrick's shoulders bobbed so hard, he spilt his chocolate. It toppled, splattering him and Kaitlin as the cup dropped to the floor with a thud.

Unprepared for the shock of hot chocolate, Kaitlin bolted with a screech.

The laughter died when Derrick jumped from his chair and went to cower in the corner.

"Hey now, what's this," Kaitlin asked, forgetting the mess on herself. When she stepped toward the boy, he began to moan and shied from her touch. For a moment she thought she heard him say no, but surely her ears were playing tricks. "What's going on?" She looked at the others.

"Poor tyke's been disciplined too many times for spilling," Margaret answered with a frown.

"What?" Kaitlin was aghast. "But he's only a child. I spill more than he does." She turned back to the boy and caressed his shoulders. He tensed under her fingers. "Sweetheart, it was an accident. I'm not going to punish you for that. Come back to the table. Come on, I'll get you another cup of chocolate." He looked up at her with such pain in his eyes, she wanted to cry. Then when he looked at her soiled dress, it was all she could do to dam the tears. She flicked her dress. "Derrick, this will clean. I'm only concerned that you might have been burned. Were you?"

With a sigh, Derrick shook his head and blinked back tears.

Kaitlin touched his cheek. "Good, then we're both okay. Come with me." She held out her hand and sighed a praise when he took it. As she led him to the table, all she could think about was finding whoever had hurt the boy so badly and wringing their necks.

Once he was settled in his chair, Kaitlin caressed the sweaty mop of hair from his face.

"It's all right," she whispered as she laid a kiss on his brow. She turned with a need to cry herself and went to get him another cup of cocoa.

"I spill all the time," Bradley said with a cherubic grin, a dribble of chocolate running his chin even then.

"So do I," Tilly commiserated. She leaned forward slowly and winced. Kaitlin wondered if her back wasn't still tender.

"Here, let me help you clean this up," Louisa offered and began to wipe up the mess. "See, all gone," she added with a grin to Derrick.

Kaitlin set another cup before him. "This one isn't so hot." To make sure, she bent over and blew on it for good measure. When she sat back down Derrick leaned into her side and sighed.

"You're welcome," she whispered and looked up to find Devlin in the doorway.

"Mr. Clayborne." Perkins was out of his seat. "Sir, you shouldn't be up. You're..." He caught the defiant look in Devlin's eyes and offered him his chair.

"Would you care for some cocoa?" Margaret said, rising.

"There are cookies," Marla added quickly.

"Don't get up." Devlin waved them off with a tired hand. "I was curious to see what all the laughter was about."

He made no mention of the spilt chocolate. But Kaitlin knew he'd heard all just by the way he looked at her now. He was tired, but his eyes were alight with tenderness. She was glad the table hid her dress otherwise she might have turned beet red. She met his eyes.

His brows hitched. "I hoped to see you sometime today."

She knew why. He probably wanted to be rid of her as soon as possible. Probably wasn't too happy with her finding out about Ernestine and how she kept her away from him. "The children and I spent the day outdoors."

"Yes, I know," he said with a tired grin, which threw her. If he were angry, he didn't show it. But what did that smile mean?

"Are you sure you wouldn't like a cup of tea, sir?" Perkins asked, taking Devlin's stare from Kaitlin, allowing her time to breathe.

"I can make it straight way, sir," Margaret replied.

He shook his head. Although the smell of dinner was beginning to play on his senses, he wasn't sure if he could eat. He looked at the stove then back to Perkins. "I'm fine." Which was a half-truth. He was growing weary, had overtaxed his body, but he didn't want to go. He leaned his elbows on the table and rested against his hands. When he found Kaitlin's gaze again, he noticed he had the attention of everyone at the table. His son included. He smiled. "And how are you, young man? Is that good cocoa?"

Derrick's head bobbed. To prove his point he lifted the cup and took a sip. He was extra careful when he set it down. A movement his father didn't miss.

"I like my chocolate, too," Bradley informed him. "You can try it," he added and generously held up his near empty cup.

"That's very kind of you. But a growing boy like you needs all the chocolate he can get."

"You used to drink your share," Margaret quipped. Devlin missed those days. The days before the darkness settled on the manor.

"And more as I recall," Devlin added with a soft smile for the old cook.

"He tried to drink his brother's chocolate as well," Perkins added.

"Like you do me!" Bradley exclaimed to his brother. Carter frowned. In youthful exuberance Bradley turned in his chair to get a better look at Devlin. "Is your brother younger, too?

"No, he's older."

That acknowledgment stunned Bradley. "And he lets you take his chocolate?"

Devlin laughed. "No, he takes my share now." He was surprised his brother wasn't there in the midst of things. He knew Eldon couldn't handle being in the sunlight, but he could handle the dim light in the kitchen. Where was he?

"Did you have a sister, too?" Bradley asked.

Devlin shook his head. "Just my brother."

"How come he lives in the dungeon? When did he move there?"

Devlin looked to Kaitlin.

"The basement," she clarified.

"Bradley, maybe you shouldn't--" Tilly tried to rein her brother in.

"It's all right, Tilly." Devlin smiled in understanding. "My brother lives in the dungeon, as you call it, because too much light hurts his body and eyes. He started living there when he wasn't much older than Louisa." Louisa flushed at the mention of her name. "People were cruel to him. Some people don't accept what is strange to them and what they don't understand. So we made up the room for him so he wouldn't be bothered."

"I want a room like that," Carver proclaimed. "Then I wouldn't have to share a bed with my brother." He had to balance himself when his sister elbowed him.

"You might want it now, but in time you'd miss your brother," Devlin replied. "Who would you boss around if he wasn't there?"

Carver had to consider that.

If Kaitlin hadn't been taken in before, she was completely besotted now. He did well with the children. So why did he continue to hide himself away from his son? Although that was mending. She realized just how much when Devlin asked if he could carry the child to bed once he saw him nodding off against her side. Twice in so little time.

"It won't tax you too much, will it?" Kaitlin asked when she saw him push off from the table. The staff silently asked the same question.

Devlin shook his head. "A mite like that? I need to be going up anyway. So it wouldn't hurt to help you get him in bed."

"Is it that late already?" Louisa asked, meeting Devlin's eyes before she bowed her head.

"Not so late, it was just a long day," Kaitlin replied. Derrick wasn't the only one trying to rest at the table. Bradley had taken his fill of chocolate and his eyelids seemed heavy. His head drooped to his chest. While Kaitlin wanted to go on sitting there, like a family, she felt the day and the days prior. A rest before dinner would be in order, but first she had to get the children home.

Tilly yawned, which in turn made Louisa yawn. When the yawn reached her after making the rounds, Kaitlin chuckled. "Looks like others might take to bed early as well."

"Not me," Carver assured her soundly. He proceeded to yawn again.

"I better get you home." Kaitlin wished Eldon would show so she could help Devlin, but he wasn't about.

Devlin looked toward the door, started to frown then rising, reached out for his son. "If I head off now you might be home by the time I reach the top of the stairs," he teased. His smile was so brilliant. Kaitlin wanted to sigh. She did when Devlin pulled his son's warm body from her side. She nearly hugged herself to keep the warmth from where Derrick lay from dissipating too fast.

"Looking like you are, sir, she just might." Perkins retorted. When Devlin scowled at him, he rose with a contrite smile. "Let me at least help you."

Devlin seemed almost relieved that Perkins had come along with him. The boy might be little, but tucked against his chest Kaitlin was sure he was mighty heavy. Still, Devlin wouldn't relinquish his hold. Twice in so many days he'd carried his son in his arms, Kaitlin doubted he wanted to go back to months without touching him.

"Kaitlin, I'll see you when you return," he said, causing her heart to flutter in a crazy manner. If she knew exactly why he wanted to see her it would help. Or maybe not. He said his goodnights to the children and left. She saw his outline long after he was gone. She told herself to concentrate on the children. Concentrate on getting them home.

Devlin was heavy on Kaitlin's mind when she returned. Her heart rioted in her chest. Was he mad at her? Did he wait because he wanted to kiss her again? The cacophony in her chest ebbed on a sigh when she found him sleeping with his son tucked in his arms. Derrick was still dressed, only his shoes had been removed. From the looks of it Devlin was more exhausted than he let on. But still she smiled. It was too beautiful a picture not to. She wanted to crawl right up beside them and rest herself. But she didn't want to wake them. Besides, watching them had inspired her. With a second wind, she left the room and went down to see that the snow seed they'd planted earlier would bloom.

Chapter Thirty-One

Devlin woke with a start. He looked down to the boy in his arms and studied his sleeping form. He languished in the warmth of his child folded in his arms, nearly drifted off again when the clock chimed ten. His eyes flew open. Where was Kate?

With gentle movements, he moved his son from his arm and rose to find her. When he found her room dark and her bed empty, he thought the worst. Had she run away? Had she met someone on a...? He shook his head and crossed to her window. Perhaps she'd gone to see Eldon? He could join her there. Stubbing his toe on the box before the window seat, he swore softly. What were the blasted contraptions doing in every room in the house anyway? He stubbed his toe on nearly every one of them. He stopped to rub his toe and catch his breath, before he took the long journey down the stairs again. He rose to go when something made him turn to the window. When he looked down, he found all he'd been searching for.

His forehead pressed to pane, he watched as Kaitlin carved a new statue in the snow. With the moonlight hitting her hair, she looked rather like an angel come down from heaven. Under her gentle hand the snow seed blossomed.

She worked the snow. He swore he could feel her touching him. And perhaps she was, because she'd planted a seed in him and miraculously it was growing. When she turned for the house he slipped back into Derrick's room and lay there feigning sleep. But he couldn't rest. He didn't care how weak he felt. He wanted to see what the hand of the angel had wrought before the night was over. First he wanted to see her.

He grinned when he heard the door to Derrick's room open. His body warmed when she came over, and gently made sure the blankets were tucked about them both. He wanted to tell her he was awake, but lay silent, unwilling to give her an excuse to run away. He was flooded with joy at his decision when she leaned over to kiss his son then rounded the bed and dropped a whispered kiss on his cheek.

He kicked himself that he hadn't turned his head at the last minute, thereby taking the kiss on his lips, but no matter, the one on his cheek kept him warm. The one on his cheek gifted him with a hope of more to come.

The kiss felt warmer still when he stood before the snow statue. There in the moonlight, rising from the petals of a rose was he and his son. But something very important was missing. He caressed his cheek then caring not for the cold, or his exhaustion, he added the most important part. He would be at the window come morning to see her reaction.

*****

Kaitlin went down to put the finishing touches on her statue. She believed in snow seeds and miracles herself when she saw the family of three, a father a son and a mother, blossoming from the center of the rose.

*Was it a sign? Surely no heavenly visitors had come down to...*With a deep sigh, she touched the statue. *But who could have... Eldon perhaps? Was he, or whoever had finished the statue, watching now?* She turned quickly, took a sweep of the yard, and looked up at her room. All the windows were empty. But the warmth on her back was not erased so easily. It was strangely disconcerting, and strangely wonderful.

She let her gaze fall to the statue. She studied the workmanship, letting her finger glide across it as if it were fine china. The addition complimented her part of the statue. It was done by talented hands. The likenesses of herself, Devlin, and Derrick were astounding. She wanted ask if anyone knew who the artist might be, but decided she would find out their name in due time. She was impatient that they come soon.

She started for the house, a sigh billowing in the air before her and came to abrupt stop when the ladder was tossed from the open window. The bottom rung rapped the base of the house as it landed.

"What are you doing, you little dickens?" She laughed when she saw Derrick scurrying out. At least he had the good sense to put on his coat, even if his pajamas peeked out from beneath it. She pulled him from the rope when he was close enough then looked up expecting his father to join them. He'd been sleeping in Derrick's bed when she slipped in that morning, when she'd been tempted to kiss him. "Was your father with you?" she asked, disappointed that no one else followed.

His head bobbed. He pressed his cheek to hers and gave her a kiss.

"Well, good morning to you." She kissed him back. "Where is your father?"

He blinked, and folded his hands and rested his cheek upon them.

"Sleeping, huh?" She laughed. Derrick's head bobbed again with his grin. "Well he's still weak." Derrick frowned. "But he's getting better. We'll go up and see him after breakfast. Maybe we can persuade him to watch you race your steeds?" Derrick liked that idea. "In the meantime, come see what the snow seed blossomed into."

Derrick's eyes widened. He twisted in her arms so strongly she had to sit him down. He ran to the statue and stood staring at it in awe.

"Pretty." She heard him whisper in a soft voice that touched her heart. Her heart was warmed further when he slipped his hand into hers. Derrick's gaze drifted to the lake and back. Kaitlin saw tears in his eyes.

"Sweetheart, are you all right?" He looked up with a sad smile then reached out to touch the forms in the statue. His fingers caressed the snow then his hand stopped on the face of the small boy captured there. Kaitlin realized who he missed.

"Dee," he said simply as he touched the petals of the rose, confirming her suspicions. She wanted to ask him to say it again. To tell her what he knew. He was content to study the rose and she let him.

They stood in silence, unaware of the cold, both silently wondering if the seed would bloom some more and fill in the missing piece.

Wrapped in a quilt, Devlin stood at the window. Watching the woman and child below, he too thought of his missing child, of all that had been lost to him. But there in the shadows of the morning mist stood a new beginning. One he was ready to reach out and take. He only hoped, no, he prayed that Kaitlin was as ready as he.

"It's beautiful," Eldon announced his presence. He'd seen Kaitlin and Devlin working on the statue the night before. He slipped out to see it just as the light of morning came over the rise. Working together Devlin and Kaitlin created a masterpiece. Eldon wondered what might grow if Devlin and Kaitlin worked on a life together. He came to stand by his brother. "It's been a long time since I've seen you make anything."

Devlin turned to face him with a smile. "Yes, it has."

"What now?" Eldon asked, his hopes unspoken, yet, clear in his simple words.

Devlin blew out a breath. "I'm going to tell her." He turned back to the pane, and the scene below.

Eldon wanted to cheer, to cry, to shout to the heavens and did so silently. Deep in his heart he wondered what else might bloom from the rose now that Devlin had decided he could live again.

"So, where have you been keeping yourself?" Devlin asked. "I hoped you'd come save me from that stubborn wife of mine. She's a wonderful nurse, but she needs to work on her bedside manner."

"I happen to like her bedside manner. After I realized she wouldn't leave me alone I sat back and let her tend me. I can't even remember the half of it."

"What are you talking about? Kaitlin took care of you? When?"

"Why do you think I didn't come see you?" Eldon declared. "I was sick as a dog and your dear wife watched over me as well."

"No wonder she slept so soundly the other night. Perkins said she'd slept half the day today."

"She was due. Your poor wife was exhausted."

"She never said a word," Devlin said, his eyes registering his amazement.

"No, she didn't," Eldon agreed. "If you had any doubts about her acceptance of you that should certainly alleviate them."

Devlin nodded. But his doubts had been with him far too long to release them.

"I wondered what the cats have been up to with us both out of commission?" Eldon broke into Devlin's thoughts.

"Kaitlin gave everyone the weekend off, with pay," Devlin smiled. A gift Perkins had thanked him for a million times over. He'd taken the time to visit his sister. She sent Ernestine off, but that didn't mean she hadn't slipped back in while Kaitlin tended them. Nor did it mean that Gerrard hadn't stayed behind to do some snooping. He wondered if they were in cahoots.

And would do some investigating into the pair to ease his mind.

*****

"We missed you," Kaitlin said to Eldon when she met him in the kitchen later. "How are you doing today?"

"Better than Devlin, I suspect." Kaitlin met his eyes. Eldon grinned. "He always takes much longer to heal than I do. But then he's a pretty puny fellow," he added with a wink.

"You're looking pretty peaked yourself," Marla quipped, as she placed a plate of food before Kaitlin and Derrick. "With those dark rings under your eyes, you look like a raccoon that's just seen a ghost. It's good to see you out and about."

Eldon chuckled and took a seat. He flipped his napkin and laid it on his lap. Kaitlin swore she saw him blush.

"How's your appetite this morning?" Margaret turned, her face red from standing over the stove. Ringlets of sweaty gray hair formed at her temples. "I've got some fresh ham and eggs."

Eldon winced and nearly turned green, his lips twisted with his gulp. "Maybe a cup of tea. Derrick is growing so much he might need my portion," he added, causing Derrick to grin brilliantly. "How's that snow seed?"

Kaitlin looked up from the ham she cut for Derrick. "Have you seen it?" She grinned, thinking he'd finished it for her.

He cocked his head. "Yep, it's a work of art, that. Always wanted to be so talented, but..."

"You did the horses."

Eldon nodded. He held up his gnarled hands. "Years ago. These ole things don't work so well now." Kaitlin frowned. "Must have been an angel come down to carve something so lovely," he added, causing Kaitlin to blush. With a bob of his brows, he turned his attention to his cup and took a sip of his tea.

Kaitlin took a bite of her eggs and wondered, if not Eldon, who might the angel be.

"What are your plans for the day?" Eldon cradled his cup as he lifted it to his lips.

Kaitlin's fork hovered in mid lift as she contemplated his question. "The children wanted to take a walk to town and visit the children at the home this morning then take a turn ice skating on the lake."

"Sounds like fun. I love to skate, but..." Eldon's lips twisted with his frown. Memories crossed his face, etching it with pain and a semblance of joy. "How 'bout you, boy?" His gaze fell on Derrick. "Your pa used to skate rings around me. Are you as good as him?"

Derrick grimaced, his fork shook in his hand.

Kaitlin sighed. "He doesn't like the lake."

Eldon shot her a querying glance. "He used to love to skate."

Kaitlin shrugged. "He won't go near it now. I promised him I wouldn't force him. We'll probably build a snowman while the others skate."

"Hmm, I like building snowmen," Eldon commented. But wondered, as did Kaitlin, why a boy who used to love to skate, was so frightened by the ice now.

Chapter Thirty-Two

"Good morning." Kaitlin smiled as she stepped into the room leveling a tray. She'd gone to Derrick's room hoping to find Devlin and found he'd returned to his room. The same room where she'd awakened in his arms. She hoped he'd be sleeping and she could leave the tray and slip out unseen. She couldn't be a coward forever. He said he'd wanted to talk to her and she couldn't put it off any longer. It might help her if he were still convalescing in bed, but he stood by the window, trying to make some sense out of the box on which he'd stubbed yet another toe.

He looked up. His lips turned up in a smile then settled in a thin line as he looked at his feet.

"They're ladders." She set down her tray. "My husband and daughter might be alive today if we'd had one in our home in Boston." His gaze met hers. She was flustered by the magnitude of his stare. "Perkins was going to bring this in, but I snatched it from him in the hall. I don't know if you're hungry. Eldon wasn't. But there's some tea and toast if you... if you want anything else I can..."

"No, nothing," he finally said, a slight grin played on his lips. He came toward her. She backed and gave him a wide berth.

*****

"You didn't come back yesterday." He found her eyes again. "I know you were busy with the children. And Eldon. Thank you. Have you managed to rest then?"

He paused to watch her reaction. She nodded. He doubted she'd rested near enough when he considered the dark shadow beneath her eyes. He sighed deeply. "I'm glad you're here. There are a few things we need to discuss. They can't be put off any longer." Kaitlin gulped and licked her lips. He held his grin as he made a cup of tea. "Would you like some?" He turned to her. She nearly shook herself out the door saying no. He took a seat on the edge of the bed and motioned for her to have a seat then chuckled when she took the chair furthest from him.

"Kaitlin, I'm not going to yell at you." He could see from the look in her eyes that was what she expected. Still, she didn't relax too much with that knowledge. She put a hand to her chest and took a long breath.

"First, to clarify, I've never stepped out on my wife and I don't intend to."

"I'm sorry, I--"

"Kaitlin, I'm not telling you this for an apology," Devlin interrupted curtly and caught himself. He focused on softening his tone. "I can see how you might come to that conclusion given the time I've spent with

Ernestine. She's a secretary. Nothing more."

"Then I'll not mention it again." Kaitlin took another sip of air and said nothing more. He contemplated his cup and the words he needed to tell her.

She started to rise. "I know you probably--"

"Stay, Kate," he said firmly. He caught her eyes with his and held them. "There's something else I need to tell you." He took a deep breath, his lips trembled. "I know I haven't been much of a husband. Even if this is only an arrangement, I've treated you badly. I've distanced myself." He sighed. "I've given it a great deal of thought and I want you to know why. You see, I've told others what I'm about to tell you and watched their eyes fill with contempt."

"Anna?" Kaitlin barely breathed the name.

"Anna and others." He bowed his head then looked up again. "I feel I must chance telling you. Perhaps you'll understand my behavior."

"You don't have to tell me. Not if--"

"I do, Kate. I need you to know. I've decided the best recourse is to tell you and give you the time you need to think it over carefully. Then you can decide whether you want to remain here or not." Setting his cup down, he rose and began to pace. Her gaze stayed upon him, her brows furrowed. "You've accepted my brother and I thank you for that. I hope you can be as charitable with me."

*****

"Of course I would," Kaitlin responded. What could be so bad that he feared she might run away? Had he killed his wife as many had rumored? She berated herself silently for even thinking such a thing.

His smile held no cheer as he stopped before her. "That remains to be seen."

"Devlin, I know you've been hurt. I know about Anna. I know your searching for your daughter. Whatever it is, I promise I won't turn my back on you."

"Anna said the same thing, Kate. I believed it for a while. Then our children were born and she couldn't hide her contempt."

"Your children are beautiful. How could that cause contempt?"

"Yes, they are beautiful," he mused. His chest lifted with his sigh. "But not to her. The instance they were born, I thought I could never love any other being as much. Anna would have nothing to do with them. She treated Deanna the worst."

"That lovely child?"

"So you have been to the cottage," he stated with a wisp of a grin, it disappeared as easily as the smile had before. "She was a lovely child. But the painting didn't show Deanna's true beauty. Anna would not allow it."

Kaitlin was bewildered. What could a small child have that would be so hideous a mother would hide it from the world? A scar? A defect?

Devlin put out his hands. Turning them slowly before her he moved closer. "Have you ever wondered about my coloring or the coloring of my son?"

"No," she replied frankly. "Although I'll have to admit I've been envious. I lack any color."

"There's no reason for envy, Kate. Your skin is lovely as are the freckles that bridge your nose and speckle your neck and shoulders." She put a hand to her face to cover her heated skin. He noticed far more than she'd ever believed he would. "And you wouldn't want what I have."

"What could be so awful?"

"It's not awful per se, only to some." He dropped his hands to his sides. "Kaitlin," he called her name and waited for her to face him. "Kaitlin, my coloring doesn't come from the sun. My mother was a Negress."

"Full blooded?"

"No, she was the master's daughter. A mulatto, to use the most *proper* of terms," Devlin answered, his wry expression revealing more than his words. "And my father was half-Indian."

"Oh! What tribe?"

"Sioux. But that doesn't matter." He turned with a frown. "Aren't you listening? I'm part Negro and part Indian." He turned his face as if she'd find him hideous to look upon. "There's very little white in me."

Kaitlin stared at him in amazement. This should offend her? This had turned Anna from her children? The dark, dreadful secret? It was nothing of the sort to her, but the way he lowered himself on the bed, weak and afraid to meet her eyes now, she knew it was to him.

"I didn't remove my daughter's picture because I was distraught or ashamed. I removed it because it showed nothing of the child she was. A beautiful child, Kate. A black child." He sighed. "Her skin was a rich and deep as my mother's and Anna was ashamed of her. In her fear, she shunned both children. She quoted scripture, called me the son of Cain. She said that sin caused my coloring and that of our children. She wouldn't lift a finger to touch them unless she wore gloves, because she was afraid it might rub off on her. She'd be tainted for life."

His eyes fell to Kaitlin's gloved hands with a frown. She wanted to melt into the chair and fade away from shame. But she had no reason to.

"I'm not afraid to touch your son." Her chin rose stubbornly. "Nor am I afraid or appalled by your lineage. I see..."

"What, Kate?" His eyes flashed with deep anger. A deep hurt that had been nurtured over the years. He shook his head. "Don't tell me what you see. Not now. I want you to consider the depths of what I said."

She rose and moved to his side. He looked away from her. "But I have," she said softly reaching out to touch him.

He glanced back with quiet fury in his eyes, burning her hand, stilling it before he turned away. "No, Kate. Anna said the same. But she really hadn't accepted it." His sigh sent a shudder through his body. "I want you to consider it. If you find that you can't bear the consequences then I want you to tell me. Truthfully."

She backed away, tears filling her eyes. "I'll go. I'll heed your wish. But I have nothing to consider. My view will not be altered. Nor my promise." He didn't turn as she opened the door. "I don't believe that your coloring makes you tainted or sinful. Nor do I consider your son such. I love him..." *And you,* "...dearly. I'm not Anna," she choked on a whisper, before she closed the door

Then there was only the silent cry of his heart.

*****

Devlin wanted to believe she wasn't like Anna. Wanted her to come back to him and argue the point. But she stayed away and gave him the time he asked for.

He wanted to give himself to her completely, was ready to believe she meant what she said. Then he saw her with *him,* a tall, blond stranger. She wrapped her arms around his middle as they walked across the field. Derrick tripped along beside them.

He saw Anna all over again. He turned from the window prepared to wait and confront her once she came home. It had been two days since she learned the truth, she should return to his room with her answer. He wouldn't tell her he'd seen her with her lover.

She didn't come to his room though; his impatience drew him to hers. Fear of what he'd find behind her bedroom door, compelled him to stop and listen. When he heard deep male laughter, and Kate's moan, he let his mind run away with him.

"Don't do that?" Kaitlin laughed so hard she snorted. He heard a slap. "Graham, you know how ticklish I am. Now stop it."

"How 'bout this, does this feel better?" Graham inquired. "Turn your leg here. Does that hurt?"

Kaitlin sighed so hard and loud, Devlin's senses were rattled. He grabbed the knob and squeezed. "Oh, yes, now that feels wonderful. Have I told you how much I love you?"

"All the time. We both know the reason why?" Graham chuckled. "You love what I do with my hands."

"There is that." Kaitlin laughed.

"Here, let me rub your leg."

Kaitlin groaned in ecstasy. Devlin covered his ears, but not for long. He would hear every seedy detail and use it against her when he had her alone. She was lucky he didn't run to get his gun and shoot her and her lover. It took all his strength not to when he heard Kaitlin tell Derrick to bring her robe. He flew to his room on a cloud of anger and seethed.

*****

"It does burn slightly," Kaitlin told Graham as she slipped into the closet to dress. "But this liniment smells much better."

"You'll find it works better," Graham assured her. "Kaitlin, are you happy here?" After considering what they'd discussed on their walk Kaitlin knew why he asked. He was concerned.

She turned to him and smiled. He'd ask the same question several times since he arrived and surprised her that morning. "Of course I am," she assured him. And she was. Earlier on her answer might have been different.

"Are you going to show him the picture?"

Kaitlin sighed and touched the picture of her husband and daughter. She clutched it to her chest. "I should. But, Graham, I want him to accept the fact that I care for him without..." her words faded with her thoughts. She placed the picture on the mantle. Touched her finger to her lips and touched her family.

Graham put his hand to her shoulder. "I still think you should show him. But it's your decision. When do I get to meet this husband of yours?"

"Soon." She was surprised he hadn't showed up already. She made enough noise to wake the dead. "Let me finish dressing and I'll take you down to see him." She touched the photo once more and went to the bath.

"Fair enough." Graham shrugged. "In the meantime, Derrick can keep me company. So, tell me more about Eldon."

"Eldon?" Kaitlin poked her head out the bathroom door. "He has an ailment that turned his skin and hair white and his eyes are nearly blood red. He can't be in the sun because the light hurts his eyes and burns him. Sometimes he even wears dark glasses inside." She stepped from the bath, fixed her waistband and buttoned her cuffs. "He's a very nice man. I hoped he'd be up and about, but he and Devlin have been sick."

"So you don't think he'll mind meeting me?"

"I told him about you." She buttoned her collar and ran a brush through her hair before pulling it up into her prim little bun.

Graham huffed a breath. "I wished you'd leave it down. You remind me of Aunt Teresa when you wear it like that."

"That bad?" Kaitlin asked, not ready to believe him. Graham grimaced. Kaitlin quickly let her hair fall and shook her head to loosen the tresses. Aunt Teresa, well into her eighties, was the family's oldest and grouchiest spinster. She pulled her buns so tight her brows formed her hairline, putting her in a continual state of amazement even when she scowled at you. Kaitlin finger-combed her hair and worked it into a loose braid. "Better?"

"Much," Graham declared. Derrick's head bobbed in agreement.

Kaitlin rolled her eyes. "Eldon has the most wonderful laboratory. You'll find it extremely interesting. He's been searching for a cure for his ailment."

"Hmmm." Graham smiled. "I'm already interested."

"Then perhaps you might like to see it."

Graham turned with a hand to chest. He studied the white-haired man. After a moment he held out his hand. "Eldon, I presume?"

Eldon grinned as he took Graham's hand in a firm shake. "I've been waiting for you to get done so I could introduce myself. I'm of a mind to pick your brain."

"Then by all means, direct me to your laboratory." Graham winked. Within seconds he, Kaitlin, and Derrick were following Eldon down the corridors below the house. "Does he always come in like that?" Graham asked Kaitlin.

"Frequently," she answered and left it at that.

*****

Later that afternoon Kaitlin came down the stairs, Derrick's hand wrapped in hers. They were dressed for an outing and hoped to find Devlin and talk him into joining them. Kaitlin never expected the scorn in his eyes when she met him in the hall.

She swallowed hard and tried to ignore it. "We we're just on our way out. Would you like to join us?"

"You're on your way out all right, Kate, but my son will stay here with me."

Kaitlin turned to meet his eyes and wondered at the anger in them. She couldn't ignore it now. "What are you saying?"

"I should have known you'd be like Anna." Devlin replied, confusing her all the more. "I should have known you'd learn the truth and find someone else."

"I don't understand what you're--"

"You don't understand. How rich." Devlin leveled her with his stare and his words. "You bring your lover into my home, you let my son spend time with him and you don't understand." Kaitlin opened her mouth to retort but he wouldn't listen. "I told you about me. But you couldn't accept it. I told you and I find you with another man."

"He's my brother," Kaitlin said in her defense, when she finally had a voice.

Devlin laughed like one insane. "Can't you come up with a better lie? Anna used the same one."

"I'm not Anna and it was my brother," Kaitlin snapped back.

"Really?" Devlin sneered so she wanted to slap him. "Then perhaps you are worse than Anna." Kaitlin blinked and tried to understand him. "The sounds coming from the room today were rather incestuous."

Kaitlin slapped him. "He's a doctor! He was taking care of my legs!"

*****

Devlin touched his hand to his face and looked at the boy glued to Kaitlin's legs. Derrick trembled. Devlin needed to put an end to this right now. He drew a heavy sigh. "All right, Kaitlin, he's a doctor and he's your brother. Say what you will. I won't fall for your lies. I want you out of my house right now."

"No, Devlin, please I'm not--"

"What, Kate, lying? Not seeing a lover? I heard enough to know better. I want you to go. Go stay with your sister. Maybe she can put up with you and your lies and your lovers, but I can't."

"No, Daddy," his son screamed now. His eyes swam with tears. "No, Mommy, don't go! Don't go!" The hold on her legs was like a vise. Peeling him from her, she knelt down and held him to her chest. She turned pleading eyes on Devlin.

Devlin, shocked by his son's outburst and the fact that he talked to defend Kate, almost changed his mind. But he'd changed it before. Many times and all it got him was pain. He couldn't stand the pain anymore. It was best to send Kate away now before they became too attached. But, Lord help him, he was attached. From the look in his son's eyes it was evident they both were.

"Say your goodbyes, son, Mrs. Franklin must be going now."

"No, Daddy," Derrick whimpered softly and clung to Kaitlin's neck.

"Now, son," Devlin said firmly, unwilling to change his mind, or his heart.

"Don't leave," Derrick sobbed in her ear.

"Shhh, sweetheart." Her voice grew soft as she pressed her lips to Derrick's ear.

Whatever she said seemed to calm him, but he still clung like a vise when she tried to pry him from her neck. Devlin pulled Derrick from her arms.

"That's enough, son," he said firmly. He winced when his son's eyes fell on him. He wondered what Kaitlin might have whispered in his son's ears.

"I love you, Mommy," the boy said so his father could hear. Then he pulled away and ran for the stairs, paying no attention to his father behind him.

Devlin eyed Kaitlin. "Go now, Kate," Devlin said with a gulp. "I'll send your things with Perkins."

Shoulders slumping, tears hazing her eyes, Kaitlin headed for the door. "I'll leave. But first I'll say this. All you had to do was believe me. But you're so mule headed you can't see. Just can't let go of the bitterness and believe someone else might care for you." Her voice broke. "And I do, Devlin. I care," she added with a hoarse whisper. Then she turned and walked out the door.

Five minutes had barely passed when Devlin, who had the look of her pleading eyes engraved in his memory, realized how much he already missed her. But he had to be strong. He needed to talk to his son. Needed to explain and work things out between them. He turned for the stairs, hoping to do that. Hoping to eradicate the urge he had to chase Kaitlin down and bring her home. He didn't need her. Neither did his son.

Evidently his son saw matters differently. Derrick wouldn't say a word to him or look at him. He sat on the edge of his bed staring at the window and beyond. Devlin left him there, hoping tomorrow would be better.

*****

"You're a fool, Dev," Eldon spat the words, as he tried to control his anger.

"I don't want to hear it," Devlin growled.

"Well, you will," Eldon replied firmly, unwilling to back down. "How could you send her away like that? How could you treat her that way?"

"Treat her that way?" Devlin retorted. "She's the one who brought her lover into my house. She's the one--"

"Her lover?" Eldon interrupted, appalled that Devlin could be so mistaken. "The only man that has visited with her, other than you or myself, was her brother."

Devlin met his eyes wanting to believe. He shook his head. "If that man is her brother then they're in an incestuous relationship and I want nothing to do with her."

"Incestuous? What are you talking about?"

"I heard them this afternoon. I'm not stupid," Devlin returned.

"But he's a doctor. He was--"

"So she has you fooled as well. I don't want to hear another word about Kate. It's time I got my life in order. And you, too. I don't care what you say. Kate's not coming back. I won't allow it. I don't want her name mentioned ever again."

Eldon sighed heavily. He was talking to a wall. An unheeding, immoveable wall. Let Devlin wallow in his anger. He wanted to see about Kate. When he knew she was all right, he'd come back and pummel his brother for being so stupid.

"What should I do about Derrick?" Devlin turned and found himself alone. Eldon was gone. Kate, Derrick, and Eldon were out of reach. He felt every lonely minute of his self-imposed isolation.

*****

Kaitlin should have gone to Constance's, she supposed, but she hoped to give Devlin some time to cool down and return and talk to him. Besides she needed to see Derrick as she promised. But as the evening wore on she realized she was going nowhere. The reason for her listlessness started to well up in her stomach. She'd thought she would be spared the sickness, but doubted she'd be so fortunate. She banked the fire and waited for it to come.

*****

Devlin passed his son's room then Kaitlin's. He'd walked for hours it seemed, making tracks, going nowhere. His anger subsided, leaving him with remorse for his actions earlier in the day. Still he couldn't bring himself to go after Kaitlin and accept her back. He'd lived years entombed in isolation, he didn't need her now. He needed no one, save his son. But how did he get his son back? How did he get his son to give him the smiles and the words he willingly gave Kate? He raked his hands through his hair and decided the time had come to be stern. His son would thank him in the end.

That thought driving him, he pushed open the door to his son's room. His son was gone.

Derrick had been there the night before and earlier that morning when he looked in on him. Devlin knew he waited for Kaitlin. His son still wanted Kaitlin. Where he, might fault her, Derrick believed and loved her.

And now he was gone. Was it by choice, or had Kaitlin...?

Chapter Thirty-Four

Devlin slammed the door to his son's room and raced down the stairs, fearful that Kaitlin had slipped in and taken him like Anna had their daughter years before. If so he would catch her, and bring his son home. He prayed, as he slipped into his coat, that she wasn't so far from him now that he couldn't find her. That thought churning his blood, spurring him on, he nearly ripped the door from its hinges as he opened it.

He came to a dead stop when he met the immoveable force beyond it. "Constance?"

"Where is my sister?" Constance asked, her eyes fierce, her nostril's flaring. "I demand to see her. This instance." She forged ahead, forcing Devlin to backup.

Devlin's brows furrowed. "She's not here."

"Well, that's evident. Your son wouldn't be making long trips to my house if she were."

"My son, my son is with you?" He couldn't hide his relief. Nor his bewilderment. "How in the world...?"

"He used the rope ladder in his room," Graham replied, coming through the open door with Derrick in tow.

Devlin didn't care to hear, he only saw Graham, Kaitlin's lover. "What is he doing here?"

"Who? Graham?" Constance dropped her chin to her chest as her shoulders hitched in bewilderment.

"I don't want him here. I won't have your sister's lover near my home or my son," he said and reached for Derrick. His hand stopped in mid-air when Constance began to laugh.

Her eyes welled with tears. "Her lover?" She doubled as far as she could to catch her breath.

"Would you mind explaining why you find this so funny?" Devlin asked in a perturbed tone.

Constance wiped her eyes, and straightened. She put her hand on her protruding stomach and sighed. "Not funny really, but Graham *is* our brother."

"Your brother," Devlin said dryly. "Then what were the incestuous noises proceeding from her room yesterday?"

Constance laughed harder. Even the man, Graham, started to laugh.

Devlin didn't see the humor. "If you're going to stand there and laugh then I must ask you to leave. Derrick, come here." He reached for his son again, only to be stopped by Constance's hand on his.

"Really, Devlin, it's not necessary. You've got it all wrong. Graham is our brother and he's a doctor."

Graham grinned. "You heard me rubbing balm on Kaitlin's legs."

Devlin was confused. "Balm? Her legs?"

"Yes, where she burned them," Constance added with a groan, born not from the conversation at hand, but the child in her. She sucked a breath, clutched her stomach in a delicate manner, and waited for the pain to pass.

"She burned her legs?" Devlin shook his head. Constance and Graham nodded.

Derrick's head bobbed as well. "Big burns."

Devlin sighed heavily and put his hand to his head. "What a mess." He turned to Graham. "I thought you were her lover. I thought she hadn't accepted my heritage and found herself another. What a fool I've been."

"I won't deny that," Constance agreed with a sniff.

"Your heritage, you say?" Having the presence of mind and feeling chilled, Graham stepped over and shut the door.

"Yes, it is rather unique," Constance answered. "But Kaitlin wouldn't have been bothered by that."

"How can you be so sure?" Devlin asked, unwilling to believe.

"Because she..." Constance started.

"She didn't show you the picture, did she?" Graham interrupted.

"Oh yes, the picture." Constance smiled. "That would explain everything."

"I've seen no picture," Devlin replied.

"You should see it now," Perkins replied.

Devlin turned to find his household staff lined up behind him. None looked too pleased with their employer. Their fierce stares chilled him.

"I realize you might let me go over this, but I have been in this house since you were a boy and feel I must call attention to your stubbornness and let you know that we all feel you've done Miss Kaitlin wrong." Perkins played spokesman. Margaret, Marla, and Anita, their chins raised in open defiance, nodded their agreement. Devlin found himself taking a step back.

"We've brought you the picture and have come to ask you to reconsider your demand upon Kaitlin," Margaret said with a sniff, stepping forward, confrontation in her eyes and her compact posture.

"We hope you do, sir," Marla interjected. "Because we love her and miss her."

"And we want her back," Anita added.

"We are of a mind to resign our posts if your treatment of Kaitlin doesn't change," Perkins said with a piercing look that made Devlin feel rather like a child, which was how he'd been acting. Having said as much, Perkins thrust out the picture he held.

Devlin stared at it for the longest time, while everyone around him waited for his reaction. He lifted his head and shrugged. "What does this tell me? It's only a picture of one of her servant's families."

"No, Devlin." Constance tapped the frame. "It's a picture of Kaitlin's in-laws, her husband, and of her daughter, Simone."

Devlin's gaze fell to the picture once more and he fully understood why Eliot thought Kaitlin would be such a fine choice for a wife and why he now knew she was. Jean Marc's mother was a Negress and her son and granddaughter bore the same deep coloring of skin as he and Derrick.

"Oh, my goodness, I've got to find her."

"It's about time you came to your senses," Constance said dryly. "Are you sure she's not here somewhere?"

Devlin threw up his hands. "I thought she was with you."

"Maybe she's with your brother," Graham suggested.

"He's not here, either." He turned to the staff. "Do any of you know where she might be?"

Everyone shook their heads, save for Anita who took interest in her shoes.

Graham turned a keen eye on her. "Anita, do you know where my sister is?"

Anita looked up and nodded. "I'll tell you but only if he promises not to be mean to her."

Feeling properly chastised, Devlin took a deep breath. "I won't hurt her. I only want to find her."

Anita fiddled with her collar and took a long gulp. "Your brother swore me to secrecy."

"Anita, please," Devlin said softly. "I promise I won't hurt her or send her away. I realize I've been an idiot and want to amend that right away."

"Very well, she's at the cottage." Anita wrung her apron nervously. "She's been feeling poorly and Eldon has been taking care of her."

"Feeling poorly?" Devlin asked no one.

"Probably the same thing you and Eldon just got over," Graham surmised.

"Then we better get to her."

"Will you bring Mommy home?" Derrick asked. Devlin was astounded and overwhelmed with joy. Derrick had talked to him. But that filled him with sadness. His son had seen what he'd been too proud and stubborn to see.

Devlin knelt before him. "I'm certainly going to try."

"We'll see that she's home promptly," Constance declared, turning for the door.

"You'll do no such thing," Graham replied, catching her collar. Tugging her to a complete stop, he turned her. "You'll stay here and wait for Eliot to arrive, while Devlin and I see to Kaitlin."

"Make Constance comfortable," Graham ordered as he followed Devlin out the door to the carriage."

Devlin apologized profusely in the carriage. He only hoped Kaitlin would be as receptive as her brother.

"I never knew," Devlin said, his voice deep with remorse.

"I told her to show you the picture," Graham replied. "But she wanted you to accept her without seeing it. She wanted you to accept that she cared for you."

Devlin's brows rose. "Does she?"

"What do you think?" Graham looked out the window and back. "She wouldn't have stayed this long if she didn't. Nor would she have placed those ladders throughout your house."

"You mean those confounded boxes?"

"Yes. She puts them around to protect those she loves."

Those she loves. That struck a soft cord deep within Devlin. Could she love him? Did she? He wanted to get to her with haste and find out, but the carriage seemed to lumber along at such a slow pace he was tempted to jump out and run. He reached for the door when the carriage came to a jolting stop in front of the cottage.

He was at the cottage door, pounding, before Graham alighted. No one answered. Impatient to get to Kaitlin, Devlin rushed the door with such force he knocked it from its hinges. It dropped to the floor with an ear piercing thud. He stepped through the threshold to find his wife and brother staring at him.

"Devlin. Graham." Kaitlin drew a long sigh and leaned against the bedpost depleted.

Urgency abating, Devlin halted. "We heard you were ailing and came to help."

"It's about time you came to your senses." Eldon's lips twisted with his admonition then tripped into a smile. "I was coming to open the door. There was no need to break it down."

Devlin started to move toward the bed but Graham blocked him with his hand. He smiled and winked.

Kaitlin hazarded a glance at them both. "Now that you know I'm okay, could you please leave? Unless of course you want me out of your cottage?" she asked Devlin with another sigh before she laid her head back against the post. "Otherwise, Eldon has been quite kind to look after me."

"I don't want you to go, Kate. Not at all." Devlin took a step closer and stood with his arms crossed high on his chest. "Kaitlin, you don't look so well. It wouldn't be wise to leave you like this."

"I'm fine," she said flatly, barely able to lift her head. "I told you, Eldon has been helping me. So if you'd both leave." Her hand rose and fluttered toward the door before it fell like a limp noodle.

"But Eldon has to go. Don't you?" Devlin said with a voice of authority. He looked at his brother, daring him to say otherwise.

"I suppose I do," Eldon replied with a smirk.

Kaitlin frowned as the words sank in. "Well, then I'll be all right alone."

"Kaitlin, you and I both know you're not well. I could stay and help," Graham offered.

"I don't need any help." Kaitlin leveled her brother with a none to fierce look. "Now if you'll both go away and leave me alone, I'd be much obliged. Eldon, make them go away," she protested when they didn't move.

"Can't do th--" Graham started to say only to be cut off by a wave from Devlin.

"We'll be glad to go." Devlin grinned slyly. "First, you have to prove to me that you're able to take care of yourself."

Kaitlin heaved and met his eyes. "How would you have me do that?"

"Well... you'll have to walk to this door and..."

"And back again," Graham interrupted. Eldon chuckled in understanding.

Devlin gave Graham a querying glance. His smile broadened. "Walk to this door and back to bed again and we'll leave you in peace."

Kaitlin shook her head. "Just to the door and back?"

Devlin nodded. She groaned and shook her head

With a gulp she took a deep breath and slowly rose from the bed, holding herself unsteadily against the post. "Then you'll leave?" she asked as she gathered her strength. They nodded again. She squared her shoulders and stepped away from the post. Devlin noticed the way her hand didn't leave the crutch of the post until it was forced to.

"Take it slowly and you can do it," Eldon cheered. He stepped back and shut up when Devlin leveled a glare at him.

Her face stoic, her head high, Kaitlin took small, wobbly steps to the door. She looked from Devlin to her brother as she made what seemed like an endless circle to turn around. She nearly fell then, but her tenacity wouldn't allow her to and there was the door frame to steady her.

Once she had herself balanced she took another deep breath. "Now back. And then you'll go?"

"Then we'll go," Devlin assured her. Her head was bowed in such concentration she didn't see the smile that passed between the men.

"Okay," she said, trying to keep her head up. It seemed weighted. Her legs moved like rubber. "Okay," she said again and stepped toward the bed. She made it all of two steps before gravity pulled her to the floor.

"Whoa, sweetheart." Devlin caught her before she fell. He hoisted her into his arms and carried her back to the bed. "Looks like you're stuck with me," he said softly, as he carefully laid her down.

Kaitlin whimpered. She pushed her palms against him. She was in no condition to argue. With a groan she closed her eyes and succumbed to her tired body.

"How did you know she'd make it to the door?" Devlin asked Graham as he reached for the covers.

"Not only is she my sister, she was my patient." Graham sat down on the edge of the bed and felt her head. "As warm as she is, I'm surprised she got that far," Graham added with a tsk.

"I only found her this morning. I've been trying to keep her fever down," Eldon apologized.

"I'm sure you did your best," Graham assured him. "It's appreciated. Isn't it, Devlin?"

Devlin heard but his attention was drawn to her legs and the memory of her midnight walks and her tears. "The fire did this to her?"

"She told me she had scars," Eldon said as he leaned in for a better look. "It looks like she walked through hell and back."

"It was months before she could walk again." Graham smiled ruefully, "I guess it's a blessing she's stubborn."

"Yes, perhaps," Devlin agreed as he pulled the covers over her legs. Her stubbornness had been a blessing. His had been a curse. He knelt by the bed and took her hand into his own. It was then he thought of the scars on her hands. The scars she tried to cover with her mittens. The scars his son had seen and kissed. He kissed them not so long ago. He drew her hand to his mouth and laid a soft kiss in her palm. "Ah Kate, I've been such a fool."

Eldon laid his hand on Devlin's shoulder. "There's no need for that now."

"No," Devlin agreed. But he knew he'd have to apologize for the way he'd treated her.

"Just take care of her," Eldon added.

Graham nodded in agreement. He checked her pulse and laid his hand to her head to assess the fever. "We should probably head back now."

Devlin laid her hand down and rose. "You head back. Let Constance and Derrick know she's all right. Just ill. I'll stay and watch her."

Graham cocked his head. "Are you sure?"

Devlin smiled. "If I don't miss my guess, you'll have your hands full with Constance before the night is over."

"So you noticed?"

"How she was trying to cover the fact that she's in pain?" Devlin chuckled. "Yes, I don't think we should take Kaitlin back to the house while she's contagious."

"What about you?" Graham asked, rising. "You can get just as sick as the next man."

Devlin nodded. "I've already had my 'bout with this. So has Eldon. Kaitlin stayed with me. I'll stay and take care of her."

Graham shrugged and tucked his things in his bag. "I'll leave some medicine to help with the fever then I'll come by as soon as I can to check on her again." Devlin followed him to the door. "What about this?" Graham asked as he bent to lift the door.

"Tell Henry to head over and help me in the morning. For now we'll sit it back in place and hope the wind doesn't get too strong tonight."

"Will do," Graham remarked and headed for the carriage.

"Oh, and Graham, don't let anyone else come. Only Eldon." Devlin turned to his brother. "But make sure you're covered and it's dark when you do. Otherwise, come in the carriage. See that he does that, Graham. I fear he's just as stubborn as Kaitlin."

Eldon rolled his eyes. Graham chuckled. "You're leaving me with the hardest task of all."

But the task was simplified. Thanks to Constance and the baby that would not wait no matter how much Constance wanted to go see her sister, everyone was busy through the evening.

*****

While Kaitlin slept, Devlin administered a cool cloth to her fevered brow, but he wasn't nearly busy enough. He had ample time to think, to consider his failings. Eldon said there was no need, but looking at Kaitlin, having seen her legs, he couldn't stop his thoughts. He remembered their past conversations now with such clarity he hurt. To think he'd thrown her out of the house, made her leave Derrick, compounded his guilt.

Graham was within rights to wring his neck, yet, he left him alone to care for Kate. Devlin would do his best.

He stretched out beside her on the bed, listened to her breathing. "Ah, Katie, what can I do? How do I make it up to you?" Tears filled his eyes and spilled again, when he saw the Bible on the stand beside the bed.

Reaching across her, he grabbed the worn leather and pulled it to himself with a shaky hand. For a moment, he held it against his chest. He hadn't truly touched a Bible in years, hadn't heard the words written since Kaitlin read to him. He was scared to read them, scared that the words would condemn him. He was a man who deserved condemnation. He prepared himself for such, swiped his tears and opened the pages, letting them fall where they may. The pages parted at Psalms; fell open to the spot where Kaitlin read to him from before. Was it mere coincidence? He didn't think so. Swiping his eyes, he began to read to her. To himself.

'*I will extol thee oh Lord, for thou hast lifted me up. And hast not made my foes to rejoice over me. Oh Lord my God I cried unto thee and thou hast healed me. Oh Lord thou hast brought up my soul from the grave: thou hast kept me alive, that I should not go down to the pit. Sing to the Lord ye saints of his; and give thanks at the remembrance of his holiness. For his anger endureth but for a moment, in his favor is life: weeping may endure for a night, but joy cometh in the morning.*'

Kaitlin's sigh, caused him to stop reading and think of another conversation between he and Kaitlin.

"Who died the greater death?" she asked him. He or Eldon? He didn't answer her then because he didn't want to face the truth. He let his eyes drift back to the Bible. He entombed himself in anger and hurt. He shut himself off from the world, from his son and wife. From his God. But God had been gracious to him. God had spared his no account life and blessed him with a wife who truly cared. She accepted him and his failings.

That knowledge, that complete and utter vision of a God who never stopped loving him, made him weep all the more. Instead of feeling lowly, he bowed his head to the tears and turned his heart toward heaven. Doing what he hadn't done in years, he lifted a prayer. When he cried the words, he knew beyond a shadow of a doubt, that God was listening.

*****

Kaitlin sat up, rolled to her side, and opened her eyes. Derrick was smiling at her. Behind him, Eldon grinned like a possum. "See, boy, she's gonna be fine. Welcome back, Kate."

"Good morning." She found a weak smile.

"I couldn't see you last night and Daddy said you weren't sick no more." Derrick stepped closer. "Didn't you want to see me?"

Kaitlin pulled him into her arms with a grunt. "I wanted to very much. But I was tired. Your father told me to sleep." And he'd sat right there with her making sure she did as he told her. He was gone now. She looked at Eldon. "Where is he?"

"The study." Eldon cocked his head toward the door. "Didn't want to leave, but he had some business that wouldn't wait."

"We're supposed to tell him when you're awake," Derrick supplied.

"And my brother?"

"He took your sister home yesterday."

"And the baby and Eliot, too," Derrick added. He grimaced. "Are you gonna have one of them, Mommy? She was wrinkly and she cried a lot."

"Graham plans to come back later today," Eldon proceeded to say. Kaitlin nodded but she was too busy listening to Derrick. He called her *Mommy*. She would treasure that forever. Eldon looked down with a grin. "Sounds rather nice, doesn't it?"

She nodded. "Speaking of nice, I never did thank you for watching over me."

Eldon practically blushed. He bounced on the heels of his shoes, reached over and pushed the hair from her cheek. "Wasn't anything special, Kate. I did it 'cause you're special. Me and the boy here was plumb worried about you. Just wanted that brother of mine to come to his senses."

"Which he's done over and over again," Devlin said, announcing his presence. He scooped up his son and took a seat on the edge of the bed. "I'm just stubborn." He grinned, a killer of a grin that made Kaitlin's heart race. She wasn't sure what to think when his gaze fell so softly on her.

"Amen to that," Eldon said, rolling his eyes toward heaven. Devlin turned to look at him. What passed between them Kaitlin wasn't sure, but in the next instance Eldon made his excuses and tried to leave. "Well, I haven't had my breakfast. It's time me and the boy here got something to eat." He grabbed Derrick and hoisted him into his arms. "We'll be sure to save some for you. Just don't take too long, Dev." He grinned as he ducked into the hall.

Devlin rose and closed the door behind them. When he turned,

Kaitlin was sitting up, nervously twisting her hands.

"You should lie down," Devlin said softly.

"I think I'd rather sit," she told him, stubbornly holding the headboard.

He shook his head. With a heavy sigh he came to stand before her. "Kaitlin," he said her name, paced a few steps and stopped. "We need to talk." She gulped. "It's not quite that bad." He smiled. "I wanted to tell you that as of now, things are going to change. I had many hours to think about our situation while you were sick and I've come to the conclusion that we can't go on living like this." He pulled a paper from his pocket and unfolded it carefully.

Kaitlin held her breath, wondering what he was about, afraid to say a word.

"I've decided I don't want to be bound by this contract anymore," he said and promptly ripped it to shreds.

Kaitlin watched the pieces flutter to the floor and swallowed her tears. He still wanted her to go. Why? He apologized for being wrong, for accusing her of having an affair with her own brother. And he'd taken care of her. She stopped on that thought and figuring she knew why he wanted her gone, she started to cry. "Am I so hideous you don't want me in your home anymore?"

*****

"Hideous?" he asked, stunned. He dropped to his knees before her and took her hand into his own. Caressing it softly, he put it to his cheek. "You're not hideous at all. Your scars are beautiful to me. I'm the one who's been hideous and my scars are buried."

"Then why?" she choked on a hiccupping breath. "Why do you want me to go?"

He laughed softly and met her eyes. "Kaitlin, I don't want you to go." He smiled tenderly. "I was following your conditions."

"Conditions?" Her lips quirked with such endearing confusion he fought the urge to kiss her.

"You told me to tell you if anything changes. Told me to tell you if and when I can't abide by the contract." Her brows knit into a perplexed knot. He kissed her fingers. Kissed the palm of her hand. "Kaitlin, I'm informing you that I want a marriage. A real marriage with you. If you're in agreement, I should like to start courting my wife."

Her tears ran her cheeks. "Me?"

"You," he whispered. "I find I can't do without you. What do you say? Are you willing to give this fool a chance?"

Her sigh said everything he needed to hear

"Ah, Katie." He caressed her cheek. "Would it offend you terribly if I said I want to kiss you?"

Eyes wide, she shook her head. "I should lik--" she started to say only to be silenced when his searching lips found hers.

Chapter Thirty-Five

Gerrard worked his way to the rear of the house and listened through the open window. He'd seen her arrive and wanted to know what she was about. He wondered why she hadn't been to see him, wondered whose horse was tethered at the post. When he heard the voice, he knew, and listened more intently. As he listened, he became inflamed.

"Why is he taking so long?"

"He said he hasn't been able to find anything," he answered.

"But he knows where the passages are," she replied angrily.

Gerrard rose on the toes of his boots and peeked into the window.

The man inside shrugged out of his coat and began to unbutton his shirt. "Yes he does, but he hasn't been able to look as closely as he'd like."

She whirled to face him. "What if he already found the jewels?" Her hands rested on her hips. "How well do you know him? How much do you trust him?"

"Darling, he's doing the best he can," he tried to placate her.

She would not be placated. "That's not an answer. I think we should have done away with him already. We should have never hired him in the first place. We should have done it ourselves."

"You know we need him," he countered, peeling off his shirt and laying it over the back of the chair. "We can't go traipsing into that house." He stepped up behind her and wrapped his arms about her waist. His fingers splayed to caress her stomach "You need not worry, once he finds what we want, his usefulness will have ended." He touched his lips to the nape of her neck. "It's not like I haven't wanted to do away with him myself."

"Why, darling?" she asked turning in his arms, her hands making a line along his arms and up to his shoulders.

He pulled her closer in an act of possession. He gritted his teeth. "Because I can't bear to hear that you've allowed him to touch you at all."

She smiled and cooed. "He doesn't mean a thing to me. But I've had to give him something to keep him. And, as much as he'd like to, he's never shared the things with me that you have." She touched her lips to his. And found his eyes. "You shouldn't worry. I'm yours alone."

Gerrard felt darkness cover his soul. *So that's why she'd been so elusive.* She'd been toying with him. Using him. She never planned to give him a cut or run away with him. Gerrard lowered himself and leaned back against the house, breathing heavily. He desired to go in and confront them both. Put an end to their lovemaking. Even kill them. He swallowed the angry pit in his throat and having heard enough, turned from the house. He would show them. He would make them pay. He would find the jewels then do away with them.

*****

Kaitlin had an overwhelming desire to scream. And anger had nothing to do with it. No, her nervous state was born from frustration alone.

Everything was going well with Devlin. Very well. He kept his promise, and was getting to know his wife. For the past couple of weeks he courted her, wooing her with flowers, long walks, long talks and carriage rides. He visited her first thing each morning, carrying a tray laden with breakfast, so they might have time alone before Derrick rose and the day began. And he joined her each evening to tuck Derrick in, listen to his prayers, and spend some quiet moments with his wife in his arms. Then he'd leave her with a kiss. A few kisses really. Enough to curl her toes, set her heart racing, and kill her with her desire.

Fill her with frustration. Her love for him deepened. She hugged herself and smiled. She might be frustrated, but she had to admit she loved every minute of it. Still, the nights found her pacing, wondering what he might do if she opened her door, walked the long hall between them and knocked on his door.

She sat down in the window seat and stared into the darkness beyond. Only now it didn't feel so vast, so foreboding. Now it whispered calm and she had a family and a home.

*****

Devlin paced. His empty arms longed to hold his wife. His heart cherished their moments together. He'd promised to court her, woo her. He planned to keep that promise no matter how impatient he might be. Still, he berated himself for ever making the promise. But he had to admit, he was learning about her and growing to love her more each day.

He raked a hand through his hair and wondered what she was doing.

"Are we playing this game or not?" Eldon thumped the chessboard.

"Is it my move?" Devlin paced back to the table.

Eldon grinned. "It's been your move for the past ten minutes. But that's not what you've been contemplating, is it?"

Devlin dropped to his chair and stared passed the chest pieces.

"You could always go to your wife."

Devlin sneered at his brother. "I promised her I'd court her. I aim to do just that," he replied firmly, more so for his sake than his brother's.

Eldon shrugged and tipped his knight. "I doubt she'd mind."

"Do you think she's ready to be my wife in more than name?" Devlin asked hopefully. His brows knit.

"I know so," Eldon declared.

"I still have things to tell her. I still..."

"She knows enough."

Devlin wasn't certain she did. "I haven't told her everything about Anna and--"

"You'll tell her soon enough. It doesn't matter right now. What matters is that you love her. With her on your mind, you're one dreadful opponent."

"Dreadful you say?" Devlin grinned mischievously. He looked at the board, made his move, and rose. "Then perhaps I should see if my wife is still awake."

Eldon chuckled as the door closed behind Devlin. He'd never seen his brother so smitten and rather liked it. His smile disappeared and he growled low when he looked at the board. Smitten or not, Devlin had still managed to win the game.

*****

Kaitlin stretched out on her bed and studied the ceiling. She saw none of the mosaics only visions of Devlin swirled in the lines above her. Pillowing her arms behind her head she closed her eyes to get a better glimpse of her husband.

She was filled with serenity until the hand covered her mouth. Serenity was stripped away when she opened her eyes and saw Gerrard. His hand smelled of horseflesh and sweat. He clamped it tightly over her mouth to hold her scream and secure her to the bed. Bile rose in her throat.

"Don't go crazy on me. I haven't got time to do what you're thinking." He grinned and caught a strand of her hair. "Although I must admit I'm mighty tempted." Letting her hair slip through his fingers, Gerrard's smile disappeared. "But I haven't got time. Where are the jewels?"

He watched her. His brows rose and furrowed. She tried to talk against his hand.

"I'll lift my hand if you promise not to scream. If you do, my friend in there will be forced to hurt Derrick. You don't want that. Do you?"

Her eyes flew to Derrick's room, tried to pierce the darkness beyond. Was someone in there with the boy? She couldn't be certain, nor could she take the chance. She met his eyes and shook her head.

"Good, girl," he whispered and lifted his hand. She took a long coughing breath and wiped her mouth. Gerrard pulled her hand away, nearly breaking it at the wrist. "Where are the jewels?"

"I have no idea."

Gerrard's lips twisted in a sneer. "You have to know."

"But I don't. I--" Her words died in her throat as he pulled her from the bed.

"Show me where they are. Take me to them." With a heavy sigh she stared at the door then the wardrobe. Gerrard followed her stare with a smile. "Don't be expecting any help. I locked them both. The boy's door, too." She bit her lip to stave the tears her fear was feeding. He pushed her toward the adjoining door to Derrick's room. "Must I tell my friend to take care of the boy?"

She shook her head and whimpered.

"Good." His hand clamped the back of her neck, sending shards of pain down her spine. "Now where are they?"

"I told you, I don't know where they--"

He pushed her face to the bed. She fought to breath. "Wrong answer. You have to know. You're the mistress of the manor. Devlin must have given them to you."

Then ask him, she wanted to scream, her lungs felt like they would burst with the need for air. Kaitlin managed to turn her head, and gulped a breath. "His first wife took them. I never--" Her face was thrust into the covers again. Her cheeks burned where they brushed the blankets.

"Wrong answer," Gerrard growled again, his strong hand twisted her neck like a vise. "Anna never got the jewels. She was given glass."

Kaitlin's mind reeled. How did he know that Anna had only gotten glass? Was he her accomplice that night? Did he know where she was and what had happened to Deanna?

She could ask him, but more important matters needed tending. She needed air. She squirmed under his hand and turning her face, managed to suck some air and cry out. His hand clamped the back of her neck, pinching her nerves, making her wish she hadn't moved at all. Her chest burned with the need for air. Gerrard's hand made certain she got none. Her senses reeled. Just when she thought the darkness was going to take her, just when she thought she would find no air, Gerrard's hand lifted.

She heard an angry growl somewhere in the dark and a thud. She wondered what the mad man might do next. Thinking his hand might return at any moment, she gulped enough air she choked. She felt a touch on her shoulders and fought against it, stopping when she realized the hand that returned to her neck was tender and the voice that called her name familiar and gentle.

"Katie, are you all right?" Devlin whispered. She felt his arms about her, lifting her. Felt herself pressed to his chest. She heard a ragged heartbeat and a sigh. Secure, she succumbed to the warmth and darkness.

Chapter Thirty-Six

"Tell me who your accomplice is?" Devlin yelled. He clamped the bars until his knuckles were white. He wanted in the cell, wanted to throttle Gerrard more, because right now the bruises on the left side of the man's face didn't seem enough somehow.

Gerrard sat stoned faced, looking at all other points but Devlin. He took a furtive glance toward the bars and let his gaze trip around the cell again. He rubbed his head.

"Still throbs, does it?" Devlin said. Gerrard ignored him. "Good. Tell me why you were at my house."

Gerrard said nothing. He glanced at the bars. Thinking himself safe, his countenance lit with a cocky grin.

"Answer me." Devlin shook the bars. Gerrard's smile faded. He studied his nails.

"If he hasn't told now, I doubt he's going to." Eliot put a hand to Devlin's arm and pulled him back. "Sheriff Aldrich will see to him, maybe he can get him to talk." He looked at the man slumped on the bed in the cell and shook his head. "In the meantime, you should go home."

Devlin stared at the bars and back to Eliot. Yes he needed to go home to Kaitlin and his son. But, heaven help him, this matter needed to be resolved. His past had returned to haunt him all over again.

He should have told Kaitlin about his suspicions concerning Gerrard, but he never thought Gerrard would take such measures. Devlin apologized profusely for putting Kaitlin in danger and nearly getting her killed. She didn't hold it against him. Still, he felt badly, he'd failed in his role as husband and protector all over again.

He talked to Kaitlin about Anna, told her how Anna left and returned to take their daughter.

"I followed her up river and lost her in Duluth when she boarded a steamer." Bound for where he didn't know. "She returned some weeks later, crazed and incensed. Telling me she wanted to see our children. I put her in a home. Not long after, she escaped and disappeared again."

"Do you think she's behind this?" Kaitlin asked.

"No," he told her soundly. "I received a death notice not long after saying that Anna had been killed in France, but there was still no word about my daughter." His laugh held no joy.

"I received papers of annulment from Anna shortly after her death. She sent them before she died." He shook his head. "I don't believe Anna was behind it," he told Kaitlin.

Now he wasn't so sure. Driven by the ghost of his daughter and past regret, Devlin turned from the bars and the man who enraged him and headed home.

*****

"Olga, must you go?" Kaitlin tried to smile. She reached out her hand.

"I've got to." She didn't want to be there when Devlin returned. Didn't want him to see her. He might start asking questions. Kaitlin had asked enough. Olga should have never come over. But when she heard that Kaitlin had been hurt, she didn't let the bluish blotches on her neck and wrists stop her.

"Devlin might be able to help--"

"I don't need help, Kaitlin." Olga's lips twitched with her need to cry. "I fell from a horse, nothing more." She met Kaitlin's penetrating gaze and knew she didn't believe the lie she'd been stubbornly telling for the past half hour. She shrugged. "I haven't ridden in so long, I got over confident."

Kaitlin watched her with skeptical eyes and said nothing. Olga couldn't fault her for not believing her. She'd given other excuses as well. Once she'd tumbled down the stairs. Another time, she ran into the cupboard door. Olga doubted Kaitlin believed it then, or now.

"Anyway, I need to be going." Olga sighed heavily, turning so she wouldn't have to meet Kaitlin's gaze again. "I'll stop by later this week and see how you're doing." With a quick glance in Kaitlin's direction she took her leave.

*****

Kaitlin blinked tears. She had a good mind to follow Olga. But what could she do? What could she...? Olga's husband was a beast. She just hoped Olga didn't end up dead. She pounded the lump of dough before her, pulled it, pushed it, slapped it on the table and pounded it some more. What she could do was stop getting so angry her senses were a kilter. And she could pray. Maybe the Lord would show her the way to confront Orin Reinhardt? He'd better come up with something quick, because the way she felt now she was liable to take a fry pan to his head.

"Are you feeling poorly?"

"Devlin." Kaitlin looked up with a smile that melted his anger and his guilt. Her face was bruised slightly from her ordeal, and the bruises were nearly hidden now by the flour on her cheeks. She turned her dough, patted it and met his eyes.

"Have you learned anything? I'm so sorry," she said softly when he didn't answer.

"There's no need for you to be." Devlin grinned. He turned her into his arms and brushed the flour from her lips so he'd have a clear spot to kiss. Once his lips found hers and he felt the warmth of her in his arms, he was wont to hold her against him forever. Derrick's presence forced him to pull apart. He stared into his wife's dazed eyes. "You're looking much better."

She blushed crimson. "I'm feeling much better."

"You sound like you have something on your mind."

Her eyes shuttered with her sigh, she lay her head against his shoulder, leaving him to wonder about the thoughts running through her head. With his old ghosts surfacing, he wondered if she felt she'd gotten in over her head. If only he could exorcise the ghosts of his past once and for all. When she opened her eyes, he caught her gaze. She bit her lip softly like she had something she needed to say but couldn't.

She gave him a smile and the day seemed to melt away. Gerrard, Anna, even his failings. She disarmed him with a kiss to his cheek. "I was just thinking."

"If you need to tell me anything, you can."

"I know."

With another kiss to her cheek and a quick firm hug, Devlin released her. She shivered slightly. "If you're cold, I wouldn't mind holding you some more."

"Oh, you." The color rose on her cheeks as she took to working the dough again.

"What are we making?" Devlin asked, dropping on the stool by his son. He mussed his hair, raising a cloud of flour dust. "Or should I say, wearing?"

Derrick giggled. He grinned like an imp and hit his dough. Another cloud of flour swirled about him. "We're making bread, Daddy."

"Hmmm." He looked up at his wife. "If it's as good as the little bit I already tasted then I can hardly wait."

Kaitlin took a deep breath and bowed her head, not before he saw the rose bloom on her cheeks once more.

"Was that the Reinholdt carriage I passed coming up the drive?"

Kaitlin looked up, the bloom of rose drained. She clutched the dough like a snake between her fingers. "Olga came to visit. She couldn't stay long. She just wanted to see how I was doing."

"Hmm," Devlin said again, making lazy circles in the flour, wondering why Olga had spurred the horses to a run when she saw him on the road. And why she barely looked his direction when she passed. And why her neck and jaw had been bruised. "How is she doing?"

"Ah..." Kaitlin met his assessing gaze. Her eyes grew to orbs. She opened her mouth and shut it. She seemed relieved when Eldon made his appearance.

"You've returned. Any more news?" Eldon took a seat.

Devlin made a diamond in the flour. "Gerrard isn't squealing." He sighed. "Eliot says to let the sheriff have him for a time. Maybe he'll be more agreeable."

"Hmm." Eldon drew a few circles in the flour. "Have you talked to Ernestine?"

Devlin shook his head. "Haven't seen her yet. But Olga came for a visit, she--"

"Do you think Ernestine is Gerrard's accomplice?" Kaitlin asked, quickly changing the subject. Devlin frowned. He wanted to discuss Olga. He wouldn't be so easily thwarted the next time.

He smiled at his wife and turned his attention to his brother. "It would explain her midnight walks through the house," Devlin replied. "But we won't be sure until we find her."

"Find who?" Graham asked, coming into the kitchen. He peeled his gloves. All eyes turned to him. Kaitlin brushed the flour from her person and went to greet him with a kiss. "Find who?" Graham asked again when his sister stepped back.

"Ernestine." Devlin grinned, saying nothing about the flour on Graham's cheek. "My secretary."

"She's been snooping around the house and now she's missing," Eldon added.

"She's not missing. She's gone to Eden Prairie," Graham replied.

Devlin rose from his stool. "Are you certain?"

"You've never meant Ernestine. How do you know it was her?" Kaitlin asked, bewildered.

"But I do know her," Graham declared. "I saw her leaving one day and realized I'd seen her before. Kate, her name isn't Ernestine. It's Ingrid McPherson."

"Ingrid McPherson?" Kaitlin shook her head. "Why does that name sound so familiar?"

"She's the reporter who disguised herself as a nurse so she could get your story. Remember?"

Kaitlin was confused. "Why didn't I remember her?"

"You were sick? And she had black hair then."

Devlin stepped to his wife and put his arms about her. "And you say her name is McPherson?" Graham nodded. "But that's Greta name." His hold tightened about his wife. "You don't think Ingrid is Greta's daughter?" Graham shrugged.

"I wonder if they're both behind this," Eldon spoke his thoughts.

"I couldn't say," Graham replied. "All I know is she took me for a turn. Luckily, I found out before she got too far."

"So she's a reporter." Devlin cocked his head. "Do you think she's here to do a story about Kate?"

*****

"No," Kaitlin shook her head. "She got her story about me." And something else. Ingrid had stolen Graham's heart. Kaitlin sighed heavily, laid the dough on the table and covered it with a towel. "She was here before me."

"Then it must be the jewels," Eldon stated.

"We won't know that until we find her." Devlin frowned.

"Then it's a mighty good thing I know exactly where she is." Graham smiled.

His smile quickly turned south. Kaitlin wondered if he wasn't remembering how Ingrid had left his heart. What would her excuse be this time? What would he say to her? Graham laid his hand over his heart, giving Kaitlin the feeling he still cared for her. Maybe Graham shouldn't go. What if it wasn't as easy to face her as he thought? Kaitlin wanted to tell him to stay, but didn't have time.

"I suggest we go get her before she disappears," Eldon suggested, rising from his chair.

"But you can't--" Devlin started to say.

Eldon cut him off. "I've done it before. Your carriage is dark enough. There shouldn't be any problem."

Devlin shook his head and sighed. He turned to his wife with an apologetic grin.

"I know you've got to go," she replied. She knew he needed to face the ghosts of his past. "I just hope it doesn't take too long. Thanksgiving is in two days."

Devlin hugged her up with a groan. "And the house smells like a bakery." He laid a kiss on her brow. "I won't miss Thanksgiving, darling. I've missed too many already. But this has to be dealt with. When I get back we can talk about Olga as well."

Kaitlin gulped and met his eyes. She nodded. "I planned to tell you, but you've had so much on your--"

He placed a finger to her lips. "Never too much to care about my wife and those she cares about."

Kaitlin literally melted into his arms. She melted further when he tipped her chin and laid a kiss on her lips.

*****

"Mr. Clayborne?" To see Devlin was enough of a shock, but when the second man stepped into the room her heart nearly stopped. "Graham." She froze in her place and proceeded to push her hair into some semblance of order as her heart tripped in her chest.

"Hello, Ingrid," Graham replied, giving her a slow lazy grin. From the thin line of his lips, it was evident he still hadn't forgiven her. Not that she'd expected him to, but she hoped. Mr. Clayborne didn't look too happy, either. She could only guess the reason why. She knew why Graham scowled. And if she were honest, she knew she deserved every bit of his scowling countenance.

It had been three years, but she recalled their last meeting as if it were yesterday. She'd played it over and over again in her head. She assumed he knew it as well. Assumed he still believed her excuses didn't hold water.

But they did to her. She wouldn't have hired on as a nurse's maid and tried to get a story on his sister if it hadn't been completely necessary. But her son depended on her. So she'd taken the assignment. And just when things had taken a decidedly personal turn between her and Graham, Graham learned she was a reporter. He'd promptly dismissed her. She'd gotten a story, and the monies to care for her son, but she'd lost Graham.

Seeing him in the doorway only reminded her of what she'd lost.

"Oh, where are my manners." She sighed. "Do come in. Please don't mind the mess," she told them as she quickly cleared a spot on the couch. "Would you care to be seated?"

"We won't be staying long," Graham replied, shaking his head as he studied the room.

Perplexed, Ingrid scratched her neck. Evidently, the visit would be a short one. Neither man had even begun to remove their coat or gloves. Her brows knit when she wondered why they stopped to see her. She sent word to the manor that she'd be late in returning. Oh, but it wouldn't be there yet.

She sighed heavily. "Why have you come? Surely you didn't come all this way to stay for so short a time?"

"You're correct, Ern--Ingrid." Devlin clasped his hands together. "We're here to get you and take you back."

Ingrid's eyes widened. "Whatever for? I sent word I'd be late."

"Gerrard is in jail for trying to harm my wife, as his accomplice, you will be joining him."

"His accomplice? Gerrard?" She dropped to the arm of the couch in confusion. She'd seen Gerrard on occasion, had spoken to him once or twice. "I barely know the man. What am I supposed to be helping him with?"

"You were hunting for the jewels," Devlin said curtly, impatient for her to tell the truth.

"Jewels?" Ingrid shook her head. "I wasn't searching for jewels. Whatever gave you that idea?"

"You've been watched on your midnight excursions," Devlin explained. She gasped. "You were seen on four occasions. Do you deny searching my home?"

"No." Her hand flew to her chest and trembled so she fumbled with her collar. "I did snoop on a couple of occasions, but only twice. And I wasn't searching for jewels."

"What then? A story?" Graham asked, bringing the past to light in his angry words.

"I suppose that's what drew me to the manor at first. Mama and Uma told me about the ghost of Clayborne Manor. The story intrigued me. Piqued my curiosity." She shot a glance at Graham then looked back to Devlin. His scowl, though able to stand her hairs on end, wasn't as menacing to her. "But not for reasons you might expect."

"You wanted a story," Graham declared.

"No, I didn't," Ingrid said. Graham's sniff said he didn't believe a word she said. "But I didn't."

"What other reason could there be?" Devlin countered. "Other than you hoped to find this ghost and exploit him?"

"The same way you exploited my sister," Graham added with a growl.

"I swear to you," she pleaded with them. But neither one believed her. "Let me show you what I've written." She ripped the page she'd been working on from the Remington and thrust it toward Devlin. He read where she told them she'd found no ghost. Nor a vampire. And how she believed it was a ridiculous story crafted by someone who wanted to scare the townsfolk.

"I wasn't going to exploit anyone. That proves it."

"Perhaps?" Devlin set the paper aside, unconvinced. "Pages can be retyped."

"I have better proof. I can show you."

"Perhaps you aren't lying. But how do I know you won't retype it once I'm gone?"

Ingrid turned at the sound of the new voice and came face to face with her ghost. She hadn't even heard the door open. Even now he moved like one. "You are real?" Her voice was a sigh of relief, of reverence. Her smile melded into tears.

It threw the men.

Eldon nodded. "Why were you trying to find me?"

"I do owe you an explanation." Ingrid chewed her lip. "As I said, I have proof that my reasoning isn't so ignoble. Since you don't believe my letter, I'll have to risk showing you that proof. I pray you'll understand."

She turned toward the stairs and looked back to find Graham on her heels.

"Forgive me if I don't believe you," he said.

"I'm not going to run off if that's what you think." She heaved in exasperation.

"She wouldn't get far if she did," Devlin said soundly.

Graham backed slightly. "You've got five minutes."

"I'll only need three."

She returned within two.

"Gentlemen." She waited until all eyes were upon her then finished her introduction. "This is my son, Peter." She stopped on the stairs and waved for someone to join her. Once the boy was by her side, she added, "This, gentlemen, is the reason why I came to find the Ghost of Clayborne Manor."

*****

Clearly, Ingrid told the truth.

Eldon stepped forward and stared at the one, who, except for his shortness of stature, nearly mirrored him.

Ingrid caressed her son's ermine hair and pulled him to her side. His skin was ghostly white against her faded muslin dress. She met Eldon's eyes. "He's the reason I needed to find you. I hoped you might have some answers." She turned her eyes to Graham and silently bade him to understand.

Repentant as ever, Graham stepped forward. "Why didn't you tell me?"

"For your pity?" She sighed. "I realize I got into your homes under false pretenses." She let her eyes drift to Devlin and back to Graham. "But I was desperate. There's not a lot out there for a woman alone with a child. Especially when that child needs such care. I jumped at the chance to make some money. I hoped by finding you..." She turned to Eldon. "...I might find a way to make my son's life easier." She shook her head, blinked tears. "I don't want him to spend his life running from ridicule because others deem him a freak."

"So we're back to square one," Devlin groaned.

"Maybe not." Eldon drew his attention away from the boy and met Ingrid's eyes. "You say you came to find me. Why did your mother want you to come? Was she concerned about the boy?"

"No, she wanted me to find some passages in the house. I thought they would lead me to you." She gnawed her bottom lip. "Now I'm not so sure."

"Why do you say that?" Devlin asked, evidently intrigued.

"Well, my mother spends little time with my son. When she and my sister got together, they discussed the fortunes to be gained if I could turn your head." She frowned as she flushed. "I didn't care to turn your head. I feel badly for being so... well, cruel to the members of your staff and family. But Mama said you would let me go if I became too soft. She said you were a harsh man. And I needed to stay. When your wife arrived, I thought I'd be released."

"We knew you were up to something, we just weren't sure what. So it's of little consequence now. Although, you might explain your actions to Kate." Devlin pushed his hands into his coat pockets. "What I want to know is whether your mother and sister were working with Gerrard?"

Ingrid shrugged. "I don't know."

"They met with the blonde lady," Peter proclaimed from his mother's side.

"What blonde lady?" Ingrid looked down at her son in bewilderment. "Have I met her?"

"She came to see Uma when you were gone," Peter explained quietly as though he wasn't accustomed to so much attention. "Grandma said she's the one who wanted you to be in the house in the first place."

Ingrid's shoulders slumped slightly. "I got involved in their schemes when I should have been with my son." Sorrow filled her eyes.

"Don't let guilt run your life. It will come to no good," Devlin replied.

He stepped forward and the boy grabbed his mother's skirts and tried to fold himself into them. "Peter, did this woman have a name?"

Peter's eyes grew to orbs as he gulped. "Uma called her Anna."

Chapter Thirty-Seven

The weather wasn't conducive for swift travel and the team pulling the load of carriage and men was not conditioned to take the trip with the speed in which Devlin wanted to move. He encouraged them as best he could, but they seemed to plod along unaware of the mission before them.

Devlin pulled his cloak tighter, longing for his team Lucifer and Hellion. Their feet were swift, their bodies strong. It would be fitting to have them lead him to the hell he knew he was driving into. His ghosts had returned to haunt him, to haunt those he loved. He needed to be home.

He snapped the reins with ferocity and prayed he'd reach his destination before Anna.

*****

Olga listened for the water as she searched the wardrobe. Her back and shoulder's still smarted from her last run in with her husband. She moved on hesitant feet, gingerly touching her lip. The contact brought tears to her eyes. And anger to her heart.

She promised herself she'd never allow him to harm her again, yet, every time they argued it still happened. She found herself cowering beneath his firm hand. She didn't know what she'd done. Whatever it was, he'd been extremely incensed. Olga wanted to cower now and he wasn't even in the room. She shook her head. She had to stop letting her fears drive her. If she listened to them she'd never look for the letters. Lord only knew what Orin would do to her if he found her going through his things.

She didn't want to think about it.

Unable to find what she wanted, she turned for the drawers. Still nothing. Where were they? She found the stack of letters in the bureau a week before, but had been too scared to read them. She wasn't scared now. She took a deep breath to remind herself of that. She wanted to see the latest offering. The one he snatched, read with gleaming eyes and stuffed in his pocket, just before he railed at her and nearly beat her senseless.

That encouraged her to keep looking, compelled her to find it.

With a groan she dropped to her knees and searched the bed and the floor beneath it. Nothing there or under the mattress. Hunkering down on the bed, she contemplated her next step when her eyes, of their own volition, fell on the cases at the foot of the bed. Could it be so easy? Was he so foolish to keep them there? She stopped and listened for the water, for his humming, and knelt at the foot of the bed. Quietly opening the first satchel, she found what she hunted for. There in the bottom, as if he had no care they might be found, were the letters from his sister. The latest lay on top.

Maybe he wants you to find them so he can beat you again, her mind cautioned. She shook her head, but checked the sounds from the bath one more time.

With tentative fingers and a thudding chest, she reached for the envelope. It shook in her hand. Unfolding it, she shut her eyes and took a deep breath. She could read it and come away chastened for her mistrust, or she could read it and have all her fears come to light.

First she had to read it.

Her teeth clenched, her eyes fluttered open. She looked beyond the pages at first then with a heavy heart, let her eyes fall to the words.

Elegant penmanship designed the page, far from the lines of a crazy lunatic as her husband claimed his sister to be. Olga gulped back angry tears. She'd been the crazy one. She allowed Orin to mistreat her and she'd believed.

Olga didn't believe anymore.

When his humming stopped, she stuffed the paper back into the envelope and dropped it to the pile in the bag. She rose, brushed her skirt to rid it of any wrinkle or lint that might give a clue to her ransacking his things.

Shoulders squared, she sat down at her dressing table to await her husband.

Olga drew a long sigh as she pushed the brush through her hair. She should be shocked, angry. Her anger melted into relief, her shock to resolve. She deduced that her husband couldn't be trusted long before, his heavy hand attested to that fact. The letter only confirmed her suspicions. Were she to read the rest they'd seal his betrayal she was certain, but it mattered not. All that mattered was seeing that the devil had his due.

She looked at her reflection in the mirror. A broken woman with a split lip looked back. Olga touched her bruises, only her face was broken now, not her spirit. Her face would heal. Orin wouldn't be so lucky. She'd make certain.

*****

"Will you be staying long this time?" Olga turned on her stool and calmly stared at the bags her husband carefully packed. His noncommittal shrug said nothing, but he'd never packed so much for his trips before. She knew, without his answer, this trip might well take him away from her forever. She was glad of it. But she wanted him to tell her, wanted him to own up to his lies. Wanted him to pay. "Orin?"

He met her eyes. "I'm only going for a while. But the doctors say my sister is bad off, I'm not certain how long I'll be."

She graced him with an understanding smile, trying to read some truth beyond the lie in his eyes, beyond the open contempt. There was none. She said nothing as she helped him pack. When his bags were latched and sitting in the front hall, she spoke. "I could join you?"

"No," he said, quickly. He smiled and took her hands into his own. "I need you here to see to things while I'm away. Who else can I trust?" he added smoothly. "And Louisa needs you home." He shrugged into his coat and wrapped his woven scarf securely about his neck.

Olga had a desire to secure it further, to strangle him. She calmly folded her hands and encouraged herself not to laugh when she considered what he'd said.

Trust? What did he know of trust? His smile said he believed she was falling for his lines. She'd allow that for now -- even though she had the desire to take the fireplace poker and ram it down his throat -- but only because she had plans, plans that involved his sister. She needed him to lead her to the other woman.

"I shan't be too long, darling," he said as he donned his hat and laid a perfunctory kiss on her cheek. Olga stifled the urge to wipe her face. "I'll write soon," he added as he grabbed his bags and walked out with nary another word.

Olga stood in the doorway until the carriage disappeared into the night then she donned her coat and hat and followed on the horse she had saddled and waiting behind the barn.

This excursion could take her anywhere and she would follow. It mattered not how far, or how cold the night. She was determined. And the gun in her pocket kept her warm.

*****

"The snow is beautiful," Marla said, pushing back the kitchen curtains for a better look. "Have you seen it?"

Kaitlin barely nodded. She'd had a glimpse. It was soft, heavy and cold.

"Don't fret, ma'am." Margaret turned to set freshly baked pies on the counter. "He'll be here for the festivities."

"Festivities?" Kaitlin murmured. "Oh. Thanksgiving." She plumb forgot.

"Perkins found a goodly sized bird. It will be a wonderful feast. We have..." Margaret prattled on, but Kaitlin wasn't listening.

She thought about Devlin.

Had he found Ernestine -- Ingrid? Was she Gerrard's accomplice? Or was Devlin still in danger? And what of Graham, would seeing Ingrid hurt him?

"What do you think, ma'am?" Margaret cut into her thoughts with the same proficient manner she used to cut the apples she peeled.

"I'm sure it will be lovely," Kaitlin answered, not quite certain what she agreed to.

When the door off the kitchen opened, no one thought better of it. Perkins had gone to see Henry and was probably returning.

"There's a cup of coffee..." Marla started. She turned and froze.

Margaret let out a gasp, dropped her knife and the apple she'd been peeling.

Kaitlin turned as a woman, resplendent in black velvet, swept into the kitchen. Perkins followed behind her. Kaitlin started to rise then she saw the man behind Perkins. When she saw the gun he wielded, her movements were arrested.

"How very quaint," the woman replied. Pushing back her hood, uncovering a head of the blondest hair Kaitlin had ever seen, she let her gaze drift around the room, taking it in with a sniff. "The new missus, sitting in the kitchen with the hired help like a common scullery maid," she added with a tinny laugh.

Kaitlin rose to face her.

The woman paid her little mind as she addressed the staff. "I declare you two look like you've seen a ghost." She touched Marla's cheek. "Aren't you happy to see me?" She shrugged delicately. "No, perhaps not? But then you were always loyal to Devlin. I'm surprised he still has need for such a lot of old crones and side show freaks." She sighed wistfully. She grabbed Margaret's jaw and tilted it upwards. "I'd have done away with you long ago. But then Devlin is just as loyal."

"Loyalty is a rather nice quality. So useful." She puckered her lips. Tears filled Margaret's eyes as Anna roughly turned the older woman's head at the jaw. "Where's the rest of your lovely family?"

"They're off hunting," Marla answered with a sneer.

"And taken the beast with them, I presume?" Anna seemed relieved. She released Margaret and strolled through the kitchen like a grand dame on a walk in the park. When she'd taken in her fill, she turned to Kaitlin. "I gather you have a good idea who I am?"

Kaitlin nodded, gulping, silently wishing Henry hadn't taken Lady along so she could sic her on Anna about now. She remembered the gun, her gaze found it again.

"Oh look. The missus is a frightened little house mouse. I see my judge of character hasn't failed me," Anna said coolly. "Oh but I have been remiss. I haven't introduced my friend. Orin, do come in and shut that door. It's drafty."

Orin? Kaitlin's eyes darted from the gun to the man. She'd heard the name. Surely he wasn't the same Orin. If so, was Olga involved as well? Had she only become her friend to...? She wouldn't allow herself to believe that for one moment.

"What do you want, Anna?" Kaitlin asked confidently, confirming that she knew the woman before her. She'd seen no pictures, but had heard enough to have a mental picture of Anna stored in her mind. The accounts of her beauty didn't do her justice.

Neither did the adage that beauty was skin deep.

Anna peeled her gloves, waved them before her. She slapped them in her palms as she spoke. "Come now. You've been here for some time. You must know?" She tapped a finger to her lip as she studied Kaitlin. "I want what should have been mine. What I came for in the beginning." Her lips quirked. "The jewels, of course."

Kaitlin's brows furrowed. "The jewels?"

Anna stabbed a laugh. Her gaze skewered Kaitlin. "I see we understand each other."

"I don't understand anything," Kaitlin assured her soundly. "I have no idea what you're talking about."

Anna brows rose in mock delight. "The mouse isn't quite as mousey as she lets on." Her eyes darkened as she turned to Orin. "Do you hear that? She has no idea." Her gaze returned to level Kaitlin. "You expect me to believe that?"

"It's the truth," Kaitlin replied brusquely.

"Hmmm. We shall see." A smile played on her lips as she removed her cape and laid it on the counter, her attention never leaving Kaitlin. She sized up her opponent with a skeptical eye. "Perhaps with some incentive you might be more accommodating?" She sighed with disappointment. "Orin, do take care of this lovely trio."

"No wait," Kaitlin stammered, and closed the distance between herself and Anna. "I've told you the truth."

"That's not what I want to hear. Must I be more persuasive? Orin."

Eyes filled with delight, Orin raised his hand. "No, please they don't know anything." Kaitlin found a sigh when Orin's hand lowered.

"Of course not." Anna's grin was magnificent. The smile never touched the darkness of her eyes. "It seems you care for them. Why? I don't know. Still, that can work to our advantage. Loyalty does have its uses."

Kaitlin looked from Anna to Orin and back again. She gulped.

"Have we an understanding?"

"There's no need to hurt them," Kaitlin said, stalling. "I don't know where the jewels are."

Anna frowned. "I tire of this game. Let me be more specific. Orin show her how specific we can be."

"Nooo." Kaitlin tried to get to Orin. But Anna blocked her path. She met Perkins' eyes, and read fear. Hopeless, terrifying fear. A fear she was beginning to taste.

Orin's hateful eyes, darker than Anna's, were aflame as he slammed the butt of his Colt on the back of Perkins' head. Perkins crumbled to the floor with a heart-rendering groan. Orin grinned with pleasure as he caught Perkins' collar, and yanked the poor man back against his thigh. "Is that specific enough? Or will more be required?"

Kaitlin shook her head, breathless as she waited for the revolver to strike again. "No, please, I don't kn--" she stopped herself when Orin lowered the barrel to Perkin's temple. "All right. I'll show you where the jewels are." She had to look away from Marla's blinking stare. "Please make him stop."

"That will do for now," Anna said with a regal wave as she again leveled her opponent with her gaze. Kaitlin's heart coursed with fear. "Well, will you take me to them now? Or should Orin be more persuasive?" Her menacing stare drifted to Marla and Margaret, then back. "The choice is yours."

Kaitlin wasn't sure how to answer. If she told them the truth, the truth they had yet to believe, others would be harmed. Even killed. She couldn't allow that. She met the terrified eyes of her staff in turn then nodded.

"I knew you'd see it my way." Anna's sigh was wrought with pleasure and relief. "Orin, do see to them. Mrs. Clayborne and I will be taking a walk." Anna's grin held an edge as she pulled a small derringer from her cuff. "So you don't get any ideas," she warned. She glanced at Orin. "I doubt it will be necessary."

Most unnecessary, Kaitlin wanted to assure her. She might delay Orin, save her friends for a time, but what would happen when Anna realized she didn't know about any jewels? What would happen when she realized that Kaitlin had led her on a merry chase, to stall for time?

"Let's go then." Anna said, pressing her derringer in Kaitlin's shoulder. She stopped and turned to Orin. "Oh, and Orin, if we're not back in ten minutes, shoot one of them." Her assessing eyes fell on Kaitlin. One brow arched in a silent taunt.

Kaitlin froze. Ten minutes left her precious time. She had to find the jewels. Where did she start? Her room? Derrick's room was next to hers. She didn't want to endanger him. Would Anna go to his room? Would she remember her son and want to see him?

Kaitlin didn't want to give Anna any reminders or put Derrick in danger, she chose the room furthest from the boy. Devlin's.

*****

Trepidation mounting, Olga leaned against the rear of the house, calculating her next move. What kind of an idiot was she? Thinking she could handle Orin on her own. Now he was in the Clayborne Manor doing Lord knew what. Was Kaitlin involved? Or in danger?

Either way Orin was still in the house, intimidating the staff. Intimidating her and she wasn't staring down the barrel of his gun. She hated being intimidated, especially by him. She wouldn't allow it. Though she'd resolved to face him -- several times in the last hour -- her hand still shook when she reached for the knob.

"Please, Mr. Reinhardt. Let me see to his head," Marla pleaded. "He's bleeding."

"That's none of my concern," he sneered. "It will dry soon enough."

"But he's..." Marla watched Perkins' eyes roll high and tried again to reach Orin's heart. If he had one. It was doubtful. But she had to help Perkins.

"I wouldn't if I were you," Orin said coolly, causing her to freeze in her spot. He checked the clock and smiled. "Won't matter in a couple minutes." He rubbed the barrel of his revolver on his sleeve. "If you catch my drift?"

"You can't mean to?"

"Oh, but I can." His brow's arching in pleasure, he grinned like the devil. "If you're mistress doesn't hurry, I'll see that you two join him. You better hope she finds those jewels. I doubt she'll get here in time to save Perkins." He glanced at the clock once more. "In fact, I know she won't," he added slowly, aiming his gun.

"Noooo please." Margaret tried to shield Perkins. Marla, too, jumped to protect her friend.

"Have it your way," Orin said calmly. "It doesn't matter to me who goes first."

Glancing at the gun one last time, Marla stubbornly threw her arms about Perkins, her back toward the gun, and held on. Prepared to die, she closed her eyes and prayed. She screamed at the gun's echoing report, and waited to feel herself slipping away.

Orin groaned

Marla raised her head.

Slumping against the wall, trying to stop the flow of crimson from his gut, Orin raised his head with a whimper. "Olga? Why?"

Olga stood, frozen in place, the gun shaking in her hand, tears streaming her cheeks. "You know why. Tell me about the woman."

His eyes wide, he stared at his arm then his wife. "Olga, please I'm bleeding. I could--"

"You're not going to die," she said harshly. "Not before you tell me about that woman."

"She's my sister."

"Don't give me that." Olga waved the gun in front of his nose for emphasis. "I want the truth."

"She's my sister," Orin said again, in a whisper.

Olga cringed. It was too sordid to be true. "But I saw you together."

Orin was shocked. "You saw... us?

"Yes, I did." Olga returned smugly. "I followed you. Now tell me the truth. We both know that isn't your sister."

"But she is," Orin said plainly, silencing those with him.

*****

"I've got to go..." Kaitlin bolted for the stairs at the sound of gunfire. She turned pleading eyes to Anna. And found no compassion.

"It's none of your concern." Anna clutched a handful of Kaitlin's hair and pulled her back into the room. Sticking the gun to Kaitlin's temple, she reminded her who was in charge. "I suggest you stop wasting my time, unless, of course, you don't mind losing another member of your staff. Good help is so hard to find," she added with a vindictive smile.

Kaitlin blinked tears of understanding and turned to resume her search. She'd been hopeful when Anna followed her to Devlin's room -- putting a long hall between her and Derrick -- to search there first. Hopeful she'd stumble on the jewels. She'd found nothing. All that remained were the echoes of a gunshot and the terror of not knowing who had possibly died and who would be next.

"Enough of this," Anna said impatiently. "Where have you hidden the jewels Devlin gave you?"

"He didn't." Kaitlin turned, her fury mounting.

"Don't lie to me," Anna said sternly. She stared around Devlin's room, shivered and shook her head. "This room is so dark and sullen still. Why haven't you given it a woman's touch?" She started to laugh. "You don't even sleep here. Why I let you lead me here, I don't know? Now take me to them. And no more stalling. They have to be in your room. Devlin must have given them to you by now. He must have." Muttering to herself, she pushed Kaitlin toward the door.

Kaitlin stared down the hall, with mounting angst. Had Derrick heard the gun blast? She expected him to come flying down the hall to find her. She found meager hope that he was still in his room, away from his mother's wrath.

But for how long?

A plan, weak at best, flitted crossed her senses. She had a box of faux jewelry in her room. Anna had accepted fakes from Devlin. If she could make Anna believe that she too had been given glass, Anna might give up the search. Or another person would be shot, killed. The report of the gun resounded in her ears, keeping time with the surging of her blood. She didn't want that on her conscience.

If she knew where the jewelry was she'd gladly give hand it over.

Then you'll all die, her heart warned.

"Here we are," Anna replied, breaking into Kaitlin's thoughts as she pulled her to a stop. Presuming Kaitlin would use the same room that had been her own, Anna stopped Kaitlin in the hall outside the empty room. Her gun at Kaitlin's chest, she pushed the door open, only to find it empty.

Her gaze hard, she turned to Kaitlin. "This isn't your room. What game are you playing?"

Kaitlin started to remind Anna that she'd stopped at the wrong door, but held her tongue.

Anna cocked her head and assessed Kaitlin through narrowed eyes. Her brows furrowed in concentration. Did Kaitlin know Devlin's dark secret? She savored the idea of sharing that tidbit of information. Savored the idea of seeing horror in Kaitlin's eyes when and if she did.

"Where is your room?" she said, she turned as if she expected to retrace her steps down the hall. Kaitlin pointed to her door. "There!" Anna was surprised. "By the nursery?"

She grinned at Kaitlin and yanked the door open.

Kaitlin's shoulders slumped with her frown.

"Does my son still sleep here?" Anna said, coolly, pushing Kaitlin into the room.

Kaitlin nodded slowly, for the first time since Anna's arrival she found reason to smile. The room was empty. The chill from the open window told her Derrick had managed to escape.

*****

Derrick's heart tripped in his chest as he ran down the road.

He'd been happily on his way down to see Kaitlin, when he saw her coming from the kitchen. Then he saw the monster. He thought he'd never see the monster again, but he'd seen it clearly ever since that night, each time he closed his eyes. Each time he dreamed.

Now the monster had returned and it would get Kaitlin.

Derrick ran back to his room, crawled under his bed and with his hands over his head prayed to be invisible, prayed the monster wouldn't find him.

He heard the loud blast and screamed -- a scream unheard beyond the ears of heaven. Scared to face the monster, he'd lowered the rope ladder and fled. He hoped Kaitlin wouldn't hate him for running like a coward, hoped he could find a way to save her. Save them all -- like he hadn't been able to save Deanna.

Derrick's hands burned and there was a pain in his rump from falling the bottom three rungs, he didn't care, he needed to find some help. He ran to the barn, it was eerily silent. His lungs bursting with fear, he turned for the road to town. His vision blurred by tears and snow, Derrick ran into the dark, seeing the horses only when they were upon him.

Chapter Thirty-Eight

His sister! It was the truth, but Olga didn't want to believe it. Her husband carried on an affair with his own sister. She felt ill, sicker still, that she couldn't get to Kaitlin. Not with Anna carrying a gun.

"What are you two after?"

"Anna wants her jewels." Orin bobbed his head until his chin rested on his chest.

"Her jewels?" Marla cocked her head.

"She has no jewels here," Margaret added in an angry rush.

"She took everything she wanted when she left. Even her daughter," Marla spat. "What more could she want?"

"Devlin gave her some jewels, but the rest was glass." Orin groaned, and tried to resituate himself. "She wants what should have been hers. Ours."

"What are you talking about?" Olga hissed through her teeth. She grabbed Orin's chin and forced him to look at her. "And don't think of lying."

Orin gulped. He closed his eyes.

"Answer me, Orin. What do mean *ours*?"

"We planned this years ago." Orin slowly opened his eyes.

"How long ago?"

"How long?"

"Yes," Olga snapped. "How long have you and Anna...?"

Orin studied his chest. "Since we were teens."

"Teens? Why did you marry me then?"

"And Anna married Devlin," Marla added in disgust.

"As I said, we needed money," Orin answered bluntly. "We were in danger of going to debtor's prison. Anna met Devlin and he seemed so enamored, we decided to take advantage of it."

"So she married Mr. Clayborne." Margaret shook her head.

"Why me?" Olga asked with a sneer. "Wasn't Devlin's wealth enough?"

"The money and lands belonged to Eldon then. You remember the older brother?"

Olga blinked. She remembered. She had befriended him years before and he'd disappeared. The last she saw him was just before his death. She still wondered about him.

"But Eldon is dead."

"Not soon enough," Orin said hastily.

Olga calculated the timing. Eldon was buried around the time Anna disappeared. "So you were forced to marry me." She shook her head and started laughing. "But you didn't count on Father's will."

Orin groaned. "Whoever heard of a man leaving his money to his grandchildren when his daughter was still living?"

Poor Orin, Olga shook her head. She wasn't allowed to touch the wealth. Neither was he.

"Only his grandchildren could touch the money," Olga stabbed a laugh.

"I hoped you have my child, but..."

"I couldn't conceive. And you deemed me weak. But you were the one who couldn't conceive. I have a child, Orin." She jutted her chin. "And she'll have the inheritance." Olga tilted her head. "I'm surprised you didn't try and marry her. Why did you even stay?"

"I stayed for Anna." Orin heaved a sigh. "She couldn't return to Devlin so..."

"You'd never get my money so you waited around hoping to find a way to get Devlin's." Orin's eyes told her all she needed to know. "You're pathetic."

"Beyond pathetic, I'd say."

"Mr. Clayborne, you're..." Olga stopped when she saw the ghost. Her mouth gaped. A smile broke on her face. "Eldon?" But he was rumored dead, he was... She ran to him and took his hands into her own. "You were dead."

"A mere technicality," Eldon replied, squeezing her hand. "I'll tell you about it some time."

"Where's Kaitlin?" Devlin asked.

"She's above stairs with Anna," Margaret answered.

And for the first time that evening, Olga's heart stopped beating in her throat.

*****

"Where is my son?" Anna yelled the words. "Are you hiding him from me?"

Kaitlin shied from the raised gun. She backed until she felt the cool wood of the carousel horse behind her. "He's not here."

"Oh, he's here," Anna said flatly. She moved slowly as if she could sense him. "Derrick, come out. It's me, your mother."

Kaitlin grasped the horse's rein and took in the room herself, praying he'd taken the rope ladder. Was he hiding? "He's not here I told you?"

Anna eyed her skeptically. "Yes, and you also told me you knew where the jewels were. But we both know you were lying."

"But he's--" She stopped when she felt the horse's mane, the stones in the bridle. She fought the urge to turn around.

"He's what?" Anna asked, the rage building in her eyes.

"He's with his father," Kaitlin replied, hopeful that Devlin would arrive at any moment and prove her correct. She traced the reins and lowered her hands. Stepping forward, she narrowed her eyes. "I thought the boy meant nothing to you."

"That's true." Anna sighed. "But he would have been a wonderful addition to our game, don't you think? Or do my eyes deceive me?"

"What are you talking about?"

"You're glad the brat isn't here," Anna explained. "You care for him?" Kaitlin couldn't deny it. Anna sniffed. "I suppose you care for his father." She sounded like a cackling witch when she laughed. "Oh my, my. He is rather handsome," she said dryly. "You should know he bears a devil."

"I thought he got rid of it when you left?" Kaitlin said soundly.

A blonde brow rose in amusement. "You amaze me, mouse." Anna's lips puckered in disdain, her finger slid along the barrel of the gun. "If you were wise, you'd watch your tongue."

Kaitlin was tired of being wise, tired of waiting for Anna to decide her next move. "Perhaps I'm not wise," she said, her tone brimming with bravado and sarcasm.

Anna put her hand to her throat, taken aback. Finding her composure, she sighed heavily. "What do you know of it? You've been here for barely two months. I was stuck here for three years. Three!" She blew out a heavy sigh. "I lived with the devil, slept with the devil and bore the children of the devil. When I learned about his horrible secret, I never let him touch me again." She leaned forward with a sneer. "If you knew the truth, you wouldn't be so bold."

"What truth are we speaking of?" Kaitlin inquired, certain she knew already.

Anna's eyes narrowed like a contented cat, she grinned like she was about to burst. "Devlin is handsome as sin because he is sin. His mama was a slave." Her lips twisted with disgust. "Part negro." She spilled her news then stepped back, expectant eyes shining with malicious triumph, waiting for Kaitlin to be appalled.

Kaitlin smiled. "If that's your great secret, you've wasted your breath." She stabbed a laugh. "Did you actually believe that would matter to me?"

"You think him so handsome you'd overlook his past? His heritage?" Anna seemed almost ill as she lowered her hand and grabbed her skirt.

"Devlin is handsome, but I would overlook it even if he wasn't. Unlike you, I wasn't looking for a handsome face or money. You see, Anna, my first husband was part black."

Anna gasped. She was appalled and Kaitlin rather liked it. When Anna's eyes flamed, she knew the pleasure wouldn't last.

"You would sleep with the devil?" Anna waved her gun in emphasis. "Then you're no better than the devil himself." Her lips arched in a wicked grin when she aimed her gun. "Maybe this will surprise you? Live with the Devil, die with the Devil."

"He's not the devil. And you well know it." Kaitlin's chest heaved with anger and fear. Anna might shoot her at any moment, as yet she'd only threatened. Kaitlin would have her say. "How can you stand there and talk about his sins after all you've done?"

"All I've done," Anna replied coolly, as her hand flew to her chest once more, perhaps to cover the darkness. "What have I done?"

"You talk of Devlin's betrayal. But you were the one who left him for another man. You were the one who left your husband and son behind. Now you've returned with yet another man, ruining yet another marriage." Her eyes narrowed. "And who knows what you did to Deanna."

Anna's gun lowered slightly. Her reply was laced with bewilderment. "I did nothing to my daughter. You should ask Devlin where she is. And I never left with Teddy. Why would I? He was a detective. I wouldn't have taken him with me much less told him about my plans."

Kaitlin blinked. "But he left the night you did. And no one has seen him since."

Anna heaved. "Another question for Devlin. Perhaps you don't realize it, but he's a murderer?" Her grin was sardonic. "You won't believe me, but a group of townspeople were out that night. They saw him murder his brother."

"His own brother you say?" The deep voice arose in the adjoining room.

Anna turned, horrified. "Devlin?"

"It's not a pleasure for me either," Devlin commented coolly as he stepped into the room.

Forgetting about Kaitlin momentarily, Anna turned her gun toward Devlin. "You stay right there." Devlin hovered as if barred by an imaginary line then took a step into her circle. Anna set the barrel at Kaitlin's temple.

Devlin raised his hand. "We know you won't kill her." Cocking his head, he chanced another step.

Kaitlin shot her husband a querying glance. Anna looked like she could shoot her and feel just fine about it. And Devlin's movements weren't helping.

"Don't tempt me, Devlin," Anna hissed. "I'll kill her without batting an eye."

"You're not a murderer. Isn't that what you just told Kaitlin? I'm the murderer. Not you."

Ann's nose crinkled. "You're right. I have little taste for blood." Her chin jutted. "But there's always a first time."

"You're stalling," Devlin pressed. Kaitlin held her eyes to a minimal roll. The gun at her temple, she couldn't quite concur with her husband. "Gerrard or even Orin might have the stomach for it, but not you. You couldn't even stomach your own children."

"Enough," Anna shouted. "Orin is not a murderer, Gerrard maybe, but Orin, never. As I recall you never had much time for your children, either," she finished smugly.

*****

Devlin had no defense for her accusation. His work kept him away far too often. It was no excuse. It kept him away from his son and wife even now. What must they think of him? He didn't care what Anna thought, but her stab had hit its mark. He avoided comment on it, and avoided Kaitlin's eyes, lest he find greater cause for shame.

"How can you be so sure about Orin?" he replied, his jaw firm.

"I just know." Anna shrugged. "He would never kill anyone."

Devlin's laugh was angry. "Maim them, beat them, but never kill them. If you didn't take our daughter or the good reverend's son, where are they now?"

"Had you been the father and husband you should have been, you'd know," Anna's return was venomous.

Devlin was poisoned by it, no matter how hard he tried not to be. "Don't talk to me about propriety, just tell me where Deanna is?"

"Perhaps that's a question I'm better prepared to answer?"

"Greta," Kaitlin gasped.

"Don't even think about it," Anna hissed when Devlin turned for her mother. He stepped back and waited as the woman stepped from the door to the hidden staircase and drew to Anna's side.

"You just had to come out here, didn't you?" Greta's smile was cool as her hand slithered up Kaitlin's arm. She pinched. "Had to get in the way. Devlin was hardly here until you arrived. And the boy never--"

"Mama!" Anna interrupted to stop her. "Why are you here?"

Devlin wanted to know more about the boy, but he was grateful for Anna's interruption. Greta stopped pinching Kaitlin's arm.

"Yes, Greta, why?" Devlin asked.

Ignoring Devlin, Greta turned to Anna. "I saw the carriage racing here and came to make sure you and your brother were all right." Her lips thinning, she turned to Devlin. "So you know, Anna may be squeamish, but I have no qualms. Never did." Having said her threat, she pulled her pistol from her pocket and took aim at Devlin.

"What do you mean?" Devlin asked, reading more into her words.

"Yes Mama, what are you saying?" Anna asked.

"Oh dear, girl," Greta brushed her hand along Anna's cheek. "I've always taken care of you. Haven't I?" Anna head bobbed with emphasis. Greta smiled. "And I will continue to."

"Yes, Mama, but--"

"The detective got too close. Asked too many questions. I couldn't let him take my children. I couldn't let him hurt you."

Anna looked as stunned by her mother's declaration as anyone else. Her mother caressed her cheek.

"And Deanna? Did you hurt Deanna?" Devlin asked.

"Stop it, Devlin. She wouldn't do that." She covered her mother's hand with her own. "Would you, Mama? Would you?"

Greta's silence became unbearable. Her dark eyes spoke volumes.

"Nooo, why?" Anna pushed her mother's hand away.

"Oh my, sweet girl, you know how much I love you. She was coming between you and Orin. And she was tainted. Even you said so." She paused as if to remember, then met Anna's eyes. "I never meant to kill her. She wouldn't stop crying. Just wouldn't stop." She shook her head, seemingly lost in her own thoughts.

"So, for the last few years you've been spreading lies. Telling everyone that Devlin killed his daughter," Kaitlin spoke the obvious. "You wanted us all to believe he was a murderer."

"He is. The whole town saw him shoot his brother. Poor beast didn't have a chance. And neither will you."

"Before you kill me. Where is my daughter?" Devlin pleaded.

"What does it matter? You'll join her soon enough."

"No Greta, you will," Eldon said, stepping into the room through the wardrobe door.

Horror filled Greta's face. "You, but you're dead. You're..." Her arms dropped to her side.

"You'd like for me to be," Eldon replied slowly, removing the pistol from her limp hand. Devlin took it and turned it on Anna. She kept the gun at Kaitlin's head.

"I saw him kill you," Anna seemed dazed.

"You saw what you wanted," Eldon explained.

"I knew someone wanted him dead. I always thought it was you, Anna," Devlin explained. "I realize you had a part in it because you wanted his money, but there were other reasons weren't there, Greta?"

Anna shot her mother a bewildered look. "Mother?"

"You haven't told her the truth either, have you?" Devlin inquired further.

"Mother?" Anna was impatient.

Greta's lips pursed. "I won't speak of this."

"You met Eldon before," Devlin continued.

"Never." Greta sniffed.

"Never?" Devlin pressed.

"Stop this," Greta pleaded. "Don't listen to him," she implored her daughter.

Eldon's brows furrowed. "What are you talking about? I first met Greta when she came to work at the manor after you and Anna were married."

Devlin met his brother's eyes and shook his head. "You were with Father the day he went to offer his condolences to Greta for the loss of her first husband, Charles Minnard. Father's friend. Anna and Orin's father."

Eldon brows drew a line as he tried to recall. "Charles Minnard? I might recall him, but her... That was years ago."

"Not so long in Greta's mind." Devlin rubbed his chin. "She couldn't forget." Eldon scratched his ermine head. Anna's mouth gaped in confusion. "Because there's more to the story," Devlin went on. "Charles was murdered." Greta's face paled to white. "There was a trial. And Greta was the prime suspect."

"Mother?"

"Hush, child," Greta snapped. "I was acquitted."

"Yes, you were," Devlin agreed with a predatory smile. "But you weren't so lucky with the second husband." He tapped his lips. "The twins would have been seven around the time you married your third husband. Did they know what you did to him? I often wonder what you told them about their father. Did they know he'd been poisoned?"

Anna glared at her mother.

Greta eyes bulged. "He's lying to you? Where are you getting your misinformation?"

Devlin shook his head. "Why would Uma misinform me?"

"Uma?" The argument died in Greta's throat, her lips twisted into a snarl. "Why that--"

"Hush, Mother," Anna scolded. She started to cry. "How could you? You said Daddy got sick. You said..." her voice faltered, she couldn't finish. She took a deep breath and straightened. "We'll discuss this when were finished here."

"What do you plan to finish?" Devlin inquired. "You know I can't let you take anything else. And I won't let you leave if you try."

"I'm not asking for permission." Anna sneered. "Since I'm still holding the trump card, I doubt I'd need to anyway."

She jabbed Kaitlin's shoulder blades. Devlin and Eldon stepped back to let her pass. She hesitated, seemed to carefully study her options.

"Well, let's go," Greta urged.

"In good time, Mother." Anna's eyes flashed contempt. Greta stepped back as though the force of anger in her daughter's gaze slapped her with a physical palm. "First I want you to tell me what happened to Deanna."

Kaitlin met Devlin's gaze, then fixed her eyes on Greta.

Greta's sigh rattled her body. "What does it matter? I told you I didn't mean to do it. You didn't even care for the girl."

"Mother," Anna said solemnly.

If a word could be laced with any more venom, Devlin didn't know how.

"All right," Greta growled. "If you must know, Orin had eyes for the girl. That's why he wanted to take her along."

For the first time in Devlin's remembrance, Anna looked appalled. Devlin wasn't sure if it was because of Orin's desire for Deanna or lack thereof for Anna. He doubted it had anything to do with the morality of a grown man with a small girl. Her relationship with her brother attested to her warped senses already.

"Then what?" Anna's voice was hard.

"I couldn't let her break up our trio."

Devlin's lips thinned at her confession. Who was the most warped? Greta seemed to think her children's relationship was healthy. She'd killed a small child trying to keep it. Devlin wasn't certain he wanted to hear the rest, but he had to.

"I thought if I could get her away from him. He'd soon forget her. I had a buyer who wanted a small girl for..." Greta stopped, her eyes drifted to Devlin. He held his expression, his hands were clenched at his sides. Greta's voice became shaky. "The child didn't want to leave without her papa and brother. She started crying, wailing, and I was forced to silence her. I didn't mean to kill her."

"The same way you didn't mean to kill my father or the others?" Anna gasped in rage.

Devlin held his rage, his expression was pure granite, and tears filled his eyes. Eldon rammed his fist into his pockets.

"Honestly, Anna, I was only thinking of you," Greta cried and reached out to touch her daughter. Anna backed away.

Devlin's stomach turned. He thought about a small boy, crouched in a dark wardrobe, watching.

No wonder he never uttered a word.

"Where's my daughter?" Devlin demanded, with a thin handle on his emotions. He moved toward Greta.

Greta ripped the pistol from her daughter's hand and waved it at him and Eldon. "I will not say." The gun passed between them again. Her eyes gleaming with unspoken hatred, Greta turned it on Kaitlin. "Perhaps it's your darling wife you should be worried about?"

Devlin waited for Kaitlin to move but she seemed frozen in place. Devlin rushed Greta, pushing Kaitlin as he went. He and Eldon reached for Greta.

Greta's scream resounded through the room, like a banshee out of hell. The gun's report echoed the manor over and then there was silence.

Chapter Thirty-Nine

Devlin stared out the window, his eyes locked on the twisted body in the snow. He gripped the sill and sighed. He learned more than he ever wanted to this night, yet, he felt a great loss. Greta, body bent and broken, lay beneath the window. Crimson seeped into the pristine snow. She'd taken her secret with her.

He would never find his little girl.

Devlin turned with a gulp, trying to dam his tears.

"I didn't mean to push her out the window," Eldon replied weakly, wincing as Olga cleaned the gash at his side where he'd taken the shot meant for Kaitlin. "I'm so sorry."

"I know." Devlin sighed once more, but he was near broken. "I just wished I knew where to find her body." He tried to smile, it wasn't in him.

It was silly to be so grieved after so many years. But he was. Kaitlin was alive, as was Eldon, but that didn't ease his grief. Kaitlin tried and her touch was warm, but he hurt. His heart was a mixture of ice and fire. Heaven help him, he wanted to bring his daughter home. Wanted to bury her body. He hadn't been there for her in life, he wanted be there for her in death.

He would get the answer somehow. "Anna?"

Anna had given up without further argument. She looked up at Devlin, crossed her arms high on her chest. "Don't you dare look at me like that, Devlin. You can demand an answer from me, but I don't know. I'm ill from the whole affair. I lost Orin and Mama." She sniffed and turned her head. Then bowed it and started to cry.

Devlin started for Anna to make her answer. Kaitlin put her hand on his shoulder, compelling him to stop.

"There's no need to ask her. We might know where she is." Kaitlin gulped.

"We do?" Devlin blinked in disbelief. He shook his head.

Kaitlin nodded. "Derrick has been trying to tell us for quite some time."

Devlin wasn't following her line of reasoning, but Eldon understood.

"The lake," he replied. "That's why he won't skate. Let's go there straightway."

Olga caught his arm. "You need to rest."

Devlin shrugged in bewilderment. "How would Derrick know?"

"He was in the room that night. Hiding in the wardrobe. He saw... something," Kaitlin choked on the words.

Understanding hit him squarely between the eyes, Devlin's throat burned. "Did he see Greta kill his sister? Did he see...?" His heart couldn't contain his sorrow. What did his son see? His sister broken and..."Oh, dear Lord."

"Devlin, he's okay," Kaitlin assured him. Cupping his face, she met his eyes.

"I should have been there for him."

"He's okay," she repeated.

"Did he say he saw Mama put her in the lake?" Anna asked in a raw whisper.

"No, but he's terrified of the water," Kaitlin answered. "Unfortunately, that's our only clue." She touched her husband's cheek. Tears slid along her cheeks. "But I, I hope... I..."

Devlin's hopes were dim. Would his search for Deanna end beneath a frozen lake? If only his heart could be as frozen and unfeeling now.

Anna cocked her head, there was pain in his eyes. Was she beginning to understand? To feel? Devlin shook his head.

"I might not have wanted the child. But to think her dead. To think her... He used to love the lake," she replied, her voice distant, rasping with sorrow. She bowed her head to her hands. "What have I done?"

Devlin wanted to tell her it was her selfishness that left them all with so few memories of Deanna. Her selfishness and greed for the jewels that encrusted the reins and saddle of the toy horses in Derrick's room had ruined several lives. She would live with the memory of loss for the rest of her life. Devlin wanted to find some vindication in that, but the sorrow that touched Anna's voice and melded her soul with her eyes, made him aware that this was one memory she didn't want to have.

Devlin's gaze drifted from Kaitlin to Anna and back. He remembered how Deanna had loved the water. Now it was her tomb. He caressed his wife's hand then slipped his free from hers and returned to the window.

*****

Next morning, though the wind howled, whipping the frozen earth along a bleak landscape, though the sun hid behind gray clouds of fury, Devlin set out to find his daughter. He would lay her to rest, if he could. Lay his search to rest.

He was digging holes in the ice on the lake when Kaitlin came to help him.

"I don't want you to freeze," he told her stubbornly.

"You shouldn't be out here, either," she yelled over the rising gale.

"My daughter is," he shot back.

"You don't know that."

"I do," he cried, his wail lifted on the wind. He swore he felt her the moment he stepped on the ice. Her distant cries rang in ears now. In his heart. He turned to his wife, who was trying to cut another hole with the saw. "Go inside, Katie," he whispered. Taking the saw from her, he pulled her scarf back over her face and pointed her home.

Tears stinging her eyes, she started to leave then turned. "If you must be so stubborn at least drink the coffee I brought so you'll stay warm."

He nodded slowly, fixed his scarf about his face then turned to his task -- another hole, another drop of his line. Nothing. Searching for his daughter in this weather, under the frozen lake, was like hunting for a shard of glass in the desert.

He had to find her. Though numb in his hands and feet -- in his heart -- he dropped to his knees, to start another hole. When Eldon and Perkins found him he was kneeling over yet another hole, weeping.

The coffee was half-frozen in the cup.

"You've got to come in," Eldon said. "No one can find her until spring." With his hands in Devlin's armpits, he lifted.

Deadweight, Devlin sobbed. "I can't wait. I need to find her. I won't fail her again."

"What if she's not here?" Eldon argued.

"She's here. I feel..." He put a hand to his heart. "I feel her. I don't want to leave her here. I don't want to fail her again.

"You didn't fail her," Perkins replied, reaching in to help Eldon.

Devlin's body slackened further. "I can't leave her."

"Do you want to join her?" Eldon asked. "Is that it? Do you want to die?"

Devlin met his eyes. Did he? He probably deserved to.

Eldon stopped trying to lift him. "Go ahead then. But what about Kaitlin and Derrick? You can do nothing to change Deanna's death. Are you willing to stay out here with the dead and forget the living? If you do, you'll fail them. How selfish of you."

How selfish of you. Like the hatchet on ice, Eldon's words struck Devlin, giving glimpses of a man he didn't want to see. Everyone always believed Eldon to be the ghost of the manor. But maybe, he, himself, walked the halls, maybe it was he who had paled so far from the man he used to be. He was the one who was lost. Rising slowly, he wiped the icy tears on his cheeks. His knees were numb. His heart was thawing.

"You're right, Eldon," he said solemnly. This will have to wait until spring." His heart needed attention right now. He would be of no use to anyone until he took a deeper look at what the holes, bored into his frigid being, had uncovered.

Kaitlin and Derrick waited for Devlin to find his way in from the cold. Derrick had succumbed to his heavy eyelids and was sleeping in her lap as she studied the lake. Watching Devlin. How long could he keep up this pace before he broke? Before the lake gave? She was growing weary, but a heavy heart kept her awake. She caressed Derrick's sweaty curls and worried. Would Devlin ever stop searching? Was she losing him? Each time the pick struck the ice she swore she felt it.

When she saw Eldon -- who had no business about in the early evening -- and Perkins cross the lawn, she moved Derrick from her lap and rose. With a cheek to the glass, she whispered a prayer.

When she saw Devlin fighting even them, she grew distressed. Her prayer lifted with all the more fervency. Devlin left the lake, heading for the barn across pristine lawns of moonlight, and she nearly shouted, "Hallelujah". It rang in her heart as she slipped from the nursery and grabbed her coat to follow.

Fearing for her husband and herself, she pushed open the barn door. Ready to face Devlin. Ready to cross any distance necessary to restore what she feared was crumbling.

Devlin, in the stall with Cotton, only added to her worries. Thinking he'd completely lost his mind, she started for him, when Henry pulled her into the shadows. His finger to his lips, he silenced her. She wanted to know why, but she did as bade. Instead, of racing to his rescue, she took the time to watch Devlin, who was now stroking the horse's nose ever so slightly. So gently.

When he leaned against the horse's neck in tears, Kaitlin struggled to hear his whispered groaning. She struggled against envy. Why hadn't he come to the house? She'd have given him her shoulder to cry on. She'd have offered him the solace of her arms.

He was finding it on the strong neck of an unruly beast.

Devlin ran his hand along Cotton's mane, cooing softly. Then he fixed the oat sack for the horse, and after grabbing some gear, left the barn.

Kaitlin came to her senses only after he was gone, and tried to catch him. "Dev. Devlin, please. Don't go. Don't leave me."

Again Henry took her arm. "He's not leaving you, ma'am."

Her heart in agony, she stared at the door. "Then why is he walking away again? Doesn't he know I want to help him? Why is he...?" Her voice breaking, she took a deep breath and met Henry's gentle gaze. "Why didn't you let me go to him?"

Again, Henry put his finger to his lips.

Against her better judgment -- because she really wanted to scream about now -- Kaitlin complied. His answer had better be good.

It was excellent, but terribly long in coming. Kaitlin waited as Henry returned some gear to the boxes.

"It ain't that I didn't want you to go to the mister, ma'am." He wound the rope about his hand and elbow as he spoke, but ol' Cotton there is still a mite temperamental. Didn't want him to get skittish and hurt the mister."

Kaitlin's eyes flew to Cotton. "Then you were right to stop me. I don't want him hurt, either."

But he was hurting in other ways.

She had a good idea where he'd gone and was impatient to follow. As soon as Henry was finished, she would.

Henry seemed to read her thoughts. "I said he ain't leaving you, ma'am." He stowed the last rope, closed the lid and sat down. He motioned for her to do the same. She felt like she was wasting time. Devlin needed her, but something in Henry's eyes told her to take the moment.

When she settled beside him, he took her hand into his own. "See the mister, he's like ol' Cotton there. With layers and layers of hurt."

"But I thought things were worked out between us."

"Oh, ma'am, they are." Henry smiled reassuringly as he squeezed her hand. "But that's only scratching the surface. Things ain't worked out so neatly between the mister and himself."

Kaitlin blinked in confusion.

Henry released her hand and brushing his knees, rose. "Do you know what freedom is, ma'am?"

She nodded slowly. "We've fought several wars because of it."

"Yes, there's that." Henry scrubbed his chin. "But there's a personal freedom allotted to each man."

"You mean, in Christ?"

Henry nodded. "There's that. Don't get me wrong, ma'am. Mister Clayborne knows the Lord." He scrubbed his chin again. "But he forgot how to lay his trouble down. He's just too stubborn." He drew a long, shuddering sigh. "Mr. Clayborne has offered a sense of freedom to everyone working at this manor. Now granted, he went through a time where he balked at the church, but I don't fault him for it. Still, he's given compassion and shelter to us all. Even a cantankerous old horse has found a home. He would go out of his way to protect any of us. But he doesn't allow himself the same freedom? He rides himself unfairly. In all his failings, even if they ain't his, he thinks he's supposed to face them alone. Do you understand?"

Kaitlin nodded. Her husband would pour himself out for the hurt and lowly, he'd be the first to offer them grace and mercy, but he didn't ask such things of himself. He didn't believe he was worthy.

Henry sighed. "He's gone to face his deepest fears, ma'am. It's a place a body goes alone, so as he can face the Lord. I suspect he'll be back in due time."

Kaitlin gave a long, hopeful look at the door her husband had passed through earlier and told herself to give him the time he needed. To lay him in the hands of God. Didn't Henry say Devlin would be back soon enough?

Chapter Forty

Soon enough turned into a few days and hovered closer to a week.

In the beginning, Kaitlin determined she wouldn't meddle. She would see to it Devlin knew how deeply he was cared for. Thomas kept the woodpile at the cabin stocked. And Perkins delivered warm meals, direct from the kitchen.

Kaitlin gave him space, praying that God would get a firm hold on her husband's broken heart and do so in a quick efficient manner.

Heaven help her, her own impatience drove her crazy. And Derrick's constant inquiries about his father did nothing to allay her anxiety.

Eldon promised if Devlin didn't return soon, he'd take matters into his own hands, even if it meant dragging Devlin home kicking and screaming. Given the scowl he wore upon making the promise, Kaitlin doubted sending Eldon would be a good thing.

But she was terrible at waiting. At her wit's end, Kaitlin decided to do the one thing she could do -- beyond dragging him home herself. Bundling herself and Derrick, she and the boy went to town.

She was exhilarated when she arrived at her sister's door nearly a half hour later

"I've come to join you and Eliot," she told her sister soundly.

Constance was ready to cry. She stepped back and welcomed them in. With a hand to her heart she said, "I say it's about time someone came to their senses. All this waiting and wondering. No one should ever have to go through such." She leveled her husband with a curt nod, daring him to defend Devlin -- the scoundrel, the deceiver of wives and children.

She took a look outside before closing the door. There was no carriage, no bags. Her brows furrowed as she shut the door and turned to her sister. "How long will you be staying?"

Kaitlin choked a laugh. "Constance, I'm not moving in."

Constance frowned. "You just said you've come to join Eliot and I?"

"Not to live here."

"You mean you're going to stay there while he... even though..." she sputtered to a stop when she found Derrick and her son, Michael, watching. "How long, Katie?"

"With Devlin? As long as it takes," she replied bluntly. "With you? I came to join you at services, I hoped with a lot of us praying together we could move the process along."

Constance's nose twisted in disgust. She would belabor the issue, but her daughter Grace's cry rang out above the stairs.

"Bully for you," Eliot praised when his wife was gone. "I've been praying for this for years."

"Well, don't quit yet," Kaitlin grinned. "'Cause I, for one, would like my husband home."

*****

Devlin faced the man in the mirror. How the mighty had fallen? His eyes were blood red and his hair unkempt. A week's worth of beard stubble on his chin. He looked like some crazy derelict, had he not known himself he might well believe he was one. He lifted his hand to his hair, to finger-comb it and nearly choked on the rank smell emanating from his underarms.

Lord, have mercy, he needed to bathe. He studied his reflection and smiled. The Lord did have mercy, for such a stubborn beast as himself. He'd offered Devlin what Devlin believed he could never have, grace, love, and mercy for his failings.

It took a time of deep soul searching and heart surrendering to get him to this place. Thankfully, the Lord had been patient, yet firm in His dealings. He studied his reflection and wondered whether Kate had been as patient.

His eyes widened, his mouth dropped open. "Katie. Derrick." In all this, he'd forgotten his wife and son. He raked his hands through his hair. What kind of man forgot his wife and son?

There was stark fear in his heart and in the eyes mirroring him. He heard the cry of his soul and felt at peace. His family was waiting for him, they had to be. He'd been mindlessly lost before, now he could return home and be a husband and a father again.

He tugged at his soiled clothes and decided it would be better to greet them after cleaning up. He was a new man when he entered the manor, hopeful and exhilarated to be among the living. Even his home looked different in the light of a restored soul. His hope rose. It would be better still if Kate were by his side. Better still, to know for certain she was there for him. His hope dwindled when, with a search of the rooms, he couldn't find his wife or son anywhere. Had she left him anyway? Had God been mistaken?

*****

"Where's Kate?" Devlin roared into the chamber like a storm. He'd searched the house over and had found neither her or his son.

Eldon and Perkins -- who'd tracked the gale while languishing over a chess game -- met each other's gaze over the board for a mere second before Perkins made his move.

Eldon could practically feel his brother bristling as he paced, but still took his sweet time answering.

"She's not here."

"Not here?" Devlin came to an abrupt stop. The invisible storm raging around him intensified. He clapped the edge of the table, the combatants on the board shuddered. "Where is she?"

Perkins cocked his head to Eldon, conceding the chore of answering. Eldon would answer in due time, he studied the board again.

"Well," Devlin roared impatiently.

Unable to concentrate fully, Eldon calmly lowered his knight and leaned back in his chair, stretching until his hands came to rest on the ball of his head.

"She grew tired of waiting for you to return from your self-imposed exile and decided to undertake a course which might better benefit the situation."

"What?" Devlin straightened. "Speak English, man."

Eldon only shrugged.

Devlin started to pace again. His head shook slightly as though he wasn't sure what he'd heard, given his frown he believed he'd lost another wife. "What was she thinking? Didn't she know I didn't want her to leave? Didn't she know I--"

"No, Dev. I mean yes, Dev," Eldon added quickly when Devlin whirled on him. "She knew you didn't want her to leave."

"Never doubted it for a moment," Perkins interjected with a curt nod.

"Then why?"

Grinning, Eldon shook his head. "Devlin, she hasn't left you. Though, given the length of your pity party, who would blame her?" His tone was as patronizing as his grin. Devlin returned a scowl. "You can't deny it."

Devlin stopped. He couldn't deny it. He'd locked himself off for days, trying to find himself again. Trying to get a better look at the man whose reflection had become so distorted.

Without a clearer perception of himself and his terribly lacking spirit, he'd be of little value to anyone. But with prayer and humility, he'd stepped before the mirror and begged God to define the reflection. It was much clearer now.

"As I was saying," Eldon picked up the queen and twirled her between his fingers, she hasn't left you. She and Derrick have gone to the church to pray, especially for you." His hands fell to his lap with a shrug. "I'd have gone myself, but... that's where they are."

"Now don't you go running after her half-cocked and angry," Perkins replied in an authoritative tone, sounding very much like Devlin's father might. "She has your best interest at heart and don't you forget it."

Devlin wouldn't. He was out the door before anyone could say another word, but not before both men were able to read the fire in his eyes. Both silently prayed Kaitlin wouldn't get scorched by the glare.

*****

Devlin stopped before he crashed through the front door of the church. The fire was still in his eyes, coursing through his veins, when he took a deep breath and stepped quietly into the church. He noticed his wife and son's bowed heads on the second row, but decided against going forward and interrupting them. Instead he took a seat on the last pew and listened.

Funny how all his searching had brought him to this point. Funny how, when he looked into the mirror of his life, he could see Kaitlin's beautiful image clearly beside his own.

There she sat, her lovely head bowed and leaning against Derrick's. He took hope in the fact that she hadn't boarded a wagon and left him. Had his exile caused him to lose her heart? He would go to any lengths to get it back.

When Reverend Marlow's prayer ceased, he made his move.

Stunning everyone, he walked to the front of the church.

Kaitlin, her head still bowed in earnest prayer, had no inkling he was coming to do battle for her heart.

First, before he could win her, Devlin felt he must face the reverend.

"Devlin." A dazed Reverend Marlow managed to say.

Kaitlin's head popped up in time to see him pass. He didn't look her way, stunning her further.

Awed, Derrick merely whispered, "It's Daddy."

Yes, Kaitlin nodded, because she couldn't speak. Derrick's daddy was in the church. Why?

"He looks mad," Michael declared. His perception was of little help.

Kaitlin agreed. He looked rather solemn. She gulped. Was he there to take her to task for coming? He'd been very clear he didn't want her to set one foot in the church. Would he confront Reverend Marlow? She looked to Constance for solace, then finding none, looked to Eliot, He wore the same bewildered face as his wife. The same stare graced Reverend Marlow's features.

Feeling sorry for him, Kaitlin started to rise to his defense. She took her seat, clutching her sister's hand, when Devlin cleared his throat.

"Reverend Marlow, I'm sorry to intrude and apologize for detaining you," he bowed slightly to the congregation," but I've come before these witnesses of men and God to beg your forgiven for the anger and mistrust I've carried of you."

The death grip Kaitlin had on Constance's hand went limp. The room gave a collective gasp, and waited.

Reverend Marlow stood momentarily silent then cleared his throat. "I'm humbled and grateful that you seek my forgiveness. You have it to my utmost, Devlin. You had it long ago," he replied. The room shuddered with another gasp, as he struck out his hand. Tears were in his eyes.

Devlin took the hand, clasp it tightly. "Thank you."

Sniffling could be heard from the crowd now. Michael boldly stood on the seat and peered round the room. Derrick peeked back then looked up at Kaitlin. He seemed confused and disconcerted.

She patted his leg and sighed softly. A prayer had been answered. She praised heaven.

The parishioners prepared to leave, when Devlin turned and begged them to stop. "I'm not finished," he announced loudly, causing everyone to settle in their seats.

Michael, upon hearing his uncle's authoritative voice, dropped to his rear and gaped.

Kaitlin could not settle, nor move, she just stared at her husband. A man for the most part foreign to her. A man who held her attentions. Who held her heart.

God, please don't let him break it.

He spoke to the congregation, "I must also, with you as my witnesses, apologize to my wife." His heart in his eyes, he knelt before her and took her hand into his own. "Seems I've said this before, but I haven't been a very good husband to you. I want the chance to be that." She sniffed, the tears flowed along her cheeks, to her neck, but she didn't turn from his stare, from the heart she saw there.

"I realize," his voice faltered, "our marriage was born of convenience, not love. But..." he paused. She drew an unsteady breath as he lifted her hand to his lips. "But I'm willing to change that. I'm willing to for the sake of love." He kissed her hand. "Because I love you, Katie. I'll marry you again, right now. So there'll be no doubt."

Kaitlin let go the breath she'd been holding, and started to cry in earnest.

"Kaitlin Michelle Dupree, will you marry me?"

With a hiccup, she started to laugh and cry all at once.

Derrick crushed himself to Kaitlin's side. "Kay," he whispered, his voice laced with concern.

With his free hand, Devlin caressed his son's shoulder then let his fingers toss the silken black tresses haloing his son's cherub face. "It's okay, boy. There's no reason to be scared. Kaitlin is okay. I've just asked her to marry me. And be your mommy forever."

Derrick blinked in wonderment. "My mommy?" He pushed away from Kaitlin's side, and looked up at her, waiting for her answer.

While Kaitlin could feel every eye in the congregation upon her, she was strangely at ease when she gave her answer. "The marriage was very real as far as I am concerned. I need no other proof of your love. But if you need proof of my--"

He covered her lips with his fingers. "I know you love me. I just needed to tell you where my heart is. I couldn't bear to lose you."

Her smile brightened. "You won't lose me. But I do have one request."

His smile faltered, then rose when he replied, "Name it and it's yours."

She asked for a honeymoon. He said he'd take her to see the world. She considered his offer, than chose a simpler place.

"A week in the cabin with you is all I ask."

In the cabin? He hated himself, but thoughts of Anna rose unbidden.

He'd built the cabin for her, and she had spurned it and his love. And hadn't he just wrestled with himself there? It harbored the past, it was a mess. It was no place for a lady, no place for Kaitlin. He opened his mouth to say so.

"I'm not Anna." It was not a reprimand, or said in anger. Only a soft gentle reminder of the woman she was. Of her love.

He shook his head. "No, you're not." He hoisted her into his arms, called for his son to follow and with the cheers echoing through the church, carried his wife out the door.

Kaitlin would help him clean the cabin of its cobwebs and ghosts. Anna, who was languishing in the regional penitentiary, never haunted him so again.

If only Deanna's voice would fade as easily. He dreaded the spring, but decided to take it one day at a time. Besides, given the smile from the woman in his arms, the evening was shaping up rather nicely.

Chapter Forty-One

Spring seemed like it would never show, but came much too early for Devlin's liking. The lake thawed, the dragging began. This time though, he didn't have to face what might be discovered alone. Kaitlin was there beside him and the church and half the town turned out to help. After two days, the remains of Reverend Marlow's son were lifted from the waters. By week's end, there was nothing of Deanna to be found. Devlin began to believe they'd find nothing and began to hope she was alive.

But Derrick, finally able to share what he saw that night, remembered Greta taking a limp Deanna to the lake and dropping her body in the waters.

From the horror still evident in his eyes every time Derrick mentioned his sister's name, Devlin knew he had little reason to hope. When they drug Deanna's red scarf to the surface, he knew he had none.

The body of Reverend Marlow's son and a worn red scarf were reverently buried and with the pallor of death and uncertainty hanging over the manor gone, life began anew.

Ingrid remained on staff and moved into the manor so her son, Peter, could be near Eldon. Graham moved his practice west, so he might spend more time in research with Eldon and with a certain young lady.

Uma, Ingrid's sister, came for Greta's funeral then disappeared without a word. Though she tried not to, it was evident that Ingrid worried. She considered hiring a detective to find Uma, but it was too costly. Uma would reappear when she wanted and not before.

Olga, too, visited when things weren't so hectic on the farm. She took to helping with the research and since Orin was out of her life now, serving time in a cell, took the time to reacquaint herself with an old friend.

Eldon was only too pleased to reacquaint himself.

Kaitlin spent her days getting to know her husband, finding how much she loved him. To have those feelings finally returned, made loving him even easier.

The manor lost its aura of gloom, love and laughter filled the halls. Kaitlin longed to fill it with more children. Her and Devlin's children. But for all her prayers, that desire seemed unattainable.

As hopeless as bringing Deanna back from the grave.

Kaitlin rubbed her stiff legs and thanked the Lord that Devlin loved her in spite of her scars. In spite of what she might never be able to give him. It would be nice to have another child. Perhaps a girl? But who was she to think that a child could take the place of those loved and lost. She laid a handful of flowers on Deanna's marker and thanked the Lord for the ability to lay her to rest. Devlin still bore the pain of losing her, she was certain. Just as she still bore the pain of losing Simone and Jean Marc.

"I'd bring you back to him if I could," she told the stone. She traced Deanna's name with her finger then rose. When she turned toward the house, she was astonished to see a small party running toward her. Ingrid led the pack, her hand held high, a letter flapping in her hand. Graham, with Derrick high in his arms, Margaret, Henry, Marla and Perkins followed.

"Miss Kaitlin, you must see this," Margaret yelled breathlessly as she hurried to keep pace with her husband who had a tight grip on her hand.

"I've received word from Uma," Ingrid said excitedly.

"That's wonderful," Kaitlin replied, giving her a quick hug. "How is she?"

"She's fine. She's going to be in Minneapolis June fourth."

"Why, that's today. Oh, Ingrid, I'm so happy for you," Kaitlin said sincerely. For reasons she couldn't understand everyone else was happy as well. "Will you need time off to see her?"

"Yes, but only if you join me."

Kaitlin's brows rose in bewilderment. Uma was barely an acquaintance. "Whatever for? Surely you want to--"

"Read this," Graham suggested, cutting her off. Taking the letter from Ingrid, he pushed it into Kaitlin's hand.

Kaitlin shrugged and did as bade. "Oh my," Was the only response she could form. She was so astonished she read it again to be sure.

"Isn't it wonderful?" Marla exclaimed.

It was beyond wonderful, Kaitlin decided. It was a miracle.

A miracle she had to share with Devlin right away. "You're right, Ingrid, I must join you. But first I must get to Eden Prairie."

Henry grinned like a possum. "We thought you might, ma'am. We sent Thomas to Miss Olga's for her team.

"And we've taken the liberty of packing you and the boy a bag," Marla added.

Kaitlin suddenly felt ill, overwhelmed. It was wonderful but... She took a deep breath and prayed for her taut nerves not to fray.

"Here's our carriage now," Graham replied as the carriage shuddered to a stop in the drive. He put his arm about his stunned sister. "Didn't I tell you I was coming along?"

She shook her head and stared after him like a simpleton, but strangely, to know he was joining her, calmed her. Kaitlin leaned into his side with a sigh. "I'm glad of it."

When Olga stepped from the carriage and crossed the lawn, Kaitlin wondered if they wouldn't have another on their journey. "I had to come and see you off," Olga replied, her eyes shining with unshed tears. She put a hand to her heart. "It's so miraculous. I never thought..." her voice faltered. "I'm only sorry Eldon won't be able to join you."

"Eldon," Kaitlin said his name in a pathetic squeak. She'd forgotten all about him. She started for the house. "I've got to tell him."

Graham caught her arm and pulled her to a stop. "He knows. He says you're to be on your way. His prayers are with you."

Kaitlin fought the urge to cry. Such a magnanimous happening and he couldn't go along. Had they the Manor's special carriage, he could have. But Devlin had the carriage. Devlin was in Minneapolis and she needed to be there.

*****

"He's still in trial," Kaitlin informed Graham as he came down the hall at the courthouse. "What should I do?"

Graham's coat grew taut on his shoulders with his shrug. He stood beside her and took a peek through the small windows into the room. Devlin was questioning a witness. "Maybe we should go in and get him?"

Kaitlin shook her head. "We can't interrupt him. He's in trial."

"This is more important. Eliot's there, he can finish the proceedings," Graham argued.

"It's unethical. It's..." Before she could form a proper protest, Graham pulled her into the courtroom. Her mouth gaping, she stood at the back, flustered. When the judge noticed them there, the fever rose further in her cheeks until she could feel them burning.

Luckily, Eliot noticed them. He motioned something to the judge and slipped back to them.

"What are you doing here?" he asked in a low whisper.

"Oh, Eliot, I have--" Kaitlin caught herself and lowered her voice, "I have some important news for Devlin." She quickly pulled the letter from her pocket. "You must read this."

"Oh my," Eliot exclaimed when he was finished, arresting the attention of the full court, Devlin and the judge.

"Mr. Dunlevy, this is not your personal arena," the judge reprimanded. "We have legal matters to attend to here. Might I know why you are interrupting my court?"

Eliot gulped. "Sir, might I approach the bench?"

The judge considered it and gave a nod. Devlin watched Eliot pass then met his wife's eyes. She answered the questions she saw there with a chagrined smile.

"Mr. Clayborne, would you approach the bench please," the judge's directive caused him to turn.

"Your honor," Devlin said as he reached the bench prepared to grovel for his job and excuse his wife's interruption. He wanted to ask Eliot what was going on, but he kept his eyes on the judge.

"Young man, your partner has made quite an argument in your favor. Such that, I'm inclined to agree to your leaving."

Devlin shot Eliot an askance glance. "Is someone hurt?" He took a quick look at his wife. She seemed well enough. Was it Derrick?

"No one's hurt," Eliot assured him.

"No one's hurt? Then I have a trial to finish," he returned to the judge.

"No sir, you must go with your wife. Mr. Dunlevy can finish the argument in your stead."

"But--"

"It's a most important matter," Eliot said softly.

"Most important," the judge added. "Now off with you before I fine you for interrupting these proceedings." This he said with a smile and wave of his hand. But Devlin knew he meant every word. He took his leave.

Devlin couldn't fathom it. If no one was hurt then what could be so important his wife had to pull him out of trial. He was certainly going to find out.

When he reached his wife and started to take her hand, Kaitlin looked ready to run. He caught her before she could bolt, as he moved her into the hall.

"Darling," he said in a low menacing voice. He acknowledged her brother. "Graham." He returned his gaze to his wife.

Graham smiled and shrugged apologetically. "Sorry we had to interrupt."

"We wouldn't have, if it weren't utterly important," Kaitlin added quickly.

"Eliot tells me no one is hurt. Has the house burned down?"

"None of the above," Graham answered.

Devlin's brows furrowed.

"But it truly is important," Kaitlin added hastily. "You must trust me."

Devlin studied her face. The importance of this remained to be seen, but trust he did.

When they reached the carriage to find Ingrid and Derrick waiting, Devlin's confusion mounted. He took a seat and pulled his son into his lap. "What is this? A clandestine operation?" he said with a hint of a smile.

"No," Ingrid said soundly. "We're on our way to--"

"The hospital," Kaitlin cut her off. She slipped her arm through her husband's and stared at him with hopeful green eyes. "Where we'll tell you everything. I promise."

Devlin studied his wife as the carriage lurched along. Confounded curiosity had dried his mouth. No one was hurt, yet they were going to a hospital. No one would tell him anymore, but it was of the utmost importance. His mind, working overtime, he formulated an answer. Admittedly, it shouldn't have swayed the judge, it wouldn't have been important enough. But it meant the world to him. If it was her excuse for pulling him from court, he could forgive her. He would forgive her anything.

Grinning, he shifted his son on his lap and slipped his arm about his wife. "You're with child, aren't you?" Her mouth unhinged so he wasn't sure what she would say. "If you are, I'm elated. I even forgive you for pulling me out of court. How you swayed the judge, I don't know."

She smiled, even as her green eyes misted. "Devlin, I wished I was carrying your child. Our child. There's nothing I want to give you more in the whole world. Except..." she paused as the carriage bumped to a stop at the hospital. Her fluttering hand crossed the window, inviting him to look and stopped aloft, pointing to the walk. "Except that," she replied her voice breaking.

Devlin followed her hand. His mouth dropped open and he began to cry.

"Deanna," came his hoarse whisper, just before he gathered his son to his chest and alighted.

With his son in his arms, he raced across the drive, drawing to a stop before the astonished child and a very nervous Uma. He wanted to take his daughter into his arms and hold her, but her deep brown eyes filled with bewilderment. Fear. He hated it, but the girl clung to Uma. When she turned into the folds of Uma's dress with a whimper, Devlin wanted to cry. Not wanting to scare her further, he dropped to his knees, wondering how to reach his daughter.

His daughter. Although she was the same age as Derrick, she stood perhaps three inches smaller. She seemed to have been well taken care of, but she was skinnier then her brother. Dressed in her white dress with a blue striped ribbon coiling through her deep black ringlets of hair, she reminded him of a little doll. A doll he wanted to pull into his arms. If only he could reach her.

He cried when Derrick managed it for him, by simply calling her name. "DeeDee."

"Yes, son, it's DeeDee."

Deanna pushed back the folds of Uma's skirts and peered out. Confusion turned to wonderment. She smiled at the boy in Devlin's arms, and in a voice barely above a whisper, a voice hesitant to recall why she knew him, she said, "Dari." She put her hand out slowly to touch what seemed so unreal.

"Yes, darling girl, it's Dari," Devlin replied. He wanted to touch her and reached out. She disappeared into the folds of Uma's skirts again.

"It's okay. This is your daddy," Uma sought to assure her all was okay. Deanna didn't seem to hear or care.

Devlin's heart broke. He'd been looking for her for years, had thought her lost. Here she was alive, two feet from him, but an eternity away. How did he cross this chasm? How did he make this child understand how much he loved her? He begged the Lord for words, for the way. When his son pulled from his arms and stepped to the girl.

"DeeDee," he cried her name, and softly touched her shoulder. Again his words and childish smile did what Devlin could not. The girl turned and faced him. "I'm Dari, 'member?" Deanna's head bobbed. Derrick looked to Devlin and added, "That's Daddy."

Deanna studied Devlin, her lips twisting as she debated whether or not Dari spoke the truth and whether it mattered or not.

Considering the time she was taking to decide, Devlin began to doubt he'd ever reach her.

Kaitlin came to his side and knelt down. "Do you remember your daddy, sweetheart?" The little girl shrugged. "Do you remember Dari?" Deanna pursed her lips and nodded. Kaitlin smiled. "Well, Dari is your brother. And this is Dari's daddy, which makes him your daddy, too. He takes care of Dari and wants to take you from here and care for you. He wants to take you home."

Deanna frowned. Clutching Uma's skirts, she looked at the hospital behind her. "Home?"

"No, sweetheart," Kaitlin called her. "That's not home. That's not..." Deanna wasn't listening, she couldn't tear her eyes from the big white building.

"Deanna." Kaitlin smiled.

Devlin found hope when the girl turned to Kaitlin.

"Deanna, I have a little girl, too. Would like to see her?" Kaitlin lifted her locket from the bodice of her gown and held it out for the child to see.

"Pretty." Deanna smiled, and, paying little mind to the man beside her, moved to Kaitlin.

Devlin had to smile. He shook his head. His little girl was already enthralled by jewelry. If only she'd give him the attention she gave that locket.

"This is my baby girl. Her name is Simone."

"Simone," the girl echoed and touched the picture.

Kaitlin covered Deanna's hand with her own. Devlin waited for Deanna to shy away in fear, but felt elation when the girl didn't pull away.

"I loved her very much. But I lost her," Kaitlin continued.

"Lost?" Deanna blinked long dark lashes.

"Yes, she had to go to heaven. And I miss her." Kaitlin's lips thinned. Deanna frowned, and gulped. "But you know what?" Kaitlin found a smile again. "God gave me Dari to love." Deanna sighed with satisfaction. Kaitlin put her arms about the girl. Devlin was again astounded when the child remained. "And I love him very much. Just like your daddy loves Dari. And he loves you, too, Deanna. He loves you so much. Now that we've found you, I should like the chance to care for you and love you, too."

Deanna eyes grew to orbs. "Like Simone?"

"Just like Simone." Kaitlin caressed the child's arm and took Devlin's hand into her own. "And your daddy would like to do that as well. Will you let him?"

Deanna looked at Devlin. Derrick had crawled back into his embrace, he wasn't afraid of the big man. The lady didn't seem scared either. But

Deanna wasn't so sure. Her lips puckering again, she looked to the hospital then to Uma, to a slightly familiar face.

Uma visited her in the hospital sometimes, but she never stayed. And she never took her away. This pretty lady and this man, her daddy, wanted to take her home.

Home. She wasn't sure what that meant, but strangely, she wanted to be there. She leaned into Kaitlin's shoulder with a sigh borne of relief, her body melting against Kaitlin's in complete trust, and nodded.

Epilogue

Kaitlin sat on the lawn fanning herself with her straw hat, watching Derrick and Michael run across the lawn. Deanna, hair bouncing around her head, ribbons flying, ran after them.

It was a beautiful sight to see.

When they brought Deanna home, Devlin feared she would never truly open up. Who could blame her after being placed in an asylum? Devlin was angry with Uma for putting the girl away, but it slowly gave over to forgiveness and forgiveness melted into thankfulness.

Kaitlin ran her fingers along the dog's belly that lay content at her feet and considered what might have been.

If Uma hadn't been near the lake that night, Deanna's remains would have been dredged up with Reverend Marlow's son. But Uma had pulled Deanna from the water and taken her for her own, telling no one lest her mother try and kill the girl again.

She should have let Devlin know, but she wanted a child. Had Devlin married her when she came to work for him, she would have told him about Deanna. But he wanted nothing to do with her. Uma angrily decided to keep the girl for her own. She'd saved her and since she couldn't have children, Deanna became God's gift to her. Payment for all her troubles.

She thought that up until the time she stood over her mother's grave. Then, somehow, her conscience had been pricked. She had tried to ignore it for a time, had disappeared, hoping to find a place for her and the girl, but her conscience gnawed too strongly.

How was she going to care for the child anyway? The girl had problems. Near strangulation had left her slower than most children her age. And Uma, while she wanted her, didn't have the monies or the patience -- she realized -- to care for her. Besides, if she was ever going to get on with her life, ever going to face herself in the mirror again, she needed to come clean. So she'd written to Ingrid.

Kaitlin and Devlin were grateful she did.

Yes, Deanna had special needs, but with care and love she was blossoming. She even learned to trust Devlin. Who was still humbled and overwhelmed with joy when not only his son, but now his daughter ran to his arms. At times, one wouldn't even know the girl had problems, and other times, like when she stood shuddering near the lake or the nights when she woke up screaming and wetting the bed, one remembered all too clearly what the child, what they'd all, been through.

Deanna flew past in pursuit of a butterfly now and Kaitlin lifted a silent praise to the Lord. Like the butterfly, the girl, though her legs still didn't move in a proper gait, was growing into her wings. The anxious moments and years of wondering were behind them.

For which she offered a silent, *Amen.*

When the girl loped to the pasture, following the boys -- who were now trying to climb on Cotton -- she still didn't worry. The old cuss was a pussy cat now. Love had healed him. Kaitlin thoroughly believed the old Morgan came to the edge of the pasture each day hoping the children would come visit him. He was rarely disappointed. If the children didn't get to him, someone else would.

What made Kaitlin anxious now, was her husband. Not that there were problems between them -- only the day to day rigors of living and loving. But Devlin had been so secretive of late, he nearly drove her crazy crazier still, because she couldn't, even after using all her womanly wiles, draw the secret out of him. He left three days earlier for a court date, promising he'd tell her when he returned at week's end.

She turned the house upside down looking for his surprise, had even asked the staff who's mouths would not be pried open wide enough to give her a hint. Even Eldon wasn't swayed, and she'd sicced the children on him then sent Olga down to try.

"You have to wait for Devlin," Eldon had snickered.

"Not even a little hint?" Olga asked demurely. "For me." Eldon just shook his head. Olga snorted, and shrugged. "Well I tried."

Kaitlin, hoping Olga had weakened his resolve, took up the challenge. "Just a tiny hint?" She held up her hand, and putting her forefinger and thumb nearly together, asked him again. "An itsy bitsy one?" The space between her thumb and finger disappeared and Eldon still wouldn't tell.

He took a long breath. "You have to wait for Devlin. Can you do it?"

"Of course," she assured him soundly. Given their laughter, neither Eldon nor Olga believed her.

They were right not to, she was dreadfully impatient for Devlin's return. But that was all right, she decided. As of this morning, she had a secret of her own. She leaned back with an impish grin and reveled in her solitude. She would be a vision of complete calm when he returned and was just beginning to believe she'd accomplish that feat, when the carriage pulled into the drive -- a day earlier than expected.

When Devlin alighted, looking far more handsome than she could remember, her exhilaration and anxiety mounted.

Mercy, but he could unman her.

With a deep breath, Kaitlin rose and following the children, the dog, and the horse -- that followed the children out the gate -- went to greet Devlin.

Clutching her hat behind her, she grinned coyly. "You weren't expected until tomorrow."

He winked and picked up Deanna. "I can always leave and come back when it suits you."

"No, Daddy." Deanna giggled and pressed her cheek to his. "Please stay."

"I'm not going anywhere, darling," he told the girl while his eyes took in his wife.

Feeling his gaze on her skin, Kaitlin flushed. She tried to ignore the sultry grin he graced her with. Acting nonchalant, she said, "Since you're home early you might as well show us the surprise."

Devlin set his daughter on Cotton's back behind the boys and, chuckling, pulled his wife into his arms. "Can't stand it, can you?" He kissed her cheek and her neck. The children giggled. "Well, can you?"

"She's been ankcy," Derrick informed his father.

Devlin met her eyes. His brows bobbed. "Antsy huh?"

"We 'splored the house and everything," Michael, the traitor, told his uncle.

"'Splored the house hmm?" Devlin teased.

Kaitlin couldn't hold her laughter. She threw up her hands and her hat sailed cross the yard. "All right, you win. I'm terribly curious."

"And terribly beautiful," Devlin complimented, before kissing her soundly.

Flushed, Kaitlin reminded him of the children who sat in wide-eyed curiosity on Cotton's ample back. She ran her hand slowly along Devlin's neck. "I have a surprise as well." His reaction pleased her. Her chin jutted. "I'll tell you *after* you tell me."

"Ah, so the lady has the upper hand." He crushed her against him with a laugh. "Well, then we best get to it." Taking her hand and laying another on Cotton's mane, he led them all to the barn. "It's in here."

When Kaitlin saw the still covered secret in the middle of one of the stalls she wanted to kick herself. Why hadn't she thought to look in the barn? "Has it been here the whole time?"

"No, Thomas and Eldon moved it out last night." Devlin told her as he lifted each child from Cotton. "I guess you didn't 'splore the whole of the house?" He laughed and pointing Cotton to a stall, swatted him in that direction.

Kaitlin's nose crinkled in confusion, as she considered where the surprise had been. She had looked so carefully.

Not carefully enough it would seem.

"What is it, Daddy?" Derrick asked. He dropped to his knees and tried to peek beneath the cover.

"Now, none of that," Devlin said to his son and Michael, who tried to lift the cover. "First you all have to close your eyes."

"Ahhhh, do we have to?" Michael groaned.

"Yes. If you want to see the surprise," Devlin added, looking directly at his wife. He waited until they'd all complied then lifted the cover. "Now, no peeking." He made sure Kaitlin's hands covered her eyes. "I'll count to three then you can look."

He counted too slowly for Kaitlin's liking, but as soon as he said three, her eyes were uncovered and opened.

The children started with gasps of surprise, then stood back and tried to decide if was as special as Devlin made it seem. It wasn't a toy, a new dog, or a pony. It didn't even move. They took a walk about it then went to feed the horses.

It moved Kaitlin. Her feigned nonchalance dissipated. With eyes welling, she took a turn about the statue. There in the unfolding petals of a rose was the likeness of a family. Her family. A reminder of the snow statue all those months ago.

She turned to Devlin. "You carved the statue in the snow?" He smiled. She reached out and touched the faces on the stone. When her hand fell on his likeness, Devlin could almost feel the warmth of it on his skin. She turned, wiping a tear. "It's beautiful."

He took her into his arms. "For my beautiful wife." He cleared his throat. "I want you to know how thankful I am for you. How much I love you." She laid her head against his shoulder, and reveled in the warmth of his arms.

"So, what about my surprise," he whispered moments later.

She pulled from his arms and taking his hand, led him to the statue. He followed with a bemused grin. "I wonder if you could carve another person. Here." She took his hand and laid it on the empty space on her carved image.

Bewildered, he studied her. "Here?"

Gently lifting his hand, she guided it upwards to the statue's arms. "Perhaps it'd be better here? A child needs their mother's arms."

He pulled his hand from the statue and turned to his wife. "Child?"

"Child." She took his hand, placed it on her womb.

"Our child?"

She nodded.

He pulled her into his arms, crying and laughing at the same time. Tears lining his cheeks, he raised his face toward heaven. No, he decided, this wasn't a surprise, it was a gift, a miraculous gift from heaven.

He wasn't speaking about the child, either.

His gift arrived at his door, sputtering wet and mad as a hornet, a little over a year before. She'd stubbornly stayed, stubbornly wormed her way into his home, his heart. His life had been changed, and graced with love because of it.

Had he known she'd upend his life, he would have opened the door sooner.

The End

About Tina Pinson

Tina Resides in Arizona with her husband of thirty-plus years, Danny. They are blessed to have three sons and seven grandchildren.

Tina started her first novel in elementary school. Beyond her love of writing she also find creative outlets in poetry, songs, drawing and woodworking. Tina has been involved with American Christian Fiction Writers since 2003.

Her WWII story *Trail of the Sandpiper* won third place in the 2003 ACFW Genesis Contest. An excerpt from *Counting Tessa* took 1st in its category for the 2009 CWOW Does Your Story Have Bite Contest.

In the Manor of the Ghost, Touched by Mercy, When Shadows Fall, and Shadowed Dreams, books 1 and 2 in the Shadow Series are available through Desert Breeze Publishers.

To Catch a Shadow book three of the Shadow Series about the Civil War and the Oregon Trail will be available June 2013. *To Carry her Cross* releases January 2013, *Then there was Grace* a Sept 9/11 type story will be available September 2013 and *Christmas in Shades of Gray* is slated to release in Dec. 2013

Read more about Tina at http://www.tinapinson.com or visit her blog @ http://tinapinson.blogspot.com

Made in the USA
Charleston, SC
17 July 2015